Beneath the Gods' Tree

by S. Kaeth

Published by:
Hakea Media
350 W 6th St #932
Dubuque, IA 52004
hakeamedia@gmail.com
www.hakeamedia.com

Print ISBN: 978-1-955220-07-1
Ebook ISBN: 978-1-955220-05-7
Library of Congress Control Number: 2024900300
First Edition

Cover by Dave Brasgalla: https://www.davidbrasgalla.art
Author's website: www.skaeth.com

Content Warning:
Includes descriptions of systemic injustice (classism), animal abuse/death, fantasy violence/injuries, fantasy discrimination, anxiety, instances of vomiting, menstruation, theft, bullying, abuse.

To Mister and Missus. Thank you for all your support and all you taught me. Teachers like you are pure gold.
Commas are still magic, though, sorry!

1

AMANAH BIT THE inside of her lip to hide her wince as she handed over a good chunk of her savings to the leather goods stall owner. His gaze raked over her again, suspicion in his eyes as they lingered over her intricate braids, which would indicate higher class, and then on her too-large, practical clothing, more common for the lower classes. And yet, she was purchasing high quality thaa oil, which the rich used to keep their leather goods supple and in good condition. The strict hierarchy of the city of Arruk confined them all, and she longed for the freedom of the wilderness.

"Thank you," the merchant said, eyes still sharp on her. "Have a good day."

She nodded in return, gaining herself a scowl for poor manners, but it was better not to speak. If he heard her speak, the small differences in the way she pronounced words or phrased ideas could betray her wilderness background. His suspicions that she did not belong here would only increase. As it was, she had to hope he figured she was a maid doing the shopping for a well-to-do employer. She hurried away, slipping the precious bottle of oil into her bag. It had been far too expensive, but it would keep her brother out of trouble, and that made it worth it.

This market was filled with goods from far-flung places or master artisans, things she could never afford but which delighted her senses anyway as she passed. She always enjoyed patrolling the higher class wells of the city when she was on duty. Her shift today only included the training yard, though, and the strain of being out of place with the expensive fabrics and fashionable styles all around itched at her.

Once she was well away from the stall, she let out her breath and pulled her scarf from her bag. She needed to cover her braids before heading back to the market near the river harbor. That market centered around one of the havi wells of the city; it was safe.

The breeze caught one end of her scarf, sending the strip of fabric fluttering. As she wound it up, claws caught the end. A sandcat cub mewled as it pounced again, razor sharp claws shredding her only headscarf.

A sandcat was death in the wilderness. Even though this was just a cub, Amanah's hand went for her knife.

"Stop that!" scolded a woman. Belatedly, Amanah realized the cub wore a jeweled collar attached to an embroidered leather leash.

The woman holding the other end of the leash gave Amanah a strained smile as she tugged the cub away. "My apologies. At least you're in work clothes, hmm? No harm done!"

Holding her ripped scarf, Amanah blinked as the woman dove into the market crowd, tugging the sandcat cub behind her. If Amanah actually belonged in this market, thriving around this higher-class well, she'd likely have three or more scarves, all much nicer than hers, and the scarf would be easily replaced. But she only had the one, and now she'd need to get a new one or find thread to try to repair it, all with hardly any coin left.

She had to get out of here.

But at least she'd gotten what she'd come for and her brother was safe.

Emin had made a mistake. A few days ago, he was on patrol with another guard and had mentioned that he needed to rub oil into his boots because they were cracking. When they got back to the guardhouse, his partner had handed him a bottle of oil, and, exhausted from the long day, Emin hadn't been paying attention. He thought it was the cheap oil the guardhouse provided, and so had used it and passed it along to another guard who needed it, just as they would do at home. He hadn't realized the bottle was the guard's personal supply until he asked for it back.

Since Emin couldn't give him the oil back, the guard wanted it replaced, which was fair, but Emin didn't have the money, especially since the guard got his oil from a high-end supplier. Emin had been trying to barter or scrounge up the coin, but it was slow going, and the threat of being charged with theft, even as a guard, was hanging over his head. Thieves who couldn't pay the fine were whipped.

Amanah hastily tied the scarf so it covered her braids, careful not to rip it further. The soft thunk of her bag with the precious oil inside was comforting against her thigh as she hurried out of the market. It had been

2

nice to wear complex braids again; the weave patterns her mothers had taught her made her feel at home, as if she could carry a part of that peace around with her in the roiling dangers of the city. But in Arruk, the more interesting plaits were for nobles only, though they relied on maids to accomplish them, and therefore she seemed pretentious for wearing them. At home in the wilderness, intricate braids were simple self-respect.

It'd be easier if she just left her hair loose, the way Emin did. It let him blend in more easily in the city, with nothing showing where he came from, who his family was. Emin was proud of being only himself in that way. Only the quality of his clothing spoke of his havi status, though neither of them had shed the wilderness accent that spoke of their nomadic roots. For her, losing the patterns from home or even thinking of not wearing braids felt like killing a precious piece of herself.

Once she got to the market near the river harbor, her shoulders relaxed somewhat. Every section of the city was centered around a well, because wells were important when one lived in a desert, and this was a havi well.

Amanah wove through the crowd, heading for the tents clustered at the edge. Hopefully, the timetable for removing them hadn't been moved up. They were supposed to have three more days, but the tightness in her chest didn't ease until the tents appeared through the shifting mass of people, holes in fabric and drooping supports matching the patched clothing of those going about their day.

As she passed a small grill where two men tended strips of mystery meat on skewers, their conversation reached her. "Perhaps Murihat's Hand will send them some mischief."

The other man stabbed a chunk of meat and turned it. "They got my son out of a trap his employer set for him. Helped him find better employment. Risk didn't stop them. Maybe we should risk more."

Amanah tried not to stiffen. Soon after arriving in the city, she learned people could easily be in danger, targets of the nobles's wrath. There were already small groups working to help in each well in the poorer parts of the city, and Amanah had helped them organize into one large network, sharing dangers and resources. Together, they shuffled those at risk of nobles' retribution from well to well until they could get them out of Arruk and away from the influence of the nobles.

The people had begun calling them Murihat's Hand, after the deity of deception, mischief, and mercy. If the identity of anyone in the Hand was known, the nobles would demand vengeance paid in suffering, so she didn't even let Emin know about the extent of her involvement with the group, lest it put him at risk. Only a few knew she was associated with them, and those that did thought she was just one of the hundreds of occasional messengers the Hand used.

Swallowing hard, Amanah passed the grill, hoping the men weren't planning anything foolish. The last thing they needed was for the nobles to come down hard on the havi for true threats—even imagined threats caused enough pain.

Little Aaya squatted on the very edge of the square, her open hand out, face smeared with tears and dirt. Amanah's heart clenched, as it did on each visit. The girl should be free to run, rather than confined to begging in hopes of helping her family afford another meal. Amanah dropped a coin in her hand and patted her shoulder as she stepped past into the tattered tent.

"Amanah!" Aaya's mother knelt by her husband's side, spooning broth into his mouth.

"Hello, Anila. How's Gitu doing?"

"Not good, I'm afraid." The woman's face was carefully blank.

"I'll be fine," wheezed the man, holding his ribs with the effort of speaking.

Amanah knelt beside Anila, pressing a small bag of coins she'd collected for them into her hand. She included Gitu in her gaze. "Here. It should be enough for a healer. Not one of the bimnas, but a decent healer."

"Oh, thank you," Anila gasped, tears sparking in her eyes.

The man grimaced with pain, reaching out. Amanah took his hand, and he squeezed it hard. "It'll take us a while to pay this back."

Amanah shook her head. "Once you get a healer, you must run. Murihat's Hand can help you get out."

"The rumors then?" Anila asked.

Gitu had worked for a powerful lord of the Asi clan when a work accident had shut down the mill and Gitu had been fired. Now, rumors were flying that Gitu had sabotaged the lord's mill, causing the accident. Gitu had lodged a complaint with the magistrate only a few days ago, only to be hit by a wagon on his way home. They couldn't prove it was retaliation, but they all knew. It'd be a matter of noble pride now, to make Gitu and his family suffer and prove that havi couldn't stand against the nobles.

Amanah gave a single nod. "They'll send someone for you when it's all set. But tell no one, or it's all ruined."

"We shouldn't be the ones running," Gitu said.

"The noble you angered won't rest until you have another accident. And this time it will be worse than being run over."

"He had it coming."

"That doesn't matter. For now, lay low, avoid risk. Avoid attracting attention."

"Our son," Anila said, "you remember, he's working with the masons? He was going to get another job, try to bring in more money. We might be able to pay this back then."

Amanah shook her head again, trying to press the importance of her message on the little family. "If he gets another job, are you leaving him behind to run? If you stay, I'm not sure it matters if he makes more money. It'd take all Hayzanu's favor to keep you safe here now."

Anila shivered, her gaze dropping to the bowl of thin soup in her hands.

Gitu scowled. "We've heard you advising others not to take better jobs unless necessary, not to find better housing unless it's needed. Are you happy with keeping us in the dirt?"

"What? No!" Amanah sat back. "There are far too many traps—jobs that sound wonderful and disguise horrors. I can't dictate what you do— and I wouldn't. I just deliver warnings."

She gritted her teeth. That was too close to the truth. Rumors travelled quickly in the guardhouse and she overheard things on the streets, enough to sometimes discover traps before they closed around the unsuspecting. When she did, she told the Hand and other havi she saw—while pretending she had just overheard it from a member of the Hand.

"You don't think that's dangerous?" Gitu's eyes narrowed on her.

She shrugged. "It's worth the risk."

If she couldn't use her position to help others, what good was it?

"We're grateful for the money," Anila said, stroking her husband's hair back from his face. "We just don't want to be indebted."

Amanah nodded. "So when you get home, when your family is safe and you have extra coin, you pass on the help to the next family in need. You're not indebted to anyone."

"We'll talk about it. The leaving part. But thank you for the money for the healer. It's very kind of you to arrange."

"Gitu." Anila frowned at him.

"Our son can work his way up," Gitu said.

"And then pay for his father's funeral?" Tears shimmered in Anila's eyes. "I don't want to lose you. This shouldn't be a question. We should go. We've already stayed too long."

Gitu grimaced.

"It takes time to set plans into motion," Amanah said. "I don't say this to pressure you, only—"

"Do it. We'll run." Gitu sighed, looking smaller somehow. "We'll start over somewhere else."

Amanah bowed. "Someone will come tomorrow night and tap this rhythm for you." Her. It would be her, but no one needed to know that.

Amanah drummed her fingers briefly, unsure if Gitu and Anila knew the tapping language or not. If not, they could match the rhythm, at least. "Do as they say. Hayzanu look kindly on you."

"Or maybe Ahunah. We could use some vengeance," Gitu suggested.

She scowled at him. "Arruk could evict your entire clan."

"Would that be so bad?" He grimaced. "No, it's just the pain talking. We won't seek vengeance."

Anila brushed the hair off her husband's forehead, and then smiled at Amanah. "Tenah smile on you."

Bowing her head in respect, Amanah left the tent. There would be others who could serve as backup if she couldn't be there for the little family, but she took on as much as she could. At least then, if something happened or a mistake was made, she wouldn't be relying on someone who might not come through.

Her woven bag bounced against her side as she moved back into the market. She lifted the strap and pressed the fabric to her nose, inhaling the spices that infused its fibers. The scents of home. And the colorful weave of the fibers... She could picture the marks her mothers would have worked on the bag before its completion, from the tight, capable weave that screamed of Renesa to the whimsical pattern winding down the straps that would have been Newin's input, and the braided rope that closed it bore Mina's signature half-twist.

The breath of home was needed here in the city. Amazing how the capital almost seemed a foreign land. She and Emin had come to the city thinking they knew what to expect. They'd answered the queen's call for more guards, not only to see beyond what could be seen from their family's travel routes, but also to prove themselves. Their father Tumaw had wanted more for them, and after the accident stole his life, it was easy to convince their father Ifel and their mothers to send them with their blessing, to honor Tumaw.

Emin had looked forward to the opportunities the guard could give him, and Amanah had thought she could leverage her guard position to gain access to train in the bamimri. She could almost laugh at how wrong she'd been.

Clutching the strap tightly, she wove through the crowd of the market, searching for a new headscarf. The Festival of Dark Nights wasn't too far off, and she'd definitely need one to cover her braids. Emin would trawl through the trash heaps if she mentioned her need, but he had enough to worry about with the guards' trials, and besides, he preferred spending the evenings with friends, nagging her to join them.

By the time she found an affordable headscarf she liked, the market sundial indicated Emin's team would be returning any moment, finished with their guards' trial. Her own group had been given the morning off, but three days' time would give them their own challenge. Borlim, head of the Arruk city guards, was evaluating them for formal war bands and leaders.

On cue, laughter rang out from the direction of the harbor. Stepping up on the edge of the market's fountain, she spied them, the ten men shoving and jostling each other as if they hadn't been exercising all afternoon—swimming, by the way their clothes were drenched. Probably the river warfare lessons Borlim had threatened them with, complete with capsizing or sinking. Their attitudes gave no sign of whether they'd passed their trial or not, but that wasn't unusual—she swore not a one of them was able to be serious.

Shouting and shoving away those nearest him, Gurseh, Emin's boyfriend, cleared a space and then leapt into the air, doing a backflip and landing in a bow. Hoots and shouts echoed around him, the others slapping his back. Taunos, one of Emin's current friend group, led and ended the congratulations, then gestured for space. He cartwheeled with no hands, leapt up into a forward flip, and twisted to land facing them with arms wide as if to welcome the cheering that followed.

Amanah snorted, crossing her arms over the strap of her bag, tugging it close. Taunos was a show-off. Ever since that first day Emin had brought him to test for a position in the guards, Amanah had given him a wide berth. He made friends far too easily—including with the nobles. He was dangerous.

Unwilling to be left out, Emin jumped up, trying a forward flip of his own. He rotated too little, and Amanah cringed as he fell, still upside down. Taunos reached out, and with a tug, caught him, Emin's rear barely missing the cobbles.

Emin clasped his arm as Taunos brought him upright, and then the whole crowd of them cheered again. Borlim needed to assign them more laps to run.

Something tugged at her bag. Her fingers tightened reflexively on the strap, but as she turned to see who'd grabbed at it, a boy careened into her,

7

knocking her off the lip of the fountain. She barely caught herself from falling on her face on the market's cobblestones, but when she found her balance again, her bag was in the grip of a different black-haired youth, the strap having been whipped away from her shoulder while she'd stumbled. Standing behind him was the boy who'd run into her.

Not her bag! It was worthless to anyone except her, but to her it was worth more than the city itself. Ifel would have spent much coin to send it to her along with Emin's new knife. And those gifts had only come last week. The city took much from her. She wouldn't let it take her bag, too. Especially since inside it was the oil Emin needed.

She snagged the dangling strap and yanked hard, just as the thief whirled to go. The strap burned her fingers, but it also brought the thief up short in his escape.

The thief looked at her and narrowed his eyes. His clothes fit him well and she saw no patches or repairs. His boots were well-made, though dirty, and of middling quality. His necklace was of Guma clan design, and outrage gripped her. Guma clan was one of the clans currently in power on the queen's council. Sometimes wealthier people entertained themselves with those less fortunate. Why couldn't they do something normal like go swimming or have a mud fight, instead?

"Thief!" he cried.

Amanah went cold. "You're trying to steal my bag!"

"Nice story. That's my sister's bag. Saw you take it off my brother as he went past. Now let it go."

"Yeah," said the boy who'd run into her, standing just behind his brother.

Amanah's fingers tightened further around the strap in her hand. She should have been more watchful. She'd known better. And the more attention that came her way, the less likely things would go well for her. If the noble classes began watching her, figured out what she was doing with her position as guard, they'd surely stop her.

But she couldn't part with the bag. Her mothers' fingers had woven that cloth, and her father's coin had shipped it to her. Worse, Emin would be whipped if he didn't replace the oil. But she couldn't let on that something so valuable was inside. She could be accused of stealing it, and even if she wasn't, the thief would be even more invested.

"It's mine," she said. "It's not worth anything to you. Please. It's my bag."

The thief sneered. "Why don't we let the magistrates figure it out, hmm?"

Despite herself, Amanah looked around, but there was no escape. No one would help her, because no one could—unless she yelled for Emin, but that would put him in harm's way. The best she could hope for was the magistrate doing their job.

Not relaxing her grip in the slightest, Amanah nodded. "Fine."

She wouldn't get justice—not by a long shot—but she wouldn't give up her bag without a fight, either.

The next well over was significantly nicer than that of the havi market, full of administrative buildings. The Gods' Way stretched before them, temples rising from the sides of the wide street. Lanterns were being set out as the Way readied for the Festival of Dark Nights to come. She'd always disliked the Festival, as the stars died and there was that moment of breathlessness, when the fear came that the light might not be born again this time.

The first time she'd walked the Gods' Way, seen the palace and the High Temple facing each other across the courtyard, she couldn't believe her luck. The palace, the library, the guardhouse, and the famous bamimri with its students of healing, all in one square with the gilded roof of the most famous temple in Far Dahutad, and she would get to see it every day.

Now she knew better. Her quarters at the guardhouse might be close to the bamimri and the library, but she had no more hope of getting into either of those places than she had of sleeping in the queen's bed.

They didn't go to the end of the Gods' Way though, not this time. The magistrate's office was only halfway down the road, and the thief tugged her inside by the bag neither of them would let go of. Still, her throat was dry by the time they were shown to a small room full of dark wood paneling and thick rugs.

The magistrate was a little man perched behind a massive desk. He looked down his long, thin nose at all three of them as the thieves told their story. Finally, he held up a hand and the youth and boy fell silent. The magistrate gestured, and Amanah explained what had happened.

The man's lip twitched as she spoke, and once she was done, he turned to an official who stood near the door.

"What's in the bag?"

"Thaa oil and a scarf," Amanah answered.

The official nodded. "She's right."

The thief scoffed. "Only because she peeked inside the bag. That's why she tried to steal it. How could a havi afford thaa oil anyway?"

The magistrate raised his eyebrows at her. "Your clothes say havi, and there's wilderness in your voice. But your hair says middle class or higher, from what I can see. Are you running some sort of scam?"

Amanah's hand went to her hair. She should have taken some of the braids out. "My mothers are very good at weaving. They made the bag these two tried to steal from me, and they taught me their skills. The thaa oil is for my brother—I had to use nearly all my savings to purchase it."

"You used your savings on something like thaa oil, not something you'd find more useful, like clothes that fit better?"

Amanah drew in a slow breath through her nose for patience. She'd bought the most durable clothes she could afford when she came to the city, and the set she was wearing was one of her better sets—decent enough to get in and out of that market this morning. Her belt made the oversized shirt fit well enough, and the color wasn't that far off from the dyes she'd seen sold in the fancy market, was it? "I'm a guard here. You can check with Borlim at the guardhouse. These two tried to steal from me."

"I don't see your vest."

"I'm off duty!" And she was going to be late for training at this rate.

"Of course you are. The queen and Borlim allow just about anyone in, but I also know people like you try to turn that to your own advantage."

Her nostrils flared, but Amanah shut her mouth. Of course they did. The nobles tried to turn things to their advantage, too. The difference was, they got away with it.

The magistrate eyed her critically. "It's one thing to come to the city to better yourself, but another to do so without respect. It takes time to work your way up—time that allows you to learn the rules the city runs by, to follow the proper etiquette, to learn how to speak properly. Shortcuts just won't do—they're lazy."

To embrace the city's ways felt like cutting out a core piece of who she was, and she refused to do that.

An official stepped forward and cleared her throat. "Excuse me, magistrate, but these two, from the Guma clan, were accused of theft three months ago. The records are in the system: they paid fines instead of going to trial."

The magistrate pinned them with a suspicious glare, and then flicked his gaze to Amanah. "And her?"

"Two accusations, neither verified. It appears she was once sent for Jattanu's justice, but the record for why is blacked out."

Amanah chewed the inside of her cheek to hide a wince—all three incidents had followed her trusting someone in the city to help her with one thing or another. Not all of them were malicious—one of the theft

10

accusations was a misunderstanding—but this was why it was safer to do everything herself.

"She's been in the city for six months with a brother, both in the city guard—Havi Amanah Teek and Havi Emin Teek of the Kanhu clan."

"Only six months in the city and already causing trouble? As a guard, you should know better than to run afoul of the law—this makes more than once every two months." The magistrate waved a hand irritably. "Let the gods decide it. A race between them."

"Jattanu requires justice to be clearly fair, magistrate," the official said.

The magistrate glared at her. "The Kanhu are largely nomadic still, yes?"

Amanah nodded, but he wasn't even looking at her, his gaze fixed on his official, who also nodded.

"Archery then, from horseback. And we will provide the horses and bows. Clearly fair enough for you?"

The official nodded, and the clamp around Amanah's heart eased a little. She'd been riding since before she could walk, and shooting from horseback as long as she could remember. No one in her clan was as good an archer as she.

The magistrate tucked his hands behind him. "At dawn tomorrow, then."

Amanah nodded reluctantly—it wasn't like she had much of a choice. The official reached for the bag, and the thief dropped it with an air of disgust. Amanah clenched her teeth, forcing her fingers to open.

The woman offered her a small smile. "This will be placed in the safe. The winner will get it back tomorrow morning."

All she could do was nod. The two thieves stomped out after the official, and Amanah followed with her stomach churning.

Now she had to hope the gods' justice was a far sight better than that of their representatives in Arruk. And if their representatives were so corrupt in the very capital of Far Dahutad... She pressed her lips together. This was not a useful line of thought. She unraveled a few braids from their weave into the rest of her braids. It looked slovenly and would get in her way, but it was better than being thought to have aspirations.

Amanah hurried up the Gods' Way—there was her late afternoon sparring to get in, even if she was otherwise off duty today, and now, she was late.

When she entered the sparring field, Borlim grunted at her and circled his hand three times. Holding back a sigh, Amanah obeyed, taking off on the first of her thirty laps. Her sandals slapped on the smooth stone of the shaded walkways that circled the Royal Garden. It was completely enclosed by the square of buildings forming an unbreakable perimeter: the palace, guardhouse, library, and bamimri. As she passed the last, the sharp scent of alcohol used to cleanse utensils stung her nose. Inside, bimnas hurried past the large windows, tending to the sick and injured in their care. Amanah turned her head away, denying the impulse to peek further.

Footfalls sounded behind her, multiple sets. She glanced behind to see Emin and Taunos, racing while shoving at one another. Emin surged ahead, and Taunos responded with a laugh and another boost of speed. They parted to pass her, and she couldn't help but speed up to match them. They should have been close to off duty for the day, but clearly they'd earned a punishment.

"What did you do, Emin?" Amanah asked. He could never learn to simply stay out of trouble—not that she was doing that good of a job herself.

"Me? Why do you think it was me?" Emin asked with mock affront.

"It's always you, Emin," Amanah said.

"She has a point." Taunos laughed. It was a nice laugh, carefree and heard often. Jealousy pricked in her stomach, and she fought not to scowl at him. It wasn't his fault she wished she could laugh like that.

Too many of Emin's friends were loud and brash; they'd stoop to associate with Emin, to embrace the novelty or to relax. Amanah gathered the higher classes often had stricter rules depending on the clan and situation, and those didn't apply in Emin's company because he couldn't care less about protocol. In the wilderness, where no one cared as much about hierarchy, she and Emin had far more freedom, and Emin extended that philosophy to everyone in his circle. But his "friends" rarely stuck around for long.

No doubt Taunos would be the same, but he was harder than most to ignore.

"Look, I was trying to distract Borlim," Emin said. "You were the one who was late."

"I had a little trouble in the market," Amanah said.

"I had a little trouble distracting Borlim." Emin rubbed his shoulder.

"You were trying to distract him from my tardiness?" Amanah asked. Her brother was unexpectedly sweet sometimes.

"Yeah. The weapons rack hit back though. It's not supposed to do that."

"You didn't make sure the weight was balanced evenly," Taunos said.

"And why are you here?" Amanah asked, eyes narrowing.

"I was part of the distraction." He grinned at her, full of dazzling arrogance.

Amanah focused back on the course. "Sorry it didn't work."

"It's all right." And the funny thing was, it really seemed like it didn't matter to him. What kind of a person didn't care about anything? Amanah fought not to roll her eyes and instead, sped up.

The men, of course, matched her.

She gave Emin an apologetic look. "I got that oil, but someone stole my bag in the market."

Emin cursed. "Amanah, I told you I had it handled."

"You clearly did not." Although, neither did she, it turned out.

"What oil? Do you need me to head to the market?" Taunos asked.

Emin's strategy to avoid trouble was to send a friend—usually Taunos—for the shopping if he couldn't find what he needed at a havi market. The thought of relying on someone else like that made everything in Amanah tense at all the things that could go wrong.

"I haven't been able to get the money together to afford thaa oil, but I'm working on it." Emin admitted the truth as if he was standing barefoot on hot sand.

"I have a few people who owe me favors," Taunos said, a splash of cool water. "And if those don't pan out, I can owe someone else a favor."

"The magistrate decided the ownership of my bag would be determined by a horse race tomorrow," Amanah said. "If I win, you get your oil. All I have to do is win."

"You didn't have to do that, Amanah," Emin said. "But you're the best rider I know. And if not, Taunos, I'll owe you."

"No need," Taunos waved him off. "I'm pretty sure I owe you already. We'll be even."

"Bet you a jug of Mekkl's wine I finish the laps before you," Emin said.

Taunos snorted. "You're on."

And just like that, the two were off, sprinting head to head as if they'd been assigned only a lap or two. Except their shirts were dark with sweat, testament to the several laps they'd already run. Amanah shook her head and reined her thoughts back to the present. She needed to focus on the laps and then get through practice. That was first. The rest could wait.

But her thoughts kept going back to her bag, locked away in a safe with people who surely wouldn't care if her possessions went missing or were damaged. The loss of her money and her new headscarf was only a small insult compared to the bag itself and the oil for Emin. Her anger and frustration fueled the rest of her run.

Panting for breath, she made her way back to the sparring ground and paused to lean a hand against the wall. Her legs ached from the run, and her lungs screamed.

In the yard, men and women sparred with a variety of weapons. Arrows thunked into targets at one end of the open space, and the clack of wooden weapons striking each other mingled with the clang of blunted metal ringing together.

And of course, Taunos whirled and lunged with an opponent, seeming more to dance than to fight. As if the very gods themselves conspired against her, the sun shone through the clouds to ring him with sunbeams, setting him alight and glowing. His opponent struck, and the man laughed, as if it was all a game.

Amanah shook her head. He was too good to be true, and she wouldn't waste another breath thinking of him. At the first nuisance, he would reconsider being friends with a havi, like all the others before him. Amanah already knew this tale by heart.

After practice, she informed Borlim of the magistrate's decision, which would make her late for tomorrow's assignment. He grunted assent, but his gaze followed her out of the training yard, his expression unreadable. She resisted the urge to shudder. Would he fire her for being too much trouble? If so, that was the undoing of all her plans, the last death knell of her once-bright dreams. But there was nothing she could do to stop it.

Trying not to think about it, she went back to her dormitory, which was now full of women changing shifts—some changing to sleep, others gathering fresh clothes for the baths as they came off work or practice. Amanah followed the flood to the baths, but she couldn't relax even in the steam of the water. There was no good conversation to distract herself from the trial in the morning. The others were polite, but distant. She never relaxed with them, because their ideas for entertainment tended to be too expensive, or she didn't have the right clothes. Besides, it was easier to work your way up in Arruk when you didn't associate with havi, especially havi from the wilderness.

Amanah unwove her braids and rewove them in a simpler pattern, twisting down her back. Clad in clean clothes and with her small money pouch in her pocket, since her bag was gone with most of her coin, she headed for the Royal Gardens. Perhaps she would find the peace she craved there.

Music drifted from the gardens, drawing her through rows of perfectly manicured shrubs and blooming flowers caressed by the evening light. Only so close to the river could such ornamental plants survive in a desert.

The unfamiliar tune drew her onward, and she followed it to a large tree—one of those gnarled giants that provided blessed shade. And on one of those branches, one leg drawn up and the other dangling carelessly, Taunos sat playing a pipe of some sort. His eyes met hers and the edges of his mouth curled upward, though he continued the tune.

She paused. She should leave him to enjoy his time alone, though if the guards caught him climbing a tree in the gardens…

She knew how it felt for small transgressions to be magnified just because you were not one of the rich and powerful. And Taunos was not Dahuti, which should put him at more risk than even her. His face was too wide, his nose broader and flatter than Dahuti—more like the Hinanuri nomads her family traded with, but not exactly Hinanuri, either.

Mirth lit in his eyes, the curl of his lips deepening.

Her cheeks heated. She'd been staring at him. She tore her gaze away.

He finished his tune and lowered the pipe. "Hello."

Jattanu's judgement on him, he could fill that word with so much ease and laughter. But she never got involved with Emin's friends on principle. So why did she always linger until her stomach fluttered with his smiles? And did he know? Was that why he smiled and laughed so often?

She drew a deep breath, forcing herself straight. "The guards will not like you in the Gods' Tree."

"Is it forbidden?" He tilted his head to the side.

"Not as such, but… it's the Gods' Tree."

Mirth rolled out from him like a wave. "Surely they have enough trees."

She frowned at him. "Do you not realize that the powerful rarely stop at 'enough?'"

He tilted his head, thoughtful for a moment, then nodded. "You're right."

With that, he shoved away from the branch he'd been sitting on, dropping down in front of her. She took several steps back as his scent filled her nose. It wasn't a bad smell. In fact, it reminded her of rain and growing things. But he attracted attention everywhere he went, and she needed to stay out of that spotlight.

She turned abruptly, stepping away from him.

"Are you joining us tonight?" he asked.

She didn't feel like celebrating. She felt like mourning, but moping never helped anything, and she hadn't lost yet. It was just impending. She took a deep breath and nodded—the distraction would be good for her, and Taunos was nothing if not distracting.

"I'll be there."
He beamed, and she fled from the sunlight in his smile.

2

THE NEXT MORNING, Emin joined her in front of the magistrate's office, along with Taunos. Two horses were held by young boys, but Amanah's stomach sank as she looked at the mounts.

"Emin."

"I see it," Emin growled.

"What?" Taunos asked. "What do you see?"

Perhaps it wouldn't be obvious to someone who wasn't raised among horses like she and Emin had been. "Look," she said. "The bay there—"

"Which?" Taunos's confusion was scrawled across his face like the mural across the wall of the Hall of Small Courts.

"The... brown one."

He nodded, his eyes flicking back to her, warm and earnest, as if he actually cared. Amanah pushed the part of her that began to hope for decency down deep, where it couldn't hurt. "The brown one has been drugged, something to lend it speed. See the feverish gleam in its eyes, the quiver to its pace?"

"That's not excitement?"

She shook her head. "The grey one is near broken-down. It might not last the race, even. That'll be the one they give me."

She braced herself for his doubt, but he simply nodded again, his expression hardening.

Emin started forward. "I'm going to talk with them."

"Emin, wait." She grabbed her brother's arm.

"That's not even pretending to be fair!" he shouted.

She winced. How many people were looking at them now? She'd

barely bothered to weave her braids together today. Her mothers would have hated to see the messy work she'd made of it, but it was better than repeating her mistake of yesterday. Unless her brother made a scene, maybe she could get through this.

Amanah sidled a little farther from Emin but kept her eyes on his. "You can't. It's too dangerous."

Emin raked his hand through his loose black hair. "Of course it is. But this isn't right."

"Emin!" she hissed. "They will lash out in revenge. I'll take the broken-down horse. You know I'm good. I'll give it my best and the rest is in the hands of the gods. If, on the off-chance, the gods pronounce judgement on them, they can't dispute it. But if a havi does... It's only a bag and oil, Emin. You're my brother."

Losing her bag would be terrible. Losing the oil would make trouble. Losing her brother, though... She couldn't see a future without his far-too-loud parties, his awful jokes, and his easy support.

Emin clenched his jaw. "It's not right."

She nodded, keeping her hand on his arm. "I know."

With a sigh, he squeezed her arms, touching his forehead to hers. "Go with the gods, Amanah. And let them taste the dust from your heels."

The last sentence was a growl, and she smiled. "I will."

But as he released her, she turned to Taunos. "Keep him out of trouble. Please."

He was possibly the worst person to choose to keep someone out of trouble, but there were no other options.

"Good luck, Amanah." Taunos nodded, though Emin rolled his eyes.

The shorter man reached up for Emin's shoulder and steered him toward the track—and away from the magistrate's bench. "Come on Emin, let's find a good spot."

Amanah let out a breath. Then, drawing herself up straight, she turned around and approached the bench.

The magistrate, the same one from yesterday, scowled at her. "Do you mock me, havi?"

She froze. What had she done? Her clothes were neat and clean under her guard's vest, which she wore because she had duty right after this. She didn't have a bag to tuck her vest into anymore, though she supposed Emin could have held it for her. Her skin was clean, her braids were messy to avoid notice, and she was on time—not too early, which would appear impatient, and not late, which would give offense... What had she forgotten?

The magistrate's scowl deepened. "You dare to come with your hair all a-tangle after putting on airs yesterday? I scolded you yesterday for disrespecting the city's ways. The solution is not to give up your self-respect but simply to have a little humility."

"I—" She bit her tongue. Arguing would only bring trouble. She knew her own worth, and it was greater than what the city assigned her—they only saw her as a havi. But that clash only ever brought trouble, with the city seeing her as arrogant and rude, like the magistrate had yesterday. She bowed her head. "I apologize."

The magistrate hmphed. His eyes shifted to a point behind her, and she turned, making sure her expression was composed. The thief approached from behind. Late.

He stopped next to her without looking at her and bowed his head. "Magistrate."

"Good, now we're all here," the magistrate said, giving the thief a stern look.

Amanah bit down on her frustration. The thief wore the braid pattern of the Guma clan today, flaunting his status. Of course the same rules wouldn't apply to him.

Standing, the magistrate raised his hands, the threads of his robes catching the sunlight and setting off a dazzling array of glittering shimmers. "May the gods look upon us and grant their wisdom. May justice be done here in Jattanu's sight."

Amanah fervently prayed along. If justice couldn't be found from Arruk's magistrates, the gods were her only chance, however slim.

The magistrate flicked a coin high into the air, the metal catching the light as it spun. "Let the gods choose the mounts. For the man, grey or brown."

The coin fell, and he caught it on the back of his hand. He raised it up, the brown side clearly visible, which meant she got the grey one, as she'd guessed. All she could do was her best, like usual. Anything else was out of her control.

The thief grinned at her, swaggering to the bay horse, but she focused solely on the grey one. She checked the saddle, her fingers snagging on the leather girth. It was cracked nearly through. Shaking her head, she removed the saddle and dumped it on the ground. The last thing she needed was the strap to snap mid-course, leaving her to fall and possibly be trampled.

The magistrate frowned at her. "What are you doing, havi?"

Telling the truth would do no good, particularly since this magistrate was so set against her.

Amanah smiled politely. "I'm of the Kanhu clan. We ride bareback."

A woman stood beside the magistrate, practically dripping with jewelry. She leaned over his shoulder. "Oh, don't worry, dear. Let her ride bareback if she wants to. It's not like it will give her an advantage, will it?"

"No…" The magistrate frowned, and then nodded, patting the woman's hand. "All right, fine."

He turned and walked toward two chairs on the side of the street, linked arm and arm with the woman. Amanah watched them go, staring at the intricate weave of the woman's braids. She had clearly struggled with a noble-level design, perhaps on her own or with the help of a maid who wasn't very skilled at weaving braids together. Her hand went to her own hair. She'd done better yesterday. Sweet Nannil, goddess of night, help her, she'd shown the magistrate's wife up without intending it. No wonder he had it out for her.

But there was no way she could take the offense back. The rich of Arruk would continue to see themselves as the peak of culture, regardless of their reliance on servants from the lower classes to twist their hair just so, make their fancy clothes, and cook their food. Instead of accepting that reliance, they enforced strict rules to keep their fragile egos intact, assuring themselves that they were indeed better than those who had less.

The horse next to her lipped one of her braids. She turned back to him, pressing her forehead against his neck. If she had any power to save him, she would, but she couldn't even save herself. Anything she did to irritate the magistrate further now would only bring down more pain, more danger, and the grey wouldn't be spared either. And her brother needed the oil—she wouldn't allow him to be whipped. She stroked the horse's neck, whispering prayers to the nine gods. If she gave it her all, maybe she could win their favor enough to help her win despite everything. Maybe they'd have mercy on this horse and help him through, too.

"All right my beauty," she said finally, smoothing the horse's mane. "It's you and me now. I'm sorry to ask this of you, but can you give me one last run?"

The horse snorted at her. She gave him another pat and then led him to the starting line to spare him her weight for as long as possible. Bad enough she would have to push him for speed soon.

An official stood by the starting mark, tall and stern—not the kind woman from yesterday. "Riders! You will follow the red flags for the trail. If you do not grab each numbered red flag, you will be disqualified. At the end of the course is a target. A center shot shall be 75 points, on down through the rings by tens to zero points for the edges of the target. Then ride back here, grabbing the numbered blue flags on your return. Fail to grab one of each and you are disqualified. Grab multiples of the same flag and you are disqualified. The first to the end gets 50 points. The rider with the most points wins and shows the favor of the gods. Do you understand?"

Amanah nodded, swinging up on her horse. The thief nodded as well, grabbing his reins too tightly, too short. He'd over-control his mount, but she couldn't do anything for the bay right now. She kept her eyes on the official, who gave each of them one arrow and a strung bow.

"Ride at the sound of the horn and not before." The official raised a hand in the air.

The still air waited expectantly. A few people watched from the sides of the course, among them Emin, who stood with his arms folded and a scowl on his face, and Taunos, with his stare too intent.

The blast of a horn made her mount shiver, and the other horse leapt ahead, galloping down the street.

"Hup, hup, hup," Amanah urged her horse on, using her knees to guide him and keeping her balance instinctively.

By the time she hit the first flag, snatching it easily mid-stride, the bay horse was already around a corner. She coaxed more speed from her mount, praising him as he hurtled into a gallop. He had trouble with the corners, and she had to slow him to avoid him falling and hurting either of them. At the back of her mind, urgency pounded like drums. The stakes were too high to lose.

Her mount was short and compact, but he responded quickly to commands in the Mahyami style, the nomadic clan that roamed the borders of the Hinanur Empire and Far Dahutad's lands. Amanah's family traded and squabbled with the Mahyami on a regular basis. She'd raced them throughout her childhood, each clan pitting their horses against the others'. Taking the grey's training into account, she was able to communicate her needs much more effectively. She sent prayers to the gods in gratitude to the Mahyami childhood friends she'd played with when the two clans mingled under water-peace.

Two more checkpoints flew past. She snatched the flags with ease while slowly gaining on her competitor, who grew more and more visible through the twists and turns of the course.

The fourth flag was pushed down nearly all the way to the ground. A groan escaped her, but she gritted her teeth to keep the flare of irritation inside. She shouldn't be surprised. No doubt she was expected to dismount and grab it, but she'd played similar games as a child. Amanah gave her mount the command and scooted forward, hooking her knee around his neck and locking it with her other leg. Then, she twisted down beside him, one hand brushing the ground while her other grabbed the flag, ripping it free of the wooden post. With her leg tight around the horse's shoulders, and the horse prepared for the maneuver, she was able to right herself without trouble.

A cheer sounded from the side, where a couple onlookers stood. Despite herself, she grinned with pride before setting her mind back on her task.

The next five of the flags were at varying heights, raggedly pushed further into the ground, but none posed a problem, and soon she was racing only a couple lengths behind her competition, leaving him no time to sabotage her. The course opened up into an alley with the target visible at the end. The thief pulled back his bow quite capably and let fly, and then wheeled his horse around, barreling back toward her as the arrow hit the center of the target. Amanah nudged her mount out of the way, but still the thief's horse hit them, slamming her leg into the wall and drawing a grunt from her stumbling mount. She cried out in pain and surprise, hatred welling in her as the thief sneered.

Then he was behind her—ahead of her, really. She needed to focus on the target. Amanah coaxed her horse around, wanting to save him some distance, and shot from her position, far though it was. She hit the inner circle, and then mimed a second shot with an arrow she didn't have. Nine arrows at the targets, they always did in her youth, for the nine deities. But this time, she only loosed two—one real, one a prayer. One for Jattanu's justice, and one for Murihat's mercy, and may the others forgive her for overlooking them. She'd let prayer flags fly tonight, she promised, even though the people of Arruk despised that as a Hinanuri custom.

Amanah urged her mount back along the course, this time snatching the blue flags. She needed more speed, so she kept herself low beside the horse's shoulder for those that were close together, to pluck the flags from their posts. Matching her horse's motions, she urged him on, faster and faster, tearing around the curves with her leg aching. There was her bad-tempered competitor, riding low as well, his coat streaming in the wind behind him.

She shouted encouragement to her mount, and the thief looked back, missing his next flag. As the thief turned around for the flag, she murmured commands, and by the time he grabbed it, she was sailing past, having already snatched hers. A bellow of rage rang out behind her, but she kept her focus on the finish line. Only a little way to go, even if he had the faster horse. She was so close to winning.

Hoofbeats sounded loud in her ears behind her, along with the thief shouting abuse at her and his mount. But they were only five lengths from the finish line, then four, then three.

And then, the grey stumbled. He didn't even scream as he went down, sending Amanah hurtling headfirst toward the cobbles. She pushed off from her mount's neck and landed, running with her momentum, stopping just past the chalked line.

"Amanah!!" Fear threaded through that shout, from both her brother and Taunos on the sidelines.

She threw herself toward them, just as the thief's mount passed through where she'd been. Something hit her, boosting her momentum out of the way, and she hit the ground, groaning as pain flared. She hurt in too many places for it merely to be from the fall—the bay's hooves must have clipped her in passing, and if its shoulder hadn't helped nudge her out of the way, she'd have been trampled.

Shaking, she turned back to the grey, who was still lying on the ground just paces from the finish line. She knelt by his head, stroking his neck as he frothed, fighting for breath. He was done—frankly, it was a surprise he'd lasted the race. He deserved more than all she could give him, which was a quick, painless death.

Amanah bent to kiss him, murmuring to him as Emin and Taunos approached.

Emin swept her up in a tight embrace. "You did it!"

"That was amazing!" Taunos agreed, and though she searched his face for derision, she found none.

From behind them, the magistrate's wife called out. "Don't cry, dear. At least you tried."

Amanah bowed her head to hide her rage. A horse had been ruined needlessly, and the woman next to the man who allowed it, if not organized it, offered her condescension? And what did she mean, she tried? She'd done more than that—even though the cost was high.

"Are you all right?" Taunos asked.

"I need your knife," she said to Emin. She was not all right, but if she let it show, the magistrate would pounce on her weakness.

"I'll do it." Emin drew the blade he kept at his hip.

"No. He did this for me. I owe him." She held out her hand, keeping her gaze on the horse, and a moment later the smooth wooden handle of Emin's knife slid into her palm.

"What are you doing?" the magistrate's sharp voice sounded behind her, but Amanah had eyes and ears only for the dying horse, stroking his muzzle one final time before plunging the knife up into his neck.

The grey was gone a moment later. Amanah closed his eyes, patting him one more time, before giving Emin his blade back.

"How horrible!" The magistrate's wife clutched at her husband's sleeve, her other hand covering her mouth.

Straightening, Amanah turned to the magistrate, too aware of the splashes of the grey's blood on her guard's vest and covering her hand as she presented her flags to the official. The official eyed Emin warily, only relaxing once her brother had cleaned and sheathed the knife. Silently, efficiently, the official counted and verified each of her flags, and then the thief's. Then, the official turned and consulted with the magistrate, frowning for a moment before nodding.

"The gods see all," the official said. "And this was a test for justice. Therefore, the bag which was the apparent item of dispute is decreed to belong to Nawu of the Guma."

Amanah's mouth dropped, though she scolded herself for daring to hope. Of course the gods wouldn't force the outcome in her favor. In fact, perhaps they were in league with the magistrate and those who ruled the city the entire time.

"What?" Taunos shouted. "She was first!"

"The rules said very clearly that each participant was to ride the course. Her horse did not finish the race," the official said.

"He fell! He never should have been forced to race in the first place, and certainly not against a horse drugged for speed," Amanah objected.

"And then you murdered it," the magistrate said. "I should charge you as a horse thief, as well, since your mount was only borrowed, I remind you, not yours to discipline so brutally."

"He was suffering," she said, straightening her back and raising her chin. "I wasn't about to let him suffer when he gave his all for me, with all the odds stacked against us. Not only was I given a run-down mount who should have lived out his retirement in a pasture, but my flags were also tampered with!"

The magistrate scowled. "Your horse was chosen by chance, if you recall, and any tampering of your flags cost your opponent time as well. Or are you accusing a magistrate of Arruk of cheating?"

Boots scraped on the stone cobbles behind her, where her brother and Taunos stood. Emin's voice hissed something she couldn't hear, and the movement stopped.

"Another objection and I will see you lose what little protection the guardhouse gives you." The magistrate glared at her.

Amanah gritted her teeth, lest her tongue land her in more trouble.

"This is not justice," Taunos objected.

"Back to your homes," the official shouted, waving his hands to disperse the gathered crowd. "The gods' will has been seen."

"The gods see you, and so do I," the magistrate said, leaning toward Amanah. "I will let you go this once. Consider it mercy. But if you test me any further, I will charge you as a horse thief. From now on, any havi thief will be subject to five lashes, understand?"

Amanah's nostrils flared, but she should have known. The remnants of hope within her withered and went cold. Arruk wouldn't know justice if it walked up and shook their hands.

She and Emin could still go home—havi who kept their heads down could leave at any time, assuming they had supplies to survive the wilderness to their destination. It was only the ones who had caught the attention of nobles who would be arrested if they tried to leave. Although, perhaps she'd ruined that now, with this display. Would they be allowed to leave if they tried? To have any chance of that, Emin would have to figure out how to return the thaa oil, or they'd be seen as thieves running from justice.

The official handed her bag, handmade by her mothers, to the thief, this youth who profited from the prejudice of others. He dipped his hand inside and pulled out the precious bottle of oil and her new head scarf, flashing her a smile.

"Good, the oil's still here," the thief said. "My sister will be so glad to get her scarf and bag back."

Pressing her lips together, Amanah turned away, pushing past a scowling Emin and Taunos. The thief likely didn't even have a sister. All she could do was maintain her dignity as much as she could. Her ribs and shoulder ached and she was certain her leg was bruised. It barely held her weight.

"That's horrible!" Taunos's voice was sharp with vehemence.

Amanah looked back, blinking. She'd been bracing for some joke from him, to help her shrug off the loss as if it meant nothing. But Emin was holding him back by the arm, while Taunos's mouth was twisted with fury, the muscles standing out on his forearms as he clenched his fists. She'd never seen him this worked up about anything. He'd always laughed off the pranks others played on him, and he joked with Emin when one of Emin's pranks landed him doing the worst chores alongside the true culprit, her brother.

So much, he took in stride, but this, someone treating her like, well, like a nomadic havi in the city, had apparently awoken his rage.

"It's not going to help. It'll only get us in more trouble," Emin was saying.

"I could talk to some of the nobles," Taunos began.

"No," Amanah said, but her voice was muted by the tears she was holding back. Best case, the nobles would pretend to help, only to snare her and Emin in a trap.

Emin snorted. "They won't care. And that'd make things even worse. Trust me."

Her brother let much of the city's annoyances roll off his broad shoulders, but he did care. Amanah dashed tears from her eyes. Her hand trembled, tremors travelling down to her taut shoulders. She needed to get out of the public eye—shaking and blood covered, she'd only present another target.

"They set it up so you couldn't win, rigged it from the start. They can't get away with this." Taunos stepped forward, against Emin shoving him back.

Amanah went back and caught Taunos's arm, tensing for a backlash that never came. "They already did. Anything less than acceptance will only prove them right. That we are not to be trusted with anything."

"Besides, they'll charge her with horse theft," Emin said. "You heard the magistrate. Five lashes. Provoke them, and there's too much risk they'll upgrade the punishment to Jattanu's justice—lashed in front of the temple, then left there to bake in the sun all day."

Amanah shuddered again, meeting her brother's gaze for a long, pained moment of shared memory.

A muscle feathered in Taunos's jaw, but then he deflated. "Are you hurt?"

She swallowed hard, avoiding his gaze.

"I'm sorry Amanah," Emin said, letting go of his friend but keeping an eye on him. "Our mothers will make you another bag though."

"That bag was made for *me*." Amanah's voice cracked. "It wasn't even worth anything. And they stole it. And you needed that oil. They together, all three of them, stole it, and there's nothing we can do about it. And now all havi will suffer for my folly."

"You can't control other people," Emin started, and she snapped at him.

"I can't even stay out of trouble by controlling myself and my own risks!"

Her shoulders shook, and the tears began in earnest. She didn't know who began the hug, but then she was wrapped in an embrace made up of four strong arms, two beating hearts surrounding her from either side, forming a wall of care until her pain subsided to where she could handle it again.

Once her grief and outrage were under control, she became all too aware of the fact that she was pressed close to Taunos. The heat of his frame, his cheek on her braids, the scent of him—sweat and green, growing things—enveloping her. Crying on Emin's shoulder was one thing, but Taunos? She stepped sidewise, away from their encircling arms, rubbing away the remains of the tears.

She cleared her throat. "I'm all right. Thank you."

Taunos's eyes were shining, his voice a rumble like thunder. "It's not right."

A bitter laugh escaped her. "Oh, I know."

"What can I do?"

She stared at him. He was just a friend of Emin's—a far too handsome one—but none of Emin's friends had asked that of her before. Not once they saw the weight of what she and Emin dealt with.

"Would taking your mind off all this help?" Taunos asked.

"She likes dancing," Emin said, nudging her with an elbow.

Taunos's eyes lit up. "Pamun has a party tonight. We should go!"

Emin snorted. "Pamun? As in, one of the richest merchants in the city?"

"He sent me an invitation," Taunos said, as if it was nothing. He took her hand, squeezed it gently. "Come with me, both of you."

It took her a moment to fully comprehend it. Taunos had received an invitation to a rich man's party, somehow. A social climber known to only invite rich and influential nobles.

Taunos was rich; he must be. Probably a noble, wherever he was from.

She withdrew her hand from his. "We're havi, Taunos. They'd never let us in."

His brow crinkled, and gods above, his confusion looked real. "Even with an invitation?"

"Yes, Taunos, even with an invitation." She clapped him on the shoulder, a distancing move, reminding herself he was only another guard. Another guard and Emin's friend and possibly a noble—all strong reasons why she should not be noticing how deep the brown of his eyes went. But the ridiculousness of the idea had lightened her soul just a bit, and she was grateful. She hoped it was apparent in her tone. "Go and have fun."

He shook his head. "No, I'm not going, then. What are we doing instead?"

"Taunos, it's Pamun. You can't get an invitation and then not go," Emin said.

"We need to get to guard duty," Amanah said, shoving them forward.

"Why not? Is it illegal?" Taunos asked Emin, allowing Amanah to herd him along. He walked on one side of her, and Emin on the other, both staying close. The pains in her muscles were still there, but they were somehow easier to bear as they walked back toward the guardhouse.

"No, it's… people would literally kill for that," Emin said, gesturing expansively. "For the chance to go to his mansion? To shake his hand? To drink his wine?"

Taunos shrugged, as if all that were nothing. "I don't care. If he won't let you in, I don't want to go."

"How do you have an invitation anyway?" Amanah asked.

"I helped him out with something," Taunos said airily.

She furrowed her brow. "Uh huh, and he was very grateful."

"I suppose," Taunos said.

"And how did he know to ask you for this favor? Why do the nobles like you if you aren't one of them?" Emin asked. "I've never been able to figure it out."

Taunos chuckled, spreading his arms. "I'm a fun person to be around!"

Amanah rolled her eyes. "He's rich, Emin."

"I'm not," Taunos said. "I think."

She snorted. That last part gave him away. "How much money do you have hidden away?"

"I spent my last coins a couple nights ago, during that party. Oh, but remember those drinks? I didn't know drinks could glow like that."

Amanah frowned at him. They'd all hung out at the market, and Taunos had indeed brought by trays of glowing blue and gold drinks, enough for the whole table to try them. But he'd done it without thinking, not like it was his last coin.

"Wait, wait, so who's the first noble in the city you found an in with and how? Maybe I can do it, too," Emin said.

Taunos shrugged. "I was about to cliff dive into a pool. I don't know, have you heard of the Cauldron, south of here?"

Amanah's eyes widened. "That's a drop of twenty paces!"

Taunos grinned. "Sounded fun. It was fun, actually. But as I was about to jump, a man came running, chased by thieves. Running right for the edge—I'm not sure he even saw it. I grabbed his arm, swung him around to keep him from falling, and then tossed the thieves over."

Emin was staring. Amanah was too, she realized, and made herself look away.

"Then what?" Emin asked.

Taunos shrugged again. "Checked to see that the man was all right, traded names—that was Lord Guri—and then I dove."

Emin burst out laughing, slapping Taunos's shoulder hard enough to make him stagger.

Amanah burst out too, spreading her hands at his folly. "That was so dangerous! You didn't know those men, the pool, nothing? They could have been anyone!"

"Sure," he shrugged. "So could I have been, from their point of view. I was surprised the man was waiting for me at the top after I climbed back up. The thieves hadn't waited—I think they thought I was chasing them."

"Weren't you?" Emin asked.

Taunos laughed. "No, I was there to dive! Well, I was going to help them out of the water if they needed, but..."

"But... but there was so much... you could have..." Disaster after potential disaster crowded her tongue. Amanah finally settled for shaking her head.

"When life hands you an opportunity to enjoy yourself without the expense of others, why think twice?" Taunos asked, his eyes gleaming. Then he snapped his fingers. "Oh, that's right! I heard a rumor there would be honeyfish that glow like stars—like those drinks—migrating past the harbor. Should we watch that?"

Amanah couldn't help but snort a laugh. This man was turning down an invitation from high society to hang out with them and watch a honeyfish migration?

"How did you hear about this?" she asked.

"When I was in the market. I listen to people talk," he said.

She didn't doubt it, though she hadn't heard this rumor. He spoke easily with rich merchants and nobles, and then in the same breath, with havi, servants, and dockworkers. All without blinking an eye, like it wasn't unusual, like the strict social hierarchy of Arruk was nothing but an illusion that had no hold on him.

And she had to admit, the honeyfish did sound intriguing.

"Let me think about it?"

He smiled at her and nodded. As they entered the guardhouse and Taunos and Emin headed to the sparring yard, conversing together in low tones, Amanah paused on her way to get a clean vest, watching them go. Honeyfish. Taunos made it seem so easy, so safe to join him. She shuddered. That's how Arruk got you—it seemed like a place of opportunity but instead, it was a cage, a pit of traps.

3

AFTER THEIR DUTY shift that day, they were filing into the guardhouse when Borlim intercepted them. "Taunos, Emin, Amanah, my office. Now."

Amanah shot a glance at Emin, but he looked as curious as she was—curious without the undercurrent of anxiety, the horrible feeling something else awful was about to happen to cap the terrible day. She swallowed down her feelings and followed the guardmaster's broad back to his small office.

Borlim's office was utilitarian, with just a few trinkets resting on his shelves from his family. It wasn't meant for so many people, and it was a good thing Amanah and Taunos were smaller than the other two men. As it was, there was no room to sit on this side of the desk, so the three of them stood. Amanah kept her weight on her less-bruised leg, and her mind firmly off the topic of a hot bath to soothe her aches.

Borlim flipped through the neat stack of papers on his desk and withdrew a letter, sealed with wax as the nobles did. The seal had been broken, and he unfolded it, looking at them from over the top of the paper.

"Haari Taunos, this is a message from Minister Ehu of the Asi clan, requesting your services as escort for two Asi nobles from Ukish to Gahimbli." Borlim scanned the paper and then nodded. "Lords Inuwe and Lamyi. The rest of the escort will be up to you to decide. You will decide on Emin and Amanah, two knowledgeable guards with complementary skills who just happen to be havi. You will add at least one other, no more than seven total."

Taunos's brow furrowed, but he nodded.

"Nobles are requesting guards, now?" Emin asked. "I don't expect they'll be happy with your—I mean Taunos's—choices."

"I don't care," Borlim said. "I'm allowing this because it solves a problem for me."

He turned his gaze on Amanah, and she stiffened with dread. "Amanah. I have a letter here from a certain magistrate who thought it was a good idea to scold my poor judgement in hiring havi. Apparently you're a thief and if you step out of line again, I'm to dismiss you from the guard or send you for Jattanu's justice."

Amanah bowed her head, swallowing down bile.

"The bimnas have seen you loitering outside the windows again."

Amanah's face heated. She wanted to learn, that was all, but what story had they made up in their heads? "Sorry sir. Nasri's been teaching me silks and I've been teaching her banner dancing in return."

"There are other places to practice dancing—including more suitable places with beams for the silks."

But none that would allow her to accidentally eavesdrop and pick up as much information from the bimnas in the bamimri as possible. Maybe she was a thief, but if so, she was a thief of knowledge that never should be hoarded in the first place. "Yes, sir. Sorry, sir."

"This is a little more than sorry." Borlim sighed. "You're an asset to us, Amanah. You're hard-working and dependable. But this letter from a magistrate cannot go ignored."

"I understand." She winced. She'd lost everything. He'd have to dismiss her to please the magistrate, and she'd never get more lessons—even covertly—from the bamimri. She wouldn't be able to help the needy in the city avoid trouble as easily, wouldn't have the resources to send their way. And would the guards at the gate even let her through? Tears pricked her eyes. She should have let her bag go, but Emin's oil was in there.

"No, you don't," Borlim snapped.

She looked up, brow wrinkled. Oh no, was it going to be even worse?

"I'm not letting you go. But the magistrate... I need to get you away from here until things cool down, and even after a few months it may not be safe."

Borlim wouldn't actually believe she was a thief, would he? "I didn't steal it—it was my bag."

"It doesn't matter. You publicly challenged him. There are already rumors he fixed the race and you still won. I don't know where those rumors came from, but they are lemon juice in the magistrate's wounds, and he is aching to hurt you. When powerful men like that want to hurt havi like you, they will find a way."

Amanah's mind raced. "So this is why you're sending us to Ukish."

Borlim's gaze flicked to Taunos. "I was lucky enough to be sitting on this request, trying to figure out how to deny it without drawing the wrath of the Asi and their allies down on my guards. But your absence would put Emin at risk. I won't have anyone targeting Emin because they can't get at you, so you both must go. But be careful. I can't guarantee the magistrate can't reach you there. And I can't guarantee his claws will be sheathed when you return."

Emin and Taunus nodded.

Amanah offered a tight smile. "Thank you, sir. For trying."

"Until then, be invisible," Borlim said.

"Yes, sir."

"I don't mean 'try.' I mean 'be.'"

"Yes, sir."

"That means staying away from the bamimri, Amanah."

She ducked her head to hide a wince. "Yes, sir."

"Ukish will be easy enough—you'll sail from our harbor, down the river and around the coast to theirs. I'll give you a letter that will secure you passage on a ship called the Squall. Gahimbli is the problem. Hinanuri forces are in that area. You must ensure the safety of the nobles, no matter what."

A tiny kernel of excitement unfurled in her, underneath all her concerns. She'd never been on a boat before. And whatever else happened, they'd be sailing, not just down the river but on the coastline, too! The longer she stayed in the city, even with its faults, the more a desire to see more of the world grew within her, spurred on by the variety of market goods from countries near and far. The more exotic goods were usually at the higher class wells, but she could at least catch glimpses during her guard rounds. What might she see on this journey, away from the confines of Arruk?

"Why are they going?" Taunos asked.

"That's for them to tell you, if they deign to. Regardless, there's pressure on this from the highest places. But you need to travel quickly, which means a small team. Taunos and Emin, you two are exceptional fighters. Guard those nobles with your lives. Get them there and back safely.

"They specifically requested Haari Taunos, so you are nominally in charge. You'll be reliant on the information these two can provide you to make up for the cultural details you don't know. However, Emin, I want a verbal report from you when you return. The quality of your report, along with other reports I will receive, will tell me whether you are ready, as I suspect, to command your own war-band. If it won't disrupt the nobles too much, Emin is to be clearly in charge of the guard, while all liaison with the nobles is to go through you, Taunos. All, are we clear?"

Taunos nodded firmly, as Emin fought to contain his smile.

"But you," Borlim eyed Amanah. "I'm not sending you just to get you out of the city until things cool down. You're one of our fastest riders, with skills hard to match, as you so capably and publicly demonstrated this morning. If things go badly with the nobles' visit so close to the border, you are to ride back hard and give us word of what happened. Do not stay and fight. Ride and do not spare the horse."

"You would have me run from a fight?" She bristled.

Borlim raised his eyebrows. "I would have you carry news so we can send support and keep those nobles alive."

Amanah bowed her head.

A thunk sounded as Borlim tossed a bag of coins on the desk in front of Amanah. "There's your budget. You leave at dawn in two days, so you have tomorrow to pack and prepare."

The guardmaster flicked his hand at the three of them, dismissing them.

"We can do a supply run tonight," Emin said as they exited. "Amanah, help me with the list and we can go—"

Just before his door closed, Borlim interrupted from the office. "Invisible!"

She winced.

Emin folded his arms. "I was hoping for one last night at the market."

Amanah turned her apologetic gaze to Taunos. "So much for honeyfish."

"We could be boring," Emin said, his voice hopeful.

She patted his arm. "You have more than enough fun for three people most days, so I think in the greater scheme of things, you'll be fine."

Emin grinned, but his flash of mirth quickly drained to concern as his eyes darted over her face. "You ok?"

"I'm fine." She smiled, trying to take the bite from her words. "I don't have another bag to be stolen."

His brow furrowed. "You're not ok."

"I will be, though." She rubbed her forehead. "I'm not used to being smuggled out of the city. I guess that means I'm special."

"Of course you are. And the rumors mean people know it," Taunos said.

She narrowed her eyes at him. "It only made the magistrate angrier. More dangerous. Be careful with who you send on the supply run, Emin. We're supposed to keep our heads down."

"I will, I will. Stop worrying."

Saying it was harder than doing it, though. She and Emin ran through the possibilities with Taunos for the additional members of their team, and finally settled on Gurseh, partially because he could write, but also because Emin trusted him—they were dating, after all, which was a bonus Amanah teased her brother about. Amanah was worried about adding too many members to their team and the possible delays that would bring, so Taunos decided on just the four of them. Emin got Gurseh, and they spent the evening meal together, planning what supplies they'd need from the guardhouse and what, if anything, they needed to buy tomorrow.

By the time they had a decent list, it was late, and Amanah's eyes were dry and tired. Everything hurt, especially the leg that'd been crushed between the wall and her horse, but also her shoulder, ribs, and hip on the other side from nearly being trampled. Her aches had only gotten worse as stiffness set in, despite how she tried to stretch while planning.

She bid the men good night, but her evening wasn't done. Gitu and his family still needed to get out of the city. She wouldn't be able to help them. It was against Borlim's advice. She could have taken Emin up on his wish to head into the city to make this task easier, except she preferred to keep him far from her activities, far from suspicion if anything should go wrong. This was even riskier now, but she couldn't have the lives of Gitu's family on her conscience.

With cautious steps, Amanah slipped back into the city, limping for the well nearest the river harbor. It was the closest well with a Murihat's Hand messenger station nearby. She didn't know the identities of the other leaders of Murihat's Hand, and she doubted the places she met them to send or receive messages were their actual homes or workplaces. The smell of fish filled her nose as she hugged the shadows, rounding a smokehouse, and tapped a particular rhythm on the door. She waited, leaning her back against the wall to take some weight off her bruises, cloak pulled high, eyes darting among the people still walking the streets.

A knock answered—the same rhythm she'd tapped out. Using the nomadic tapping language, she passed along the message. Since at least some of the Hand, like Amanah, were illiterate, the tapping language kept their faces and voices secret from one another. Any time she needed to pass on information, she went to the few buildings she knew a Hand member might be near and tapped it out.

35

When the confirmation came, Amanah nodded to herself, though her eyes went toward the market where the tents would be. She'd done everything she could for Gitu and Anila. She had enough to worry about now just keeping herself safe. She pushed off the wall, slinking through the streets and pausing at other houses to loiter for a bit, just in case, before heading back.

~

Though she had to dodge a patrol, she made it back to the guardhouse without incident. Still, her nerves buzzed with tension, her mind turning over all the myriad dangers, fueled by impotent anger. Amanah opened the window at one end of her dormitory and leaned out, bracing her good shoulder against the stone edging the window, closing her eyes as the night breeze whistled around her to mingle with the snores of the nine others. She wished there was music tonight from the garden to soothe her soul.

A scraping on the wall below made her eyes fly open. Someone was carefully scaling the stonework of the guardhouse. He looked up and waved, the carefree motions easily identifying him. It was full dark, and had been for some time. What was Taunos doing in the garden? He knew the rules against it. Not to mention this wall-climbing.

"Someone needs to tell Borlim how easily this wall can be climbed. It's a security hazard," Amanah whispered dryly when Taunos got to her.

He flashed another grin. "Maybe tomorrow."

"What are you doing up here?"

"I wanted to see how you were."

"Trying to sleep."

He quirked his eyebrows at her. "I can't say I've ever found sleeping while standing to be very comfortable. And here, seems like you'd risk falling out the window."

She snorted at him.

"What's your favorite flower?" Taunos asked.

"What?"

"I didn't get to take you dancing or help take your mind off of everything today, and clearly you're still upset. So, what's your favorite flower? Maybe the scent will help calm your mind so you can get some rest."

What made him care so much? Today he'd seen first-hand how havi were treated. That was enough to make people run.

36

Worse, Taunos hung out with nobles. If he fell out of favor, Emin, being his friend, could get roped in as a casualty of the carnage that would follow.

"A rose," she lied. The only roses nearby were those in the garden—forbidden to be cut. She was as off-limits as the queen's roses.

He nodded and she watched him go. As he blended into the shadows, she blew out her breath and rubbed her eyes, turning her back to the window, to the garden, to him. That would be the end of it, and they'd face the mission to come with pure professionalism. And she wasn't sad about it, because he was just Emin's friend. Nothing to her. Just a friendly face that would leave one day and never think of her again. She banished the memory of his strong arms around her earlier that day, shielding her from the pain of injustice until she could collect herself.

A scrape from the wall made her whirl back around. Taunos was nearly up to her window again, his progress made clumsy by the potted rose he cradled in one arm.

He set the pot in her windowsill, switching his handhold to stretch out his fingers. "I have to put it back, but I thought a little time with a treasure is better than none."

She stared at him. What kind of person did that sort of thing? She should be nothing to him.

"This is ridiculous. I'm coming down." The words were out of her mouth before she could think better of them, but sleep seemed far away and maybe conversation would help. And she definitely didn't want to disturb her roommates.

He grinned at her and nodded, then took the rose and disappeared, back down the wall once again.

She threw on a long-sleeved shirt against the chill of the night and grabbed her sandals, carrying them as she silently made her way through the hallways. The world was made silvery by the light of the two moons, already past their zenith. This was a stupid idea. She should be getting sleep so she'd be ready for whatever tomorrow brought her, not slipping into the garden. It wasn't a rule largely considered important, and the doors were kept unlocked at all times to provide easy access across in case of emergency, but still, she hadn't dared before. If the guards caught her, Borlim would surely lecture her on the meaning of the word invisible. What was making her take this chance now, beyond a mind muddled with anger, worry, and sleep? She probably wouldn't be able to find Taunos in the garden anyway.

But she did find him, before she could talk herself out of it. He was in the center of the garden, leaning against the white bark of the Gods' Tree as if it were any common tree, because of course he was.

"What are you doing?" she asked, trying not to show her unease at his casual disrespect of the Gods' Tree.

"Waiting for you. Want to walk a bit? You can carry your rose."

She took the pot gingerly. "Where did you get it from?"

"Just over there," he said, waving toward the palace.

She eyed him. Surely he was jesting with her or it was a trap. No one was so dense as to not realize you don't walk off with pots outside the palace. It was bad enough to move them in the garden.

"Let's get this back," she said, trying to hide the stiffness and pain of her entire right side.

He watched her, something glimmering in his expression for a moment that she couldn't quite identify, and then it was gone, smoothed away.

She set the rose back in the empty place among its siblings, and he shadowed her as she turned back to the path, hurrying away from the looming palace. It was a near perfect night, the cool breeze a caress, and her stiffness eased a little as they walked. The caged nightbirds throughout the garden sang, their jeweled daytime companions glimmering quietly in the moonlight as they slept. Heat radiated off Taunos beside her, and she found herself drifting closer to him, having to force herself away.

He grimaced as they passed another dangling cage, and she tilted her head. "You don't like the birds?"

"I think they should be free to live their lives, not confined for someone else's enjoyment."

She watched his expression, but his eyes were on the cage, his face carefully blank. His voice had been rough, as if he were speaking a truth important to him, and she pondered that. Did the city count as a cage? It was a trap, certainly, but she also found it difficult to leave, despite her struggles here. Did he think the same? If so, he had never shown it.

Her feet stopped under the spreading white branches of the Gods' Tree clothed in silver leaves. It, like the man lounging below it, simply couldn't stand to be normal either.

"I wish I could have stopped it," he murmured.

"Stopped what?" she asked.

He gestured beyond the guardhouse, frustration pinching the corners of his mouth. "That farce of a trial."

"It wasn't yours to stop. The magistrate was responsible, and he's decided to make me pay for it."

"Still, I—"

"Wishes come easily," she cut him off. She needed to be strong right now, not to cave to the crumbling of her heart.

Would she even be welcome back in Arruk after this? Maybe it was time to name this experience a failure and go home. Surely she'd never get anywhere close to the bamimri to learn any more, and havi were in even more trouble, thanks to her. At least for a little while, until the magistrate's pride was assuaged.

Taunos let out a breath in a long exhale.

The silence between them weighed on her. He'd tried to cheer her up with a flower, but she'd been dishonest with him. She cleared her throat, looking away. "I lied to you. I don't like roses. I was trying to send you away."

"If you want me to go, all you need to do is say." His words were soft.

He shifted, his warmth receding, and she caught his arm. He paused, head tilted, brow furrowed slightly above the darkness of his brown eyes. She could get lost staring at him.

"Stay."

His shoulder pressed against hers as he leaned against the tree, settling in. So near.

She fixed her eyes on the stars instead, firmly not looking at him. To distract herself, she said, "I've heard sailors ride across the seas navigating by stars, just like we do across the desert."

Taunos's smile was evident even in the dark. His voice was low, a comforting rumble she shouldn't appreciate so much. "Some people believe the stars are doorways through which spirits of old visit us. Or even where our spirits can see the future. But maybe it doesn't matter if they're right or wrong—maybe what people think of the stars tells you enough about who they are."

"Who said that?"

"There was an old man I shared a meal with once, far from here. He wandered around thinking about people and life. A philosopher, they called him."

Amanah shook her head. He just casually spoke of rubbing elbows with philosophers in far off lands? Was he boasting? But it was like when he'd mentioned the party earlier, as if he didn't realize what it was he was saying. As if he didn't realize the social norms it seemed he broke with every moment of his existence.

Well, here anyway, she could play along. "I heard someone once say the stars were pinpricks from a giant needle used by the gods."

"Who said that?" he asked.

"A drunk in the market yesterday," she said.

He chuckled, and the sound made her grin.

"I heard a poem once, in a land where the people only travelled at night," he said. "About stars. Would you like to hear it?"

Caught off guard, she nodded.

His words washed around her, his voice soothing in a lyric rumble, but she had trouble paying attention. She couldn't stop staring at him. Most of Emin's friends didn't care much about seeing far-off lands. They were happy where they were. Emin could be content here in Arruk too, she knew. She'd come for the bamimri, until all too cruelly she learned that dream was never to be, not for a havi, even if they were a guard. So she adapted, instead stealing every secret she could from the bamimri windows. A growing appetite for secrets, for learning, grew in her month by month, but could she actually get free of the city and travel, to see everything there was to see? It would mean no longer having access to covert learning from the bamimri, and she wouldn't be able to help Murihat's Hand. They would be fine, but it would be a disruption, and in that disruption, people would get hurt. Already this trip increased the risk that the plans for the people in the tents might fail, and she worried for Gitu.

No, people depended on her now. She couldn't drop everything and leave.

Maybe the city was a cage after all.

And then there was Taunos, who fit in so well with Emin's friends, so easily. She'd never really given him much thought, except to affirm to herself that no matter how dashing a figure he cut in practice, with all the heads he turned, he was far too dangerous to get involved with. But all this time, hidden away within him, were memorized poems and the words of philosophers?

His poem ended, and she fixed her eyes on the stars. "It's lovely. The poem. Maybe someday, I'll see lands where the stars are different."

"Why someday?"

Her brow furrowed. He was clearly well-travelled. Why didn't he understand? "Because. It would be nice to see new people, new places. To do things I've never done before, to meet people who live differently, who see the world differently, to experience all there is to life."

"So why *someday*?" The question was gentle, with more emphasis on the last two words this time. "What keeps you from just walking out of the city gates, especially after what I saw today?"

"I don't know, imminent death?" she said dryly. She eyed him, and then turned to face him more fully. "Were you listening at all to the list of supplies we need? If Borlim hadn't given us money, we couldn't afford them, and we certainly can't cross the wilderness without them. If dehydration didn't get us, an animal would."

Taunos hummed. "That is a good point."

"I know. That's why I made it." Her eyes narrowed. "How did you come to Arruk, anyway?"

"By ship." He grimaced. "Hopefully this one won't be so bad since I'll be there entirely of my own free will."

"So far as being under orders go, anyway," Amanah said.

His teeth flashed white in the darkness before he sobered. "So supplies are what's holding you back, then?"

"It takes time to prepare for a trip like that. Money. How would I pay for a horse or passage on a ship? Where would I sleep? How would I find my way back? And things keep getting in the way." She couldn't tell him all the ties that bound her here, the duty to the people who depended on her.

He chuckled, and she narrowed her eyes at him, but he didn't seem to be laughing at her, just in general. "It's an adventure," he said. "If you know all about it in advance, where's the fun?"

"Knowing nothing in advance is folly that will get you killed," she returned.

"Maybe. Maybe not. But you'll have lived, right? Lived your dreams."

She shook her head. "I can't."

"If you don't want to, or if you don't want to right now, that's one thing," he said. "But if you do, you can find a way, or make it. Maybe get help with the needed supplies."

"Maybe for you."

"What do you mean?" That furrow in his brow was back, honest confusion in his eyes. "You already know what's needed, and you made it here in the first place."

She sighed, her hand going to her braids, and leaned against the trunk of the white-barked tree. How could she reduce all her troubles to words that would sum up the reality she faced each day without hinting at things he had no business knowing?

She couldn't tell him any of that. Couldn't risk others' lives. And the rest of her troubles were all tangled up together.

The words wouldn't come.

Taunos nudged his shoulder against hers; thankfully he stood on her less bruised side. "Maybe out there, people will see you for you. All the brilliance of you."

She turned, eyes narrowed. "I'm not brilliant."

"You're incredible," he said, his words a soft murmur. "You're a masterful archer and rider, and you care so much about people, even if you don't like them individually. You do what you think is right and stay true to your principles. Your mind is always working. Maybe a little too much, if Emin's right, but maybe exactly enough."

Amanah snorted. Here she was, out in the gardens with him, alone, at night, because her mind was running too much to let her sleep. And suddenly, she was aware of how very close he was, how she'd been drawn in by the heat of him again. She resisted leaning in, but with her next breath, his scent filled her nose, far better than that of roses, which were too sweet. He smelled like places she'd never been, scents she had no name for, but which seemed to her green, rich, and filled with possibilities.

The nomadic clans knew that pairs who smelled good to each other were good matches. Prospective suitors would often first leave a shirt out for the other. Only if the recipient enjoyed the scent would the relationship progress, regardless of any past interactions.

And Taunos didn't just smell good. He was handsome, too, the brown of his skin gleaming, taut with muscle, and his brown eyes warm and kind, with a third shade of brown for the hair he was growing out to fit more in the Dahuti style.

But she couldn't get involved with him. Not *him*. The rich of Arruk would see her getting ideas above her station. She could bring down pain on all havi. More than she already had today.

Taunos gave a little hop, springing easily to the lowest branch of the tree. He swung himself up in fluid motions, then grinned down at her. "Want to join me?"

Again, him and climbing the tree. She closed her gaping mouth. "I don't know how to climb. Trees, that is."

His grin only broadened, and he extended a hand to her. "Here, I'll help you."

"This is the Gods' Tree," she objected. "If we get caught…"

"That's half the fun, isn't it?" he asked. "Besides, we're already breaking the rules by being here."

A recklessness rose in her. He was right. She'd already be in trouble if they got caught, but Taunos seemed to excel at not getting caught. Besides, following the rules hadn't worked for her so far today, because the rules were stacked against her. All her efforts had only brought more pain.

Rebelliousness became daring, and she reached up and took his hand.

It was warm, his calloused grip strong and sure around her wrist as he lifted her, distracting her from the pangs in her ribs. Her feet scraped against the bark as she grasped for the tree limb. As soon as she was clinging to the branch, he swung higher into the tree as if it were as easy as walking.

The limbs were closer together now that they were in the tree's canopy. Feeling like a child, she followed him, placing her hands where he did, feet where he did. He stilled for a moment, head turning, and then beckoned her, angling for the tightest clump of branches. She headed that direction, pressing her lips together when her bruised hip objected. Sticks snapped with her passage. He hushed her, mischief in his eyes.

"What's that?" someone below asked. Royal guards.

She froze. She was too low in the tree still. The guards coming would spot her easily, whereas the next branches were thick with leaves to shield her—if she could get there. But if she moved, that also might give her away. She needed a plan, but there was no time.

Taunos beckoned again, indicating the spot next to him on a thick, sturdy-looking branch near the trunk. As silently as possible, she moved toward him, but her foot slipped, her sandal getting caught in the crook of two branches. If it dropped, the guards would see where they were. She tugged ineffectually, and then finally jammed it deeper into the crook of the branches. Carefully she slipped her foot out and abandoned it there, catching Taunos's hand. He tugged her easily to his side, catching her so that she didn't bruise herself further against the tree. She pressed herself against the trunk, breathing as quietly as she could, while below them, guards prowled.

"It's past sundown," one called. "Garden's off-limits."

"It's probably just an animal." The other sounded bored.

Amanah scowled, recognizing the second guard. He'd sneered at her before for listening outside the bamimri, even though Nasri was also there. He'd stepped on her foot, too, but there was no recompense. Royal guards weren't under Borlim's command like city guards were. Her eyes went to her abandoned sandal, sitting there like an accusation. Trouble.

"Come on, let's check in with the interior guards," the second guard said.

"You mean check in on the cups of hot yeru."

The two guards' casual bickering was slowly swallowed by the night as they ambled away. Amanah grinned. She'd gotten away with it—a minor rebellion, but still. Even though she'd left her sandal behind, the guards hadn't caught her.

Taunos's eyes were on her—she could feel the weight of them. She wanted to avoid them, to avoid the contempt that would come from her ineptitude with climbing—nothing at all like his obvious skill. But when she finally met his gaze, they were only full of carefree light, as if it were him and her together, laughing at the world.

Humor filled her in response—this was, after all, quite ridiculous. She held it in until the guards' voices faded from the breeze, and then it came bubbling out quietly, the stresses of the day lifting from her. Taunos shook silently next to her, eyes crinkled at the corners.

He tilted his head toward her sandal. "It did its best, didn't it?"

"To get us caught, perhaps," she said.

He threw his head back, silent laughter in every line of his body. Completely carefree but for the stealth of him.

Goddess help her, she wanted to kiss him. Lightning filled her, her body rigid with anticipation, charged by the nearness of him. The danger of him was an elixir, a little voice within her asking, hadn't she been cautious long enough? And if she was going to take a chance, might it be on him? Borlim did allow romantic entanglements so long as they didn't affect work.

But no. Anyone romantic with Taunos would be the opposite of invisible, and they had the mission coming up. The last thing they needed were distractions. Besides, Taunos drew attention wherever he went. He also associated with nobles, even if he had hated how the trial today went. Even if he had comforted her.

He returned her gaze, his head tilting to the side.

Words blurted from her mouth, more to keep her self-control alive than anything else. "You were just here yesterday. How many times have you done this?"

Her hands stayed on the tree limb beneath her, but her arm brushed against his. She shied away from the contact, but he didn't press, and the next time she bumped him, she let it be. What was the danger in a little stability so high up? She'd often climbed cliffs before, but they didn't rock in the wind.

"Many nights," he answered, his eyes turned upward.

She followed the strong lines of his neck, his jaw, following his gaze through the leaves to the stars that peeked between the moving green. Everything moved up here.

"Why?" she asked.

"It reminds me of home. I spent my childhood climbing trees."

"You have many trees there?"

44

"Forests."

Her eyebrows rose, but he didn't elaborate. She knew by now how he'd deflect if she asked where he came from. He always did, and she had secrets too, even from Emin.

What would it look like, to have these gardens as far as the eye could see? That's what a forest was, wasn't it? She'd never seen one, for her family lived among the rocky cliffs and canyons, and the Hinanuri clans they travelled and traded with occasionally lived on wide open, windswept plains.

And how would it feel to come from living in a massive garden to living in Arruk? Did he miss home, or was he tired of trees, craving the new and interesting?

The heat coming off him caught her attention again as she began to lean into it. He was like a fire. Abruptly, she frowned, pressing her hand to his temple before she thought about it.

He shivered, leaning back. "What?"

Blood rose to her cheeks, setting them aflame to match his heat. "Sorry. I... you're warm. Do you have a fever?"

He shook his head. "No, I'm fine."

"But you're burning up!"

"And you're freezing," he said with another shiver. "If I had my cloak, I'd offer it to you."

Amanah eyed him critically. "It's a cool night. You're sure you're not sick?"

"I promise. I just run a little hotter than most people, I'm told."

The tension in her shoulders loosened with that assurance, and she tore her gaze from him. Her cheeks surely were as red as his infernal roses. Why did knowing he was well fill her with relief?

But her eyes returned to his, caught by his gaze flickering across her face, eyes so dark she could drown in them. He tilted his head toward her, a curve to the corners of his mouth. His words breathed across her skin like a perfume. "I very much want to kiss you."

His hand was warm on her wrist, but not confining. How would his lips feel on hers? Soft? Firm? A thrill ran through her core, begging her to find out. He leaned closer, and their breath mingled, and gods all around her, her head swam. Was he some magic creature, some sea-wizard to enchant her?

She leaned away, swallowing hard, and pressed her back against the tree, trying to regain her composure.

"What's wrong?" he asked, concern clear in his face.

Tearing her eyes away from him, Amanah focused on the breeze blowing past the whispering leaves, the rough bark of the tree beside her. She couldn't get involved with him. What had she been thinking, to come here, to climb this tree? She hadn't been.

"I can't," she said. "I... Everyone loves you. If we were together, people would think less of you."

"I'm not interested in what anyone else thinks. I'm interested in what *you* think."

The way his voice went all husky combined with the intensity in his gaze sent a shiver through her.

"But I'd be the cause. I don't want that."

"That doesn't make sense." Disappointment swam in his eyes, along with something else. Embarrassment? Then he nodded, pulled in a deep breath, and stepped back, one foot on a different branch. For a heartbeat, she feared he was leaving, that she'd placed enmity between them where they'd had, almost, a friendship. Because she needed more enemies. But he stayed there, just a step away. "But all right."

"All right?" She needed to go. Too much of her wanted to snatch hold of his wild recklessness, to throw away her caution. To change her mind and say yes instead. She was lingering too long on his full lips, on his shining eyes, on wondering what his hair would feel like if she ran her fingers through it. He was interested in her, but worse, he was *interesting*.

"Your answer is no, and I accept that, even if I don't understand your reasons. It's enough." Leaning his head against the bark of the tree, he stared upward again, releasing her from his gaze.

He didn't understand... and yet, he didn't argue, either? Disappointment welled up where he had filled all the space, and it surprised her. She wasn't supposed to feel like that. It should only ever be so easy. No one even associated with nobles took "no" as an answer so quickly, so calmly. Not in Arruk.

Unless it was easy because it didn't matter to him. He was just playing with her. She knew better than to fall for such a trick. Humiliation flared in her.

She scowled. "You're teasing me. You don't actually want to kiss me at all."

"Is that what you think?" His rumbling voice was colored with hurt, or maybe offense. "You think I would do that to you?"

Tight shoulders and a frown replaced his earlier relaxation. So similar to how he'd looked at the trial earlier when she'd noticed the horses, but he leaned his weight on the far branch, away from her. Giving her space. If it wasn't a trick, if he was true, he was still willing to give up something he so eagerly wanted to try for, because of her misgivings?

She focused her thoughts back on what was important. Surely a man who partied with nobles would take the nobles' view of havi. There were so many reasons not to take even one step more down this road with him, and she couldn't forget them.

"I am not a toy to be played with and discarded when no longer amusing."

He slid down to sit on his branch, his scent no longer hemming her in and making her dizzy, her thoughts no longer clouded with desire. He tilted his head back to look up at her, his hands hooked around one knee. Exasperation ran as an undertone to his voice. "I never intended you to feel like a toy. I am coming to this with sincerity, not as a game."

"I am not looking for honeyed words. I am not looking to be saved."

"Why would you need saving?" His brow creased, deep furrows in his brown skin. He looked baffled.

It shook her. She picked at a leaf near her fingers. "I don't, but... Why else would someone like you want to be with me?"

"Why wouldn't I want to be with someone who gives her heart to every endeavor, who speaks her mind, who looks for not just trouble but solutions to the trouble? But you said no, so no it is."

"You're all right with that?" she asked, her gaze fixed on his face, ready for the ugliness of hate.

Instead there was only that little frown and the furrow in his brow. "I'm after something real, not something forced. Why would I want to force you into a situation you don't want to be in?"

"Because you have power."

A laugh broke out of him, short and slightly bitter. "That's no reason to do anything and plenty of reason not to." Then he stopped, the rumble of his voice low and filled with grieved realization. "Today. The horse race... that wasn't just one bad judge, was it?"

"No."

He took a deep breath, as if collecting himself, and then leaned his weight on the farther branch, opening up more space between them, his voice shedding its harsh edges to clothe itself in gentleness and serenity again. "I know you don't want saving, but, if you do need help, I hope you know you can ask me. Are you in some tr—no, sorry."

"I'm sorry." She sank down to sit on the branch and let out her breath in a long sigh. She shouldn't be sharing this with him. It'd be used against her, surely. And yet, somehow, the words flowed from her. "Some people like to raise little havi up, to have us in their debt. Kindness always costs more than it seems."

"But you're happy as you are," he said. "I'm sorry, I didn't realize what you and Emin deal with. I never saw, I guess."

"We're always at the guardhouse or at the havi market, places where it's not so bad, when we're off-duty. And on-duty, we're guards. Besides, Borlim tries to be careful about where he places us while we're working, especially havi from the wilderness, like Emin and me." She tried to shrug, as if it didn't matter, as if her stomach wasn't twisting inside her.

"I will continue on this path," he said. "We can stay friends for as long as you'd like—all our lives, if you wish it, and I will cherish your company. If you do change your mind, if you do want more, all you have to do is tell me. Whatever you need, even if it's me gone, please, will you tell me?"

Tears blurred her vision but she nodded. Her throat was thick, her relief full of disbelief, but true nonetheless. It was that easy with him? Even though she'd seen the passion in him, heard the hurt. He hadn't belittled or explained away her view, or twisted her words into something he liked better.

The city had almost made her forget what it felt like to be respected, seen for more than just her class.

She couldn't stop staring. She'd been in company with him and the rest of her brother's friends for weeks, both in days and in nights, both at work and at play. She knew the warrior in Taunos from practice, from the hard edges that showed when he came up against injustice. She knew the boy within who came out when he threw himself into contests and challenges with Emin and his friends, laughter continually pointing to where he was among a crowd. But she hadn't guessed at the poet, and she hadn't guessed at the extent of his support during the race or after.

Homesickness flooded back through her, and yet at the same time, she felt that with someone like this beside her, perhaps she could face anything. Perhaps some day she could simply step onto a boat and leave without a plan, not knowing where she was going to sleep or what she was going to eat next.

But not now. He'd have to deal with the disappointment, because she couldn't handle taking that leap into another romance likely doomed, not with a man who rubbed shoulders with the nobles. It was the highest folly.

Nannil, goddess of night, she was tired.

She cleared the thickness from her voice to speak. "Thank you. I promise I will let you know what I decide, what I need. I can't promise you'll like it."

An easy grin formed familiar creases around his mouth. "I will, because that's all I want. You're an inspiring person, Amanah. Even simply being your friend is worth more than the jewels in the palace."

How did one respond to such a statement? It was in error, clearly, and yet it wasn't a jest.

So she sat on her branch, resting her head on the trunk behind her, and stared up at the stars visible through the rustling leaves. The tension fled her shoulders as the stars moved above, and Taunos told stories until her muscles were languid. She drew in a deep breath and sighed it out. She hadn't expected to find peace at all today. Certainly not while up in a tree with her brother's friend. It didn't make the loss of her case with the magistrate hurt less, but it made it easier to bear. This had been a far better use of time than if she'd stayed to toss and turn in her bed, but now, it was time to get some sleep.

"Thank you," she said.

He glanced over, eyebrows up, that curl at the corners of his mouth so familiar now.

"I did need this," she admitted. "It was a hard day, but I feel better now."

"My pleasure." And it seemed, incredibly enough, like it actually was.

4

UKISH WAS A port town, and the smell of salt in the air filled every corner of it. Amanah breathed in deep and loosened her tight grip on the ship's railing. Showing her enthusiasm for something was a good way for that thing to be taken away—at least in Arruk. She'd rather assume it was the same in Ukish and be proven wrong than fall for traps she should know enough to avoid.

Borlim had sent them to Arruk's riverside harbor with a note which Gurseh said gave them passage to Ukish. Gurseh's reading ability was immediately handy, for Amanah couldn't tell which ship was which, but Gurseh guided them along, turning in at the boat with presumably the correct name on the side. Indeed, the captain of the vessel read over the note, squinted at the four of them, and then waved them aboard with a grunt.

Once she'd found a spot out of the way, Amanah had spent the ride curled up by the edge, watching the land go by. It was all part of Far Dahutad, but it was her first time on a boat. She couldn't help but smile as they sailed down to the delta and around the coast until they berthed in Ukish's harbor late the next afternoon. Taunos provided entertainment, regaling them all with the story of how he'd come to Far Dahutad aboard a pirate vessel, only to trick them into sailing to Arruk, escape, and turn them in for their crimes. The belt of Emin's laughter at Taunos's adventures loosened something tight around her heart, just as the bruises on her side from the race had begun to fade. That tension was loosened further as Taunos and Emin tossed mock insults back and forth circling entirely around oil—apparently the guard Emin had borrowed the thaa oil from had found a new bottle in his possession and thanked Emin before they left.

Stepping off the docks in Ukish and trailing behind her brother, Amanah kept craning her neck, trying to catch every detail of the bustling area. One whole section was roped off—Gurseh said the sign designated it for sea-wizards only—with three normal-looking craft docked there. Another boat sailing away was clad all in metal, its deck empty, but Amanah thought she caught a glimpse of shiny green skin in a porthole for the briefest of moments. Two square-sailed Ifreesian boats sat in the middle of the harbor, the sound of their argument carrying over the water even if the words were unintelligible. Amanah had longed to see Ifreesians or Kelm since she was a child, and she craned her neck to catch a glimpse.

It was too bad they'd only be here until morning. And after the job was done, they'd head back to Arruk immediately, lest they prove that havi were as faithless as the city people said they were. But for a little while, at least, she could enjoy the new sights and sounds.

Just so long as it didn't turn into trouble.

Emin led them to the town's station office to report. The guardmaster's gaze caught on his worn boots, the patches on his pants, and his ripped-off sleeves, and her lip curled ever so slightly. Emin interrupted her scrutiny by handing her the letter, scrawled in bold script Amanah assumed was Borlim's.

Her gaze passed over Amanah with a wrinkle of her nose and Amanah bit back a sigh. She and Emin were wearing the nicest clothes they had, but clearly it wasn't enough, even if Emin hadn't torn a hole in his pants on the ship, necessitating sacrificing his sleeves to make patches.

The guardmaster's assessment lingered on Taunos and Gurseh, whose clothes were patch-free and without a frayed thread to be seen. Her tone became almost polite, though still crisp with annoyance. "Haari Taunos?"

Taunos dipped his head courteously. "That's me."

A blink, and the guardmaster fixed her attention on him. "Asi lords Inuwe and Lamyi are at the Cedes Rush Inn waiting for you. They'll be ready to leave in the morning, but you are to call on them as soon as you arrive."

"Thank you."

Taunos turned to go, but Amanah asked, "Where will our lodgings be for the night?"

Taunos raised his eyebrows, and she amended, "I'm sure the lords would not sleep in an inn that would welcome Emin and I. Maybe Gurseh would be fine there."

An angry spark lit in Taunos's eyes, but the guardmaster nodded. "The lords have made an exception for you at their inn, Haari. There's another inn closer to the gates that would be suitable for these three. The Reeds."

"There's no guardhouse here?" Amanah asked.

"Unlike Arruk, Ukish can't house all its guards together," the guardmaster said stiffly. "Each has a home in the city."

No wonder it was harder to get into the guardhouse here—you had to have enough money to purchase property, instead of being offered a bunk in the guardhouse. She and Emin had gone straight for Arruk, since it had more positions available and offered lodging and meals.

"The Reeds is a decent place," the guardmaster continued. "Not fancy, but they clean the floor mats weekly."

Amanah carefully kept her expression blank. Weekly floor mat changes —did they also change out the bedding monthly? The bamimri talked about how important it was to sweep the floors and change bedding daily, no matter how the laundry complained. Keeping her muscles tense, she avoided shuddering. At least it was only one night.

As they stepped back out into the bright sun, she lifted her face to the light and rolled her shoulders.

Gurseh let loose a dramatic sigh. "There's going to be a lot of this, isn't there?"

"Probably," Amanah said flatly. Gurseh could probably get into the nicer inn if he leveraged the fact that he was Guma clan. But she didn't want to point that out, didn't want to cause Emin pain if Gurseh took the chance to abandon him for a nicer bed.

Emin turned to Taunos. "We'll head to the inn. You can bring the nobles in the morning."

Taunos snorted. "I'm not sleeping anywhere that won't allow you. If the nobles want our escort, they can come to us."

"Taunos, you can't leave them waiting," Amanah said. "They're expecting you."

"And I'm not going inside if they won't let you in. That's ridiculous."

Amanah blew out her breath. "You've gone plenty of places that wouldn't allow us, it's becoming clear. This isn't new. We might as well start the journey without needling these nobles unnecessarily."

Emin shoved Taunos's shoulder. "Besides, they hired you to guard them. Someone has to stay in their inn, or they aren't adequately guarded."

"Maybe these lords won't turn out to be all that bad," Gurseh said.

Emin laughed. "We can hope. In the meantime, I want dinner, drink, and a bed."

"Me too," grumbled Taunos.

Emin waved a hand at him. "Go meet your fancy nobles and then come find us later for supper. The quality will be worse but the company, probably better."

Taunos waved him away and set off, holding his bag by its straps over one shoulder, the dust on his cloak shimmering into the air with his movements.

"Come on," Emin said, nudging her ankle with the toe of his boot. She turned to follow him and Gurseh through the streets.

Ukish was much smaller than Arruk. She'd known that but had forgotten how different it would feel. It reminded her of the small towns her family stopped at occasionally for trade, though now she was seeing it with eyes that had grown used to the ebb and flow of people from all sorts of places, voices mixing in a joyful sound.

It reminded her of the dreams that had drawn her and her brother to Arruk in the first place, dreams that had been ignited by the stories Tumaw would tell them before sending them to bed, laughing at their groans and pleas for one more tale. How she and Emin had whispered at the possibility that they might catch sight of Kelm gnomes or Ifreesian dwarves, attracted by the commerce of merchants from dozens of nations all mingling in one place. Emin dreamed of making a name for himself, but he didn't care to play the city's games. Similar to how she had dreamed of the bamimri, only to find out that was never an option.

Hopefully things would be alright while she was gone. Hopefully Gitu and Anila's family was safe. She'd find out when she returned, but that would be two months of wondering, and they weren't the only ones in precarious positions.

Quickening her steps, she squared her shoulders. She couldn't do anything about that now. She was out of Arruk, with less to worry about as far as city politics, at least—the only danger would be the nobles, and she could stay away from two nobles, couldn't she? Instead, there would be more of the kind of hazards she was good at looking out for: hazards from the environment and negotiations with the nomadic clans that roamed the land. Had she accounted for most of the possible dangers? The nobles would bring much uncertainty with them that she couldn't plan for.

"Amanah, want to get some horses?" Emin asked. "Gurseh and I will check for any last minute supplies, and if we're lucky, something nice for supper tonight."

"Not tumi fruit." Amanah pointed a warning finger at him.

"Yes, Amanah, I'll get your favorite. Otherwise you'll nag me until I die of shame for forgetting the tumi fruit." He smirked.

She gagged at him. "Do we know if the Reeds has a stable?"

"You can check first to make sure. I know you will anyway."

Amanah flicked him a rude gesture, and he laughed.

"I know you're itching for a chance to ride. Got your water and sun gear?"

She nodded. Of course she had it, but she didn't chide him. It was strange how the role of war-band leader seemed to naturally fit Emin, even though he was new to it. Hopefully Borlim would promote him permanently at the end of this—he deserved it.

"I'll see you at the inn," she said.

Amanah checked out the Reeds first, as Emin had known she would. It was less expensive than she'd budgeted and had a small but serviceable stable in the back. The purse Borlim had handed her for the trip's funds—because Taunos would lose it and Emin would spend it—would hardly notice a night's stay in two rooms, even with the stabling fees.

The horses might be a different matter, though.

She paused to fill her water pouch from the public well, then scooped an extra dipper of water and let the cool liquid slide down her throat. She was still carrying all her meager possessions on her, afraid that her room at the inn—which didn't lock—would be visited by a thief and more of her precious things would be stolen. Unwinding her torn scarf from her waist, she wrapped it around her hair to deflect the heat of the sun, binding her braids back. Now, to hunt for the stables.

By late afternoon, she'd found all three of Ukish's stables and perused the stock they had to offer, quickly rejecting those drugged or otherwise tampered with to look livelier than they were. It was a refreshing task—not just being among horses again, but also the grooms, for they only tried the normal tricks that were played to separate those who knew what they were doing from the pretenders. No added suspicion was turned her way, no jokes about her speech or phrasing. Just respect for her knowledge once she'd proven it, and they in turn quit playing games with her. In a short time, she had only sound, trained options, narrowing them quickly to only the best they could afford.

She chose a quick Hinanuri-bred horse for herself. Ifel would have scoffed, but she wouldn't have been able to afford even the worst of her father's horses anyway. For Emin, she chose a gelding that looked more bluster than brains—Emin would have fun with him. She found a steady mount for Gurseh—she'd seen him ride, and refused to saddle any of the more sensitive, fleet horses with him. The last horse she chose was for

Taunos. Since he was only slightly taller than her, he'd need a smaller horse like hers for him to be able to mount easily. Remembering how he avoided riding horses whenever he could, she finally settled on a gentle horse that looked to be able to keep up with the rest of them but would handle easily, without too much spirit.

As she'd expected, the mounts cost most of the purse. They'd have to be frugal from now on, but good horses could be the difference between life and death during their journey.

In the morning, she led out the horses, bringing them to the gate to wait. Emin and Gurseh took theirs, and then they waited for Taunos and the nobles to appear, taking shade under the sprawling branches of a tree. The sun was well up by the time the nobles arrived, with Taunos walking alongside them. The two lords rode expertly on expensive, enormous mounts that no doubt would overheat on the way, their two pack horses laden near to overburdening. Amanah winced, glancing back toward the stables, but she had no time or money to get an extra horse to help the poor beasts out.

The nobles moved on past them, out the gate, but Taunos paused beside them. He looked at the extra horse Amanah held and groaned.

Emin poked him with an elbow. "You need practice."

"I can just run," Taunos said.

"She's quite gentle," Amanah said. "A baby could ride her."

Taunos fixed her with a flat look. "I *can* ride. I just prefer not to."

"You'll be fine," Emin said. "And you're welcome."

"Pfft. See, you ruin it." Amanah nudged her brother. "No one thanked you, and no one will."

Emin snickered. "All right, all right, let's get going. Mount up!" He paused, as if remembering that Taunos was nominally in charge. "Er, yeah, boss?"

Taunos snorted and waved him on. "Get out there."

Grinning like a fool, Emin touched his heels to his horse, and he and Gurseh followed the nobles, easily catching up to them. Taunos turned to the mare, patting her and then swinging himself astride fluidly.

Shifting her weight, Amanah cued her gelding forward. Taunos's followed without the need for a nudge, and he grimaced, gathering the reins up.

"Talk to her by name," Amanah suggested. "Maybe it'll help."

"What is her name?" Taunos asked.

"Rose."

He glanced at her. "You don't like roses."

She leaned forward to pat his mare's forehead. "I like this one."

With a chuckle, Taunos trotted Rose forward, past Emin and Gurseh and then on past the noblemen to scout ahead. Amanah watched him go with a critical eye. He wasn't a terrible rider, she supposed, but his timing with the reins was off, too tense, so that he argued with the mare the whole way. That, and he bounced.

The morning sun was still gentle, and the tension eased from Amanah's back and shoulders as she rode, reveling in the feel of the wind in her face. As they gathered in around the nobles and their horses, Amanah adjusted her scarf to make sure it covered her braids, which were woven in the intricate pattern for Hayzanu's luck and Jattanu's favor. She stroked her horse's mane with nervous fingers. She'd braided the portions she could reach from his back, and she now smoothed them out, fearing they were too ornamental. The last thing she needed was another confrontation like with the magistrate. She couldn't forget that the danger of the city loomed, and it would for the whole trip. At least it was just these two nobles, rather than an entire city's worth.

The nobles were handsome men with rich robes, both clearly competent riders—which meant they should know better than to overburden their horses. They barely glanced at Emin, Amanah, and Gurseh, instead saving their few words for Taunos. Amanah mostly ignored them in return. Too much attention on them would invite trouble, but at the same time, one had to keep an eye on dangerous predators.

From their map, Amanah had expected little protection from the sun on the way between Ukish and Gahimbli. The land proved that correct—short blue-tinged grass clung to sandy, dry soil, with only a few brave trees here and there. The horizon was broken by large, colorful buttes with layers of stone in red, orange, and slivers of green or yellow jutting up from the sandy dirt, marking where the ground broke into canyons and more difficult ground. Perfect for bandits and raiders, but at least they'd provide a little shade at times.

She and Emin quickly donned their sun protection, smearing the slimy concoction on their skin, and Emin finally wound his scarf around his head. While Gurseh and Taunos applied the brown protective goop as well, Emin helped Gurseh adjust his head covering. Amanah helped Taunos with his, making sure the fabric extended well beyond the collar of his shirt.

Emin glanced at the nobles, who still rode bare-headed. "They need some, too. And they should cover their heads."

Taunos straightened. "Oh, right, I need to be the one to tell them."

"You're the one who has a chance."

"So unnecessary," Taunos muttered. Still, he reined his mare alongside the two lords and offered them the jar and the advice.

"No. That jar smells foul," one of them said.

A concerned frown creased Taunos's brow. "Do you have anything to cover your heads?"

"It's too stuffy under there," the first said.

"And it'll mess up my braids," the other said.

His braids were fabulous, Amanah had to admit, with every strand in place and each plait oiled to a gleam. All that oil would cook his brains in the heat, though.

"We'll be fine—far cooler than under more fabric." The first one waved Taunos away. "You should embrace Jattanu's light instead of hiding from it."

Taunos's frown deepened. "Why wouldn't you listen to the advice of people who live in these lands?"

The first noble snorted. "It's all Far Dahutad, and it's hot in the city too. It's fine."

"There's shade in the city," Taunos noted, but the noble kicked his horse ahead, leaving dust swirling up behind him.

Handing the jar back to Amanah, Taunos made a face and took a sip of water. Emin shrugged at Taunos and nudged his mount forward to take the lead for a turn, riding ahead to check their direction and scout for dangers.

Amanah grimaced at the noblemen's backs as she put the jar away. If they didn't follow common sense, the wilderness would happily make them suffer. And if the nobleman suffered, all of them would. Punishment on one fell on all: that was how the rich and privileged ruled the land. But how could they make the nobles see sense—especially while she was to remain invisible?

The sun rose higher, and every attempt Amanah made to coax the lords into even so much as pulling up their hoods was ignored. Taunos attempted to persuade them as well, to no avail. Near midday, one of them glared at her as he poured water on himself, and she eyed the reddening of his skin, pressing her lips together. It was a waste of good water, but also a waste of her words.

Taunos started toward him, but Amanah caught his sleeve, quickly letting go when he turned in his saddle.

"You can't protect someone from themselves," she told him.

One side of his mouth quirked, though his eyes looked almost sad. He nodded, but his gaze often returned to the nobles.

Emin stopped them not long after in the shade of one of the rock pillars jutting up like a giant's fingers. "This is a good place to set up camp for a bit. We'll wait out the heat of the day and then continue. If we're lucky, we'll have moonlight and be able to travel at night, depending on how the horses hold up."

Taunos nodded and swung down from his horse. The haste with which he did so was not lost on Amanah.

But the nobles scowled at Taunos. "What are you doing? We have business, and we need to be on our way. Don't let the laziness of this man slow us down!"

"If you keep pushing on, your horses will fail in the sun," Amanah said, dismounting. "They need rest and water, and so do you."

"I give the orders here." The nobleman drew himself up.

Taunos stepped between the nobles and Amanah and Emin. "Lord Lamyi, they know what they're talking about. If they say we need to stop, we need to stop. We'll get farther faster by listening to their wisdom."

Lamyi scowled, but the other—Inuwe—shrugged. "I could do with lunch. Cook me up some eggs and ham, please."

Amanah resisted the urge to rub her face with her hands. It was hot, and even properly dressed, sweat was trickling down her back, yet they wanted to cook? Checking on her horse, she caught Emin rolling his eyes, safely hidden from the nobles' view behind his horse. She smiled in agreement; what could they do but keep their heads down and bear it? They tethered their horses in the shade of the rock finger and set about unloading their mounts.

"Wait! Who's going to cook?" Inuwe said behind them, his voice rising as he checked his impeccable braids in a hand mirror. "Haari, why are your people walking away?"

"They're guards, not servants," Taunos said. "I told you yesterday you'd need to cook for yourselves."

"But who's putting up the tent? Surely you can spare them for a bit," Lamyi said. "They're havi, anyway. They'll know how to do it."

"They are not servants," Taunos said. "You need to put your own tent up. They have their own tasks to handle."

"I'll help with the tent," Gurseh offered.

Amanah glanced up from giving the horses water. Gurseh was already making his way to the pack horses, untying the unwieldy supports.

"Emin, do you need Gurseh for anything?" Taunos asked.

Meeting her brother's gaze, Amanah mimed taking care of the mounts, but Emin bellowed back, "Nope. I'll scout around while Amanah takes care of the horses."

She'd meant Gurseh should help with the mounts—if the nobles got their way, they'd continue to expect it all trip—but she shrugged. She could take care of the horses on her own well enough, and that would keep her out of the noble's sight. Honestly, not a bad way to begin the trip, though of course it couldn't last long. Emin headed off to prowl the rocky columns and she headed to the pack horses, helping Gurseh haul off the bags and crates strapped to them.

Lord Lamyi leaned in to Taunos, but his words still carried well enough. "I don't often tell others their business, but you need to get your guards in line. You don't make a very commanding presence. A firm hand, or you fall into disorder. Everyone knows that."

Amanah pressed her lips together, tugging on the last strap, which was stuck. It came free with a jolt, dumping the pack on the ground and covering Taunos's reply.

"Be careful with that!" Lord Lamyi shouted. "If you've broken anything, I'll take it out of your pay."

"You're not paying them, or me," Taunos said. "You paid the guardhouse. You'd do well to treat them with respect. If you have something fragile, you might want to handle those bags yourself."

Amanah kept her back turned to the nobles, gathering the reins of the horses and biting her tongue. She knew better than to confront a noble, but they were being ridiculous.

At home, her family was well regarded. None of them had much, but what they did have was respect and honor. She was known for being a hard worker and generous. And they were in the wilderness once again. This was where she knew what to do and what to watch for.

But Taunos muddled it all up. She wasn't sure how to feel about him at her back. Would it bring trouble, unintentional or not, like in the city? Or could she trust his support to be true and without a cost?

Gurseh's horse jostled Emin's, which shied sideways, pulling her from her thoughts. One of the horse's hooves hit the edge of the bag as they passed, and something clinked inside. Amanah glanced back, her eyes meeting the noble's irritated expression.

"Be more careful. I can have you whipped, you know," Lord Lamyi said, taking a step toward her.

"You will not." The words came sharp and cold from Taunos as he sidestepped, blocking Lamyi's passage.

Amanah led the horses into the deepest part of the shade as if she didn't have a chill in her back. She retreated as much from the threat as she did from the hissing venom in Taunos's voice as he continued speaking, though too quietly for her to hear. The best place to be was out of sight, certainly not in the middle of two powerful people at odds.

Gurseh's horse tossed his head and tried to step on her foot, but the rest were well-mannered enough, including the nobles' horses. She took her time with them, half-listening to Gurseh struggle to get the nobles' tent up and Taunos's reasoning with them. Lord Inuwe actually tried to help with the tent for a bit, until Lord Lamyi scolded him for it. Finally, Taunos had to help Gurseh wrestle the fabric and frame upright.

Amanah trained her attention firmly on her gelding, who she named Nakii after the wind that brings rain. She shouldn't get attached to him, and yet, he was proving such a fine horse. She'd finished watering the horses, and rubbing them down, and checking their health by the time Taunos and Gurseh headed over to her. Shortly after, Emin returned, his sword still in its sheath. All clear.

With one last pat for Nakii, Amanah sank down in the shade, sharing it gratefully with the horses, and pulled out some bread and cheese from her pack, passing around the rations. She'd found some dried fruit in Ukish, and Emin exclaimed in delight over it. He snagged some fruit out of Gurseh's hand, laughing at his objection. Tossing a piece in the air, he opened his mouth to catch it, but Gurseh snatched it and popped it into his mouth with a smirk.

There was a peace here, with the wind whistling past and the company of the horses, tails flicking to shoo away the insects. Letting her eyelids droop, Amanah settled against her pack.

"It's beautiful here," Taunos said, awe touching his voice. "The columns of stone jutting into the sky, they have all those layers of color, almost as if they were painted. Do you know why?"

She glanced at him out of the corner of her eye. "Different kinds of stone, I think?"

"I've heard many different stories from many people as to why," Taunos said. "What do your people think?"

She shrugged. She'd never paid much attention to it before, though now she was curious as to these tales.

"Who cares? It's just rocks," Gurseh said.

Disappointment flashed across Taunos's expression, but he lifted his face, gazing toward the top of the pillar beside them. "I know someone who would love to see them. She'll have more questions than I'll have answers for anyway."

Amanah considered him for a moment. She had questions too—but curiosity got punished in Arruk. Even though they weren't in Arruk anymore, she still couldn't ask them. Doing so would open up far too many possibilities, and she wasn't sure she wanted that.

"I wish we'd brought a tent," Gurseh grumbled, popping the last of the fruit in his mouth.

"Don't need one," Emin said, resting his arm over Gurseh's shoulders. "The country gets rougher between here and Gahimbli. We'll be able to shelter in the shade of cliffs and canyon walls. Amanah you brought the canopies right?"

"Tarps. Waterproof," she said, closing her eyes.

"Good," Emin said. "We can stretch those between rocks if we can't find shade at midday. The sun's at an angle this time of year, so at least it won't be directly above us."

"A tent would be nicer," Gurseh grumbled.

"You could share with Inuwe and Lamyi, then," Taunos suggested.

Gurseh snorted, showing he had some amount of sense. "Right."

It took Amanah a moment to realize Taunos was serious. She sighed, opening her eyes to fix him with a frank look. "Taunos, none of us can share with the nobles. Not even you, I bet. But I'm worried—they're going to get sun sickness."

Emin nodded. "We'll just have to try to catch it early."

She grimaced, remembering their reddened skin. "Too early and they won't believe us."

"Too late and we'll lose too much time," he said. "Honey, salt, and water—that'll cure them. We have salt, right? You made sure?"

"Yes, Emin, I made sure." Amanah tried not to roll her eyes until she saw her brother's grin, and then she did.

Taunos stood, stretching out his back. "I'll go talk to them again."

"You might as well wait. We're not moving for a couple marks," Emin said. "Here, pass me the water, Amanah."

"Trade you for the map," she said.

She grabbed the map he offered and tossed the water pouch back, then rolled onto her stomach, map spread out before her. She traced their route with her finger, marking the landmarks and calculating how far they'd come. The others reclined against the rocks or lay back with their heads on their packs, and the horses were quiet but for the occasional stomp of a hoof.

Taunos grimaced, shifting position. "I forgot how much I dislike riding. I mean, the horse is nice. And you look like you were born to it."

"We were," Emin said. "Amanah and I, anyway."

"I was riding in front of my parents before I could walk." She smiled as Taunos's eyebrows rose.

"Here, hand over the bag of nuts," Gurseh said, changing the subject.

Amanah packed the bag away, instead. "That's all I rationed for us for this meal. This should last a few days and then we'll get our salt from the jerky."

"You planned out our snacks?" Taunos asked.

Amanah furrowed her brow but nodded. Of course she did.

He chuckled and she scowled at him. What, did he think it was funny to be prepared? They'd see how he felt about it if they ran into more trouble than she'd been able to account for and had to scramble for necessities.

"We'll need to make better time. We're going to run out of rations at this speed," she said after double-checking the map.

Emin yawned, stirring from where he'd been dozing. "What? Amanah, it's the first day."

"Yes, and everything is planned out. We have food for a month, and there's water for twenty days—twice what's needed if the streams are clear —but at this rate we'll take more than a month to reach Gahimbli, and that's assuming nothing goes wrong." She shuddered.

Emin frowned. "We can't take too long or we won't be there before the rain of the gods."

"What's this?" Taunos asked, suddenly alert with curiosity.

"The rain of the gods, when the stars fall from the sky?" Amanah prompted.

"I've seen it. What does it mean to your people?"

"The rain of the gods contains the fragments of the nameless god, eternally dying, bringing bad luck and the gods' displeasure to any caught beneath. Everything hangs in the balance. If all the stars fell, there'd be only darkness, forever and always."

"That's why we have the Festival of Dark Nights. Everyone stays indoors while the rain of the gods falls. We keep lights burning and we dance and sing and eat and drink. We live life as loudly as we can," Emin said.

Amanah nodded. "We pray to the gods to hear us living, to catch the stars and scatter them again into the night."

"But that'll be impossible if we're still out here in the wilderness," Emin said.

"So there's a tension during this time, then, for you," Taunos said. "It's viewed differently in other places."

"We have to make it to Gahimbli before then," Amanah said. "That doesn't help our supply problem with this pace."

"We can find food and water," Taunos suggested.

"And hunting will take still more time," Amanah pointed out.

"Not if we hunt while on the move." Emin tapped the map. "And look, there's a river here. We can fish."

"There's no guarantee we'll catch anything," she said.

"We can't move faster," Emin argued. "You saw the pack horses."

"We can unburden them," Amanah said. "The nobles brought too much."

"I convinced them to leave some bags back at Ukish as it is," Taunos said. "They won't leave anything else. Can some of our horses take some of their things?"

"Yes," Amanah started.

"No," Emin said. "First, they wouldn't allow it, and if anything happened to go missing, that would be really bad for us. See, I do listen—we're supposed to lay low." He made a face at Amanah and she wrinkled her nose at him in return. "Second, we need to be able to move fast. If we run into more trouble than we can handle, we leave the pack horses and run. If our horses are also burdened, they'll be slower. And third, I want the freedom of scouting."

Amanah scowled but he made good points. She just wished there was a way to help the pack horses. "I suppose we'll have to go slow then."

"We can use my horse as a pack animal to share the load," Taunos said. "I can run. I'll be fine."

Amanah turned a blistering glare on him. His suggestion rankled more than it should. "I picked her especially for you. To ride."

He shrugged. "Plans can change, and we need another pack animal."

With effort, she resisted scowling at him. "If you run, you'll get tired, and if trouble comes, it won't do much good to have you tired. Besides, the nobles will lose respect for you."

"I honestly couldn't care less about that last part."

She snorted. How did he get through life not caring about so much? "It's not a game."

"I know it's not a game." Frustration underlined his words, and he abruptly shifted to a new position.

"You're supposed to be the leader," Gurseh spoke up. "Leaders don't walk."

Taunos rubbed his face with both hands, but at least he gave up the foolish notion. "Someone could go back for an extra horse."

"No," Emin said. "We need to remain together, and Amanah will have spent all of our budget."

"You're welcome." She smirked at him, trying to push away her annoyance.

"What about the nobles' money?" Taunos asked.

"You can't spend it for them, Taunos, gods!" Emin chuckled.

"They ordered this mission," Taunos said. "They want to get to Gahimbli, surely. This is one of the costs, isn't it?"

Shaking his head, Emin lay back down, and Amanah folded up the map.

"What now?" Taunos asked, twisting his back in a stretch, one leg out in front of him and the other pulled up.

"Now we sleep," Emin said, one arm over his face, holding Gurseh's hand in the other atop his chest.

"I'll go scout again." Taunos stood, brushing off his clothes.

Emin snorted. "I just did."

"And now I'll make extra sure," he said.

"More scouting's fine," Amanah said.

"And unexpected," Emin said drily.

Taunos waved Emin off as he walked away.

Amanah turned to her brother. "What's that about?"

"He gets bored easily." Emin said. "He'll probably do lots of scouting."

"That might be useful. It might help us make better time," she mused. And it definitely could help with the prospect of animal or bandit attacks. A thought struck her. "He's fine at your parties."

"People don't bore him. Doing nothing does."

Gurseh raised his head to look at her. "Ever notice when there's downtime, he's telling stories or starting up contests or games? Or when we have to wait for Borlim, when there's no games, he brings along something to do?"

No, she hadn't noticed that. Thinking back though, she could remember.

Emin grinned at her. "Why the sudden interest?"

"Just want to make sure there won't be trouble," she said, turning her back on her brother.

Somehow, they got through the day. The nobles finally covered their heads, though they resisted help, and they had to stop early that evening because the lords were feeling sick. Thanks to Emin and Taunos's close watch, they caught the dehydration before it became too serious. Emin scouted the campsite, Amanah took care of the animals, and Gurseh cooked, while Taunos remained in the tent with the nobles, their muffled voices low and tense, the words indistinguishable.

Eventually, he emerged and sat with them, weary and slump-shouldered. Emin shoved a bowl of stew over to him.

"I was starting to think you'd stay in there," Gurseh said.

Taunos shook his head, taking the bowl with quiet thanks and shoveling food into his mouth. Emin and Gurseh soon resumed their conversation—something about boots Gurseh wanted to buy when they got back to Arruk.

After Taunos finished eating and cleaned the dishes, he turned to them during a break in the conversation. "What's the protocol for noble requests?"

"What do you mean?" Amanah's words came cautiously, her every muscle tensing.

"They had a lot to say in there," Taunos said, rubbing his hands over his face. "I don't know enough to… I don't want to get you in more trouble by accident."

"By not giving in to their demands?" Amanah asked.

He nodded.

"What are they asking?" Emin asked.

"There were a lot of things, from shoes to hair to bowing when they pass."

Emin snorted.

Taunos shoved a hand through his hair. "I tried to reason with them, but they didn't want to listen."

"You can't argue every little thing," Amanah said. "We can humble ourselves for their pride."

They'd have to.

"Nothing that will compromise safety though," Emin said. "If they have a problem with our gear, for instance, or our sun protection, tough."

Amanah nodded. "By only arguing some things, you can make a more effective line with them, versus battling over their every little demand. Bowing to them when they pass won't hurt us."

"You shouldn't have to—" Taunos cut himself off, blowing out a breath.

"What were their nonsensical demands?" Emin asked. "The ones we can give in to safely."

A grimace cut across Taunos's face, and he pulled out his knife and an oil cloth, working away at the blade with smooth strokes as he spoke. "Starting later in the day. Cooking their food first, then our food. Setting up their tent and taking it down—I already told them you wouldn't be packing and unpacking their things, though. Grooming their horses and checking their hooves."

"I'm already doing that one," Amanah said.

He flashed a ghost of a smile at her, but it withered and died like a frog left in the sun. His eyes fixed on his blade. "No more than three braids in your hair, with no more than three strands in each braid."

The world seemed to stop turning. Amanah felt like she'd gotten kicked in the stomach. Her hand reached up to brush past her woven together plaits, lingering on a single one. Emin and Gurseh had worn their hair loose today, and Taunos always did. This had been targeted at her. She'd only done five braids, and her scarf had covered them all day, except for where they'd trailed together down her back.

"Three times three is still nine," Emin pointed out.

Nine was an important number for Dahuti. Nine deities. Nine blessed illusions. Tumaw had told her when she was little that Far Dahutad had once been Fa Dahutad, with nine letters to honor the blessed. The r had been added later, when everyone forgot. The loss of her father was still fresh enough to be a near physical ache at home, a gaping wound where he should be. He would have used three braids of three strands each to flaunt the symbolism, like Emin had mentioned.

Taunos's voice was quiet. "I'm sorry, Amanah. I know your braids mean a lot to you."

She should have taken more care with that blasted pack she'd dropped on the ground earlier. Her voice seemed to come from far away as she shoved away her grief and regret. "It's fine. I'll do only three."

Heat blazed through Emin's tone. "Anything else?"

"Nothing that wouldn't put us all in danger," Taunos said.

Emin blew out a breath. "We can do all those things except leave later —the heat of the day makes that too risky."

"I thought so," Taunos said. "I warned them that wouldn't be a good idea, but they're insistent."

"Otherwise, it's fine. We'll make it work."

Taunos rubbed his brow, clearly hating the idea, but he nodded. "All right. I'll tell them."

"We can practice the tapping language before turning in," Emin said.

"Great—give me full sentences this time," Taunos said.

"What?" Amanah shook herself from her thoughts.

"I'm teaching him the tapping language," Emin said. "He was curious."

"It's a fantastic idea," Taunos said.

Bemused, Amanah watched as they tapped out messages, Emin occasionally giving far more force to his taps than necessary, which eventually devolved into a scuffle.

Gurseh met her gaze. "At least two of us are adults."

She snickered.

Emin shoved out of a headlock and brushed dust off his pants. "Speaking of adults, who wants first watch?"

"I'll take first watch tonight. I'm not very tired," she said.

Emin tilted his head at Taunos. "Second?"

He nodded. "Thank you."

Amanah raised her eyebrows at Taunos as Emin and Gurseh sorted out the third and fourth watches. He pulled out another knife to oil and didn't meet her gaze.

She turned back to Emin. "Should we rotate through the watches day by day? Will that make me fourth or second watch tomorrow night?"

Emin shook his head. "You, me, and Gurseh can rotate, but Taunos is always going to be on second watch."

"Why?" Gurseh asked before she could.

"He's always up then anyway," Emin said.

"It doesn't make sense to have two people up," Taunos said. "Since I'll be awake, the rest of you can sleep."

That made sense, but why was he always awake at that time? At least Emin had known about it. Arms around each other, Gurseh and Emin left the pool of firelight, and Amanah fed the fire. Her gaze kept turning back to Taunos, though.

"Why are you always awake at second watch?" she asked.

He looked up, then put his oil rag away. "I've always gotten up in the middle of the night for a little while. Can't go back to sleep for a bit. Works well when I'm travelling alone," he explained, his voice a low rumble.

"Do you often travel alone?" she asked. "Sounds dangerous."

"I do."

With natural ease, he drew her into conversation, asking her about the day ahead of them and the nomadic clans that lived in the area. She found herself drawn into the companionship. But soon enough, Emin and Gurseh returned, and the three lay down to sleep, leaving her on watch. She stared into the night, listened to the scurry of night creatures, and her thoughts wandered back to the puzzle lying with his back to the fire just a few paces away from her. He'd come to them for advice and had listened to their thoughts on how to handle the nobles. His job. He'd remembered what she'd said in the garden and asked to make sure he didn't put them in danger.

How did he seem so safe and familiar? Or was she only seeing what she wanted to see?

5

TRAVELLING WITH EMIN, Taunos, and Gurseh, it was inevitable that a wrestling match would begin at some point. Emin's excuse was that they needed to keep their skills sharp.

Amanah stayed out of the way.

They were stopped for midday again, four days out from Ukish and still travelling far too slowly, but the pack horses needed a break, and soon the heat of the day would be too much for any of them to continue. When Emin discovered a nearby stream that didn't appear on the maps, Amanah's arguments about water rations had dried up.

In the cleared space, Gurseh swiped for Taunos, who slid sideways out of reach, laughing. Only a few months ago, the advanced moves had challenged Taunos, but he'd thrown himself into studying the Dahuti style of wrestling, and with Emin's tips, he'd improved greatly. He still dodged more than a Dahuti would, though.

Gurseh scowled as Taunos evaded him again. "Are you dancing or wrestling?"

"You have to be able to touch me to pin me. So far, all that's happened is me throwing you," Taunos said with a grin.

Beside Amanah, Emin laughed. He was watching intently, waiting for his next turn. She'd never been interested in wrestling—she preferred keeping opponents away from her with a bow or whip, though she'd rarely touched a whip since being in Arruk. But wrestling was Emin's favorite sport, so she ended up watching a lot of it with him.

"Only because you slip away like a fish," Gurseh said.

He rushed in, feet making a flurry of dust, so that Amanah had to throw her hands up to block her eyes. When she could see again, Gurseh slammed Taunos down hard on his back. Taunos twisted away and sprang up again before Gurseh could pin him.

Eyes sharp on his opponent, alight with his love of a challenge, Taunos fell easily into a ready stance. "That was nice. Do that again?"

"What?" Gurseh asked.

"Do that again, will you?" Taunos beckoned, voice filled with eager anticipation. "It worked."

"That's why I'm not teaching you how to avoid it." Gurseh grinned. "So no. You'll just have to be faster."

Emin spoke up. "You're quick, Taunos, but what about when someone actually gets hold of you? Remember the first time I tackled you?"

"I think the ground still has the impression of my face." Laughing, he screwed up his face, tongue hanging out in a mock impression.

"All you have to do is watch his hips." The words were out before Amanah could think twice.

Emin raised his eyebrows at her, a grin curling his moustaches, and she hurried on to explain. "The shoulders, feet, and hands—that's all misdirection for Taunos. His hips point the way he's going to go most often."

Emin leaned forward, eyes bright on hers. "So, Amanah. Tell me more about watching Taunos's hips."

Face burning, Amanah made herself smirk at him. "It's okay that you're unobservant, Emin. I'll look out for my big, dumb brother."

Roars of laughter from all three answered her. She glanced back at the tent, where the nobles had taken their tea. Surely the nobles would poke their heads out any moment now and their laughter would die, like so many good things when touched by Arruk nobility.

Gurseh clapped hands with Taunos, signaling he was done, and Emin took his spot in the ring. This time, Taunos barely made a move before Emin took him down in a crash that made her wince. Taunos, who'd nearly managed to dodge the sudden rush, lay gasping, the wind knocked out of him, until Emin claimed victory and reached to help him up. Taunos's foot snaked out and swept Emin off his feet. He was up in a moment, while Emin landed on his back.

Laughing, Emin grabbed Taunos's offered hand with a tug, pulling him nearly off his feet yet again.

"I still win," Emin said. "And now that I know this lovely tip, I'm going to wrestle you for every slight until you're beggared."

Amanah snorted. "I'm not your get-rich-quick charm."

Dahuti culture had a simple way to deal with personal disputes and blows to the pride—public wrestling matches. It was no wonder Emin's ego was so overgrown. If the incident in the marketplace had just been an insult, she could have asked Emin to stand in for her and wrestle for honor money. She wouldn't have, of course, for it would only have created more problems for them.

"I need some of these valuable insights!" Taunos said, still chuckling. He rubbed his back, but the loss—even in view of the nobles' tent—didn't seem to phase him any more than it did in the training yard. He turned to Amanah, eyes bright. "A little help?"

Why was he asking her? Probably because she'd been watching from the sidelines instead of distracted.

"Oh, Emin's easy," she said. "When he puffs up, he's about to charge, and always in the direction his left foot is pointing. I'm surprised you haven't noticed."

"I've been busy getting the air crushed out of me," he said, grinning mischievously at Emin. "You hit like a landslide."

"Thank you." Emin matched his grin. "Go again?"

"Of course!" Then Taunos paused, turning back to Amanah. "What about Gurseh?"

"He's easy, too. When he's misleading his opponent, he pulls his arms in tight to his sides."

"Excellent."

Gurseh scowled, but Amanah shrugged at him. Fair was fair.

A few rounds later, Taunos bowed out, he and Emin both sweating and breathing hard as they grabbed water. Amanah shook her head at them as they dropped down on the cleared ground near her and Gurseh. It was far too hot for exercise, but at least they'd shown enough sense to stop before the heat got really intense.

"What would you do if you could go anywhere, do anything?" Taunos asked, stretching out his legs.

Emin spread his arms. "I'm doing it! Well, maybe all I'm missing are some goats. With the gold horns, preferably, but the double red-horned kind are nice, too."

"A goat herder?" Gurseh asked, his lip curling for a moment.

"Emin likes stubborn animals? I'm stunned!" Taunos laughed.

"He smells about as good as a goat, too," Amanah teased.

Emin crashed into her, his thick forearm blocking her head from hitting the ground. "I'll let you go when you say I smell like roses."

"She doesn't like roses," Taunos pointed out.

"And you smell like dust and sweat," Amanah said, pushing at him even though it was useless. Emin was why she avoided wrestling. "Get off!"

"Why goats?" Gurseh asked as Emin released Amanah and she sat back up, shoving his shoulder.

"Why not?" Emin asked. "You bring your food and drink with you, and you get to travel all the time. The only thing is to make sure to stop at markets plenty."

Gurseh bumped Emin's shoulder with his. "Yeah, you'd get lonely with only yourself to talk to."

"What about you?" Emin asked him.

"I think I want to stay in Arruk." Gurseh passed around the snacks. "It's so quiet out here. Not enough people, not enough opportunity to make money, to move up in the world."

Emin elbowed Amanah. "You'll be shocked to hear Amanah's plan for the future."

"Amanah? Have a plan?" Gurseh put a hand on his chest, mouth comically agape.

She shot her brother a look. "It's not feasible. Life in the city's harder than we anticipated."

"I'd love to hear it anyway," Taunos said, stretching his other side. "No responsibilities, no duties. What would you do? What would you see?"

She shook her head, focusing on her food. Her stomach twisted with the grief of dying hopes. After the horse race, it was clear that dreams were too dangerous while she was in Arruk. If she showed how capable she was, if those in power began to watch her, they'd realize how she was undermining them, helping their victims escape their traps.

No, speaking her dreams would only hurt more when they were crushed. "It doesn't matter. The question is foolish, because there *are* duties and responsibilities. The fact is, we can't go anywhere and do anything, so why waste time dreaming?"

"Because sometimes dreams are all that get you through the day," Taunos said. "Sometimes they're a way to push back. I don't think dreams should be easily given up on."

"It wasn't easy." The words were full of bitter regret.

Something flashed across his face. Empathy maybe, or apology. "Maybe there's still a way for you to achieve this plan, I mean."

She glanced toward the tent. No doubt the nobles could hear them talking. The last thing she wanted was them hearing anything precious to her.

"What about the gnomes? The dwarves? Meeting them was a dream," Emin said, poking her in the shoulder.

"Yes, it was." She shrugged him away, trying to hide her pain and annoyance behind a flat expression.

"Why do you want to see gnomes and dwarves?" Gurseh asked, brow wrinkled.

She stared at him a moment. Why wouldn't someone want to meet people who travelled all over, who experienced life in a way she never could? His dismissal twisted in her gut like a knife, making her words come out short. "I was dreaming. But it's not to be, so that's that."

Taunos's voice was low but rich like honey. "You don't have to tell us this plan of yours. But I also think it would be amazing to meet Ifreesian dwarves. And... gnomes? I haven't heard of them."

"They're said to live in the sea and know many incredible things," Amanah said. "So I always thought it'd be interesting to meet them, to learn from them. Same with the Ifreesians, since they go everywhere. See everything."

"Is this trip helping? I know you told me it's been difficult to plan, but..." He leaned back against a rock, twisting a frayed rope back into shape, his legs crossed in front of him at the ankle.

Emin watched her, worry in his eyes. Beside him, Gurseh munched on a handful of nuts.

Amanah shrugged away from their attention, digging through her pack just for something to do. "Yes. I don't mind it so much because of that."

Taunos tilted his head. "What's to mind out here? Have the nobles been bothering you?"

"No." She frowned at him, waving a hand and lowering her voice. "It's the strain of worrying about what might go wrong. Avoiding the ire of the nobles while also keeping them safe. And there's all sorts of things to prepare for. Things that need to be anticipated. What if one of the horses breaks a leg? An animal attacks? Sickness? Falling down a canyon? And that's not even including the risk of attack from Hinanuri. And if anything happens to the nobles..."

"Yes, all of those things could happen, but you've been extremely well prepared. Is there anything more that can be done to prepare, or have you done everything you can to avoid these possibilities?"

"None of you worry over these things, so someone has to."

Taunos shook his head, visible in the corner of her vision. "I'm not saying these things shouldn't be thought about, planned for. And I'm happy to listen and help prepare for emergencies. But maybe there can be balance instead of you carrying all the worries. You might not get the chance to travel in the future, you said, but you have it now. And we're here in case any danger comes—we're still watching for trouble too, you know. Why not enjoy the freedom now, the chance to just be you without the confines of the city?"

She grimaced, glancing behind her toward the nobles' tent. The flap waved in a slight breeze, and she pressed her lips together. The nobles could overhear. Dreams spoken died.

She had to turn the attention away. She narrowed her eyes at Taunos and all his pushing. "I don't know. Why, what would you do?"

He tilted his head at her, watching her for a long moment. There was something sad there, and she ripped her gaze away.

Still, the tension of the moment lessened as Taunos hmmed as if in thought, his eyes roving over their surroundings. Like he sucked the attention away, off of her. She struggled not to sigh in relief, shoulders relaxing of their own accord.

Taunos smiled before he spoke. "If I could be anything, I'd be a wanderer."

"…a haari?" Amanah raised her eyebrows, looking at him askance. Haari was his nickname in Arruk, and it meant wanderer. Apparently it was more true than it even seemed.

He chuckled. "Yes, it's my second favorite name I've been given."

"Second favorite?"

His eyes sparked with humor. "Well, I am partial to my own true name."

That was an odd way to phrase it.

Something slipped behind her, pebbles cascading like falling rain. Amanah twisted to look, her chest clenching at the sight of Lord Inuwe coming down the small incline from the tent toward them.

"You should sweep these up," he commented lightly. "Someone could fall."

Amanah blinked. Sweep up… the pebbles? Was he serious? Should they clean away the dirt too?

"Maybe you should do a sparring match with your guards, Haari Taunos," Inuwe said.

"That's too dangerous," Taunos said, his tone just as easy as it had been moments ago with her. "Having everyone tired would leave you vulnerable."

"You were just wrestling," Inuwe said. "Lord Lamyi and I heard."

"And now we're resting." There was an edge to Taunos's voice, a finality.

Amanah glanced at him. How was he able to be so firm with them? How did he not fear the consequences they would rain on his head? Probably, he managed to escape even rainstorms unscathed.

"Well, fine, maybe another time," Inuwe said. "I thought I'd ask. Anyway, now I'll need one of you to sew up my slipper when I get back. Looks like the heel tore."

"Where are you going?" Taunos asked.

"To the latrine."

"Be careful," Emin said. "Do you need a guard?"

Inuwe drew himself up, his immaculate braids gleaming in the sunlight. "Excuse me, but I have been toileting on my own for over twenty years. I'm not about to change that now. All I need from you is someone to sew up my slipper after. One of you should know how, no? I imagine you repair your own clothes all the time."

Her gaze dropped to his feet, clad in silk slippers. The blue-grey dust from the rocks in this area had coated the bottoms of his yellow slippers. Or was that gold? Who in their right mind wore gold silk to go to the bathroom?

Taunos glanced at Emin, then returned his attention to Inuwe. "We'll discuss who. Call if you need us."

Out of the corner of her eye, Amanah watched the noble go, heading around to the other side of the tent. She quickly returned her gaze to the others, but her back prickled as if she had a target on it.

Meanwhile, Taunos, of course, seemed completely at his ease. He gestured at the buttes and canyons that broke up the land around them, picking up the thread of conversation from before the noble's interruption. "I'd go everywhere, if I could. See all the lands, meet all the people. Learn all the stories, all the songs. Play all the games."

She shook her head, though his enthusiasm drew a small smile from her. "Alas, some of us must be grownups."

"Boring." Emin's voice was light, his grin broad.

"I think it's a great name for you, Haari," Gurseh said. "It's a friendlier version of slacker."

"Who carried you last time we patrolled together?" Taunos asked, leaning back on his elbows. "I distinctly remember it not being me who was carried."

"I would not have gotten stabbed if you'd been there!" Gurseh said, all teasing vanishing.

"I told you I was going to check on something," Taunos said. The edge to his voice was back, to match Gurseh's.

Amanah sighed. There had been an incident a month ago in the city, but she hadn't realized Gurseh held a grudge.

"I didn't tell you you could go," Gurseh snapped. "You're supposed to watch out for your partner's back!"

"It was a scratch, Gurseh. I only carried you because you got light-headed."

"Yes, and now everyone knows I'm the guard who faints at the sight of blood. Thanks for that."

"Only your own," Amanah said. "And it's not that uncommon."

"Besides, you prove your skills in other ways," Taunos said.

"You should have been there," Gurseh said.

Taunos frowned. "You didn't have to try to take down the thief alone. It could have waited, since he was holing up."

"Everyone has to look out for themselves as well as their partner," Emin said, sitting forward.

"What did you see?" Amanah asked.

"What?" Gurseh asked.

She kept her gaze on Taunos. "You said you left because you were going to check on something. What was it?"

Taunos shook his head, and Amanah raised her eyebrows. For Gurseh's pride, he had to say it. He had to admit to whatever it was and hope it was a reason good enough to draw away a guard.

"There was a small, potted tree—I thought I saw it, anyway. A white tree."

"Like the Gods' Tree?" she asked, shock chilling her. It was supposed to be the only one of its kind.

"Did you find it?" Emin asked, leaning forward eagerly.

"Was it pretty?" Gurseh sneered.

Taunos shook his head. "It vanished in the crowd as I was going toward it, and then I heard the scuffle and got back as soon as I could."

"You didn't even get a good look at the bit of fancy that drew you away?" Gurseh scowled.

Regret filled Taunos's expression, and he rubbed his face with both hands. Mumbled words came from behind his hands, sounding something like, "It was important."

Amanah flicked her gaze between the two. Taunos had apologized and paid for the bimnas to check Gurseh's injury out, though he hadn't even needed a bandage, and Borlim had assigned Taunos punishments.

It had been stupid to leave Gurseh, but Amanah couldn't honestly say she wouldn't have been tempted herself, if not fully drawn away. Someone carrying a Gods' Tree through the city? That seemed like something the clans in power would want to know about. She'd certainly want to know more.

"Aren't we taking this a little far?" Emin asked.

"I'm not important?" Gurseh asked, challenge in his voice.

"What would make it up to you?" Taunos asked.

"Your humiliation, just like you humiliated me. It's only fair."

Amanah rubbed her forehead. "Gurseh, you got distracted by that barge worker last time you and I patrolled."

His tone became sullen. "I messed up, but we all have to look out for ourselves, too."

"Then that applies to you, too," she said.

Emin stood up abruptly. "Stop this. This is not the time or the place—not during this mission when we all need to work together. Gurseh, if you really want to push this, you're going to have to wait until we get to Gahimbli and wrestle Taunos for your pride back in front of a magistrate there. Understand?"

Gurseh folded his arms.

Gaze locked with Gurseh's, Taunos's lips flattened, but he merely gave a single nod, as if in acknowledgement.

Emin frowned at them. "I won't have this compromise the safety of this team. We all need to work together. Is that clear?"

Amanah nodded, as did Taunos and Gurseh.

A bell rang out from the nobles' tent, crystal notes breaking the air. The nobles had taken to ringing a bell when they needed something from Taunos—usually just to scold him about something. They couldn't deign to just shout like a normal person.

Emin looked around. "Inuwe's been gone a while. I'll go to scout the perimeter just in case."

Blowing out his breath, Taunos stood, his gaze lifting on the shadowy cliff-face next to them. "I'll see what Lamyi wants."

In short order, both he and Emin had disappeared among the rock columns.

Gurseh watched Emin go, pride in his eyes. "He's going to be a great leader someday. All he needs is some ambition."

She agreed, but that last sentence struck her. Taunos's words came back to her from the garden, the sentiment so much the opposite. 'You're happy as you are.'

"Don't try to change my brother," Amanah said. "He deserves to be loved for who he is."

"I do. But I also see who he could be." Gurseh eyed her. "You two need to stop letting Haari Taunos drag you down."

"What do you mean?"

"All this frivolousness won't help you work your way up."

Anger heated in her again. "Maybe we don't have the same desires, but that doesn't mean what Emin and I want out of life isn't worthwhile."

Gurseh stood with a sigh. "From what I can tell, you have no goals. Not even to get rich enough so you can prove yourself to these nobles."

Amanah shook her head. No ambitions? She had far too many, at least according to Arruk. She just couldn't talk about them. "I'm off to check the horses."

Still, his words followed her, stuck in her mind amidst a flurry of frustration.

She was tired of passing up opportunities for fear of drawing attention. Tired of her worth, her dreams, being questioned or outright sabotaged. Tired of what she cared about and who she cared for being used against her.

And all that meant she was overlooked, instead, which was its own irritation.

But Taunos saw her. He'd listened to her fears about water shortage. Yesterday, they'd all realized he drank more water than any of them except the nobles, so he'd tried to match his drinking rate to theirs. She'd seen him watching them closely but hadn't figured out why until later. When she caught him paling, his skin drying in the first signs of sun sickness, she'd shoved a water canteen into his hand and ordered him to drink. He downed the mess of honey, salt, and water that Emin gave him without complaint or question, even though he gagged as it went down. And still, his first question had been that of whether there would still be enough water for all of them if he drank what he needed.

She'd been right to reject his offer in the garden, hadn't she? Because how could she tie herself to someone who was so visible, so loud? And yet, he brought with him a sense of optimism, and she found she missed that sort of hope. He seemed to respect her and, so far, took her advice often. Something she'd wanted desperately. Something she feared wholly.

She sighed, resting her head against Nakii's neck. The horse was yet another ephemeral happiness she couldn't hold onto. Why had she bothered to name the gelding? It'd only hurt worse when she had to give him up. Still, her hand stroked his neck, and she smiled when he turned his head and nuzzled her.

"Are you all right?" Emin asked, walking up behind her.

"I thought you were scouting the perimeter."

"I am. But also, I'm checking on my sister."

"There's no need." But she wasn't able to keep the strain from her voice.

Emin nudged her with his elbow. "I'm just worried about you. You've been more and more closed off. Arruk is wearing you down, and we're not even still there."

"I'm surprised it isn't wearing you down, too."

"See? That's what I'm talking about. You're growing more cynical. Back home, you were happy, but now, you're all stressed out and worried."

She didn't want to be. It's just that happiness seemed so far away these days. When had her joy and wonder died? Probably when she muted it to avoid notice. The time she spent with Emin and his friends staved off the bulk of the darkness caging her in, but she'd stopped searching for other ways to enjoy herself.

She turned to face him. "Why doesn't the city grate on you so much?"

"I focus on what I like, so the good outweighs the bad. There's still light and laughter and love, you know."

"I know."

"Come on. You talk yourself out of opportunities all the time."

"I do not!"

"The trip to the harbor?"

She folded her arms. "There was that sickness going around, and the families couldn't afford the bamimri."

"That city-wide archery competition?"

"If I had won, they'd have said I cheated, just like the horse race before we left Arruk."

"Okay, bad example. What about the training for leadership evaluation?"

She scoffed. "Like anyone there would follow me. Most of the guards have money and therefore wouldn't follow a havi."

Emin crossed his arms and stared at her. He'd done that training, and here he was, potentially in line for leadership.

She sighed, shoulders slumping. "Fine. Maybe I do, sometimes."

"You're becoming a ghost, wasting your life away while still on your feet."

"But this? This is folly. You know how they play with us in Arruk."

His brow furrowed. "What are you talking about?"

She blew out a breath. Great. She hadn't meant to actually get into this with her brother, but once he saw the promise of something to embarrass her with, he was stubborn.

"Taunos. He wants more." She confessed it to the rocks past her brother's shoulder.

A grin pulled at his mouth, and he looked far too satisfied with himself. "What do you want?"

"I'm not sure. I'm not even sure I want to have this conversation with my brother," she said, glaring at him.

He chuckled. "Fair enough. But, for what it's worth, you two might be good for each other."

"You don't need to set me up with your friend, Emin. You could date him." She scowled.

"Nah, I have Gurseh. Besides, Taunos is way too short."

Amanah snorted. Taunos was significantly shorter than many Dahuti men, though he had a way of carrying himself that made him seem taller, filling the room. It was refreshing to be able to look into Taunos's eyes without craning her neck.

She shook her head. What was she thinking?

"But he's friends with nobles. We're havi, with nothing the city considers as worth."

"He's not a noble, though."

"Who else carries themselves the way he does, like the world will stand aside for them? Like they're just wading into the pool for the fun of it? He's not part of the world of common people."

He shrugged. "Still, even if he is rich, he's always been decent."

"For now." She'd learned all too well not to trust nobles.

As part of the Hand, she'd seen plenty of traps—more than most. The jobs with good pay that abused their workers and framed them for crimes when they complained. The servants who weren't allowed to go home or see their families once they accepted the position. The jobs that seemed safe right up until the contract was signed, after which the danger was revealed. Kindness in nobles was like bright colors on poisonous fungus— a promise of pain and suffering to come.

"You're doing this job for nobles."

"Borlim assigned it. And you know what happens when you say no to nobles. Which is another reason why I should not get involved with Taunos, even if he's condescending to join us."

But nothing had happened when she'd said no to Taunos. Nothing had changed. He was holding to their agreement in the garden and had somehow avoided awkwardness between them.

Emin grinned. "Should not, I see. Not cannot or will not."

She glared at him. "He wants something, like they all do."

"You want things, too." Emin shrugged. "So long as you're both honest about it, I don't see the issue."

"People will talk. People will stare. They won't be happy."

"They do that anyway." He waved his hand, as if batting away her argument.

Amanah scuffed the ground with her boot. "I wish I could take a peek at the pattern the gods weave in time. Then, I would know what choice to make. What's safe." She made a face at herself, at how ridiculous this fanciful wish was.

Her brother's hand landed heavily on her shoulder, a solid weight to ground her in the now. "Just because it's hard doesn't mean it can't be good and right. Relationships are hard and messy and scary, sometimes."

She frowned at him. "Are you and Gurseh all right?"

Emin laughed. "Don't turn this around on me! You're as bad as Taunos."

She snorted. "I'm pretty sure that's impossible."

"Do what you want, Amanah." He squeezed her shoulder. "Whatever that is, whoever that's with. The rich in Arruk, they have so much already. We can keep them from stealing our little moments of joy, though."

"Yet another reason to stay away from Taunos."

He frowned. "Has he done something?"

"Not yet."

"Don't judge him for the faults of others. That's not fair. Judge him for his own faults—there's plenty of them." Emin chuckled. Her brother couldn't manage to be serious for more than a couple breaths.

"Oh, I know his faults." She shook her head. Emin had a point, and Amanah hated it. Especially as he knew it and grinned insufferably at her.

A sigh broke from her. "How much do you really know about him?"

"As much as I need to."

She raised her eyebrows, and he ticked off his fingers. "He's terrible at playing ija so that's always a good laugh. He holds his alcohol better than he pretends, so if you're looking to take advantage of him, he turns the tables on you quicker than a blink. And he's generous—at parties, he's always giving people money to bring their favorite dishes back to the group to share, and I've never seen him turn anyone away from food, no matter who, even after a practice."

She'd seen that, too, a few times. Taunos delighted in trying anything and everything new. And Emin was right—he often handed out handfuls of coins like they were flower petals. Who did that if they weren't rich enough not to care about money? But what noble shared the way he did, either?

Emin ruffled her braids, dodging when she swatted him away.

"Look, I won't push; it's not mine to have a say, anyway. Like I said, I just want some happiness for you, whatever form that takes. You work so hard to bring it to others, and you deserve some for yourself. Just, don't let fear of risk keep you from some joy, is all." He walked away, back on patrol, leaving her alone once more with her thoughts.

It'd been a long time since she'd opened up her heart. She'd taken a chance on someone in Arruk before and still carried the scars. She was far more comfortable being needed by others, instead of needing them. Even with things she wanted, she weighed the risks and often decided it wasn't worth it, even for a new scarf.

She didn't have to decide anything about Taunos right now—that situation was too complex anyway. But in the meantime, she'd take the advice and enjoy this break from the city. Enjoy the sun on her face, the wind in her hair, seeing landscapes she hadn't seen before.

Maybe she had been suppressing her curiosity and sense of adventure for too long. Maybe despite all she gave to those who needed her in Arruk, she needed to give to herself, as well, to take some chances to really live again. Maybe preparing for trouble didn't have to mean the death of joy.

If Emin was right, that was going to be so annoying.

6

"AMANAH! HURRY!" EMIN bellowed, jolting her from her thoughts.

She snatched her pack and ran, ignoring the snorts of spooked horses at her sudden motion. Her brother's voice had come from behind the noble's tent, and she charged past it, then paused. Between the boulders and the towering rock spires, no one was in clear view. Voices carried, however, and one of the nobles was howling.

"It bit me! Why was there a snake here?"

She headed in the direction of his voice, her heart hammering, eyes sharp on the trail for any more snakes.

"This is their home—we're only visiting," Taunos replied, his voice soothing. "Stay calm. Amanah's coming."

"And how exactly will that help?" someone snapped.

Around a huge boulder, Taunos was holding one of the nobles—Lamyi —by the shoulders, while the noble was shouting and cursing and trying to shake Taunos off him. Beyond them, Emin was backing away, dragging a writhing snake by the tail.

"What kind?" Amanah asked Emin.

"Viper." His tone was grim.

Great. That was all they needed. "Careful."

He nodded, still dragging the venomous snake away step by cautious step, and she headed for Taunos, where he struggled to hold Lamyi. If it wasn't a dry bite, all the activity would only pump the venom through his system faster.

But Taunos met her gaze and shook his head, then tipped his head toward the other noble.

Lord Inuwe sat on the ground, his leg outstretched in front of him, staring wide-eyed at his ankle. His silk slippers had completely shredded on one heel. "Am I going to die?"

"Not if I can help it," she said, kneeling in front of Inuwe and setting her pack beside her.

She'd seen this before, spying in the bamimri, where sometimes the injured person was the calm one while the onlooker panicked. Normally, the bimnas would then give the panicking person something to do, but the nobles weren't going to take orders from her. At least Taunos was holding Lamyi back so he wouldn't get in the way.

"What did I pay you for?" Lamyi shoved Taunos, trying to shake his hold off. "Do something!"

"I am," grunted Taunos, blocking his way with one swift motion. "Amanah, what do you need?"

"I have a snakebite kit for exactly this reason in my pack." She lifted it in explanation. "But we should move him back to the tent. I need space to work and there might be more snakes here."

"You *expected this*?" Lamyi shouted. "You could have at least warned us. Unless you intended this to happen?"

Inuwe began to get to his feet, but she held out her hand. "Don't move. You'll need to be carried."

"And who's going to carry him? You?" Lamyi snarled.

"Me, if you'll let me," Taunos said.

Lamyi paused in his fury, eyes darting to Taunos. Taunos carefully let go of Lamyi and nodded when he stood still. He crouched beside Amanah. In one fluid movement, Taunos picked Inuwe up in his arms like a child, ignoring the squawk of startled protest from the noble.

Taunos looked at Amanah. "The tent?"

She nodded. "That ground's already been cleared, so it should be safe."

His stride ate up the ground quickly. Lamyi shouldered past her with a fierce glower, stalking after him, and she took a moment to breathe before hurrying after them both. Emin would dispose of the snake and then come back to camp. She just hoped he'd stay safe and she wouldn't have another snakebite to tend, as well.

Taunos ducked into the tent and gently set Inuwe down on the carpets the nobles had covered the ground with. Now the slippers made a smidgen more sense, but still. Lamyi hovered over Taunos's shoulder, so Amanah went around Inuwe's other side to kneel beside his leg.

"You can't seriously be intending to let her do anything," Lamyi said.

"I hear wilderness in her words—does she even know how to read? Has she had any schooling?"

Taunos stood up carefully, pressing Lamyi back, away from Inuwe and Amanah. Giving her room to work. She tried not to sigh with relief.

She gestured to Inuwe. "May I see?"

Pale, breathing hard, he nodded.

Lamyi's voice filled the tent, strident with worry and accusation. "There's no way she knows what she's doing."

She couldn't focus on Lamyi and on saving Inuwe's life at the same time. She'd have to trust Taunos to deal with Lamyi. Doing her best to shut out his dramatics, Amanah gingerly rolled up the cuff of Inuwe's trousers. On his left leg above the ankle were two round holes, the skin around it already beginning to redden.

She opened her bag, grabbed the bottle of alcohol, and poured some on the wound. Inuwe jerked away, kicking her in the jaw as he did so.

"What are you doing?" Lamyi struggled, but Taunos grabbed his arms once more, keeping him at bay.

"Stay still," Taunos warned.

Her jaw ached, warmth blooming with the pain across it, but she tried to ignore it. Her hands shook as she reached out for Inuwe's ankle again, but he shifted away from her. Chasing him would only worsen his chances.

"I need to clean it," she told him. "We have to hope it's a dry bite—no venom—otherwise there's nothing we can do."

"What do you mean?" Lamyi asked.

"We have no antivenin. All I can do is clean it."

Inuwe stared at her, eyes wide, trembling. He suddenly looked very young in his terror.

"She's not a bimna," Lamyi said. "She doesn't know medicine. There has to be something that can be done!"

"She's learned from the bimnas," Taunos said.

The lie came smoothly from his lips, shining a light on her, the sort of light she'd always avoided. If the nobles discovered how she'd learned, she wasn't sure even Borlim could protect her. This sort of visibility—helping nobles with a snakebite—was exactly what she was supposed to be avoiding, yet here she was. She glanced at Taunos, barely keeping her rising fear under control.

"What was her supervisor's name?" Lamyi demanded. "Havi can't be bimnas, and it's clear she hasn't even acclimated to the city yet, not with that attitude."

Taunos caught her eye for a moment, but continued speaking to

Lamyi. "Unofficial learning. Cleaning and such, but she's right. This will help Inuwe—unless you keep arguing."

Somehow, his words helped her find her steadiness once again. Snake bites were not an uncommon danger in the wilderness. She had done this before, and she'd eavesdropped on the preparation of snake balm in the bamimri to make her own. She took a deep, steadying breath.

Staring at Taunos, then at her, Inuwe nodded and relaxed his leg, but Lamyi shouted, pushing Taunos back a couple steps before Taunos managed to stop him. "The bamimri would never allow you to listen in. You have to pay for that kind of training!"

"Get him out of here!" Amanah said, pouring on a little more alcohol to cleanse the wound.

Inuwe screamed into his fist.

"If you hurt him, if he sickens, I swear to Jattanu himself I will ruin you," Lamyi said, scuffling with Taunos until Taunos finally succeeded in dragging him out of the tent.

Amanah took a deep breath. Now that it was quieter, there was room to think again, instead of wondering when she'd have to switch from trying to save a life to avoiding an attack.

"I'm sorry it hurt. The worst is over now, all right?"

Trembling, Inuwe nodded.

Giving him a quick, supportive smile, Amanah poured water over the nobleman's ankle to rinse away the alcohol. She reined her thoughts firmly to just her tasks, just right now, and grabbed her pot of snake balm, massaging it into Inuwe's skin.

"Thank you," he breathed.

Amanah glanced up at him. He'd thanked her? That never happened —where was the trap? She forced her gaze back to her work, wrapping a strip of fabric around the noble's thigh.

"But I'm not hurt there." His voice shook but he didn't move, didn't fight her.

"This is to compress your leg. Hopefully, it'll keep any venom—or infection—from your heart. Don't remove it." It wasn't likely to work, but it wouldn't hurt either, unless she kept it on too long. At least it would help the nobles feel like she was doing something, even though there was nothing much to do but pray.

Taunos stepped back into the tent as she began to bandage the nobleman's ankle, covering the salve. His expression was tight, his gaze flickering over her as if to check if she was hurt. "Do you need anything?"

"Can you help him stand?"

He nodded, scooping up the nobleman once again and then setting him on his good foot, keeping him steady with one arm. She shifted to work around them, winding the bandage around Inuwe's ankle.

"You'll need regular care on the bite—it'll need cleaning, more snake balm, clean bandages," she said to Inuwe. "We'll keep your foot far below your heart to increase your chances. If we can keep infection away, you'll be fine."

If not, or if there was venom, they'd punish her for sure. She pressed her lips together. There was no time for these emotions right now. Not here. It wasn't safe.

Inuwe nodded, leaning against Taunos.

Taunos gave him one of his brilliant smiles. "I've never known Amanah to do a half-job at anything. I'm sure you'll be fine."

"You only chose the best for this mission, hmm?" Inuwe asked, his voice tremulous.

"Of course," Taunos said. "Each of them is exceptional."

Amanah glued her gaze to her work, fastening the bandage securely. Lamyi's threats made sense; Taunos's admiration did not. It'd be easier if she could predict him. He kept seeming to waffle between seeming like wilderness havi and seeming noble, familiar and dangerous.

She shook the thought out of her head. She didn't have time for this now. Somehow, she just needed to learn to keep her head down, not to marvel at Inuwe thanking her, or how it felt to be called exceptional in front of others.

Still supporting Inuwe with one hand, Taunos reached out, indicating her jaw. "Are you all right? That's probably going to bruise."

"I apologize." Inuwe sounded sheepish, like a child caught being naughty.

She blinked at him. First gratitude and now an apology?

The nobleman was still talking. "I do thank you for the help. One must make do with what one has, hmm? Especially in the wilderness. It was just… unexpected."

"I'm all right." She waved them both off, even though her jaw ached, especially when she spoke. "Where's Lord Lamyi?"

"I handed him off to Gurseh," Taunos said. "I need to go check on Emin, but I also wanted to check in on you."

She nodded, keeping her expression blank. Only the work. Focus only on the work. She'd figure everything else out later. Amanah took the lord's arm as Taunos passed him to her, stepping past her to the tent's entrance. The flap rustled, and he was gone.

"Can I walk?" Inuwe asked her. "On this, I mean. Is it wise?"

"We'll have you stay as still and calm as you can for a while. Let me know if you get dizzy."

"You mentioned infection?" Inuwe asked.

"We need to give the balm time to work, but we'll wash your wound again in alcohol tonight. We'll have a better idea of infection by then. I'm sorry it hurts."

"Better than being bitten again. I mean, by the snake."

She forced a smile at him, studying him with one hand as she bent to grab her pack. Her things spilled out all over the ground, and she groaned.

"Just get me to my horse, then you can clean this up," Inuwe said. "No one needs to hold me up if I'm in the saddle, right?"

"It's still too hot to move," she said.

"Then I'll just sit."

And his horse wouldn't get a break.

But she'd already gathered far too much attention to herself today, so she bowed her head and obeyed.

She moved aside the tent flap and carefully negotiated the exit with Inuwe, wincing when he slipped and hissed in pain. Emin and Taunos were walking back into camp together. Both seemed fine, and a flash of relief washed over her. Gurseh was in Lamyi's way, his hands flying through the air as he spoke to the noble, and Amanah trained her gaze on the horses, instead. All she had to do was help Inuwe over there.

But the nobleman was trembling with the stress and fear of his ordeal, and as they navigated the path, he stepped wrong and slid again, exclaiming in sudden panic.

She steadied him. "Remember, be calm."

With a quick motion, Lamyi broke Gurseh's hold on him and stormed toward her, but she couldn't leave Inuwe, or he'd fall. He needed her support to hop along on his one leg.

"What are you doing to him?" Lamyi shouted.

"Lamyi," Inuwe started.

"Inuwe, are you alright?" Fear and anger warred in Lamyi's face and voice.

"I'm fine—"

"What's that bandage?" Lamyi's focus switched to her. "Did you cut into him? He kept *screaming*."

"I didn't—" she started.

"Don't lie to me. I have eyes and I have ears." Lamyi flung out his arm. "Did you enjoy his pain? Get away from him."

Amanah tried to untangle herself from Inuwe, but he held onto her, unbalanced on his one good leg.

"I can't," she said.

"Your insolence is not appreciated," Lamyi said. "I warned you what would happen if you harmed Inuwe. And you'll pay for the rugs you ruined. Bad enough my aunt's ceramic vase was chipped when you dropped it."

She winced. Lamyi was only a couple paces away now, and Inuwe was still holding onto her.

"Lamyi, I'm fine—" Inuwe began.

But she had to get away. She couldn't remain trapped in his grip, not with Lamyi stomping toward them. She pulled Inuwe's fingers away from her shoulder, and he yelped in surprise.

Rage flared in Lamyi's eyes. She winced. He raised a hand, and she didn't wait to find out if he'd actually hit her or not—she lifted Inuwe's hand from her shoulder and stepped back, behind him, out of reach.

At the same time, Taunos tackled Lamyi. They crashed to the ground in a cloud of dust, and Amanah tightened her grip on Inuwe as he wobbled, eyes fixed on the scene.

"Gurseh!" Emin bellowed. "Get Lord Inuwe to his horse."

"How dare you?" Lamyi shouted, spittle flying, as he rose.

Taunos sprang back to his feet, glancing back at her and then planting himself between Lamyi and her, every line of his body tensed. Amanah struggled to remember how to breathe. Confrontations with nobles always went badly. She'd learned to avoid them, and now... Well, now, it was all going to escalate.

Gurseh hurried up, quietly taking Inuwe's arm and helping the sputtering noble away from them, toward the horses.

Emin touched her shoulder lightly, eyes grave on her jaw. She shook her head, but before she could explain, he joined Taunos in front of her.

Her blood roared in her ears. This was all bad, and the longer it went on, the more angry Lamyi would get. Which meant the worse it would be for them.

"I'll make sure you're each whipped for this," Lamyi snarled. "Paid to protect us and instead you attack us?"

"I told you, no one is being whipped for your mistakes," Taunos growled.

Amanah stepped to the side, backing up to give herself space to maneuver. She'd rather see the danger, even if the promise of pain in Lamyi's eyes tore the breath from her lungs.

"She cut into Inuwe, harmed him! Don't even try to tell me she didn't —I heard his tortured screams."

"She saved Inuwe's life." There was a cold kind of fury in Taunos's voice, and his stance was set for fighting.

"My father is—" Lamyi began.

"Not here." Taunos stepped forward. "Now, you can apologize and we'll move on with no more attacks. Or, we can—" Emin nudged Taunos, and Taunos quickly amended, "Or I will tie you up and you can spend the rest of the journey slung over your horse's back like a package."

Lamyi puffed himself up, like a viper. That was probably unkind to think toward vipers. "You won't get away with this. You're protecting her after she knifed the man she's supposed to protect? You left him in there with her alone!"

"Amanah did not cut Lord Inuwe." Taunos didn't even look back at her to be sure, but Lamyi did. She gave him a shake of her head, for all the good it would do her.

The noble's eyes narrowed. "There's a bandage around his thigh."

"It's preventative," she said. There was no sneaking away from this attention. Taunos wouldn't know, no doubt, and if Emin spoke up, he'd be targeted. She wouldn't let him be threatened for her. "Just to keep any venom from his heart."

"I have difficulty believing that," Lamyi said. "And your attitude… You're no doubt the worst servant I've ever seen."

"She's not a servant," Taunos said.

Lamyi was undeterred. "No one will want to even speak to you once I get back to Arruk."

Emin's hands curled into fists, but Taunos shrugged. "There will be people who will. I'm not worried about your threats, Lord Lamyi."

How could he be so cavalier about it all? Amanah couldn't stop watching the horrific spectacle playing out in front of her. Taunos and Emin were being fools. Even if her brother at least had the sense to keep his mouth shut, he was still visibly defending her.

"Your job is to follow orders!" Lamyi snarled.

Taunos's voice was flat. "No, my job is to make sure you and Inuwe get to Gahimbli safe. Amanah did excellent for her part, and you attacked her for it. If you insist on trying to follow through on your threats, or on attacking any of us, well, I can deliver you safely through the gates of Gahimbli trussed hand and foot and tied to your horse's saddle on your belly."

"You wouldn't," Lamyi hissed. "And if you even tried it, I will make each of you pay dearly."

Taunos leaned in, voice low. His fists clenched so tightly, his knuckles were white and the muscles on his forearms stood out. "Lord Lamyi, let me assure you, you have no idea what I will or will not do. And if you attack anyone else on this team, I will stop you, however I need to."

"Don't hit him." Amanah's voice cracked, it was so sharp.

Taunos turned from Lamyi, eyes narrowed, mouth opening.

She cut him off. "Not on my account. Hit him for your own sake if you must, but never mine."

He, at least, might be able to make it out unscathed, but not the rest of them. And at least saying it showed she wasn't stirring up trouble. For whatever little that would be worth.

Taunos stilled, eyes holding hers for a moment, then nodded.

Time to try to put a stop to this. Drawing in a steadying breath, Amanah bowed low to the noble, avoiding his gaze. "Lord Lamyi, please forgive me. I will try to stay out of your way for the rest of the journey."

Taunos's narrowed gaze bore into her as she straightened, and Emin glanced at her, eyes full of worry and indignation. She turned away from both of them. She needed to leave, to collect herself before she shattered into a million pieces. She needed to be out of sight before the shakes came, so no one would see her distraught.

But where could she go? Inuwe and Gurseh were with the horses, where she'd normally go. She shook her head. She just needed to leave camp for a bit. Her feet carried her away from Lamyi's posturing, away from Emin and Taunos's concern. She walked among the buttes, winding her path without caring much which direction she was going. Just away—far, far away.

How was she going to recover from this? Inuwe wasn't so bad—for now, at least. Perhaps he really was the sort of noble who could show honest gratitude and apologize.

But even in that case, Lamyi would eventually convince him to hate her like he did, and she couldn't do anything about it. She'd just have to figure out how to go back to staying out of their sight.

~

Amanah sank down on a boulder, gingerly rubbing her sore jaw. The pain brought tears to her eyes. Blinking them away, she crossed her arms atop her knees and stared across the desolate landscape. She'd walked a long way from camp, farther than was probably wise, but she didn't want to risk coming across Lamyi again too soon.

Using the bits of healing knowledge she'd cobbled together would go against Borlim's orders to stay invisible, but she *wanted* to use those skills. And gain more. If anyone else got hurt and she had the chance to save them, she couldn't keep healing skills to herself. She wouldn't. Besides, there were only the six of them—she couldn't exactly hide in a crowd.

Lamyi's anger wasn't surprising, really. He was scared and wasn't thinking straight. But he had power, and his lack of reasoning made him dangerous. Clearly he cared about things and about Inuwe, but that seemed a mark against her, instead of for her.

A plan forward continued to elude her.

She was no nearer a solution and instead had hit the post-crisis shivers when Taunos found her.

He perched silently on the boulder beside her, holding out her pack. "Everything inside is all messed up, but I think I gathered it all. Are you all right?"

Amanah nodded, but the lie crushed the breath out of her, and she switched it to a shake of her head. Swallowing hard, she clutched her arms closer to her, trying to stop her trembling.

"You wouldn't really tie him up, would you?" Maybe it was all empty threats, but Amanah couldn't tell. If she hadn't known he was lying about her bamimri training earlier, she might have believed him.

"I can't stand adults who are bullies." He sighed, looking at her. "I'm not going to hurt him, not unless he tries to hurt someone again. Not unless it's necessary. Is that what you think of me?"

She narrowed her eyes at him. "But you'd tie him up?"

He rubbed his hands over his face. "Not unless there's no other option, but he doesn't need to know that. Reason wasn't working. Sometimes bullies only respond to threats in return."

"They paid for protection," she reminded him. "We have a duty."

"Then so do they—to not attack the people they're employing to keep them safe. Besides, they can have their money for all I care."

Gurseh would be livid if he heard, but Taunos was matter-of-fact about it.

"You'll be disgraced if Lamyi gets his way," she said. "You're going to stand by us even if it's your downfall?"

He tilted his head as if she'd testified that the sky was beneath them and overhead was the ocean. "Why would it be my downfall? I will always choose to stand with those who are true and noble and kind. Not those who call themselves noble and are none of those things. And if that makes me less popular, well, good, because those people didn't see me anyway."

She blinked. He took care of the nobles, making sure they had what they needed, but he didn't curry favor with them the way Gurseh sometimes did. And yet, he'd let go of their regard without a second thought? Even though, surely, them thinking highly of him would make his job easier? Was he really willing to fall from the heights, to lose his party invitations, the respect so easily afforded him, all on account of her and Emin?

He was watching her, too. "Do you have anything? For the bruising?"

She wrenched her gaze from his, looking down at the bag by her feet. "In my bag."

Her hands would shake as soon as she let go of her arms, and she felt like she might entirely lose her grip on her emotions. She'd come undone.

Taunos remained a statue of serenity next to her. "Do you want me to get the medicine?"

No. What she wanted was the comfort she'd felt from him the last time she'd felt so adrift, when Emin and Taunos had sandwiched her in an embrace between them, shielding her from the world and all its problems for just a little bit.

But how could she ask for that, especially when she knew he wished for more from her? And yet, she still craved that snatch of peace. Maybe he could pretend she was Emin. Maybe she could pretend the same with him.

"This is going to sound silly," she began.

"I'm good at silly." One corner of his mouth lifted crookedly.

She drew in a shaky breath. "Can I just have a hug? Nothing more?"

The crooked smile became full as he stood, opening his arms. "Just a hug, nothing more."

She rose, trembling with the movement, and stepped into his arms. They wrapped around her solidly, though he shivered.

He squeezed her gently, humor filling his voice. "You're still so cold."

A laugh broke from her, past the soreness in her jaw. "You're still warm."

Somehow, she could breathe a little easier within that circle of warmth and comfort, surrounded by the scent of him, like rich soil, like trees and water. The weight in her chest eased. Safety. That's what it felt like. Like he was a cave in a storm, a place of refuge in a tempest. A place where she could stitch her composure back together without melting into a pool of tears first. Time enough to build a plan.

The closeness to him felt too good. Embarrassment welled up in her. What must he think of her—and why did she care at all?

She fumbled to explain. "Deep pressure helps with shivers, especially after an event like that."

He just nodded. Slowly, his relaxation, his comfort and warmth, ate through her embarrassment, and the tension and shivers began to lessen.

"You were amazing back there," he murmured.

She laid her head down on his shoulder and closed her eyes, securing her arms around his waist. "Thank you for backing me up."

"You did all the work," Taunos said with a shrug, his arms shifting across hers. He swayed, ever so slightly, back and forth as her trembling melted away. She let it lull her. "You didn't need me at all—they should have listened to you."

"I'm havi. They're nobles."

"That's what Emin says, too. It doesn't make sense."

"You've asked Emin?"

Taunos nodded.

Amanah sighed. "He's terrible at explaining things."

A light chuckle shook his arms around her.

"You know how the cities of Far Dahutad are run by clans? Each clan keeps its clan members in line, or that's how it's supposed to work, anyway."

He hmm'ed an affirmative.

"Well, the cities also assign you worth based on how much you have. Property. Your own personal guards. Servants. That sort of thing."

He remained silent, but she could feel the weight of his attention.

"Any clan member can become havi—low class. Poor. All they have to do is make mistakes, mistakes big enough the rest of their clan won't cover for them. They can climb out again, too, of course, particularly if they can promise their allies or family or clan leaders enough to persuade them to lend a hand."

"Your clan won't help you?" he asked.

She pulled back a little to look at him, but not so much to leave that circle of safety entirely. "My clan doesn't have much power in the cities. Various members might move up, and they take titles from their work instead of their clan name in the city. Outside of the city, most everyone is havi."

"Why do some clans have the power and others not? Money?"

"Money, favors, blackmail. The usual."

"And you don't have those things. Hopefully, especially the blackmail."

She couldn't help the flash of a smile at that. "Most of my clan doesn't have lots of money, or own land or buildings. Nothing that Arruk counts as wealth. We aren't owed big favors, and we're not considered important enough—usually—to blackmail. My family moves with the seasons, with the herds. We aren't around the cities long enough to make either friends or enemies, generally."

The explanation was fumbled, but a light of understanding dawned in Taunos's face. "Ah. My people also move seasonally."

She tilted her head. "Really?"

"Why does that surprise you?"

She glanced away, fumbling for a reason. "You get along so well with the city folk."

"I was, hmm... nineteen? No, twenty, when I saw my first city." He shrugged. "Anyway, it seems natural to move, to me."

It drew a ghost of a smile from her. "Me too."

His grin was like the sun dawning, hot and radiant.

So he was also a nomad. And apparently, she'd seen cities and towns even before he had. He was only three years older than her, after all. But why did he spend like he never had to worry about money? Her father Ifel was careful with money—he'd taught her well—even though some of the towns they visited bartered instead.

She caught her breath, realization striking her. "You barter, don't you? Or trade? You're not used to money. That's why it flows through your hands like sand."

"You might be too observant for my own good." But he sounded delighted about it, and his eyes crinkled with his smile.

She found herself sharing in that smile. It all made sense suddenly, and giddiness filled her. Emin was right—Taunos wasn't noble. He was a lot like her family. That was a lot less daunting, less dangerous. When she found allies in her work in Arruk, they were invariably havi. Not that she hadn't seen cruelty among the lowest classes, too, but most of what she saw came raining down on them from above.

She considered him carefully. "If you're havi too, why aren't you treated that way? Or have you moved up in class while Emin and I haven't yet? But you wander, and you aren't even from Far Dahutad. People in power usually care about that, especially recently."

He shrugged. "I'm still learning your system."

"It has to be the charm, and the confidence, the way you carry yourself like a noble. That must be why you're Haari Taunos, not just another havi. And the worst part is, I can't even hate you for it."

His voice dipped to a low rumble. "I think I'm grateful for that last point."

Abruptly, she realized what she'd just done. How had she fallen into flirting with him so quickly, so easily? Her face heated, and she pulled back, looking away as his arms dropped from around her. Was his impulsivity contagious, like a disease? She knew better than to do this.

She struggled to keep her voice steady and light. "It's easier, I think, for those who have already had status to regain it, like the nobles who fall temporarily to havi and then regain their status and power. It's easier to climb up when you already have a network of connections than when you arrive with nothing, knowing no one."

"Ah. That's it perhaps."

She darted a look at him. "What is?"

"I have connections in Gahimbli. Perhaps that's the true reason for the difference? But my connections, for whatever it's worth, are yours and Emin's, if it helps."

Amanah bit her lip, then winced as her bruises complained. His noble connections must be why he was treated so well, why the rules bent for him. She'd stopped trying, considering it too risky after her early attempts saw her sent for Jattanu's justice, but clearly it worked for him.

Taunos's gaze wandered over her face, and he abruptly switched the subject. "Why don't you actually join the bam—er, bimas? I can't imagine you wouldn't do well there."

"Bimnas," she said. "It costs money to apply—lots of money—and they require a permanent address for a private residence in the city. One that isn't the guardhouse." She tried to say it off-handedly, as if it didn't cut her.

"Maybe Inuwe could be persuaded to help you get in."

"He won't." Her voice was sharp, and she turned away to take a jar of balm from her bag. Hope preceded betrayal, and she didn't trust these nobles. She stared studiously at the landscape, the sunlit gullies and lengthening shadows around them, as she spread the balm over the stiffening skin on her jaw.

"We have the whole trip to change their minds," Taunos said. "Or maybe someone else would step up to help once we get to Gahimbli."

His optimism, the way he thought impossible things were possible, reminded her of how she'd been, before her brushes with nobles had educated her to their ways. Yet somehow he hadn't learned her wariness.

He rescued nobles and jumped off cliffs. She saw the rocks at the bottom.

She swallowed hard. This would be a big change, but what she was doing wasn't working. "They don't hold what you want over your head? To try to control you?"

"Some try," he acknowledged. "Some don't. Obviously, I'll introduce you to my friends, who don't."

"The others could pressure them, threaten to ruin them and make them havi too."

"So far, if that's happened, they've pushed back. Besides, you've tried to learn anyway, from the bamimri. You've already started."

It wasn't a smart thing she'd been doing. It was folly, like climbing the Gods' Tree at night. Somehow he made it seem admirable.

"I went around them. I didn't ask for a favor they'll demand payment for tenfold in the future."

"Favors work both ways." His eyes caught and held hers, compassion in their depths. "It's just an idea. It doesn't have to be your path. You'll find your way, I have no doubt."

She considered him for a moment. "Why do you believe in me?"

"Why not?" He spread his hands. "You don't brag. If you say you can do something, I trust that you can. You and Emin are two of the most capable people I know. To be dismissed simply because you don't place value in the same things they do? It shows fault only in them."

She smiled despite herself. There was no coercion she could see in that wide, honest face. She wanted to step back into his arms, to feel the warmth and safety again. But she couldn't do that until she was sure of what she wanted. She refused to play with him the way she'd been played with. She'd probably already gone too far.

"It felt good, fixing up Inuwe's leg. So long as he doesn't get an infection from it."

"Good?" He looked at her askance, skepticism evident in the wrinkle of his brow.

"Not this." She gestured to her face, then capped the balm and put it away. "That decidedly did not feel good. I meant seeing the problem in front of me and knowing how to fix it. Even if he forgets it and accepts Lamyi's view of me, I still did that. I did my best, anyway. I want to do that more. And maybe I've been thinking too small."

"Too small?"

"I've been trying not to draw attention. Because of, well, like what happened at the race. I don't want to put others at risk for my mistakes. But it means I can only do so much. This idea... I'll have to think on this. If I could have a sponsor to pay my way forward, maybe someone willing to let me use their address as my permanent address..." Amanah grinned. "I can turn their own system against them. They can't stop me then."

Taunos matched her grin for grin.

She swallowed her ferocity and shrugged it away. "Nothing will stop me from helping those who need it."

"I understand that all too well. People rely on you. And you do well by them."

Her mind was racing, hope rising in her, energizing her. If she could find a way to do more…

But Taunos drew attention wherever he went. Why didn't it fall on his head?

He, too, seemed to be letting cares wash away the optimism they'd shared for a moment. He looked back toward the camp, rubbing the back of his neck. "I need to be better. Like we discussed earlier, I shouldn't have left Gurseh on patrol, and I should have been faster when I saw Lamyi heading toward you."

She gave him a flat look. Sometimes he was utterly ridiculous. "You can't do everything."

"I know that all too well."

"We make mistakes sometimes. It just means we're human. Then we do better next time."

He grimaced, then nodded. "Thank you."

"Why?"

"Because you say what you think, and when you look at me, it isn't as Haari Taunos. You look at me as your idiot brother's idiot friend." His mouth curled up on one side. "It's good to have people around who will let you know when you're being foolish."

It drew a smile from her, though she'd have to ponder that later.

"It's just one opinion," she said, shrugging off the intensity of his gaze.

"It matters to me."

Her cheeks heated, and she kept her focus on a particularly oddly shaped rock nearby.

Abruptly, he shifted, boots scraping the stone in a way that had to be intentional, because he normally walked in eerie silence. "Are you ready to head back?"

Amanah nodded, falling in beside him.

He chattered as they walked, trading stories about some of the people they knew in Arruk. He asked about Nasri, spoke of the jeweler in the west havi well and his arthritis, he knew how one of the weavers had lost her pinky in an accident, and he reported that the old fisherman she had tended for a cough was apparently feeling better. He even knew about

Gitu, who had been seen by a healer and was expected to recover. It surprised her, at first, that they knew some of the same people, but then again, Taunos loved people, so maybe it wasn't so odd that he remembered names and families.

She tried not to look at him, but somehow, her gaze kept drifting back to him. He'd placed himself in front of her today, despite knowing she could fight, and then had come to check on her. He made her laugh, made things seem lighter when he was around, even when he exasperated her. Besides, if she didn't have help, she'd spend the whole trip looking over her shoulder, and how long would she hold out before exhausting herself?

He'd been a shield for her and Emin already during this trip, deflecting the nobles' attention. Maybe he could be even more of one.

She grabbed Taunos's arm to stop him, and he immediately halted, turning to her with concern in his eyes.

"Taunos, I need something from you. I hate to ask, but it's important."

"What is it?"

She withdrew her hand, shifting uncomfortably. "I can take care of myself, normally."

"I know."

"Emin won't think of this. After today, Lamyi... I wouldn't be surprised if he targets us. Maybe Gurseh, too, for holding him back."

Worry clouded his face. "Did I make things worse when I confronted him? I wasn't thinking. I just... I lost my temper. I didn't immediately think about what you said at the horse race."

She shrugged. "I'm not sure. But I think I'm glad you did it."

If he hadn't been there, things could have gone much worse. It was one danger or another, and this one seemed the lesser, at least for now.

He nodded, relaxing a fraction, but his eyes held hers, watching her intently.

"I need you to be a shield for us against the nobles. Just in case. I don't think they'll hit us—probably—but I do think they'll threaten us if given the chance."

"Amanah, that's the whole reason I'm here," he murmured. "To be the one dealing with Lamyi and Inuwe."

"Yes, but it's not quite the same thing, is it? And I'm telling you the danger." She lifted her chin.

He smiled, though sadness lurked in his eyes. "It would be my honor."

She forced herself to hold his gaze, to not look away from the intensity there. If she was going to rely on him, she wanted to be sure. "Don't promise me something you can't follow through on."

"I will be here." He gave her a single nod. "I will do everything I can to keep you all safe."

She nodded and let out her breath.

He gestured to her face but didn't touch her. "How's your jaw?"

"Bruised a bit, but that's all. It hurts to talk, and chewing might be fun for a couple days."

Exasperation crossed his features. "It hurts to talk? Then why—I was just trying to take your mind off things."

She laughed. "And it worked. Unfortunately, bruises lack minds."

"Well, you don't have to talk if you don't want to."

She stopped herself from giving him a shove like she would with her brother. Instead, she raised her eyebrows at him. "If I hadn't wanted to say something, I wouldn't have."

"Now, if you could somehow teach Emin the opposite, the world would be much quieter!"

She laughed, walking beside him toward camp, but the words were like a splash of ice water in the face. Out of the corner of her eye, she watched him, trying to decide exactly what he'd meant by bringing up her brother, but then again, it didn't really matter. He was Emin's friend, and she had turned him down romantically. They were just friends. She'd blurred that line a little today, and too much of her wanted to cross it entirely. But now was not the time. She had to be careful, not chase after a dangerous attraction.

However... Perhaps the way Taunos snatched attention could work for her. Perhaps, he could be the redirection so she could accomplish more.

7

THE SKY OPENED up without warning, pouring sheets of rain down on them. Amanah's mount, Nakii, grumbled, and she stroked his mane, agreeing with him. Rain brought life, but not when it was so violent, and there'd been no place to hole up since the clouds began to gather and darken above them. They should have made it to the caves marked on the map by now, but one of the pack horses was beginning to stumble, and moving any faster would ruin it. With the nobles unwilling to part with their supplies, if they lost a horse, the others would be even more overburdened, and soon they'd be stuck in the wilderness without mounts.

"We have to get out of the rain!" Gurseh yelled above the downpour.

Of course they did, but she couldn't see any options. The hillside they traversed was bare of cover and too steep to stop on. They needed to get to caves, or at the very least, high, flat ground.

"Haari Taunos!" Lamyi reined in his mount. "Have your guards pitch our tent."

Taunos shot a quick glance at Emin before shaking his head in reply. "We can't linger on the slope. We need flatter ground or the tents will be swept away."

Amanah kept Nakii toward the edge of the group, far from Lamyi. The noble had offered her a water pouch yesterday with words that implied an apology without actually being one. She hadn't been able to trust that her water hadn't been tampered with though, and she'd tried to discreetly get rid of it, but he'd caught her and taken offense. Worse, nothing had been clearly wrong with it—there'd been a few specks of dirt that could have been nothing, or accidental, and it didn't smell suspicious, but why had he had her pouch in the first place? It felt like a trap in the guise of kindness. Still, she had no evidence to support her mistrust, and it'd done nothing but put her more firmly on his bad side.

"It's pouring out here! We can't see where we're going," Lamyi said.

"We should find shelter ahead," Emin said, barely audible. "Not too much farther."

Amanah nodded, catching Taunos's eye.

Taunos spoke up for Lamyi to hear. "We're close to shelter. We need to get across the hill first."

"The tent will provide shelter," the noble grumbled, the rest of his words lost in a crack of thunder.

Nakii wickered uneasily, but Lord Lamyi's horse spooked and took off, with the pack horses and Inuwe's mount following.

Amanah tightened her grip on the reins. The last thing they needed was a headlong race in the dark and the rain, but they couldn't just leave the nobles. Nudging Nakii into a gallop, they thundered through the gloom. The sturdy horse's hooves kicked up mud, and Amanah kept her touch light on the reins, letting him have his head as she crouched low over his neck.

Gurseh, Emin, and Taunos trailed behind, their horses objecting to a run in such weather. She could sympathize. But they were gaining on the runaways. All she needed to do was get close enough to grab the reins. But ahead, a deeper blackness opened up—they were heading toward a drop-off.

"Cliff ahead!" she shouted the warning, but Lamyi still couldn't quite get control of his mount.

Pushing Nakii for speed, she flung her arm out, snatching Lamyi's reins out of his hand. He startled, tumbling from his horse, and she reined his mount in quickly, grabbing Inuwe's reins too when his horse made to pass her. Nakii neighed, stamping his hooves as the pack horses crowded him. Her heart pounded in her chest as she tried to soothe him, turning all the horses around to where Lamyi lay groaning. Did he have a head injury from falling? They didn't need any more trouble to deal with, and if he was injured, no doubt they'd all be punished.

She gathered the reins of the three mounts and tied them to her saddle, then dismounted and sent Nakii away from the edge, towing the other horses behind him. Inuwe, still hunched in his saddle, twisted to gape at them while his horse was led away by hers. Amanah ran to the fallen Lamyi as Emin, Gurseh, and Taunos charged up, Emin's horse stamping nearly all the way up to the edge before settling down, snorting and blowing. The bottom of the drop-off was hidden by the darkness. She had to get Lamyi away before he unwittingly rolled right off the edge.

"Get back from the edge. Someone needs to watch Inuwe," Amanah said.

"Gurseh, take my horse and stand guard," Emin said, dismounting and tossing him the reins.

As Gurseh headed away, Amanah took Lamyi's wrists and tried to drag him away from the edge. He shoved at her, his motions unfocused but strong, the mud slipping beneath her. Emin nudged her out of the way, then lifted Lamyi under the arms while she moved back to lift his feet. Lamyi fought them deliriously, nearly falling several times.

The mud seeped through the loose stitching keeping her soles attached to her boots. Her socks soaked up the cold damp, making her shiver.

"Here." Taunos had dismounted, too, of course. He led Rose over to them, stepping carefully in the mud. "Can you get him on my horse?"

Together, the three of them hauled Lamyi over the saddle. Amanah winced as the noble's head bounced, and she steadied him. Taunos led Rose back toward Inuwe, his boots squelching in the thick mud—the same mud engulfing Emin's boots and her own. The rain was sheeting down so hard, the ground couldn't absorb it. The land was drowning around them.

The ground beneath them shuddered.

Amanah's boots slipped, and she went down. Rose shied away, dragging Taunos with her as she ran for the safety of the other horses.

Emin grabbed Amanah's arm to help her stand, but the ground began to flow beneath them. Amanah scrambled back to her feet, gripping his hand hard. Her chest tightened, her breath coming faster. The cracking ground drew her gaze, especially as it began sloughing away down the cliff edge. Emin's grip on her became iron, but she didn't care because she was holding on to him just as tightly. Together, they ran, but with the mud sucking at their boots, they were still sliding toward the drop-off.

"Emin!" Gurseh shouted. Panic sharpened his features.

Rose shuddered to a stop with the others, and Taunos turned at the shout. Fear flashed across his mud-spattered face like lightning. He shoved the reins into Inuwe's hands, and then both Taunos and Gurseh sprinted toward her and Emin. But they'd never get there in time. She knew that, even as she kept running through the streaming mud.

Her feet were swept out from under her, tearing her from Emin's grip even as he landed hard right next to her. She grabbed his arm with one hand and clawed for a handhold with the other, but she couldn't even keep her grip on her brother. The mudslide ripped him away from her, no matter how hard she tried to hold on.

"Roll," she shouted to him. Maybe they could escape to the side. Nothing else was working.

He immediately obeyed, throwing himself sideways. Mud and rain in her eyes blinded her. She gasped for breaths that were never enough, struggling to get out of the muck sweeping her to her doom. She'd lost Emin and couldn't find him. Where was he? Where was the edge? Surely he hadn't—

Someone grabbed her arm, jerking her to the side. She was falling. Her fist clenched around fabric. Her throat closed on a scream.

The ground hit her feet with a shudder that rocked through her bones, but momentum continued carrying her around in a spin. A moment later, she slammed into rocks, bruising her back against them. Someone collided with her, arms holding her tight, and she was whirled around, only to hit rock again, and then, finally, they stopped.

"Emin?" His name was a strangled cry from her throat.

Gasping for breath, she collected her wits, trying to catch her bearings while the world still seemed to spin. She wiped mud and rain out of her eyes, shaking off the disorientation and forcing her panic down, though her heart still pounded against her ribs.

She was on her feet, leaning against a stone wall. The rain was lessened here, a shallow ledge of stone about ten feet from the top of the cliff face. Taunos was holding her, and beyond him, mud poured over the edge like a waterfall. Somehow he must have grabbed her and hurled them both off the drop and onto this ledge to the side of the mudslide, their momentum slamming her against the rock wall before they stopped.

Amanah stared at him. He'd saved her. How had he saved her? He was Emin's friend, but he'd saved *her*. He'd left behind his job, the nobles, to put his life at risk for hers. Why?

"Are you all right?" he asked, loosening his hold on her.

She had fistfuls of his shirt in her grip. Gulping, she snatched her hands away. Her whole body shook, and she wrapped her arms around herself to steady them. She was safe now, but what about her brother? Taunos held one arm out to bar her from tumbling off the ledge, but dropped it once she showed she had her balance.

"Thank you," she breathed, still trying to keep control of her terror as her gaze darted past him, scanning the landscape.

"Emin!" Breathlessness stole her voice. She tried again, panic sharpening her voice as she screamed her brother's name into the void. No response came. Her stomach twisted and she struggled with the fear of what she might find. But she had to know. "Where's Emin?"

His mouth firmed into a flat line as he looked to the side. "I couldn't reach him and Gurseh in time. They were heading the other way."

She fought for breath, to calm the terror rising in her. She couldn't have lost Emin. She should have held on to him. She had to move, had to do something, lest her emotions bury her like the mud.

They both should be dead right now, buried under the mudflow.

Taunos's gaze flickered over her. "If you're all right, we can climb up and then head that way. They might have found a similar ledge, or a gentler slope."

How could he be so easily optimistic that they weren't buried under mud, crushed by rocks far below? She shuddered and forced in a slow breath, swallowing down her panic. He was right. She had survived— maybe Emin had, too. She had to look for him.

"The nobles." Her stomach twisted at the thought of even more trouble if they were lost or injured, either through another landslide or an opportunistic attack. As if her brother in danger wasn't enough to worry about. "Are they ok?"

"They were behind me. So I think so, for now."

"We have to find Emin and Gurseh."

First one thing, then the next. Focusing on the tasks that needed doing helped drive back the flood of emotion, and if she let her emotions run wild, she'd drown in overwhelm. She had to keep a level head to have a chance at rescuing her brother so he could annoy her for the rest of the trip.

She *had* to find him. Her stomach knotted, and it felt like a boulder was crushing her chest. She swallowed hard. She was normally better at this, boxing away her emotions so she could deal with a crisis. Of course, usually Emin's life wasn't at stake. She forced her focus onto forming a clear plan. First, they needed off this ledge.

"Can we even get up top? We need to see what we're dealing with." Amanah eyed the upper face of the cliff. Mud sloughed down a few paces to the side, and below, the land flowed like a river. At least the lip of stone above them had outlasted the rain, so far.

"I can boost you." Taunos was still breathing hard from exertion, but he readied his hands anyway.

She'd have to rely on Taunos's assistance, and the thought opened a pit in her stomach. Asking others to help all too often let her down, and the stakes now were higher than ever. But she couldn't climb up alone, either, and besides, he'd caught her right out of the landslide. She had to trust him, have to hope she wasn't wrong. It was Emin's only chance.

With a shaky nod, Amanah set her foot in his hands, steadying herself on his shoulders. He pushed her higher with a grunt, and she clambered up the rocks. On her belly, she turned around. The cold rain had already soaked her through, but now it seeped into her stomach, and it felt as if she'd never be warm again. She reached down, and Taunos leapt, the gloom making it seem far higher than he should have been able to jump. He caught her hand, and it wasn't nearly as hard to drag him up beside her as she expected—he must have found good handholds to help.

That had been easy, and no trap had closed. Was it still there, waiting, or was her worry simply a product of working alone for so long? She shook her head. It didn't matter if there was fallout from working with Taunos. Only one thing mattered—saving Emin.

One task done. Now the next.

Her eyes caught on the horses, still gathered in a miserable huddle at the edge of visibility. Inuwe had his arm around Lamyi, propping him up. Good, at least they were safe, for now. Surely they could stay out of trouble for a few moments, and no bandits would be out in this weather, right? Unless they were still too close to the mudflow and got caught, too.

Tracking her gaze carefully along the edge of the mudslide, she spotted two figures huddled together on a ledge well down the drop-off and several paces to the left. Part of the cliff edge had given way, making them visible from the top. She could only barely see them through the rain, but they had to be Emin and Gurseh.

Her breath let out in a gust of relief so strong it left her light-headed. They were alive. Now she just needed to keep them that way. Every moment they waited could mean the ledge Emin and Gurseh were on washed out. The rain hadn't lessened. Even now, the attempt to rescue them would be incredibly dangerous, and the danger only increased with every raindrop. She kept her emotions tamped deep within her, where all they could touch her with was the nervous tension thrumming through her.

Next task, next problem to solve.

"We need a rope," she said.

Grimly, Taunos nodded, his gaze fixed on Emin and Gurseh. "Do we have one long enough? It looks like they're pretty far down there."

She estimated quickly. Emin was tall, but the top of the cliff extended far above his head. The rope could reach, but the problem would be the land. It was too likely to slide to risk tying the rope to one of the horses. To be that far back where the ground would be sturdy enough, there was no way Emin or Gurseh would be able to reach it. But they had to try. Who knew how much longer the ledge would last?

She grimaced as they ran back to the horses. "We'll have to make it work."

What choice did they have? Reaching the huddle of horses and nobles, she flung open the pack that held the rope.

"What are you doing?" Inuwe asked.

"Emin and Gurseh were swept away," Taunos said, his voice tight.

"You're leaving us?" Inuwe squeaked.

"Leaving? Can't leave," Lamyi mumbled.

Inuwe clutched Lamyi tighter, his features taut in his terror. "Amanah, you stay here. Haari can manage, but Lamyi needs your help, like you helped me. Please."

That pleading tugged at her heart, but it couldn't compete with the fact that her brother was in danger. Her fingers tightened over the rope until her knuckles were white. She didn't have time to argue. "Emin needs me *now*. I'll do what I can for Lamyi after we find shelter."

She glanced warily at Taunos. Would he want to stay to protect the nobles? That was technically their job, and was supposed to be the most important thing to them, more important than their own lives. She wasn't supposed to be rescuing her brother, and he wasn't supposed to be helping her.

"You have to guard us!" Inuwe said. "You have a duty."

"I have a heart, too. Stay here. We'll be right back," Taunos said to Inuwe, then looked at her. "Let's go."

Amanah nodded, some of the pressure lifting from her shoulders. They still might not succeed, even together, but at least there was a chance. As long as they worked together. As long as neither of them messed up. As long as she could trust him to pull his weight.

Leaving the noble's demands and complaints behind, she hurried with Taunos back toward the rockslide. Their boots slipped here and there on slick spots, and she began to move closer to Taunos for support. There was something about him that exuded confidence, that helped silence the niggling fear at the back of her mind that Emin was going to die, that she couldn't save him. Taunos's intense focus seemed as if this mattered to him almost as much as it did to her.

He was willing to risk his life for Emin and Gurseh, and he'd already done so for her. So easily, they could have tumbled off the cliff.

They picked their way across the rockslide remnants. More than once, one needed to grab hold of the other when rocks slipped under their feet, the drop-off calling to them. Perhaps it was angry that Taunos had stolen her from its maw.

By the time they got to the ledge above Emin and Gurseh's marginal shelter, she had bruised her knee and twisted an ankle in falls, and her wet socks and sodden boots had rubbed her skin raw in places. Her fear for them drove her forward despite it all, with Taunos at her side.

"Emin!" Amanah shouted down. "Are you all right?"

"We're all right, but we're stuck!" he said. "We can't climb out—the rocks are too slippery and there's nowhere to go but down."

"Well, don't go that direction," Taunos said.

"Thank you for that sage advice," Emin shouted back.

"I have rope," Amanah said. "Can you climb it?"

Emin looked at Gurseh, the two murmuring for a moment, and then he called up, "Yes."

Amanah nodded and tossed down one end of the rope. It dangled a few feet above their heads. There was nothing nearby to secure the other end to, though. She knew there wouldn't be, but she looked anyway.

She gnawed on her lip. Gurseh weighed significantly more than she did, and Emin was even heavier.

She winced. There was nothing for it but to try. "We can't let the rope slip if we fall. I'm going to wrap it around my hands. Can you hold me still?"

Taunos nodded. "I won't let you fall."

Amanah took a deep breath through the tangle of nerves in her stomach. Their strength combined with leverage would have to be enough. It had to work.

Making a loop in the end of the rope, she tied a knot, double-checking that it was secure. Then, holding the loop, she wound the rope around her wrist and up her forearm in a spiral for grip. Taunos tugged it taut for her.

Checking his work, she gritted her teeth and tightened it. He'd made it so she could let go of the rope without too much trouble if needed. But if she let go, or if the rope slid out of her grip, the chances of Gurseh tumbling to his death and taking Emin with him were too high. She was not going to be the cause of her brother's death. There would be no second chances.

Amanah steadied herself as far from the drop-off as she could without the rope being too high for Gurseh and Emin to reach. Behind her, Taunos wrapped one arm around her waist and reached around her to grab the rope with his other hand. She clung to his hand and the rope with her free hand in turn, feet set as much as they could be in the gravel and mud.

"Ready?" Taunos asked, his boots set right next to hers.

She nodded, her mouth dry.

"We're ready up here, Emin. Can you reach the rope?" she called out.

"Hold on!" Emin shouted.

The rope tugged hard, biting into her arm and wrist and slipping a bit. She gasped, clutching harder at it. Taunos's hand tightened around hers and the rope until her fingers went white with the pressure.

"Gurseh's coming up!" Emin yelled.

Amanah gritted her teeth, closing her eyes as the rope bit into her skin. Gurseh's weight was painful on her hands and wrists. She tried to adjust her hold, but her foot slid, heading toward the edge. She clawed for grip before Taunos caught her, and her eyes darted back toward the edge, measuring the distance. She'd only slid a hand's breadth, but it'd felt like forever.

She dug her heels in as much as she could through her boots. The rocks tumbled under her worn soles, and the pressure on her arms and shoulders was brutal. Still, she kept sliding slowly toward the edge, despite Taunos's hold on her. His feet scraped along the rock, shifting positions as he searched for solid ground. The rope slipped, burning her hands and wrists where she'd wrapped it. She was sliding, unable to stop, and then Gurseh would fall and Emin might fall in the commotion and they'd all be dead together at the bottom.

"Hold on." Taunos's voice was tight with strain. "I'm coming around in front of you."

Deftly, he switched places with her so he was nearer the edge, her stomach pressed to his back, his hands lessening the rope's strain on her arms. She steadied herself against him, increasingly desperate to find solid ground that would hold for more than a few moments. Every heartbeat thundered in her ears, every smidgen she slid magnified in her mind several times over. She couldn't fail at this. This was the one task she had to succeed in. The cost of failure—never hearing her brother's booming laugh or enduring his jokes again—was too high.

Her boots skidded out from under her, and Amanah hit the ground hard enough to drive her breath from her. She flipped to her stomach, but she couldn't claw for a handhold with the rope in the way.

A heartbeat, then Taunos caught her. He pinned her to the ground, looping his arm around hers and the rope again, his chest pressed against her back while his free hand gripped a rock, jutting up from the slick mud.

She dug her toes into the shallow ridge of stone she found. Even with Taunos's help, the rope felt like it would sever her hands and pull her arms right out of their sockets. Who would pop them back in, if so? She certainly wasn't going to let go, no matter how much it hurt.

"Hurry!" Taunos shouted behind them.

With Taunos half over her, the rain pattered less on her face, but her nose was filled with the smell of rain and mud and him, sweaty and musty from all the rain. Thankful for his tight grip on her, she focused on enduring the pain.

Finally, with one last jerk, the pressure ended, and Gurseh rolled onto the stone beside her. All three of them rasped breathlessly for several moments as rain pelted them. Her arms screamed, but Emin was still down there. She forced herself to her unsteady feet.

"Do we need to switch for the rope?" Taunos asked.

Amanah clenched her jaw and shook her head. Rationally, it made sense, but everything in her balked at the idea of someone else being responsible for her brother's life. Emin was too important for her to entrust entirely to anyone else—even Taunos and Gurseh.

"Let's just get Emin up," she said. "This wrapping worked well enough and it's already tightened on itself. I don't want to try another and have it come loose."

One more climb. One more climb and then she could yell at Emin to never scare her like this again. Tears welled in her eyes and she blinked them away, forcing her fear back down again. She had no time for that now —not until after Emin was safe.

"Come on, Gurseh. Help me hold the rope," Taunos said.

Gurseh grabbed the rope with both hands, placing himself closer to the edge, while Taunos held the rope with one hand and her waist with the other. To prevent being stunned by another fall, all three laid down, their feet jammed into any crevice they could find.

And then Emin started to climb. She knew because the rope jerked taut around her arm, biting into her bruised and raw skin even more viciously. Amanah groaned, the agony overwhelming her for a moment. Darkness invaded her vision and she could feel herself slipping. Tugging her closer, Taunos gave a grunt of effort, and the pressure lessened just a little, just enough that she didn't pass out. All she could do was hang on.

Taunos murmured at her. The words were rendered meaningless by the haze of excruciating pain, but his tone sounded encouraging. She focused on that instead of the rope tearing her arm off. She couldn't even feel the strain in her shoulders. All she could feel was the rope sawing into her skin. A wordless whimper came from her before she swallowed it back down. The darkness crowding the edge of her vision called to her, to let go of her hold, to let go of the pain. Her fingers clenched tight into the rope that felt like it was trying to become one with her skin.

"Hurry up, Emin!" Taunos bellowed over her head. There was a note of desperation in his voice, swirling around her.

"You're ok, Amanah. Just a little longer," Gurseh said.

Time lost meaning. There was only pain, cold rain, Gurseh's weight against her legs, Taunos's iron grip on her waist, and his murmuring voice like a soft blanket over it all. Finally, the pressure ended with a suddenness that made blackness wash over her for a moment, and her brother dropped down beside her with a thud and waft of sweaty Emin. Gurseh scrambled over to him to brush the hair back from his face, folding him in his arms. Amanah relaxed her fingers, relaxed her toes, relaxed everything. Shutting her eyes, she lay in the mud and tried not to drown.

"Can you stand?" Taunos asked. "I don't know how much longer this edge will last."

She flickered her weary eyes open. Taunos was on his feet, hand extended toward her and Emin. How was he standing already?

Emin puffed out his breath. "I'm getting to it."

"Are you all right?" she asked Emin, raising her head with effort to look him over with bleary vision.

"Better now." Her brother gathered himself to his feet, clapping Gurseh on the shoulder and sweeping him into another embrace.

"You're heavy." She groaned, getting to her wobbly feet. She went to rub her wrists, but pain flashed through her, making her think better of it. Her knee hurt, her back hurt, everything hurt, and the pain was exhausting.

Emin grabbed her with his other arm, crushing her to his chest as well. "Thank you."

She buried her face in his muddy shirt, clinging to his back with fingers that didn't want to uncurl. Even the pain couldn't mute the joy filling her. Tears burned her eyes and made tracks down her cheeks, and there was an impossible lightness in her chest, a need to run and shout, even though her limbs threatened her with collapse at any moment from exhaustion. They'd done it. Emin was safe. She felt she might tremble into a million pieces, shattered with relief.

"Where are the nobles?" Gurseh asked.

Taunos grinned. "We left them behind to commit acts of daring heroics."

"Them, or you?" Gurseh snorted.

"Come on. Taunos is right—we need to move back from this ledge. None of this area is safe." Emin herded them all away from the drop.

He and Gurseh were all scraped up, and Emin walked stiffly, but they would all heal. Breathing deep with relief, Amanah limped with them until they were all far from the edge. The rope was cumbersome, but she fumbled with unwinding it, hissing as it peeled from her skin. The others turned as soon as she stopped, various inquiring looks on her.

"Go ahead," she waved them off. "Get back to the horses. And the nobles."

Gurseh started back, and Emin squeezed her shoulder and then headed after him, but Taunos waited for her.

"Are you all right?" Taunos asked.

She smiled, though it felt more like a grimace. "I'm fine. Just having trouble with the rope."

Taunos reached out, gingerly unwinding it and then rubbing her skin gently to help with blood flow. She couldn't help the tears that fell or the shaking in her limbs as he massaged her cramped fingers while she tried to breathe through the pain. She kept her eyes on the distance, trying to ignore the overwhelming nearness of him even through his care. Part of her cried out for the comfort of his embrace again, but there was too much to do still.

He'd been there when she'd needed him, without question. He hadn't failed her. The thought brought on a fresh wave of tears to join the rain on her face.

"Thank you," she whispered as the pain ebbed.

He inclined his head, and continued on.

She fell in beside Taunos, trailing Emin and Gurseh by a few paces. Each of them had been beaten up by their misadventure, but Taunos was moving just a little stiffly, just a little too sharply.

"What are you doing?" she asked.

He looked at her. "What?"

The rocks rolled beneath him, and he almost didn't catch himself.

She sighed—those quick movements were all bluster, and she had no patience for it, not now. "I can see you're tired. You don't have to hide it. That's just foolish—we're all exhausted."

"I'm fine." He slowed though, shoulders relaxing jerkily, as if it was an effort not to cover for his weariness. "Just tired. Really tired."

"Me too." She felt like she could just lie down right there in the mud again and sleep for a day, even though it was cold. "The caves can't be much farther. I hope we can get out of this rain soon."

They walked a while in silence. Her back hurt, her arm ached, her soaked shirt stuck to the rope burns, and her twisted ankle cried out against her putting weight on it, so she appreciated not having to keep up with Emin. Pain made her weary and clumsy. Her eyes kept going to Taunos, watching for wounds, but he seemed fine—just with shoulders now sagging with the same crushing fatigue she felt. He'd clung with her to the rocks tight enough that she hadn't been pulled off the cliff, and before that, he'd whisked her right out of the clutches of death.

"Thank you for everything," she said. "Without your help..." She shuddered against the flash of Emin lying dead on the rocks below that stole her voice.

"I couldn't leave Emin and Gurseh out here," he said. "Nothing the nobles could say was going to tear me away."

"Me neither." She shuddered. "There'll be repercussions for walking away from duty, but I'd do anything for Emin. It's not even a question."

Taunos gave her a grim smile. "Sometimes duty must wait for a little while. This was important."

Amanah nodded.

He scrubbed his hands over his face. "I should have been faster. Again."

Amanah tilted her head. "What do you mean?"

"I should have gotten to them, too." He shook his head, grimacing. "They could have died."

Tears sparked in her eyes. Sometimes it seemed like no one in Arruk cared about those who came from nothing, like no one would shed a tear if they were all swept off a cliff.

But he would.

She laid a hand on his arm. "Don't be foolish. We just had this conversation. You can't do everything. Not even you, remember?"

"I let Gurseh down once before already," Taunos said. "I need to make it up to him."

"Emin and Gurseh had each other to help them," Amanah said. "And neither is helpless. They're both fine now, and that's what matters. You helped me save them."

He swallowed hard and nodded.

"And you saved me," she pointed out.

He smiled. "I'm glad I was able to do that, at least."

She squeezed his hand, and he squeezed back.

"Thank you," he said. "For poking me out of my self-reprimand. For reminding me of the truth."

She raised her eyebrows, specifically calling back to their conversation after Inuwe's snakebite. "For telling you when you're an idiot? Any time."

"I need that sometimes." He grinned ruefully.

Teasing him helped her ignore the complaints of her bruises, but she kept her tone light to take away any sting. "Sometimes? It'd be all someone could do, if they were to tell you every time. You might need to hire multiple people."

The sound of his laughter made everything just a little bit better. A world where he couldn't laugh would be strange and terrifying.

"Are you two cracking jokes back there?" Emin called back in mock affront. "I'm the funny one!"

"Now *that* is a joke," Amanah said, simply to set her brother off.

They caught up to Gurseh and Emin, and soon enough returned to where the nobles still huddled, dripping wet and looking miserable. The horses stood clustered together, while Inuwe sat on the ground, Lamyi propped up against him, looking half-conscious at best. Amanah let out a breath—at least no bandits had braved the weather to set upon the nobles while they were gone.

Emin eyed Amanah and Taunos. "You both well enough to ride?"

Amanah nodded, as did Taunos.

"Good. Mount up." Emin froze then, blinking, and darted a look at Taunos. "Er... yeah, boss?"

Taunos straightened, as if belatedly remembering, like Emin, that he was nominally in charge. "Right."

"What?" squawked Inuwe. "Lamyi is in no condition to ride, and what about all this rain?"

Even though riding could make a head injury worse, the weather was more dangerous, even without the risk of another mudslide.

"We need to get to shelter and off this hill." Emin shivered. "And we have to get out of this rain. It's too cold."

Taunos nodded, sighing. "Let's go. I'll ride with Lamyi to keep him from falling."

"No, I will," Inuwe snapped. "You left us out here alone."

Amanah pressed her lips together. She checked the packs on all the animals, and then swung herself astride Nakii. It'd be a miserable ride, for they still couldn't see much with all the rain, but hopefully it wouldn't be long.

Emin lifted Lamyi up into the saddle in front of Inuwe, and then mounted his gelding and they were off, forming a square around the nobles and the pack animals. Amanah watched her brother, riding out in front, occasionally shivering. So easily, they could be riding with fewer numbers now. So easily, one of them or more might not have survived. It had all happened so fast. She wrapped her arms around herself. If Emin had died, she'd be truly alone in the city. How could she bear it without him? How could she bear anything without his larger-than-life presence, his support? The world would be a darker place, filled with despair, without Emin.

Her eyes drifted to Taunos, riding ahead of her, once again straight-backed as if exhaustion couldn't touch him, while she drooped in her saddle. She remembered the way he'd braced against her, his muscles straining every bit as hard as hers, equals in a partnership to save the others. How his laughter lit the darkness, just as his heat warmed her. It had been remarkably easy, working with him. Too much so.

She might get used to leaning on Taunos if she wasn't careful, but she still couldn't see the trap in it.

8

ONLY A LITTLE while later, Nakii wickered, his ears flickering, and she followed the direction they pointed. Shadows moved, shapes blurred and hidden by the heavy rain. Amanah stroked her gelding's neck.

"Emin," she called out.

"I see them," he said.

Emin reined his mount in, closer to the nobles, and she did as well until all four of them were in a tight cluster around Inuwe, Lamyi, and the pack horses. Amanah peered into the gloom, easing the safety buckle on her scabbard and loosening her sword. If she were a bandit, this would be the perfect time to strike. If she cared nothing for weather, anyway.

"What are you doing? Why are we stopping?" Inuwe asked.

Someone called out ahead of them. Emin's head turned in that direction, but Amanah kept scanning to the sides and behind them. She didn't want to be surprised, not more than they already had been, at any rate.

"Who are you, travelling in such glorious weather?" shouted the voice from the darkness.

"We're simply caught in a storm," Emin said.

"Where are you going, and from where?" A vague figure was just visible through the darkness and rain. Hoofbeats sounded to their sides, riders moving in to surround them.

"Our business is our own." Emin's stern voice was undermined somewhat by the shivers wracking him.

Amanah grimaced. They needed to get out of this rain. The wet and cold did them no favors. Someone rode past her, close enough to see clearly, and though she didn't recognize the person, she recognized the mount.

"Yiyi!" she called.

The horse paused with a snort, head turning toward her, ears flickering.

"Who are you?" the rider asked sharply.

"That is Yiyi, isn't she?" Amanah asked.

"How do you know my horse's name?" the rider asked.

"She was born in the herds of my father, Ifel Teek," Amanah said. "I trained her."

"She's well trained," the person in front of Emin said. There was a beat, and then, "Come. Let's talk as friends, out of the rain."

"That's a wonderful idea," Inuwe said. "It's about time we find shelter."

Amanah exchanged glances with her brother, but his fatigue was clear to her even in the dim light. Besides, Lamyi needed to be looked at, and Inuwe's ankle would need tending. They didn't exactly have much of a choice, especially as she was too sore and stiff to fight well, if it came to it.

The shadowy figures surrounding them didn't speak as they escorted them through the rain, and Amanah didn't try to speak either. Dread muted by fatigue sat in the cold pit of her stomach, and she couldn't think of a single thing she wanted to say. Even Taunos was quiet.

In a surprisingly short amount of time, cliffs loomed up in front of them with the dark maw of a cave gaping hungrily. Firelight flickered from the interior as they entered, with the nobles, Emin, and Gurseh all needing to duck in their saddles to gain entrance. Amanah blinked, trying to hasten her eyes adjusting to the sudden brightness. Ten robed figures surrounded them, each with a bow leveled. She grimaced, the previous dread rearing up through leaden exhaustion.

Emin, Taunos, and Gurseh all took ready stances from their horses, while Inuwe sat, pale and frightened, his arms wrapped around the slumped figure of Lamyi, who was apparently unconscious. Amanah's stomach twisted more painfully, glancing at his wan face. If anything more happened to the nobles, there'd be no possibility they could ever run far enough to be safe.

"Please excuse our manners." The voice that had spoken to Emin before belonged to a tall figure wearing a gold chain. Their brown hair reached their shoulders, bound in many braids woven in the pattern for luck, secrecy, and health. They raised their hands, extending empty palms. "This is our current home, you see, and we need to be sure of our guests.

117

So, who are you?"

"I am Lord Inuwe of the Asi of Arruk." The noble's voice was thin and strangled. "And this is Lord Lamyi, also of the Asi of Arruk. Have you a bimna here? We need one at once!"

Amanah glanced over, meeting Taunos's gaze, who was pressing his lips together. It was dangerous to declare they were nobles. If these were bandits whose hideout they'd entered, it was an invitation to robbery and ransom.

"You will address Mapih with respect," snapped one of the riders. "They are the leader of the Lenuri."

"And these, I assume, are your guards?" Mapih asked, their tone calm.

"This one's Haari Taunos," Inuwe said, pointing him out. His voice trembled faintly with bravado, now that Lamyi wasn't able to speak for them both. "I suggest you put your weapons down, or I'll have him take them."

Taunos kept his empty palms out, clearly visible. "I don't think anyone here wants violence."

"We were caught in the rain, and then in a mudslide," Emin said. "I'm Kanhu Emin Teek, and my sister is Amanah. This over here is Gurseh from Arruk."

"The Teek name we recognize, and the Kanhu clan," Mapih said. "But who is this Haari?"

"Only one of the best—" Inuwe began.

"Just a man," Amanah interrupted, her heart hammering at her ribs. Boasts or threats would doom them. "Tired, dripping wet, and wishing you no harm. Please, may we find peace here?"

She glanced at Taunos, expecting to find wounded pride or anger on his face, but he just gave her a grateful smile. She turned her eyes back to the leader. One worry at a time.

Emin sneezed, shivering again. Gurseh reached out and gripped his shoulder, though he, too, was shivering hard.

Mapih gestured, and the warriors relaxed, lowering their bows.

"Come," they said. "You are welcome to our home, children of Ifel Teek, you and your companions."

"We're grateful for your hospitality," Amanah said.

They smiled. "Hot broth, I think, and dry clothes. Then a meal, and we can talk. We'll provide you sleeping space for the night at least."

Amanah bowed from Nakii's back. "Thank you. That would be wonderful."

Out of the corner of her eye, she saw Inuwe press his lips together. It must be odd for him, that his status gained him nothing here, while she and Emin were the ones to get them shelter for a little while. At least he had the sense not to argue.

In a whirlwind of activity, they were taken through a tunnel at the back into an enormous cavern that could possibly hold Arruk's training yard, guardhouse, and the garden with the Gods' Tree. Light from several fires lit the space, which was occupied by tens of families, the smoke rising and venting through holes in the sides of the ceiling. Stalactites glowed green and yellow from the ceiling, and large glowing stalagmites formed a makeshift fence which had been reinforced with rope, within which their mounts were stabled with the clan's horses. The nobles were set up in a small chamber off the main one, and Taunos stayed behind with them while Amanah, Emin, and Gurseh followed their guide to one of the fires in the main chamber.

Weary and shivering, Amanah sank gratefully onto the thick rugs piled up on the rough stone ground and accepted the woven blankets offered. She eased off her boots and then peeled away her socks with a hiss as angry skin protested. Her arm was swollen and she winced whenever the coarse fabric of her sleeve caught on the raw skin. Feet gripping the rug beneath her, she hunched under a blanket and let out her breath slowly.

They were alive, and they were out of the rain. They were likely safe here, or they wouldn't be treated with such hospitality. She smiled at Emin, who sat huddled with Gurseh under several blankets, arms wrapped around each other. The smells of roasting meats and vegetables and baking bread filled the area, and Amanah's stomach growled.

It didn't take long before the leader of the clan approached them once more. Mapih bowed to them, and they returned the gesture politely. Mapih knelt before them with a loaf of bread in their hands, decorated on top with the knot of peace. Amanah straightened—the welcome ritual deserved gravity, even though her muscles felt like liquid and her bruises and rope burns sent throbbing pain through her. They broke the bread, handing Amanah, Gurseh, and Emin each a piece of crusty, fluffy, steaming goodness. Amanah raised her chunk of bread into the air with Emin and Mapih's. Gurseh quickly followed suit, eyes darting between them. With all four pieces of bread touching in the center, Mapih smiled.

"May the peace between us not be broken," the leader intoned the sacred words.

"Hayzanu smile on you," Amanah replied. The god of travellers reigned in these matters.

"And on you," Mapih said. "Please eat. Broth will be brought to you, and then you are welcome to share in our supper."

Emin nodded gratefully, shivering and pale under his blankets. He sank back into Gurseh's arms.

"Thank you," Amanah said, tearing the bread into smaller chunks for the sake of the still-healing bruise on her jaw. "Are you going to perform the peace ceremony with the others of our group as well?"

The nobles wouldn't know the ceremony, which would give them protection under this roof until their stay ended. Once the ceremony was complete, they were considered temporary family, and leaders did not allow family to prey on family.

Mapih nodded. "I thought I would do it correctly first, before wrestling with city folk."

A smile touched her lips. She could understand that. "May I accompany you? They won't know the ceremony, but I can show them what to do."

Mapih raised their eyebrows. "And they will listen to the daughter of Ifel Teek, these city people?"

"Probably not," she admitted. "But Taunos will, and he can be persuasive."

"Then come, please. Follow me."

Amanah stood, loath to leave the warmth of the blankets, but some things needed to be done. She paused a moment, looking at her boots and socks, and then the red, angry blisters forming on her feet and ankles.

She winced. "I hope I will not give offense if I go barefoot?"

Mapih extended an arm. "Not at all. Your trust in the peace is appreciated."

Amanah ruffled Emin's hair as she passed, making a face at him as he gave her a rude gesture. He was well enough to laugh at her, and that knowledge eased her nerves a little as she followed the leader of the Lenuri through the cook fires. Mapih collected another loaf of peace bread, which was ritually baked nightly in many of the nomadic communities, for one never knew when a stranger might need assistance or a bed for the night. By being ready to offer such peace, they could be more assured of receiving such help themselves if they should need it in the future, regardless of how often the clans bickered. Mercy in the form of hospitality was a virtue.

Inuwe's scratchy voice carried out of the side room they'd been given. He wasn't shouting like Lamyi did, but his hoarse rebuke of Taunos still travelled. "Should have been expecting such weather, no? And been better prepared? What good is all that planning? Are we even going to make it to Gahimbli, Haari? Do you intend to let us die out here, or will you get your team in line and perform better?"

Taunos's voice was tight. "Without such planning, we'd have been in several tight spots multiple times already. None of my team is an issue. They're all doing an excellent job."

"When Lamyi lies unconscious and I was bitten by a snake and am still recovering? That's an excellent job, to you?"

Mapih stopped in the doorway, and Amanah stopped behind them, watching. Lamyi lay on a bedroll, with Inuwe fussing with a blanket over his shoulders, while Taunos stood by the wall, blank-faced under the tirade.

Taunos's gaze darted to them almost as soon as they stopped in the doorway. He cleared his throat.

"Well?" Inuwe turned. "Do you have something to say—"

He stopped, seeing Amanah and Mapih. His cheeks flushed beneath the washed-out brown of weariness, cold, and fear, but he pressed his lips together. Then, he drew in a deep breath, only slightly shuddering as he glanced again at Lamyi, as if the unconscious noble would tell him what to do.

"Well?" Inuwe said again, this time to her. "What is the meaning of this?"

"I bring the loaf of peace," Mapih said.

"Good. Put it down over there. Or Taunos can take it."

Amanah winced, and Taunos paused mid-step, swaying back to where he'd stood. He watched her, a question in his eyes.

"The peace ceremony is required for every guest," Amanah said. "It binds us together, including an oath of doing no harm to one another while under the same roof."

Understanding dawned on Taunos's face, and he turned to face Mapih. "What do we do?"

"Whatever needs done, just tell Taunos, and then please get your bimnas," Inuwe said.

"Inuwe," Taunos's voice was a rumble. "I think this ceremony needs your participation."

He raised his eyebrows at Mapih, and Amanah nodded confirmation even as the leader did.

"Fine, fine," Inuwe sighed, coming over. "What must I do? Does this take long?"

Mapih's mouth pinched, and Amanah grimaced. Taunos leaned over and whispered something to Inuwe that made chagrin flash over his features.

"Please excuse my poor manners," he mumbled to the floor.

Amanah slipped past them to check on Lord Lamyi, but he was deep asleep. She grimaced, stomach knotting. She didn't like him, but that didn't mean she wanted him to die on her watch. At least he couldn't cause too much trouble while unconscious. Maybe he'd stay that way, or at least wake in a more polite mood. She held back a scoff at her own thought. Nannil and Jattanu would likely switch places first, night for day.

Thankfully, Inuwe allowed her to coach him through the ceremony, and Taunos watched her closely, mimicking her movements and then bowing his head to Mapih at the end of the ceremony.

As Taunos was thanking the Lenuri leader, Amanah checked on Lamyi again.

"When will the bimnas come?" Inuwe asked, following her. "No one answers me. It's quite irritating."

"There are no bimnas here," Amanah said. "Who among the Lenuri could meet the bamimri's entry requirements? And what bimna would travel out here to live and work without a bamimri? Very few, if any. But this clan will have their own healers."

"But no bimnas." Inuwe frowned, pulling nervously on his beard. "Are they at least guild healers?"

A step below bimnas, healers were apprenticed and trained much the same way as in the bamimri, and they kept their secrets close as well. She'd never heard of a guild healer working outside of a city, where they could charge sums to pay their apprentice debts and surround themselves in comforts.

"No, not guild healers."

"What use will they be, then? At best ignorant, not to have the training, and at worst charlatans, or even malicious."

Amanah forced her tone to remain calm. He'd let her tend his ankle in a crisis, but apparently that didn't fully open his eyes to the fact that others could have useful information and not be found in cities. "More than you might think. Let the Lenuri healers check on Lamyi, and on your ankle, please. You allowed me to tend you, and they likely know more than I do."

Inuwe sighed, shoulders slumping. "I will consider it. Will they feed us?"

Amanah smiled. "You're Lenuri for the night now, Lord Inuwe. So long as you keep the peace, the peace will also be kept for you."

"Very well." Inuwe jutted his chin at the door, where Mapih was just leaving. "You are dismissed."

Amanah kept her face blank and bowed to him, pushing away the hint of disappointment in him. She shouldn't have expected anything more of him, even though he'd surprised her while she treated his snakebite. He was still a noble, and their situation clearly rankled him. Nobles in a bad mood were as dangerous as sandcats, and less predictable. Best to assuage his pride and then stay out of sight.

Taunos stood in the doorway, watching the cave outside and eating his bread thoughtfully, but he moved aside for her as she approached.

"Your feet are bare."

"My socks were rubbing."

"Does your family live like this?" he asked. "In caves?"

She smiled. "No, caves are rather difficult to move around."

He chuckled, then sobered. "Thank you. For the ceremony."

She nodded to him. "Are you all right?"

He gave her a grin. "I'm fine. I'll stay for a bit to make sure Lamyi and Inuwe are all right—and urge Inuwe to take your advice and let the healers here lend their expertise."

It warmed her heart, how easily he accepted that the Lenuri were skilled and capable people.

"Don't stay in here all night. They'll probably bring broth and food here, but we have some down there, too. That fire, just there." She pointed it out, and he leaned over to sight along her arm, his warmth soaking into her. She tried to ignore it.

"That sounds good. I'll come as soon as I can."

Giving him a last smile, Amanah slipped past him and walked back to the pile of blankets by the fire and the cups of broth there. Hopefully Inuwe and Lamyi wouldn't cause too much trouble and they'd be able to leave soon.

~

It wasn't too much longer before Taunos came wandering over to their fire, but long enough that they'd all recovered somewhat—warmth, safety, and hot drinks helped a lot. Still, she was surprised he had left the nobles so soon.

"Are they all right?" Amanah passed him a mug, but he sat down and set it beside him without drinking.

"Lamyi's awake, and they're both cranky. They kicked me out for a while—but at least we can keep a watch on their doorway from here, and there's no other way inside their cave." Taunos blew out a breath, putting his head in his hands. "I don't know what to do about them."

"What do you mean?" she asked.

"Lamyi's delirious, but he remembers us leaving to help Emin and Gurseh. Except he thinks you convinced me. He's determined to punish you."

Amanah nodded. "How?"

He raised his head, gaze fierce. "I am not letting you pay for my decisions."

"I made my own decision." She raised her eyebrows, tamping the icy fear deep down within her and steadfastly refusing the urge to look at Emin. Not a whipping, please. Anything else. But she needed to know the cost. Any price was worth her brother's safety, but not knowing was the worst part.

Some of the ferocity bled from his voice, and he shook his head. "I know. But you shouldn't be held accountable for mine. If they want to punish someone, they can punish me."

She shrugged further under her blankets, raising her mug to let the steam heat her face. So easily, he could let someone else take the fall, but Taunos always took his punishments. She didn't like the idea of him hurt on her account, though, even if he was acting as their shield. Sometimes he needed one of his own.

Gurseh took another drink of broth. "Aren't you the charismatic one? Convince them."

"We could run off," Emin joked. "Let them live in caves alone until they find their civility."

A snort escaped Taunos as he shook his head. He looked at her. "What do you think?"

"Why are you asking me?" she asked.

"Because you've been giving me good advice." Taunos scrubbed his hand through his hair again, leaving it sticking out in all directions. "The nobles aren't thinking straight, with Lamyi being injured and Inuwe being scared—and scared to admit he's afraid."

She twisted her lips, but Emin shoved her shoulder lightly. "It's true. Of all of us, you're the wise one."

"Well, that's not hard, given the company," she returned.

Her brother chuckled.

She refilled his mug and passed it to him. "I don't know. We need to stay here for at least the night. We need warmth and a good night's sleep, and perhaps we can refill supplies while we're here."

"If there's any money left from the pouch Borlim gave you, that might help," Taunos said.

She nodded. "As for the nobles, I'm not sure they're in a position to make good on their threats right now. Probably the worst they can do is be offensive to the Lenuri."

"We can stand guard on them even here," he said. "They'll expect that and won't suspect that we're also guarding the Lenuri from them. Will that annoy our hosts?"

Amanah grimaced. "Perhaps. I'll see if I can explain it to Mapih and beg pardon for any offense. We need to ask for details about the land before us, too. And if possible, we need to trade for another pack horse before the nobles ruin the ones we have."

"I'll talk to them. You relax," Emin said.

She started to give him a grateful smile, but he continued.

"As for the nobles, Amanah's dangerous enough if she needs to be. Or you get her angry," Emin said, ignoring her stop-talking glare. Her brother liked bragging far too much, even if he was bragging for her. "Ever since her first ribbons."

"I *knew* you're still upset about me tying you up when we were kids," Amanah said.

"It's an ever-present wound to my soul," he said. "Got some balm for that?"

"Enough for all your ego? There wouldn't be enough balm in all the world," she said sweetly.

"Ribbons?" Taunos asked.

"Among my clan, the children are taught a dance with ribbons," she said. "As the child gets better and better at the dance, the ribbons flow and flutter in beautiful ways. Then, upon puberty, the ribbons are replaced with whips. After a few years gaining mastery, we switch to the sword and at the same time, are taught the banner dances for communicating across chasms. Every child of my clan is well versed in how to kill an enemy by the time they're adults, just in case."

"And you do it with a dance." Taunos didn't sound daunted in the slightest. He sounded intrigued, the faintest of smiles pulling at the edges of his mouth.

Amanah nodded.

Emin's eyes darted from him to her and back. Then they paused on her face, the fading bruise on her jawline. "Amanah, if something happens here or on this trip, defend yourself. I know we can't do so in the city, but… I don't want you to let them hurt you."

"Are you prepared for that, Emin? For the consequences if I do?" Amanah asked. Her tone was harder than she'd like, but her brother knew just as well as she did why she ran or hid instead of fought. Her punishment had been hard on him, too, the first—and last—time she'd scuffled with a noble. Would he be able to handle it a second time?

"More so than I am for the alternative. We'll figure everything else out later." Emin's eyes bore into her, and Amanah reluctantly nodded, pulling the blanket tighter around her.

"We double up, short shifts because we need to rest, too. No one's in there alone except maybe Taunos," Emin said. "Stay outside their room as much as possible."

They each nodded, and then Taunos stood. "I'm going to find some food. Did you all eat already?"

"Not yet," Emin said.

"Did you finish your broth yet? Make sure you do." Amanah frowned at him.

Taunos tipped his empty cup toward her while Emin snickered.

"Here, I'll help," Gurseh said, getting to his feet. He turned to Emin and pointed. "You stay right there."

Gurseh and Taunos wandered off, talking quietly together, and Amanah raised her eyebrows at Emin. Her brother shrugged.

And with that shrug came the memory of losing hold on him, of losing sight of him. Of nearly losing him.

She scooted next to Emin, wrapping her arms around his shoulders. After a moment of wrestling with the blanket, he returned the embrace.

"I thought I'd lost everything back there," Emin said, resting his cheek on her braids. "You, Gurseh, my life, Taunos. Thank you for rescuing me."

"Don't make me do it again," she said.

He laughed. "I'll try. I don't want you mad at me."

She scowled at him, tears sparking in her eyes. "I'm serious. If I lose you…"

He patted her arm, and she winced, shifting so her rope burn was out of the way. "It's not easy to be rid of me. I'm like one of those burrs that get under your saddle. You know, one of the really annoying ones that get all caught up in the fabric and still have sharp edges everywhere, so it takes forever to pull them out."

"Ah." Amanah grinned up at her big brother, built like a mountain. She shrank the space between her thumb and forefinger down to indicate the actual size of the burr in question. "One of the tiny ones."

Mock affront appeared on Emin's face, and giggles burst out of her.

He shoved her, perhaps harder than he intended, because she lost her balance, falling backward. He grabbed her arm and pulled her back next to him before her back even hit the ground.

"Sorry. I shouldn't roughhouse when I'm tired."

"I'd ask who taught you your manners, but I know exactly who," she said, wrinkling her nose at him.

"Is this like when I was six and I asked you not to tell our mothers and you did anyway?"

"I was three!" Amanah poked him in the side where he was ticklish. "And you pushed me in the mud."

He snickered, and she wrapped her arms around him again, sobering, her voice quieting to a murmur. "I don't want to tell our parents anything about today at all."

"Except meeting with the Lenuri?" Emin asked.

She smiled. "Except that. Are you hurt from the fall?"

He snorted. "You're as bad as our parents, I swear."

She made a face at him. "Yes, well, someone needs to keep you in line."

With all the resigned humor he could muster, he spoke, as if heading to his doom. "I promise I will see the healers here, and I'll make sure Gurseh does also. Actually we all should, probably—and that means you, too." He snagged one of her braids and tugged it.

She swatted his hand away. "Good. I was already planning to anyway. My arms and feet need some balm and I don't want to use up what I brought if I don't need to."

Once again, his expression turned somber. "I'm so sorry, Amanah."

Poking his shoulder interrupted him effectively. "You're my brother. How could I put your fate in someone else's hands, and then not be able to hold it over you so effectively?"

Her teasing was a little flat, but he gave her a ghost of a smile anyway. The terror was just too near still to make it easy to joke about.

"I'm glad I didn't pull you over the ledge," he said.

She nodded. "Me too. If Taunos hadn't been there…"

Remembered fear threaded through his voice. "You slid when Gurseh was climbing, didn't you? For a while? I was terrified I was going to have to try to catch both of you."

"You weren't the only one." A shudder wracked through her. "But we managed to find leverage."

The way Taunos had held her as Emin and Gurseh climbed up filled her memory, along with the murmur of his comforting words against the rope burns. His determination to help, and the way he reacted even to the thought of her being punished for their rescue of Emin and Gurseh. How seriously he was taking the question of guarding them tonight, his easy deference to Mapih, and even the way he'd managed to bring Inuwe into line for the ceremony. She'd needed him to save the person she loved most in the world and he hadn't let her down.

A question slipped out against her better judgement. "Speaking of Taunos… I wanted to check if you knew his people's ways of courting. He won't ask again?"

"About a relationship with you?" Emin shook his head. "No."

"How do you know?"

"He asked me how things are done among our people, explained some things from his people. I'm here only as a culture clash buffer if needed."

"He didn't ask like a Kanhu clan member would have."

Emin chuckled. "No. He thought about it, but he was afraid one of the others in your dorm would think it was for her, and he wanted to avoid a misunderstanding. So I guess he went with his original idea to speak plainly?"

"Honeyed words. But at the same time, quite plain in his intent."

He shrugged. "Well, he won't ask again. If you change your mind, it's on you to ask him."

"I have to be sure, so don't say anything to him."

Emin grinned at her, pulling her from her thoughts. "Who, me? I never say anything."

She shoved his shoulder, but he barely moved, apart from letting her go from his embrace. Brothers were infuriating.

His black eyes sparked with mirth. "Neither of you like to depend on anyone else. You two together, if you can learn to open up, might be interesting."

Giving him a scowl wasn't nearly enough, so she added a glare. "What are you talking about? He trusts everyone."

"He also wakes at the slightest step near him. He's always prepared to be attacked, even when he's messing around. You're both the ones people rely on. You're never the ones relying on others."

"I rely on you." The words were small.

He squeezed his arm around her. "I know. I'm exceptional. You can say it."

She snorted a laugh, but Emin's words weighed on her as Gurseh and Taunos returned, laden with meats and vegetables and breads and sauces. Their fire became loud with conversation, jokes, and laughter, their voices rising and falling around her, comforting as a well-loved blanket. Life, stolen from the edge of a cliff. A smile spread across her face as she snatched portions from under the others' fingers. Just as her body warmed and relaxed, so too did her inner tension, and she found herself cheering along with Gurseh and others in a ring of watchers as Taunos and Emin joined in a Lenuri rhythm competition. The laughter that rang out with each mistake and the whoops of joy with each win eased the last of her tension.

Gurseh stood, brushing himself off, and went to check on the nobles. Emin was his backup, but they were close enough to the nobles' room that if Gurseh needed anything, they could be there in moments. Amanah gave him a wave, but allowed the game to claim most of her attention. Emin had caught Gurseh's eye and nodded as he left—perhaps she didn't have to be ready for trouble at all times. Even at Emin's parties in Arruk, she hadn't allowed herself to have this much fun, too worried she'd miss warning signs or bring down trouble. But all that never-ending watchfulness hadn't saved her. It'd just eaten away at all her joy.

Taunos was trying to get Emin to add a third rhythm into the two he had going via song and clapping, and when Emin botched it, they doubled over in laughter, the other players joining in with good-natured jabs. Amanah met Mapih's gaze where the leader stood watching, a smile creasing their face, and they gave her a nod. The laughter was as warm and comforting as firelight. Tangible in a way, pushing the darkness and tension back. The same as Emin and Taunos did when they sang or told stories at night. It wove them together in a symbol as powerful as the peace bread.

And while they gathered attention, there was nothing stopping her from doing the work she needed to do. Freedom to work in the shadows, knowing every eye would be drawn to their light. Maybe that was something she could rely on, too. She didn't want to mute her curiosity anymore. She certainly wasn't going to let herself be made so small and silent that everything that made her *her* died. That'd be even worse than being swept off that cliff.

She would travel. She would satisfy her curiosity. She would learn all the skills she could to help those who needed it.

After all, if impossible hope and brazen courage could carry Taunos, why couldn't preparation and care, with a dash of daring, bring her to everything she wanted? Her dreams weren't even that extravagant, especially compared to the noblemen who'd spent the trip sleeping in silk sheets. She could balance them with her duties to those who needed her. She had to, because she couldn't go on denying herself everything she wanted.

A roar went up as one of the Lenuri added in another rhythm, and this time Taunos failed to match it immediately. He shook his head at himself and leapt right back in to try again. Emin elbowed him repeatedly, trying to throw him off, but the cheating only made Taunos laugh harder, crowing when he managed to match the additional rhythm despite Emin's efforts.

Unable to keep the smile from her face, Amanah grabbed her bag of medicines and sought out the Lenuri healers. She wove through the clusters of people, following directions to a group sitting around a fire, grinding something into paste. Her wrist and arm were badly rope-burned, her back was bruised, her ankle needed wrapping for support, and her feet needed balm and dry socks—which hers would be once the heat of the fire finished with them. After being fixed up and bandaged, she shared the snake balm she'd reinvented from the bamimri. In no time, they were swapping recipes and techniques, and Amanah delighted in feeling so alive, making concrete steps toward who she wanted to be, instead of struggling to juggle dreams and responsibilities.

After speaking with the healers, she went to find the person who'd been riding Yiyi. In no time, she found herself welcomed around a fire by a couple of very bossy old women, sitting next to a slender young man with long, thin braids. His eyes lit with delight at seeing her, and he introduced himself as Yiyi's rider. Over dessert—because the women kept pressing food on her even though she told them she'd already eaten—Yiyi's rider regaled her with stories of the mare and news that they were expecting a foal. In return, Amanah shared tales of Yiyi's naughty exploits when she was a foal herself.

Gurseh stopped by not long after, on his way from the nobles' room, to inform her it was her turn for watch. Once she'd turned down yet more dessert and escaped the little circle of homeyness, Amanah headed to check on the nobles. Her eyes drifted over the cave as she went. Emin and Gurseh were huddled cozily by a low fire, heads together. Several fires over, Taunos sat with a group of Lenuri elders, attentively listening to whatever they were saying. She paused, mid-step, and watched as he nodded, then spoke. One of the elders, a woman with a face full of wrinkles, gestured expansively as she answered. Amanah smiled, it suddenly being all too easy to imagine introducing him to her parents, her siblings. How he might interact with her own clan, the Kanhu, with all the respect he was showing here. How perhaps, she might meet his clan one day, too. The thrill that ran through her startled her.

But things needed to be done yet. She shook herself. She had to check on the nobles, though everyone looked so comfortable. She'd stay outside, so no one would need to back her up, for now.

130

At the entrance to the nobles' cave, she stopped.

"Where have you been?" Lamyi snapped. Then he peered at her. "You're not the healer."

"It's just me," she said.

Lamyi huffed. "Wonderful. We have to leave. We have very important things to do, and we can't even rest properly on these uncomfortable beds."

Amanah tucked her hands behind her back, clenching them into fists to keep her voice even. "Our hosts are providing for you out of their own generosity."

"Where's Taunos?" Inuwe asked. "He was supposed to find the healers."

"Did they not come?" Amanah asked, brow wrinkling.

"Yes, but we want them again," Inuwe answered.

"They did not come! No one came," Lamyi said.

Amanah frowned, cold washing her newfound relaxation right out of her. If he had a head injury and memory loss, things were bad. She didn't know how to fix this.

"Let me talk to the healers." She hurried away, ignoring their objections. The best thing she could do was bring them help. Quickly, she headed for the healers, but on the way, Taunos fell into step beside her.

"Is everything all right?" he asked. "You look concerned."

"Lamyi said the healers didn't come, but Inuwe said they did," Amanah said, rubbing her bandaged forearm. "If he's having memory issues from hitting his head, he might be gravely wounded. Taunos, if he dies..."

Taunos touched her upper arm, stopping her. "The healers did come. I asked them to leave the nobles alone for a while. Lamyi was working himself up and throwing insults, and Inuwe's too afraid to really think. I didn't want Lamyi offending our hosts."

"Oh." She let out a breath. "Do you know how bad Lamyi's injury is? Gurseh didn't say anything, but maybe they didn't bother him about it."

"The healers told me it's mostly exhaustion. He'll have a headache for a while, which might be why he's even grumpier than normal," Taunos said. "His memory is actually fine."

"Why is he saying the healers didn't come, then?" She chewed on her lip, still ready to go right back into crisis mode.

Taunos glanced back at the cave. "Either he's lying to get you to bother them, or he's saying they didn't come promptly enough or the last time he asked. I stopped getting them because he wanted them repeatedly. They don't think it's anything to worry about, because when pressed or motivated, his memory is consistently fine, so I was interceding between them. I didn't realize it was time for a shift change until I saw you head in there."

Amanah nodded, already missing the nearly-carefree relaxation she'd sampled. "All was good for your watch?"

"Lamyi threw me out three times so far—it might be a record. But if it keeps the peace…" He shrugged.

"Why did he throw you out?"

A grimace rippled over his face. "He's been demanding things of the Lenuri all night. He wasn't happy to figure out I was not passing on those demands, except for the ones that seemed like necessities."

Amanah rubbed her forehead. "Tonight's going to be a long night."

"One of the healers suggested I spike his wine so we can all get some rest."

She raised her eyebrows. "Did you do it?"

"No, but I do have to say I was tempted." His eyes flashed with mirth for a moment, then dimmed. "Don't worry, he's not misbehaving enough to put you in danger, and I mean to keep it that way. Are you all right? How're your rope burns? And your ankle?"

She sighed. "It hurts, but I'll be fine. I saw the healers, and we wrapped the burns and my ankle, and put salve on my back and on my feet where my boots were rubbing."

"Your back?" he said, brow wrinkling. Then he grimaced. "When I caught you, you hit the rocks that hard?"

"It was better than hitting the bottom of the cliff. I'll be fine. What about you?"

She took his hands without thinking, turning them over. Just like hers, the edges of his nails were broken, his fingers bruised from the rocks. The hand he'd wrapped around her to hold her was scraped up on the back. The injuries were clean, though, just the rawness of fresh wounds.

And she was holding his hands. His warm, calloused hands. And he had gone very, very still.

She swallowed hard, dropping her grip on him. "Sorry."

He tilted his head, eyes searching her face. That curl to the edges of his mouth was back, a precursor to a smile. "It's fine."

She tried to think instead of drowning in his gaze. "Did you go to the healers?"

A laugh broke out of him, and he held up his hands again. "For these? No. These aren't bad, especially after washing them. Besides, the healers have had enough of a headache with Lamyi. I don't want to ask them for more, and I preferred spending my time other ways."

"Playing games and talking with the elders?" she asked, eyeing him.

His smile grew. "I'm not the one you're supposed to be guarding."

She scowled and stepped back, and regret flashed in his eyes. He was exasperating, but at the same time, he had made it a point to connect with their hosts. And she was more upset with her own preoccupation than she was with him and his teasing, in truth. Why was this draw toward him so strong?

Taunos cleared his throat, gaze travelling over the cave. He often did that, his eyes sweeping his surroundings for danger. She shouldn't notice so much. He was part explorer, part nomad, and of course, part warrior. An interesting combination. Too interesting. "Anyway, I should try to sleep again."

Her brow furrowed as she forced herself to focus on his words. "Again?"

"So I can take watches," he explained. "I tried to sleep before, but," he waved a hand at the Lenuri, who were now just beginning to settle in for the night, "it was all so interesting. And busy."

She nodded. "I'm on watch. I can get Gurseh to—"

"No." He straightened. "I'll sit nearby and doze. You can shake me awake if you need to go in there or if Lamyi or Inuwe come out. If that's all right?"

Amanah eyed him. They both knew he wouldn't need shaking awake. But maybe an out of the way place would help. "It's not going to be very restful sleep that way."

His gaze drifted across the cave full of people once more, worry returning to the lines of his face. "Maybe, but I want to give Emin and Gurseh time together. They could have died so easily. And you."

"But we didn't," she reminded him—and herself. "You can stay with me if you want, but it likely won't be very comfortable."

"I'd rather be there, in case."

She nodded. "Come on then. Find a dark corner."

Taunos grinned and soon enough was settled a few paces from the door of the nobles's room, wrapped in his cloak. He held out the blanket he'd been loaned by the Lenuri. "Need a blanket? It was cold out there. Your hands were like ice even just now."

She shook her head. His hands had been like fire. Well, more like coals —soothing heat instead of burning. Which she did not need to think about.

"I'm fine." She managed to keep her tone light, casual.

He folded up the blanket to use as a pillow and laid down. The nobles were in bed, and Amanah sat near the doorway, but her gaze kept drifting to Taunos, to the play of shadows and firelight on his features. She shifted, turning so she could account for her distraction, and his head lifted, his eyes snapping open.

A smile curved her lips despite herself. "Relax. I'll watch over you."

He chuckled, laying his head back down.

"Why does that make you laugh?" She tilted her head, though he'd closed his eyes again.

"It's not something I hear much. I'm more used to saying it." His voice was a low rumble, his eyes still closed.

"Well, get used to hearing it."

His eyes opened again, gleaming with caught firelight as he considered her intently.

She turned her face away. "Emin and I watch out for our friends."

Taunos made no response that she could hear, but when she looked back over at him, his eyes were closed again, his breathing even.

It brought a smile to her face, and her mind wandered back to something Mapih had told her earlier. "When we find people who we can share trust in, share duty with, share goals with, we bind them to us with all our hearts. We hold tight to them."

She'd certainly shared all three with him today. But holding tight to him? How tight? Taunos was laughter and wild joy, and she didn't want to lose that. She didn't want to lose him, or hurt him by playing with his feelings. He'd shown remarkable restraint. It was she who was having trouble not acting on her growing affection for him—that reckless desire to be more than friends with him. If she really wished it, she had no doubt they could continue on and he'd tease her like a friend, like a sister, like Emin did.

But she doubted that she could show the same restraint, despite her best intentions. She'd held his hands tonight, for Nannil's sake. His easy comfort and support shouldn't feel so... good, so right. And it wasn't fair to him if she kept crossing a line she wouldn't allow him to walk with her on.

Amanah scowled at herself and the man sleeping only a few paces away.

In fact, she already knew what she wanted. She was tired of carrying all the responsibility alone. Taunos smashed through her barriers with humor and persistent optimism. She wanted to kiss Taunos, to tangle her fingers in his hair, to feel his arms around her, to always have access to the warmth of his safety, the distraction of his humor. She wanted him to look at her again the way he had that night in the Gods' Tree.

And then there was her other blooming goal, which was even more dangerous: to not only get into the bamimri, but be the first travelling bimna she'd heard of. The nomadic clans had no bimna because they all stayed in Arruk, and why should that continue? She'd bring the secrets of the bamimri to clans like the Lenuri—regardless of how the bimnas felt about that—and trade for other secrets of healing. Everyone would be better off then.

But if she tried to get into the bamimri, she'd have to step away from her work with Murihat's Hand. She'd be a target, as would anyone she associated with. Just as she'd worried about with Taunos during their conversation that night in the Gods' Tree. And there'd be no going back.

Her eyes wandered back to Taunos, his features soft in the dimness. If she was reaching for one dream, what was to stop her from reaching for the other thing she clearly wanted?

She knew far too much about him. He made a game of everything he could, but when it came to people getting hurt, he often blamed himself, as if everyone's well-being was his responsibility. She snorted, for she had the same tendency. He was exactly who he wanted to be. She wanted the same chance for herself.

She wrenched her gaze away from him, training it on the doorway to the nobles' room.

Neither decision was safe, so she had to be sure. There was no sense rushing into it, and she had time to ponder all the possible ramifications, account for every risk, before setting down a path there'd be no return from.

9

Only a few days after leaving the caves, they entered an area of the country that was even more broken with cliffs and canyons than before. The Lenuri had cautioned them not to rely completely on their map, as maps of the area were famously inaccurate. The clan couldn't spare an escort, but Amanah was grateful for the advice. Still, scouting ahead when the rugged land didn't match the map and backtracking when they got turned around ate up even more time.

Emin had managed to barter with the Lenuri for another pack horse during their full-day stay with them. It meant their food supplies plummeted, but they were making better time. They'd have to stop to resupply with fresh water anyway, and where there was fresh water, there were hunting possibilities.

Amanah made it a habit to stay as far from the nobles as she could. Every time in the last several days when the nobles' eyes turned to her or Emin, or, more rarely, Gurseh, with some grievance, Taunos was always there, diverting their attention with charm and charisma, and sometimes sheer stubbornness. It was odd, but freeing, even though Taunos reported threats against them nightly—typically the same old vague rumblings evening after evening, but the anger in Taunos's voice as he alerted them still warmed her. He cared. Deeply.

She'd gotten a little too used to Taunos being everywhere: talking, laughing, sometimes being a nuisance, but also keeping her company for a short time each night when she was on watch. She'd begun to look forward to it.

She worried about Taunos, even though she knew he was capable. The nobles were angrier at him since their stay with the Lenuri, and all too often Lamyi's verbal lashings rang out from the tent while Taunos attended them.

After another long day of travel followed by Amanah scouting the perimeter of the camp, she was eager to relax for the night. Gurseh had built a fire and was cooking supper, and Emin arrived a little while later with an armful of wood harvested from the scraggly trees of the area. Only Taunos was missing. Amanah sat down wearily to eat, glancing toward the nobles' tent. They must have had yet another problem they needed to yell at Taunos for, though she couldn't hear any raised voices.

But as they finished their meal and cleaned up, he still didn't show. Emin left Taunos's portion in a covered bowl in the coals to keep warm, and Amanah frowned in the direction of the tent.

"Is Taunos still with the nobles?" she asked. He'd better hurry if he was going to get enough sleep before scouting the way in the morning.

Gurseh poked up the fire. "He told me the nobles sent him to fill up their water skins. They were out completely. I expect he'll be back any time."

Emin frowned. "How did they run out of water already, even with how much they waste? Are they feverish?"

Gurseh snorted. "Like they'd let me check their temperature."

"Where did he go for water?" Amanah asked, the back of her neck prickling. There was no sign of water nearby. Emin's frown reflected her worry.

A shrug rolled across Gurseh's shoulders before he looked up at them and straightened. Maybe the tension that gripped Emin and Amanah had finally reached him. "Some dried riverbed to the southwest has water underneath, I guess. He took one of the shovels, and he said he'd be careful of landslides and predators, of course. It hasn't actually rained again yet, so it should be fine. Right?"

Shivering in the night's chill, Amanah pulled out the map and held it out to the flickering firelight. She shared a long look with Emin. The most likely place in that direction to dig for water was a slot canyon leading from higher ground. She'd been keeping an eye on it on their maps, keeping them away from it, because unlike the other canyons they'd travelled through, this one would be perfect for a flash flood. From what she could see on the map, it was narrow and connected with several other channels that would flow into it if they held water. If it rained upriver, gulleys like that one could send enough water rushing through to wash a person away before they even knew they were in danger.

It'd been cloudy for the last two days, and after the trouble they'd had the last time it rained, they didn't need to look for more.

"Are you going?" Emin asked, rare seriousness sitting heavy on his features.

"Yes," she said. Emin could stay in camp with Gurseh—her horse was faster.

Amanah hopped to her feet, grabbing her cloak and her smaller pack with just the essentials—water, rope, medicine, some jerky. She checked her knife and then got her horse.

"Taunos's horse is still here!" she reported.

"That fool," Emin grumbled. "Of course he walked."

"I'll catch him," Amanah said grimly. "I'm taking his horse with me."

"What's going on?" Gurseh asked as she mounted. She rode out, letting Emin's explanation of the danger fade into the distance as she left the camp behind.

These nobles. Either this was a foolish prank or they had deliberately set out to get Taunos killed. She figured it was probably the former, but the blackness in her heart leaned toward holding the latter against them, especially considering their attitudes ever since the caves. Fear for Taunos pounded along with the blood rushing in her veins, crying out for Nakii to run faster.

The light of the moons struggled through the thick cloud cover, so she had to limit their pace for fear of breaking the horses' legs. It felt like it took forever to get to the canyon, where tall, steep sides descended into darkness. She walked the horses along the edge, staring down into it for any sign of Taunos, calling out for him every few steps. There were predators out here, and possibly bandits as well, but the worry of an oncoming rush of water sweeping him away made the risk worth it.

The horses' hooves on the ground echoed the pounding of her heart. Grimly, she pressed on, hoping he hadn't been in the opposite direction, but she'd had to pick one.

Finally, Taunos's voice sounded back in response to her calls. Her heart lightened with relief as bright as a flash of moonlight through the clouds.

"Taunos!" she shouted. "Get out of the canyon!"

She quickened their pace recklessly. Tying Rose to Nakii's saddle, she directed both horses down a narrow path which led down the steep side. Rocks tumbled and bounced, but in the dim light she thought she saw a shadow coming toward the edge—one she hoped was Taunos. Her boots skidded on the slope, and even the horse's hooves slipped at times. Her gelding pulled irritably at the reins, but she coaxed him forward, pulling

Rose behind.

"Amanah, what's going on?" Taunos asked. The shadow was him, thank Nannil. "Is everyone all right?"

"We need to get out of here," she said.

"This path is too narrow to turn a horse around on," he said. "You'll have to come all the way down, but it gets steeper. Will they make it?"

"They'll have to," she said grimly. She'd been foolish, but hopefully Hayzanu was on their side. They could use all his luck.

"What's going on?" His voice was getting closer.

"Gulleys like this are dangerous in the rainy season. When it rains upstream, that water comes racing through here. It can sweep away anything before it has a chance to run."

"Like the mudslide before. And it's been cloudy all day," Taunos said, an edge creeping into his voice.

"Exactly. It's far too dangerous to be here."

"I'm coming," he said.

Her boots skidded again. Nakii slid with her this time, but fortunately it was only a small jump to the bottom. Unprepared for the sudden leap, Taunos's mare stumbled on the landing and whinnied in protest.

Amanah tried to control her breathing, soothing the horses, checking them over, praying she hadn't ruined them with her fear-directed choices, but they seemed fine. And then Taunos was there, holding a shovel and a long stick in one hand. The stick was damp on one end; what he'd used to probe for water, no doubt. He'd picked a good spot—she'd have picked the same, but for the danger of flash flooding.

Shaking his head at her, he tied the shovel to his saddle along with a large water pouch. His shirt stuck to him with sweat, his hair was a mess, and his hands were caked with dirt, but he was alive and whole. For now, at least.

"Of course you brought my Rose." He flashed a grin at her, but his shoulders sagged a little with resignation, weariness, or both.

"Better to have the speed." She untied Rose from Nakii and handed Taunos the reins.

"Isn't that dangerous for the horses, running at night?"

"Yes, but it's better than being too late or lingering in the dark."

They both mounted their horses, and Amanah let him lead the way up the narrow trail, still urging Nakii to go as quickly as the switchback trail would allow without further recklessness. Her senses strained for any signs of danger, her heartbeat and breathing sounding too loud, along with every step of the horses' hooves.

"Thank you," Taunos said. "For realizing my folly, and for coming to get me."

"You didn't know," she said. "And hopefully the nobles didn't either."

The outline of his form stilled as he stiffened. "You think they did?"

"I don't know. Maybe not. But..." She sighed, trying to think how to explain it to him in the simplest way. "Do you know how Emin and Gurseh met?"

"In the guards, right?"

The words drew out of her, part of her hoping he'd understand, the rest of her on alert for more danger. "Sort of. Besides this mission, I haven't ridden a horse since arriving in Arruk. The nobles would see a havi on a horse and immediately assume they stole it. But when we were new to the city, one day a noble asked Emin to bring his horse to his stable, and Emin agreed—the money was good and we didn't see the harm. He didn't realize he was being set up until Gurseh arrived, sent to arrest him for horse theft. You'd think being in the guard would be some sort of protection, but no."

He twisted back to look at her. "That's horrible. Did he do it? Arrest Emin?"

"Emin talked him out of it and into drinks instead, fortunately," Amanah said.

Taunos nodded. "Still, that's terrible."

"A hundred petty cruelties happen every day in Arruk," Amanah said. "I see their aftermath."

"And some have been directed toward you," Taunos said.

"Of course some have been directed toward me. I'm not special."

"We can disagree on that." His voice quieted to a murmur she could barely hear.

"You keep saying that sort of thing."

"Because I think it's true," he returned, back to normal volume again. "You always speak your mind to me. You treat me how you treat everyone. I value that."

She didn't know how to respond to that and focused instead on smoothing her horse's mane. Their hoofbeats echoed as they hurried, nearing the top of the canyon walls.

Taunos's form tensed. "Amanah—"

A sandcat sprang from the rocks above them, just as Taunos raised his arm as if to shield himself and Rose. It was a big one, nearly the size of the horses, with paws past experience told her would be larger than her face. Time seemed to freeze, crushing her voice in her throat as she stared, unable to help from where she was. Taunos was going to be pulled from his saddle and dashed to pieces on the rocks below.

But impossibly, clinging to the saddle, he twisted enough that the sandcat sailed past them, claws snagging on Taunos's shirt for a moment as it fell before ripping free. Taunos clung to the saddle while Rose screamed, rocks clattering down the slope from her hooves. Amanah sent a quick prayer of thanks to Hayzanu for their luck in the cat's miscalculation. It landed on its feet just a few paces vertically down the cliff where the trail curved back around. Snarling, it bounded up the path after them.

"Go! Go!" Amanah shouted, flicking the ends of her reins forward to slap Rose into motion. She kneed Nakii after the mare, though he didn't need the prodding, and they thundered up the narrow path. There was the head of the trail, a few lengths farther on.

She glanced back, and her stomach dropped. The sandcat was still chasing them. She turned forward again, wishing she'd brought her bow. She hadn't thought to, it being a dark night, but the sandcat was close enough she could see its muscles rippling as it pursued.

They gained the top of the cliff, and Taunos turned his mare in the direction of camp, looking back at her. Nakii hurtled forward, lengthening his stride now that there was room to pass Rose.

"Go!" she shouted as Nakii shoved past. "Hurry!"

Taunos pushed Rose into a gallop. His riding skills had improved over the days as he'd listened to her instructions; he no longer bounced. Just behind her and Nakii, he leaned low over his mare's neck, matching Rose's motions, pushing her forward. But he was still handling a horse who only had so much in her. She'd picked him a gentle horse, a horse without much spirit, without much speed. In short, she'd given him the perfect meal for this sandcat. The guilt gnawed at her. She should have chosen him a horse that could actually give him a chance.

Amanah reined in Nakii, though part of her wanted to let him run, to get away from the predator. But if she did so, she'd be feeding Taunos to the sandcat, and she wouldn't do that even to the nobles.

The sandcat leapt at Rose again, and Taunos flung his hand backward, though what he was trying to accomplish, Amanah couldn't tell. Its claws sliced the mare's haunch. She bucked, kicking, and Taunos clutched at her mane, at the saddle. Amanah turned her gelding, yanking on the reins. Nakii fought her hard, bucking and twisting until her emergency bag came loose and dumped onto the sand, just as Rose tossed Taunos off her back. Taunos hit the ground, rolled, and came up on his feet as the sandcat turned from the bolting mare to him.

It sprang at Taunos even as Amanah jumped down from Nakii's back, letting him race after the mare. Clearly, the horses had more sense than she did. But she had no weapons long enough to reach from horseback, and Taunos looked unarmed. Her heart pounded in her ears, a drumbeat of foolish decisions.

Taunos dodged to the side, the sandcat kicking up dust between them. It turned and Taunos came back into view as they circled each other.

"Do you have a knife?" she called to him, drawing hers.

Gaze still fixed on the cat, he turned his hand, and the faintest glimmer of moonlight on metal caught her eye. Good, so he was armed. She should have expected that.

And then the cat was bounding for her, likely deciding she was an easier meal. She half-crouched, tracking it, its sandy-colored fur that had camouflaged it so well, its round eyes, round ears. Its enormous paws stretched toward her with each claw unsheathed.

She dodged, forced to redirect one set of claws from her face with her knife. She twisted, regaining her balance, but the cat was already beyond her knife's range, its focus back on Taunos. No time to deliver the blow that would doom it.

"Stab its heart," Amanah said. "That's our only way out."

Taunos grunted, twisting aside from a pounce, but its huge paw grabbed him. Amanah shouted, scooping up a rock by her foot and lobbing it at the cat. Taunos would be pinned there, shredded by claws... But he wasn't. The rock hit the cat's back, and it startled. Taunos slipped under it somehow, with the agility he was famous for, and it leapt into the air as if stung.

As the predator spun to face them, Taunos rose to his feet, slices in his shirt and skin, but no deep gouges. Amanah couldn't believe it.

She had known that he was fast, and she'd known he was skilled. It wasn't unusual to hear Borlim yelling at him in the sparring ring: "Taunos, if you have breath to laugh, you have breath to fight. Someone else get in there until he shuts up." Sometimes Borlim would send two or three against him—more, if the recruits were green and arrogant, or if Taunos was testing his patience particularly badly that day.

But Taunos was something else entirely when his life was actually on the line. That speed was sharpened, with an efficiency to his movements that was beautiful, sure, and fluid as he twisted and dodged.

He was Taunos though, so he still talked, even as he slid around its side, deflecting another swipe of claws. "Hold on, buddy, I don't taste good. You don't want to eat us, you'll get sick. We're too much trouble, anyway."

"We have to split its attention," Amanah said. The only way to take down a sandcat without a bow was teamwork.

She backed up, and Taunos nodded, stepping back in the opposite direction. The cat lunged for her again, and she flung herself to the side. It twisted and swiped, fast as a flash of lightning. A line of fiery pain shot down her thigh as she tucked herself into a ball to protect her head, rolling out of the way. Glowing eyes locked on her, it bared its fangs and pounced, far too close for her to be able to dodge this time.

Taunos rammed into the sandcat's ribs, knocking it off its arc hard enough that it stumbled. He flung himself after it, giving Amanah time to scramble to her feet. Her leg was on fire and wouldn't hold all of her weight. She limped to the left, while the cat once more pinned its gaze on Taunos. It was bleeding—he must have rammed it knife-first—but a hand's-width too far forward to hit its heart.

Taunos's eyes flicked to hers, the concern in them clear despite the distance and the dark. He continued talking to the cat, which turned back to face them, head low, short tail flicking.

"Over here. Stay on me. Right here," Taunos told the cat. "Unless you want to go home and leave us be?"

"Back toward me!" Amanah shouted.

The cat was huge and would wear them both down soon, unless she killed it. She could do that, if Taunos could keep it distracted while she got in close. But not if she had to chase them both all over. She forced herself to focus—otherwise they'd both die.

Taunos backpedaled, his eyes on the powerful feline, his chatter flowing all the while from his lips. It gathered itself and leapt again, and he slid to the side, away from her and just out of reach of the cat.

As it landed, forelegs outstretched, Amanah sprang, aiming her knife at the space between its ribs. Her fathers had taught her to go for that vulnerable spot, though they'd also taught her never to be caught in this situation in the first place. The blade pierced the hide of the cat and she plunged it up to the hilt, throwing her weight on it to make sure she got deep enough. At the same time, the cat shuddered against her, as if hit from the other side as well.

The cat yowled and twisted. One forelimb spasmed, smacking her away. She slammed into the dirt, tumbling far less gracefully than Taunos had. She forced herself to sit back up, braced for the cat to be on her again.

But it wasn't.

It lay in a spreading pool of its blood, ribs still, her hilt jutting out of its side.

Taunos skidded to a halt next to her, his voice breathless. "Amanah. Are you all right?"

Her head rang. She must have hit it when she tumbled. As she tried to get up, the world spun and tilted around her. She grabbed out for stability and a strong hand found hers. Taunos pulled her close, and she let him, bowing her head against his shoulder until the world stopped rotating. His chest was injured, she remembered, and made sure to rest her hands on his arms as he held her until she felt stable once more.

"Your leg is injured. Can you walk?" he asked.

She looked down. Blood soaked her pants from a long, jagged slice on the outside of her thigh, extending down to her knee. She swallowed hard and looked around, but the world spun again.

"I have… bandages. In case," she said.

"In that bag that fell before the fight?" he asked.

She nodded, immediately wishing she hadn't as the world spun again.

"You clipped your head on a rock as you hit the ground," Taunos said. "Would you like me to get your bag or help you to it?"

She grimaced at the very thought of needing assistance to get her bag, but she also didn't want to tend her wounds so close to the sandcat's body. "Take me there, please."

Taunos supported her at first, and then, when her leg gave out, carried her the rest of the way to her bag. His gaze travelled the landscape, watching for danger—like she would be doing, if she wasn't so dizzy. All she could really discern was that the horses were out of sight—probably on their way back to camp. At least she had Taunos nearby, on guard, while she removed the smaller pack of medicines from her bag.

Biting back a groan, she sank to the ground, keeping her injured leg mostly stretched out. She needed to assess the damage, but she'd need help with her head. She unwrapped her scarf to free her braids—only three, as she'd been ordered.

"My head. Is it bloody?"

Taunos crouched beside her, his fingers gently stabilizing her as he peered at the back of her head. "A little. Shall I clean it for you?"

"No, I'll do it." She rarely let people touch her hair. "Just show me where."

She cleaned her knife, then cut off a piece of bandage and poured a small amount of alcohol on it, just as they did at the bamimri, before raising her hand to her head. Taunos guided her wrist, and then pain flared like fire through her scalp. She hissed, and her eyes watered as she dabbed at the area until he said it was clean. Turning her attention to her leg, she carefully rolled her pant leg all the way up, away from the wound. Her too-large pants came in handy here, giving her room to work.

Her hands shook as she poured alcohol on them to clean them, then poured more on her leg wound. The sharp, slicing pain of it, even worse than the sandcat's claws, made her gasp. Nausea rose, and she clamped her lips shut, determined not to puke.

She did not win that battle.

Heat rose in her face. What must he think of her? Why did she even care?

Beside her, Taunos offered her a water skin, continuing to scan the landscape. Looking out for her, though there were no nobles nearby. She took it, looking up at him with surprise.

"Vomit always tastes terrible," he said. "Don't worry, it's not one of the ones I filled. It's from your bag."

She thanked him, taking a mouthful and swishing, then spitting to get rid of the awful taste. She wiped her mouth on her sleeve and handed the water skin back to him.

"So you did find water?" she asked.

"Muddy water. I thought we might be able to filter and boil it. But don't drink it now."

She chuckled—of course she wouldn't drink muddy water. Somehow, he had a way of making her feel more at ease, even with the task she now faced. The gash in her thigh would need to be stitched, and though she hadn't ever intended to practice on herself, she'd do what was needed. She always did. Scooting to cleaner ground and taking a deep breath, she steadied her shaking hands and carefully threaded a needle.

Piercing her own flesh was far more difficult than she'd ever guessed it would be. She hissed, tears filling her eyes and blurring her vision as she pushed the needle through. By the third stitch, she'd thrown up again and her hands shook so badly that she couldn't control the needle. Her skin felt hot and cold at the same time.

"Hey." Taunos's hands landed lightly on her arms. He'd crouched in front of her again at some point.

She shrugged him off. There wasn't time for nonsense. "I have to do this before we can move, or I'll leave a trail of blood for more predators. And probably weaken more from blood loss. I just have to be strong enough to do this."

"You're not weak. As I recall, you saved me from being dinner."

"And I've only managed three stitches." It was a horrible job. She'd certainly need to do better—not just to keep her wound closed now, but also in later attempts, if she was to have any chance of getting into the bamimri.

"Would it help if I did it?"

"Do you know how to sew?" She tried again to guide the needle into her thigh, but her hand shook and her fingers fumbled the needle, sticking the pad of her finger as she grabbed for it.

"If you want a design, you'd have to ask someone else, but I can do a straight line, and I can follow what you did." His voice was light, but there was seriousness in his eyes.

She bit her lip, staring at the needle, at her trembling fingers. She needed help. She hated it, but it was true. She sucked in a shuddering breath. Emin thought she couldn't rely on anyone? She'd prove him wrong. "Clean your hands—pour the alcohol on them."

Taunos knelt beside her, did as she instructed, then plucked the needle from her shaking fingers. With a murmur, he turned her leg slightly for a better angle. His calloused fingers were rough against her skin, but his touch was gentle.

She clasped her fingers together and squeezed, trying to quell the tremors. Her stomach twisted tighter, already anticipating the pain to come.

His voice came casually, relaxing her just a little despite everything. "You were supposed to run at the first sign of trouble. To get help. I was surprised you joined me."

She hissed as the needle pierced her again, the roughness of the thread catching on angry skin.

"That order was for Hinanuri scouts, not predators," Amanah gritted out. "Besides, then you would have been dinner."

"At least we'll have more provisions."

"What?" She clutched at his words for meaning, a diversion to the fiery pain in her leg as he made another stitch.

"The sandcat—we can bring it with us. It'll provide meals for several days."

"They don't taste very good."

He shrugged, pulling the thread through again. His motions were sure and steady, and best of all, quick. "No need to waste it."

He had a point. The meat would allow them to make it to Gahimbli with food to spare, unless more unexpected surprises arose. They'd just have to figure out the water situation, since the nobles had wasted theirs.

"But we can't drag it back ourselves," she said. "We'll have to have Emin and Gurseh bring out horses to collect it."

Taunos tied off the knot and sliced the thread short with her blade, then handed her the needle and knife. She sighed out her relief, gratitude welling in her for his effortless distraction.

"Thank you. Are you injured?" she asked. "Your ankle?"

"Turned my ankle, and I have some scratches, but I'll be fine," he said. "Let me guess, wash them with alcohol?"

She nodded, watching him critically as she wound a bandage around her thigh and then carefully unrolled her pant leg. His shirt was ruined, with rips across the front and holes in the back, too. He pulled it off and set it to the side, using a small piece of bandage on the scratches across his chest and then reaching around awkwardly to his back, his features tight, his movements careful. At least his wounds seemed shallow enough not to need stitching—she wasn't sure she could handle a needle yet.

"Don't forget the scratches on your back," she said. "You barely reached back there."

Taunos grunted. "I can't reach them, but I squeezed out the cloth with alcohol. I'll probably be fine."

She narrowed her eyes at him. Risking infection was not fine. "Let me see. They need proper cleaning. I can do it, if that's okay."

He held her gaze for a moment, then nodded, turning his back to her. His movements were slower, more careful even than before, and she frowned. Were his injuries worse than they seemed? The cat had clearly hooked its claws into him and left four puncture wounds on the side with minor tearing. Thankfully, none of them seemed deep enough to need stitching. She cleaned them out, trying to avoid brushing his skin with her fingers.

"I'm going to wind bandages around you to keep these clean," she told him. "Raise your arms."

He tucked his hands behind his head and stared up at the stars, still as a boulder.

"Sorry," she said, reaching around him as she worked. Her leg and head hurt too much to move around him herself.

"It's fine, Amanah." His voice was a low rumble.

But it wasn't fine. Because she had to force her fingers still, keep from accidentally brushing him. Seeing him shirtless was nothing new, but knowing he wanted more and knowing *she* wanted more, she had to fight off the impulse to caress his skin, to soothe the hurt. She wanted to wrap him in her arms to make sure he was really okay, to lean into the warmth he always radiated, to release the fear and anger that had fueled her headlong race to save him.

Instead, she tied off the bandage and scooted away from him and temptation.

"Thank you," he said, still looking upward.

"Of course," she said. "Just leave those on for a few days."

"How's your head?" He turned to face her, but every movement of that small action was slower than usual, increasingly careful.

She eyed him, swallowing the rising dread. "Getting better. I'll be fine, too. Thank you."

Taunos nodded, jaw clenched.

She frowned at him. "What's wrong? And don't you dare say nothing."

"I'll be fine," he repeated himself. "But..." He grimaced, like he was fighting some inner war with himself. Finally, he looked at her, blowing out his breath. "Can we... Is it safe to rest here for a little bit?"

"Taunos—" She reached out for him, gripping his arm. Had she missed some wound?

"I'm not seriously injured. Just tired."

"You were trying to hide your fatigue, like with the mudslide." Exasperation sharpened her tone.

"Had to finish things." He forced a smile that was more of a grimace, his sweat-and-dirt streaked face lined with tension. He picked up his shirt, finding the cleanest portion and wiping his face.

She sighed, but she understood that need to finish things first. At least he'd had the sense to ask for a rest this time. He had to have been tired even before the fight, but he'd flung himself against a sandcat without hesitation. And they still had to get back to camp, hopefully without any other surprises. They could use a little rest to regain the energy they'd need to deal with any other trouble they might run into, and his too-careful movements concerned her. Would he even be able to make it to camp if they didn't rest? She couldn't make it without help—not without it taking half the night.

"Not long," she said, answering his question. "It's too dangerous. But for a little bit. I'll watch."

"Just for a little bit." He lay back on his shirt with a long exhalation, eyes drooping closed.

That bit of vulnerability from him, so easily shown in her presence, shot another spike of worry through her. Taunos had never seemed so exhausted in practices before. Tired, yes, but this, lying in the wilderness, asking if they could rest? He was never the one to ask for a rest.

But he'd never moved so blindingly fast before, either, and the strength of his blows... A couple times in the dim light of the stars, it had seemed like the sandcat had slid to the side in midair, rather than him dodging.

Amanah tore her gaze from him. He said he was fine, and a rest could help her dizziness anyway, not to mention that walking with her leg unable to take much of her weight would be grueling. Her wounds ached, too, and she could use the time to rub more balm into her feet and on her arm. She was probably worrying too much about him. They'd had a life or death battle and escaped without serious injury—that was more luck than most got. It was a miracle he was alive, much less unharmed except for a few scratches. It was a miracle they both were. Maybe it was better not to question Hayzanu's apparent favor.

She replaced her supplies in her pack then tied her scarf back on. She glanced toward Taunos, frowning. "Let me do something about your ankle," she said. "It's a long walk."

Eyes still closed, he shifted, offering her his foot. She unlaced his boot and removed it, taking his sock, too. His ankle looked all right, and he didn't tense or wince as she gently rotated it, so it would probably be fine. Just in case, she rubbed in some bruise balm and a salve to counteract swelling, then wrapped it in bandages for support. She replaced his sock and boot, only then realizing part of the reason for her lingering unease— he was quiet. Not just quiet, but still. Either was unusual for him, but both at once were rare unless he was focused on a task where it was necessary.

It was odd, sitting in company with Taunos with him not talking. It was needed—too much noise could bring down more danger on them, but the night seemed... emptier, somehow. She folded her arms, refusing the temptation to reach for him, to tangle her fingers in his. She let him rest, keeping watch as he'd done for her, just as she had that night with the Lenuri, though this time she kept her gaze on their surroundings, instead of letting herself watch him.

10

ONCE THE STARS had moved noticeably and her dizziness had mostly subsided, Amanah touched Taunos's shoulder to wake him. He surged to his feet so quickly she wrenched herself backward to avoid colliding with him.

She gripped his arm to steady both of them. "Calm down. Nothing's wrong."

He offered her a small smile, his hand curling around her elbow to help her get her balance back, and twisted to scan the landscape. "Sorry. Time to go?"

"Are you rested enough?"

"Are you mended enough?" He raised his eyebrows at her in challenge.

She pressed her lips together against a relieved smile. At least he seemed to have recovered somewhat. "We'll both have to make do," she said.

Walking back was harder than she'd expected. Taunos's ankle and scratches didn't seem to cause him trouble, at least. That was good, because her leg did. Taunos kept one arm around her waist, supporting her as she limped along, but she had to lean on him more and more as her good leg tired of doing the work of both.

He'd walked a long way to get here, and it seemed even longer back. Every small hill was a challenge, and the rugged ground was full of dips and hazards. The last thing they needed was more injuries, but those could come from another wildlife encounter, too. She was holding them back. She struggled to increase her pace but only stumbled more and more often.

Taunos stopped, facing her. "Let me carry you."

Oh no. Bracing herself against him was hard enough. But this... That sort of closeness would be too dangerous. Too easy to relax into. His soothing heat was already coaxing her to give in. Even tired and filthy, she found somehow he took her breath away.

She hadn't been able to keep herself from getting attached. Already, the thought that one of the nobles meant Taunos harm made her irrationally angry and afraid for him. When the sandcat had leapt at him... This would only be trouble, unless she either accepted it or dealt with it in another way.

"You were taking a nap only just back there." She pointed to the spot they'd rested, a depressingly short distance away. Her leg ached.

His lips quirked up at the edges. "It worked. You were watching, and I rested."

She frowned at him.

His arm around her tightened a bit, his voice dipping lower. "I do need more rest, yes, but it can wait until we're back at camp. I can do this. I wouldn't offer if I couldn't."

"Can your ankle handle it?" she asked.

The crooked smile he gave her was soft and knowing. He nodded.

Biting her lip, she nodded in return.

He lifted her smoothly, one arm around her back and the other under her knees, careful to avoid her bandage. At least he was giving her some dignity, though it'd be harder to carry her in this position. She didn't argue with him. Amanah eased her arms around his shoulders to help support her weight, trying to ignore the nearness of him, trying not to stare at him. At least his bandages, visible through the tears in his shirt, seemed to provide enough cushion between them—her weight didn't seem to pain him. Every step he took was placed with care, so they glided through the desert, and yet still they were going faster than she'd been able to manage.

Her heart pounded in her chest. Once more, she was surrounded by the scent of him, underneath the sweat and dirt. Taunos's breaths puffed steadily with his steps, audible with her so close, whispering past her neck and shoulder. His gaze kept sweeping their surroundings, brushing past her, and she found herself wishing that weren't so. Starlight reflected in his brown eyes, glimmering. She could lose herself in looking at him. She watched behind him, instead—her position would be useful to warn him of any danger creeping up from the rear, after all.

It still didn't help. The muscles of his chest and arms flexed around her as he walked, and the heat of him soaked into her, chasing away the night's chill.

This had been a bad idea. She had to distract herself somehow. One of the two decisions she was struggling with didn't have to do with him, so she focused on that one.

She cleared her throat just as he glanced at her, opening his mouth to say something. His eyes crinkled with humor, and he tilted his head.

"You go first." The rumble of his voice vibrated right into her, and she tightened her arms before thinking better of it.

She cleared her throat again, avoiding his gaze. "Well, I thought I'd ask about your contacts in Gahimbli. I've decided to do it, to get into the bamimri, any way I can. Our time with the Lenuri proved how valuable a travelling bimna might be. The bamimri won't like it, surely, but I don't care, and by that time I'll already have the knowledge. Can you imagine how much help a bimna who learns from all the various clans could be?"

Excitement filled his voice. "That's an excellent idea. Collecting knowledge from all over, making it available to all."

The words brought a smile to her lips, but she focused on the plan instead of his praise. She'd do it even if he didn't approve, after all. "So, you mentioned people in Gahimbli you could talk to?"

He nodded. "I don't know which ones will be open to helping and which will prove... like Lamyi and Inuwe. But it might be best to start with Yadi. He'll know who to talk to first."

"Who's Yadi?"

"He's a guard in Gahimbli."

"And I suppose you met him in a fit of daring and heroics?" she asked dryly, glancing at him despite herself.

The corners of his mouth quirked.

She blinked, then shook her head at him, clenching her hand to avoid shoving him like she would her brother. And to avoid caressing the back of his neck. She curled the fingers of both hands firmly inward. "Taunos! You seem to make a habit of saving people."

He raised his eyebrows at her. "I could hear his screams. What else could I do?"

"He was screaming?"

"Not to impinge on his courage. It was his first real fight, and he was outnumbered by experienced bandits."

A lock of his hair was plastered against his forehead. She knotted her fingers together. She would not brush it away. She needed to stop thinking about touching him. "One of these days, it'll be a trap. You'll run in to save someone, and you won't run back out."

Taunos shrugged, lifting her a little with the movement. "I'm not going to stop."

She glanced up at the stars, as if Nannil could help her knock some sense into this impossible man. That might be too much even for a goddess, though. "I'm not saying to stop. You could do with some planning, though, instead of simply running headlong into trouble."

He smiled at her, that disarming smile that made her feel like no problems were insurmountable. Like she could do anything she wanted.

She cleared her throat again. "So Yadi's a good start?"

Taunos nodded. "His mother is a noblewoman of some rank, I think. So hopefully that'll give us a start."

Us. The word warmed her, even though he was speaking of practical matters: introducing her to people through which she could make her own contacts and hopefully get into the bamimri. That was all.

But it didn't have to be.

Taunos felt safe. He made her feel safe. He drew attention to himself as easily as breathing. And while everyone was looking at him, she had room to simply breathe. She could relax for a moment without the world tumbling down around her. If she had only herself to think about, the decision regarding this man was clear.

Taunos had mentioned before that he'd prefer to stay with her and Emin, but duties dragged him away now and then. Surely he understood the struggle between outside considerations and his own desires.

"What do you do when duty and heart conflict?" She blurted out the question before she could think better of it.

His glance was sharp and quick this time, piercing her to her core. He took some time to reply. "Duty isn't always easy."

She waited for more, the breeze cooling her skin and making her want to sink deeper into his warmth, but she held back.

Slowly, carefully, he formed his thoughts into words. "I'm not always sure. Sometimes responsibilities conflict with each other: I'm supposed to do one thing and also another, and I can't do both at the same time. I let people down or hurt them. Sometimes, I want something, but duty calls me away. It's hard to know for sure if I'm being selfish or if there's a balance that can be struck."

At least it wasn't just her struggling with this. She wasn't alone, and it loosened the tightness within her a little.

"It helps when there's someone to talk it out with, I expect," Amanah said. Which meant if she relaxed into an us, they'd be there to help each other through the tangles of heart and duty.

His smile tugged at her core, though his tone was serious. "It does. I think it's too easy for conflicts of responsibilities to shift you into someone you don't want to be, away from who you are. It's difficult to fight against it, but I try."

"I suppose it comes down to need?"

"Possibly. And where your values are. Which is heavier, with more impact."

She nodded. "So you can hang on to yourself through hanging on to what matters most to you."

"I think so," he said. "But no one gets everything right all the time. Or at least, I have to believe I'm not the only one who messes it up."

Arms tightening a fraction, she stared behind him, into the distance. Was it time to dive off that cliff herself? Her whole chest felt light, like wings were beating behind her ribs. Clearly, her heart had already made its decision without consulting her head first.

"What brings this up?" Taunos asked. "Idle wonderings? Distraction?"

She snorted. "If it was a distraction, you'd have undone it just then."

He chuckled, shrugging a little. She steadied herself on his shoulder at the movement.

He darted another glance at her. "I know this might be an uncomfortable situation. I don't want—"

"That's not it," she said. "I'm just thinking."

Another quick glance, but he didn't say anything, instead returning to skimming his gaze across the landscape.

She chewed on her lip. Once again, he could have died, and she'd have lost out on any chance of an "us." And in the end, that's what made her decision. Because there was precious little safety and light in this world sometimes, and she was not going to deny herself at least the chance of accepting some for herself. She didn't know where this path would end or if she'd prepared appropriately, and that terrified her, but she'd be walking it with a man who leapt into danger and came safely through the other side on a regular basis. She feared not trying for it and regretting it even more.

No, she would do this for herself. And maybe that was reason enough.

The firelight of camp glimmered ahead of them, and she tapped his shoulder. She wanted to stand on her own two feet, if she was going to do this. "Let me down?"

He did so, steadying her as she hopped once before she found her balance. His arm fell away, and she bit her lip, her words suddenly drying up. Her heart hammered in her ears. What if he no longer wanted a relationship? What if she'd considered too long and the door had now closed?

"Are you all right?" His brow creased as he looked at her.

"Maybe. I... I hope I'm not being foolish." She grabbed her water pouch and shoved it at him.

He tilted his head but said nothing. His eyes stayed intent on her as he drank, while hers were caught on the motion of his throat as he swallowed.

She threw herself off the cliff before she could fully lose her nerve.

"I said no before to a relationship, because, like with the horse race, I didn't want others to be in danger. But..." She folded her arms, nerves tangling in her stomach. "What you said before, about how I could change my mind? About a possible relationship between us?"

"I remember," he said, returning her pouch.

"I—with the hug, and the Lenuri, and just now, carrying me...I wasn't trying to play with you or test you."

He puffed out an exasperated breath. "A hug is just a hug. More is more. It all depends on what the people involved look at it as."

She narrowed her eyes at him. He'd just accepted everything, without suspicion of guile?

"Sometimes people need to be carried for a bit," Taunos said, his tone gentler. "Though I'd prefer not to carry you. Not because—" He broke off, looking away. "I just don't like seeing you injured."

"And you've been there for me, each time."

His voice fell to a murmur, his eyes flickering over her face. "Amanah, I don't want to misunderstand you. What are you saying?"

She rubbed her forehead. Why couldn't she get the words to come out right? Maybe it was the depths of his brown eyes, making her feel like she could fall right into him. Maybe it was because whenever she was so close she felt like her head was swimming—like she'd hit her head again. How did he manage to be so achingly handsome?

"What I'm saying is, I'd very much like to kiss you as well," she said.

His eyes widened and a smile began to pull at the corners of his mouth but she didn't let it complete, because she'd held herself back too long already. She leaned in to kiss him, but he pulled back at the last second.

Heat rose to her cheeks. He didn't want her anymore. She'd waited too long, and had missed her chance, and now she'd thrown herself at him like a fool, and— She swallowed hard against the painful knots in her stomach, rocking back on her heels.

"Where are we going with this?" he asked in a murmur like water. Questions burned in his eyes, a little furrow between his brows.

She blinked. He was the impulsive one, not her. "I didn't expect you to ask that."

"Hearts are precious and easily hurt. I don't want to hurt you, so I think it's best to be clear."

"I don't know how this ends, but I want to explore this, a relationship, with you. If you still wanted…" He didn't want it though, or he'd have kissed her. Her misplaced hope twisted like a knife in her heart.

His gaze darted away for a moment before coming back to her. There was that reflex of his, to hide, to deflect.

But he spoke instead. "I… I've always been choosy with my heart. From the past, I've learned to be careful. So in matters like this, yes, I do like guidelines, a plan, a shared goal. Otherwise, there's too much pain. So, for you, is this just for tonight? Just while on this trip? What exactly are you expecting?"

She stepped back, away from the pull of his gaze so she could think. She hadn't considered any reservations he might have as well, any hurt in his own past. But knowing he was being careful too, it made this seem even more possible. She wanted this more than she'd admitted.

And the way he treated this so seriously felt like yet another side of him she'd unveiled. "This isn't a tryst or a game for me. I've been considering what you asked, about courtship, for some time. I'm choosing you, choosing to try an 'us.' This is not a spontaneous decision. I'm not trying to play with your heart."

His voice was a low, smooth rumble. "I asked you back in Arruk. I don't know that you've ever made a decision lightly."

"And what do you want out of this? Does courtship mean the same to you?" She kept making assumptions about him. It was best to make sure they were in clear agreement about this.

"I don't want to pressure you," he said. "I told you before, I only want what you're willing to give."

He was hiding again. She'd thought they were getting past that.

"You want to know what I want. Don't I deserve to know the same about you?" she asked. "Besides, I can take care of myself, heart and all. If you get to ask me, I get to ask you, too."

He took a deep breath as if bracing himself, and reached out to her again, taking her hands. His grip surrounded hers loosely, his callouses rubbing hers with the shifting of his fingers. "If you were willing—"

"Of course." She needed solid ground beneath them again, to be sure of what he wanted, especially now that she laid out her own desires. Why did he have to drag it out? "We've established that already, way back in the

Gods' Tree. Otherwise, we wouldn't be having this discussion."

His eyes gleamed as he continued. "If we're compatible. If we find nothing that shows we'd be better apart. Then, I want to be with you for as long as we both can be. I want to wake up and see your face, to hear your voice before falling asleep. To work together on making life better around us. I want our stories and songs to become one, our lives entwined until death. I want to give you my heart and know it's safe in your hands."

He was such a poet, with his honeyed words. "You speak like that, and my own words feel inadequate."

A chuckle broke from deep within him. "You are the farthest thing from inadequate, Amanah."

"That's a lot," she whispered, her voice gone hoarse. He did want her still. Relief flooded through her like a flash flood in a slot canyon.

"Only if you want it, too." His thumb brushed across the back of her knuckles.

It was so similar to her thoughts, but his words gave it a weight, a gravity. He was aiming for a lifelong commitment—if things worked out between them.

He might want a lot, but so did she. And if their hearts did mesh, a lifelong partnership would be the natural end goal. He'd know he could rely on her and she'd know she could rely on him. She'd know her heart was safe in his hands, even when she wore it thin with worry.

And if it didn't work out, it would be over, but nothing he'd shown her yet made her even slightly worried that he would react badly to giving this up if it didn't work out. It would hurt, yes, but they'd have tried.

"I'm not asking for a commitment right now," Taunos said. His hold on her hand loosened, and he scratched the back of his neck with his free hand. "Just an aim. If we aren't aiming at the same target, our paths will diverge, and I just want to be prepared. I don't do well at loving halfway."

She'd been stunned into silence for too long. She squeezed his hand, stepping closer to place her free hand on his cheek. "Yes."

His eyebrows rose and the weight of his gaze made heat rush to her core.

Amanah couldn't help the smile that grew on her lips. "Let's see if we're better together than we are apart. I will share my heart with you, if yours is still up for offer."

"Only for you." Relief relaxed the lines of his face and his lips quirked upward.

His arm snared her around the waist again, pulling her to him. She pressed her lips to his, light, gentle, seeking, but he deepened the kiss until she was breathless. His free hand lifted, his thumb brushing her cheek with a tenderness that banished the last of her worries, calloused fingers gentle on her jawline. She melted against him, pulling him closer, meeting his deeper kisses with her own.

Finally, he drew away with a chuckle, panting for breath. His hand slid away from her waist and left a cool that burned like fire in its absence.

She was panting too, but her gaze caught on his parted lips. One kiss was certainly not enough. Something must have shown on her face, because he grinned.

His joy was infectious, and she fell back into his arms, leaning against him and off her injured leg. She squeezed him hard, treasuring the feel of his cheek pressed against her plaits.

But his muscles tensed around her, and she pulled back, turning to follow his gaze. A figure on horseback was riding hard toward them. Emin, with Nakii trailing behind on a lead rein.

Taunos's shoulders relaxed. He stepped back from Amanah, dropping his supporting arm, and waved to Emin.

Emin reined in beside them. His eyes were wide and wild, his voice tight. "Are you all right?"

"We'll be fine, Emin," she said, trying to scrub any annoyance from her voice. This new thing with Taunos was too precious to subject to Emin's teasing so soon. Better to divert him from whatever he might have seen. "We fought a sandcat."

"Murihat's mercy, Amanah," Emin swore. "Nakii and Rose just came back without you two and I knew something had to have happened."

"The carcass is still back there," Taunos said, pointing. "We thought you could collect it, since we were kind enough to solve the food problem."

Emin snorted. "Sandcat's better than nothing, I suppose. Let's get you back to camp first. How badly are you injured?"

"We'll be fine," Amanah said.

"We have some scratches, some deeper than others," Taunos said.

Emin's brow furrowed as he scrutinized them. "You two fought a sandcat and all you have is scratches?"

Amanah caught Taunos's look and couldn't help but grin. "We did."

"You're both trouble," he said. "How far away is the carcass?"

"That direction. I'm not sure how far exactly, but near the slot canyon," Amanah said. She'd lost track of how far —she'd been distracted both on the way out and on the way back.

"About three ithins," Taunos said.

Her gaze flicked to him. Of course he knew the distance. Fondness unfurled within her.

She turned back to her brother. "You should bring Gurseh with you—we can see the camp and ride Nakii back. But be careful."

"You're telling *me* to be careful?" Emin scoffed.

"Yes—I'm the one who killed a sandcat tonight." She caught Taunos's look and amended. "With some help."

Emin looked between the two of them, his eyes lingering a little too long, his gaze a little too discerning. "All right. But no more adventures, you two."

"Don't worry, I fully intend to be boring," Amanah said.

Emin scoffed but left Nakii and galloped back toward camp. After collecting Gurseh, the two men thundered away in the direction they'd indicated.

Taunos turned back to her, his arm around her bringing her closer. She relaxed against him, letting the larger world fade away once more in the serenity he exuded.

He tipped his head toward the fire. "Together?"

But it meant so much more than just heading back to camp. She couldn't help the smile pulling at her lips as she nodded, twining her fingers with his. "Together."

Taunos helped her mount Nakii, and then he swung astride behind her. She leaned back into him. Nakii could take as long as he wanted to get back to camp if it meant this peace never ended.

11

"How do you want to proceed with the others?" Taunos asked as he helped her down from Nakii. "What are you comfortable with?"

She didn't need the help. She allowed it for the excuse of his closeness, but things needed to be done, so she squashed the part of her that wanted to lean back into him.

Her eyes went to the nobles' tent, tension creeping back into her. "I'm worried about what they'll do if they find out about us. They might use us against each other."

"Particularly Lamyi." His lips pressed into a flat line and he nodded. "I don't like that we have to take others' actions into account in what should be between you and me. But I won't put you in danger. What about your brother and Gurseh?"

She waved a hand. "Them, I'm not worried about, though Emin's going to be annoying until he gets it out of his system."

"I think we can give as good as we get from them," Taunos said.

Tossing him a mischievous smile, Amanah limped forward to inspect the wound on Rose's flank. The sandcat's claws had sliced deep. She winced sympathetically, then checked the rest of the mare's body over for any other injuries. Emin had presumably done this already for both Rose and Nakii when they'd returned without their riders, but she wanted to check for herself.

"I need to stitch up this wound," she said. "Rose is not going to be happy."

"Is there anything you can do for the pain? I can try to keep her calm," Taunos said, stroking the mare's neck.

160

"I have a salve I'll rub in first," Amanah said.

He chuckled low under his breath. "Of course you prepared for this."

She gave him a smug glance and went to work, placing Rose on a short lead beside a large rock to prevent her from evading them.

Even with the salve, stitching the wound was a challenge. At the first prick of the needle, Rose tossed her head, though Taunos held her by the bridle, murmuring comfort. At the next stitch, though, Rose kicked out. Amanah dodged with experienced timing, but her injured leg buckled under her, shooting searing pain through her. Taunos caught her, lifting her back on her feet.

"You're not allowed to kill a sandcat and then get trampled by a horse." Taunos's tone was light, but he watched her with concern. "Just think how much fun Emin would have teasing you for that."

She breathed a laugh and allowed herself to sag against him for a moment. Then, she straightened. "All right, so I need help dodging."

"Why don't I stand next to you? I can do my best to comfort Rose while also helping you stay on your feet," Taunos said.

She nodded. With the next stitch, Rose attempted to kick again, but Taunos snagged Amanah around the waist and side-stepped, his soothing murmurings never stopping. By the time the last stitch was pulled taut, they'd developed a rhythm, with Amanah dodging stamps and kicks almost like she would normally, and Taunos steadying her from behind, helping her keep her weight off her wounded leg. It was almost like dancing, though less relaxing.

"How are you not completely exhausted?" she asked as she tied off the knot. "You dug for water, you fought a sandcat, and you carried me all the way back."

"It's the kissing." His lips kicked upward and a mischievous spark glinted in his eyes. "We clearly need to do more of that."

"You really could out-walk the horses, huh," she said, trying to ignore his words and the heat in her cheeks. "You wouldn't be as fast as them, for sure, but if you can outlast them..."

"I told you I could." That confidence of his edged toward arrogance, and yet, maybe he was simply telling the truth.

"Well, then, perhaps your preference for walking isn't *completely* foolish after all," she teased, packing away her supplies.

"My primary goal in life is to not be completely foolish," he returned, and she couldn't help but laugh.

He wrapped his arms more snugly around her, and she leaned into his embrace. "Done here?"

She nodded, weary but comfortable with her back against his chest, her cheek brushing his.

In a quick motion, he whisked her off her feet and walked over to the fire before setting her gently down. He grabbed the water pouch he'd filled and held it up.

"Filter, then boil?"

She pulled out fine mesh cloth and a pan to pour into. "We should filter it multiple times, just to be safe."

They passed the time with camp chores, building up the fire to ward off predators, especially since Emin and Gurseh would be returning with a carcass. When they finally did come riding back into camp, Emin looked at the two of them, his gaze lingering a little too long. Could he tell something had changed between them?

Then, Emin scowled at her, dumping the sandcat at her feet as he untied the ropes. "I can't believe you fought a sandcat without me."

Taunos laughed. "You sound like a child who missed out on sweets."

"He'll be jealous for days, don't worry," Amanah said.

"Exactly, which is why you get to rub down the horses." Emin made a face at her. "Maybe all the chores for a few days."

Taunos shook his head, rising to his feet. "I'll take care of your horses."

Amanah offered him a smile—she normally took that task, but she wasn't in good shape for it tonight.

Emin frowned, suddenly serious. "You said you only had scratches."

"Of course they would downplay it," Gurseh said, patting Emin's shoulder. "I'll take care of the horses. You work on that animal."

Amanah gave Gurseh a grateful look, but Emin crouched beside her, pinning her with his gaze. "Where?"

Taunos went around them, tugging on the carcass to straighten it out. Sinking into a fluid crouch, he began to skin it.

Giving in to her brother's concern, she rolled up her pant leg. "I needed stitches."

"Tenah save me, Amanah, you stitched your own leg up? What, you didn't feel you'd achieved enough for one night, what with rescuing Taunos and killing a sandcat? Next you'll be telling me you found us a shortcut to Gahimbli, hm?"

She snorted. "I wouldn't want to damage your ego further."

Emin blew out his breath, shaking his head. "You're all right though?"

"Yes. My leg just doesn't fully take my weight all the time."

He squeezed her shoulder and then turned to Taunos, clapping him on the back so he nearly fell on the sandcat. "And you? These bandages covering stitches, too?"

"Thankfully not," Taunos said, tossing him a grin. "If you're looking to aggravate me, you'll have to try harder."

"Don't *encourage* him!" Amanah covered her face with her hand.

"Fine, fine, I'll take pity on you and help," Emin grumbled, though Taunos was working quickly. It was another job he excelled at, his knife strokes smooth, hands carefully separating skin from meat. Emin and Gurseh had clearly let the blood drain and removed the organs before bringing it to camp, so part of the work was done already.

"If it'll keep you from feeling left out," Taunos said with a chuckle, moving aside for him.

She smiled, watching the two work, trying to conceal her fondness. This thing between her and Taunos was just so new. While she didn't mind Emin and Gurseh knowing, it'd also be nice to keep it between the two of them for a few marks. At least Emin had plenty to distract him.

Light-hearted insults flew back and forth as they worked, until Lamyi scowled out the tent at them. "Keep it down! It's time for sleep. At least for civilized people."

"Civilized is the word we're going with, huh?" Emin said under his breath.

Taunos shook his head. Exhaustion drew lines in his face, but they couldn't rest until they'd gotten rid of the carcass. At least she could make sure nothing braved their circle of light as they worked.

When Gurseh finished up with the horses and came over to take watch, Amanah climbed to her feet.

Emin and Taunos looked at her with questions in their eyes, and she shook her head. "No, I don't need help. I'm just going to the latrine."

They nodded, Taunos's eyes lingering on her, and she limped out into the night.

On her way back to camp, though, she passed Inuwe on the path. The noble reached out, stopping her.

"We really do need to get to Gahimbli as quickly as possible, you know."

Amanah frowned.

"It's not just us demanding it of you on a whim or whatever you might think." Inuwe gestured back to the flickering firelight. "All this... hunting and commotion is only slowing us down and putting Lamyi in a worse mood."

"You think we were hunting?"

"Clearly."

Her hands clenched into fists that she tucked behind her back, out of sight. She kept her tone even as she spoke—at least Inuwe seemed the more reasonable one. "He could have died, you know. You sent Taunos out for water, and it could have killed him. There are dangers out here that we know about—that's why we're here. We aren't stopping for fun. Every pause in this trip has been required."

It wasn't like they *wanted* to spend any longer than absolutely necessary in company of the nobles.

Inuwe scoffed. "Give him some credit. Haari Taunos is harder to kill than by fetching water."

"He's not invincible," she shot back. "Did you even notice that we both came back injured?"

"And then apparently decided to go hunting, so it can't have been too bad. You might not know the stories about him, but if even half are true, he doesn't need anyone to worry about him."

She narrowed her eyes at him and his condescending tone. "I killed the sandcat. It attacked us as we were returning from your foo—your errand. Perhaps Taunos would have been able to scrape through somehow to die alone in the desert, I don't know. But I do know that one person against a sandcat means the person doesn't return."

Inuwe frowned, glancing back toward camp before pinching the bridge of his nose and returning his gaze to her. "Lamyi's not used to being challenged the way Haari has been doing, so it was only a matter of time until Lamyi put him in his place. But he just won't listen to reason. Haari really should have known better than to extract an oath from him. He'll pay for it once we get back to civilization, no doubt, but Lamyi won't go back on his oath."

"Wait, what are you talking about?" Fear shot through her, cold and sharp.

"He didn't mention this to you? Well, I suppose it hasn't been long. Just earlier today—or yesterday, if we're past midnight." Inuwe pressed his lips together, and then sighed, speaking slowly. "Lamyi won't threaten you anymore. It's all fine, while we're in the wilderness, anyway."

It's all fine. Of course the nobles would view it as such. They were the ones causing the problems. "He's still been threatening us."

"It's only words, and like I just said, if you were listening, it'll stop for now. Anyway, try to reason with him, maybe." With a flick of his fingers, as if shooing away a gnat, Inuwe turned to go.

"With Lamyi?" Amanah swallowed hard. Climbing the sky to fetch both moons would be easier.

Inuwe turned back, his brow knitted with confusion and amusement. "No, with Haari Taunos. It's not safe to cross Lamyi. Maybe if Haari can make up to him, Lamyi will forgive him by Gahimbli."

Forgive Taunos for what? Amanah blinked at him. "Why don't you talk to Lamyi and explain that threatening his guards makes it more difficult for them to protect him?"

Inuwe snorted. "That's your job, isn't it? It's not our job to make yours easy on you. You're certainly not making our task any easier."

"And if Taunos doesn't make whatever it was up to Lamyi?"

The nobleman shrugged. "No need to lose sleep over it for now. He can worry about that later, once we make it to the city. But again, we need to make better time. That's what I'm here to tell you."

"I understand." Amanah jerked herself into a hasty bow but scowled at Inuwe's back as he continued toward the latrine. She hurried back to camp, teeth gritted.

Danger ahead and behind. Of course it would be their fault for standing up to the nobles, for crossing them, rather than the nobles' fault for being unreasonable. And why hadn't Taunos told them that the danger was increasing? Had he realized how the nobles would turn on him? Had that been why this entire disaster of a night had happened?

Her stomach turned, tight with knots that refused to loosen. Well, perhaps the *whole* night hadn't been a disaster, but clearly she and Taunos were right that they needed to keep their relationship a secret from the nobles. If Lamyi would send Taunos to die for extracting a promise to stop threatening them, she shuddered to think what he might do if he discovered that she and Taunos were courting.

She couldn't wait to get away from the nobles, and yet, now she dreaded reaching Gahimbli, too, especially if Lamyi was going to bring some horrible retribution down on their heads. But they had to reach Gahimbli before the rain of the gods fell.

She drifted back into camp, where the scene in the firelight was so different from the nightmare Inuwe had alerted her to. The skin of the sandcat was off, and Emin and Taunos worked quickly to harvest the meat, chatting and joking with Gurseh. Her unease must have shown on her face, because Taunos paused in his work.

In a flash, tension lined his shoulders, and his mouth became a hard, flat line. "What happened?"

Amanah scowled at him. "Inuwe told me you made Lamyi vow not to threaten us again."

Emin raised his eyebrows, but Gurseh frowned.

With deliberate motions, Taunos cut free another slab of meat. He handed it over to Gurseh for trimming and portioning. "I did. I was tired of listening to his daily threats."

"Why?" Emin asked.

Taunos rubbed his forehead with his sleeve, fatigue peeking through his nonchalance. "Even if he doesn't act on them, I know they've been wearing on you. You all deserve better."

Weary, she sank down by Gurseh to help salt and pack away the portions of steak. "Inuwe implied that you were in danger, that you should have known better than to extract an oath from Lamyi. So what exactly did you do, Taunos? And why didn't you tell us?"

"I was going to, but I wanted to tell all of you at once, so I thought I would wait until after running Lamyi's errand." He tried for a grin. "That went well."

Emin frowned. "What did you give in return for this oath?"

"Only my dignity. Nothing I can't handle." There was an edge to Taunos's voice at the last word, and he flicked his gaze up to meet Emin's.

"What about your dignity did you give?" Amanah asked. A sense of doom sat on her shoulders. She'd thought they were done with this dancing around answers, but clearly not. She pressed her lips together. He'd better stop hiding things from her, now that they'd entered a relationship. His own secrets were one thing—she could wait for him to trust her with those—but hiding things in her world from her? That was entirely different.

He drew in a long, slow breath, finally meeting her eyes. "I promised that I wouldn't stop him if he needed to lash out at someone—so long as it's me, there are no weapons involved, and I get to block any seriously wounding blows—and that I would support his story if he spun tales about besting me in sparring. And I promised to do what chores he needed doing from now until Gahimbli. That's when he sent me for water."

"You became our whipping boy," Gurseh said, staring at him in shock. "Well, close enough, anyway. If we annoy the nobles, they'll hurt you."

Emin dropped his knife with a scowl. "Great. That's just what we need."

Amanah shook her head, staring at the ground. Why would he do such a thing, go to such lengths for them, but do it behind their backs? How was she supposed to handle this, knowing that stepping out of line would get Taunos hurt—especially after the decision they'd made just tonight? The very thought was crushing. "I don't like it. We need you healthy and uninjured."

Taunos's eyes were hard and fierce as he sliced free another portion and handed it to Gurseh. "And I don't like seeing you hurt either. You think I don't notice the bleakness, the flash of pain in your eyes every time I report a threat? Emin, you hide it better than Amanah, but I still see it, and it cuts me like a knife every time. Especially since I'm delivering that hurt. I know it's indirect, but still, the pain comes from me. And I have felt so helpless all these days; nothing I thought of was enough. I know it's not the same as your pain, but... I would give much to keep from hurting the two of you, and now, finally, I figured out a way to stop it, at least for a little while. I didn't mean to hurt you with my solution."

She shook her head, bristling. "We're not to blame for your poor decision. We could have planned a better way, not this. Even threatened, we make plans and we survive."

A weary sigh came from him. "I'm not blaming you—that's not what I meant. I'm explaining my reasoning. You should have the chance, at least, to thrive, not just survive."

She gave him a flat look. How could he be so thoughtful and thoughtless at the same time? Because he didn't look at the world the same way she did, she supposed. Didn't see the same dangers, weigh the same risks. If he'd only talked first...

"Besides, I think he'll get tired of it eventually." Taunos shrugged. "He wants to feel powerful. This should do it—especially since he gets to brag that he bested me."

Emin glared at him. "Taunos, you are a complete ass sometimes, tail and all. Gods above, will you ever stop being a reckless fool?"

"Light, I hope not, if it saves you from harm," Taunos shot back.

"Threats are only threats, Taunos," Amanah said. He'd just told her he wouldn't put her in danger on his account, but apparently the reverse was acceptable to him.

"But they can become more. This way he has an outlet that isn't you." His voice was low and fervent. "I'd pay the cost gladly to keep you from being targeted by small-minded people, a hundred times over."

Emin shook his head. "And now we have a member of the team more likely to be wounded than not."

"I can handle some pain, and he won't seriously wound me. He's a lot of things, but he's not stupid."

"He won't seriously wound you?" Amanah hissed. She flung her hand out in the direction of the gully, only slightly mollified when Taunos deflated a little.

"If you're so eager to be hit, I can fix that for you." Emin flexed his fingers and Taunos rose to meet him, even though it was just bluster.

Her brother's desperate, impotent fear rang out clearly to her beneath his anger. Amanah rubbed her forehead, wishing she could offer him comfort. Wishing she could go back and talk this through with Taunos before he made this decision. Emin couldn't protect her from the nobles—he couldn't even protect himself. None of them could. Of course he'd react badly to Taunos putting himself in the same danger.

"If you need a sparring session to work through this, I'm here." Taunos's voice was almost casual.

Emin's face contorted. "No. You'll be hurting plenty soon enough. I'm not adding to it."

Inuwe came back to camp, and they all went quiet as the man paused, looking at them, and then headed into the tent. Someone's faint laughter spilled from inside, and Taunos stiffened.

Amanah glanced at the tent. "They want us divided. This is entertaining to them."

Taunos nodded. He was still so calm, as if he was used to being yelled at. Given the frequency with which he pulled such stunts, he probably was.

"Lamyi's been using the threats to control and distract us." Taunos sank back onto the ground, this time with his legs folded up in front of him, keeping his voice to a bare murmur. "At the very least, from their point of view, they were distracting me, trying to keep you safe. You know I've been having to spend more and more time in that tent with them. But now, I don't have to run all over trying to figure out real dangers from threats. I can help with camp chores and scouting more."

"His beating on you could be practice for us," Amanah said.

Taunos shook his head. "If Lamyi was going to escalate, he'd do so with someone who can't fight back. And now that I have his oath, he'll confine his ire to me. All I have to do is outlast his temper. I can do that."

How could they trust Lamyi's word? Had he been paying any attention at all on this journey?

"And you believe he'll honor an oath?" Emin asked, his voice dripping with disbelief.

"He will. I know that much about Dahuti nobles—they don't give oaths easily, which is why I pushed," Taunos said.

"It's true," Gurseh said, finally speaking up. "If Lamyi gave his oath, it's better than law."

Taunos gave Gurseh a nod.

"Sometimes I really—" Emin cut himself off with a growl. "They'll treat you like you're havi."

"Two of my favorite people in any land are havi. Why would I have a problem being treated equal to them?" Taunos waved a hand toward them, then picked up the knife and continued working.

Warmth rushed through her at his words, but she held on to her anger, aggressively rubbing salt into the next slab of meat.

"Because you being treated differently *was* the shield," Gurseh said.

Emin nodded. "And now I have three people in danger from the nobles. Gurseh, don't tell me you'll set aside your sense and join us."

"I will not," Gurseh said.

"Good." Emin blew out a breath.

"How is me taking the hit different than Amanah letting Lamyi hit her?"

"I dodged." Her voice came out stiff.

Taunos's gaze flicked to her. "Yes, but Emin was worried if it happened again, you would allow it."

Amanah gritted her teeth.

Taunos blew out a weary breath and rubbed his forehead with his arm, shoulders sagging a bit. "Gahimbli presents the same dangers for you all as Arruk does, right?"

Gurseh kicked his legs out in front of him. "For Amanah and Emin. I'm Guma clan—I'll be fine."

"I gave us time to make a plan," Taunos said. "It's possible by the time we reach Gahimbli, they'll have it out of their system or be so upset with me that they stop worrying about you two. And I have allies in Gahimbli."

"Why do you get to take on the danger without consulting us?" Amanah's tone was crisp with anger. He'd sacrificed for them, and the dangers of being beholden to someone roared in her head—that way led to snares of reliance, to betrayal. Perhaps she needed to learn to rely on others more, but she still wanted to have that decision, not have it taken away from her.

"Because it's my job." Taunos's gaze was as flat as his tone. "This is why I'm here, Amanah. This is my purpose on this trip, why Borlim sent me. This is what I promised you. I'm the one to deal with the nobles. I'm the one to keep you and Emin from being targeted too badly."

"I didn't mean this." Emotion clogged her throat, and she cleared it away savagely. "I meant we should, all of us, avoid precisely this situation! But you didn't even let me clarify because you didn't do us the courtesy of asking our thoughts on the matter before you decided for us all!"

"We can't change it now." Emin sighed, staring up at the twin moons. "Much as I hate it, Taunos is right. He did his job—as foolishly as possible."

Taunos's mouth quirked.

Emin scowled, standing. "I'm still angry with you. But I've said my piece. Come on, Gurseh."

"Where are you going?" Amanah asked.

"We need to drag this carcass away from camp to deter predators. And I need a moment. Can you two get the rest of this dried and packed away while we're gone?"

Amanah nodded.

Emin stabbed a finger at Taunos. "You. Stop being a fool. And don't you dare do something like this again without telling us first."

As Emin tied a rope to the carcass, Gurseh stepped around the fire to clasp arms with Taunos. "I understand. I wouldn't have done it, but I understand."

Taunos squeezed his arm, nodding.

Amanah pressed her lips together as Emin and Gurseh mounted up and rode away. It was good that Gurseh and Taunos were getting along better now, but at the moment, it was not helpful.

With a low exhale, Taunos sat down beside her. "I didn't mean to upset you. I've been training for this all my life."

"Don't exaggerate."

A wry smile crossed his lips. "All right, I've been training for as long as I can remember to do things like this. To see danger, to find a way to neutralize it—mostly things like the sandcat, true, but also bullies like Lamyi. You've been riding horses since birth, and you learned to fight with ribbon dances. I woke up at dawn to puzzle out how to keep people alive and safe, including putting myself on the line."

Gurseh had once told Emin about the school he'd attended as a child—a strict place of schedules and lessons to fill the day. A surprised laugh broke from her. "You went to hero school."

No wonder Taunos habitually flung himself into danger at the slightest opportunity. No wonder he'd handled the possibility of Lamyi purposely sending him to his death in stride. It turned her stomach.

He flashed a grin, but it faded quickly, his attention fixed on salting and packing the meat. His hands worked right alongside hers, but the distance between them now seemed a gulf.

Taunos cast her a side-long look. "Tell me if I've missed something—*when* I've missed something. But don't tell me not to be me."

"I'm not telling you not to be you," she snapped. "Unless being you is you making decisions that affect me without even asking me first."

"No, not at all. I just want to save people."

Her eyes narrowed on him. "Save people, or help people?"

He stopped then, as if struck. Blinked.

She rubbed her forehead. "Because you're acting on the former right now, but you usually claim to want the latter. I don't want to be saved. Yes, you're here to stand between us and the nobles, but I asked you to do that while communicating with us. You did this for us but without us. It's not the decision, it's that you excluded us, not considering that we could come up with a better solution together."

He blinked again, and then grimaced, packing away the last of the meat. "No, you're right. I confused the two."

She blew out a breath, looking at her hands. "Now when I annoy Lamyi, it's not just me I'm risking—I'll be hurting you. I'll have to be even more careful, because he'll take any excuse to hurt you on account of us."

He reached over, clasping her hand in his, regardless of the mess on each of them. "I'm sorry, Amanah. I didn't think about it that way. I should have asked your thoughts first."

Some of the tension drained from her, like a boil being lanced. She curled her fingers around his. "It makes it almost impossible to defend myself when you spring things like this on me. Don't keep things from me to protect me. If I can't trust you to tell me about a danger, if instead you'll go behind my back to protect me without even discussing it with me first, we can't meet the danger side-by-side."

He reached up as if to pass a hand down his face, then paused. He grabbed a cloth and the diri pulp she'd brought along for soap. Eyes on his task, Taunos began cleaning off his hands. "This is the second time you've told me you don't want to be protected. There's something more, isn't there? I want to understand you better. Wanting a choice makes sense and I shouldn't have stolen that from you. But beyond that, what upsets you about being protected?"

It took her a moment to respond, to sort out the reasons. She stared at her boots. "I guess I don't want to be disappointed."

He held out a hand for hers, offering but not touching her yet. "That makes sense."

She looked at him. "Really? That's it?"

"Really. I understand that."

With a deep steadying breath, she gave him her hand and continued. "And I don't want to be beholden to anyone."

"Beholden?" His brow furrowed, then he nodded. With smooth, firm strokes, he gently but meticulously cleaned her hands. "Ah. The people who want to raise up 'little havi' that you mentioned before, in Arruk?"

She nodded.

Realization spilled over his face, followed by self-disgust and remorse so heavy he looked sickened. "Amanah, I'm so sorry. That's not what I was trying to do. I..." He dropped the cloth and scrubbed his face with his hands as he swore. She couldn't understand the word, muffled by his fingers as it was, but it definitely sounded like a curse. When he spoke clearly again, his voice was deep and rough with emotion. "I really messed up, huh?"

"I know you were trying to help, and I know you did this before our conversation, but I need to be clear. Just because we decided to see how this thing between us goes doesn't give you the right to decide what dangers I can and cannot face. Such things will *never* work between us. I'm your equal or we're nothing."

He nodded, still looking sickened. He twined his fingers with hers. "You are my equal, Amanah. I shouldn't have cut you out. I can stand between you and danger, but you're right. You should still be able to see the battlefield and choose your own course of action. I will not be your cage." His voice dipped into something almost like a growl, filled with promise.

She squeezed his hands, tears pricking at her eyes.

"I need to make this up to you and to Emin," he said, resolve winding around the grief in his voice. "Do you have any suggestions you might be willing to give me? I don't want to fumble the apology, too. Or maybe I should ask Gurseh, so as not to put you in an awkward position."

Bungled though it had been, he had meant to help her and Emin, and without ever asking anything in return. But the feeling with which he'd argued his case and still been able to see her point of view and accept his responsibility, it eased the knot of worry in her. As long as they could move forward together, as partners, that was enough.

She raised her eyebrows at him. "Were you planning to hold this over my head?"

He straightened, eyes wide. "No! Never!"

Relief blanketed her, stealing her voice for a moment. She believed him, and it felt good to believe him. She squeezed his hands. "Then it's forgiven."

"That's it?" He frowned. "That easy?"

"No, not easy. Because now it comes down to actions. To doing better."

His gaze searched hers, slowly calming at whatever he saw in her eyes. He nodded.

She offered him a smile. "You made a mistake trying to do something to help. I see no reason to hold errors over your head. Especially since you didn't do it maliciously. If it's a pattern, though…"

He nodded again, thumbs brushing over her knuckles. "All right. I want this. This partnership. But I'm afraid I'm going to mess up. I don't want to see something hurt you, not when I could stop it. I do want to protect you. And I'm afraid that impulse will win sometimes as I learn to walk this road with you."

A frown tugged at her mouth. That didn't sound promising, but he was still speaking, words spilling out quickly.

"But you don't want protection, and you're more important to me. I want to earn your trust."

She held up their hands, their fingers interlaced. "This is about partnership, like you said. You already have my trust."

"Thank you." He took a deep breath, his composure snapping back into place. "And if I mess up and get overprotective—"

"Then I'll tell you. That's why I'm here—to look at things my way, and you to look at it yours, and us to talk about things."

"You never shy away from telling me exactly what you think," he said with a smile. "You're right. That's how my parents did things, too."

"Mine, too." She rested her forehead on his. "I don't want Lamyi to hurt you. I don't want to see you hurt ever, really. But I'll be there for you."

He leaned into her in return. "I will get hurt. I told you how I met Yadi, and there will be other times like that, times I'll dive into danger. Can you be ok with that?"

She smiled at him, remembering how he'd assured her in the Gods' Tree that he didn't want to change her. She felt the same for him. "I'm not sure I could expect anything else from someone who throws himself in front of a sandcat. This is who you are, and I don't want to change you. I love you for it. Just don't back me into a corner again—let me fight at your side."

"I would be honored to have you fight by my side," he murmured.

She closed her eyes, letting him tug her gently into his arms, letting the tension drain from her.

He gave her a little squeeze.

She opened her eyes to meet Taunos's gaze.

"First fight. I thought we'd at least last the night, but…" His eyes crinkled at the corners, and there was a lightness to his tone, a transition toward teasing while still leaving room for a return to serious conversation.

She curled her fists in his shirt. "Regretting things?"

He was solemn as he stared into her eyes, his gaze drinking her in. "Absolutely not. But are you?"

"No," she whispered. "It's often easier for me to push emotions away and just get through the day. But you bring them out in me. And you listened."

He kissed her. "Keep sharing with me. I don't ever want to stop having you by my side."

12

THEY GOT A late start the next morning, due to working through half the night. Amanah tried to avoid Taunos's gaze as much as possible. Every time she looked at him, she wanted to kiss him again, to linger in his embrace, despite the fact that there was work to be done.

"We should check Rose," she said, getting to her feet carefully. Her leg protested whenever she used it.

"I'll bring her over to you," Taunos said, watching her with concern.

She gave him a grateful smile. "Walk her past, please."

He nodded, doing so, and she eyed the mare's gait critically. There was just the faintest lurch to her step, where the mare favored her injured haunch.

She exchanged looks with her brother, and Emin shook his head, agreeing with her assessment.

"She's too injured?" Taunos asked.

"She could carry you, but it'll help her healing if she doesn't have to."

"I'll run, then," Taunos said, flashing a grin. "After all, I apparently need to prove I can."

Emin snorted. "As if you need another reason to show off."

"I don't care how we go, but we need to leave now," Lamyi interrupted, hauling himself into his saddle, as if he hadn't woken up at the same time they did.

Amanah looked at Taunos, worry twisting in her gut. "Be careful. Keep Rose with you, just in case you need speed."

He smiled, patting Nakii's neck as he passed. "Be safe, too."

His brown eyes pulled at her. Heat rushed to her face, her skin alive

175

with his touch, the memory of his lips on hers vivid and tempting. And then he was gone, jogging ahead, the smooth movement of his muscles making rippling shadows in his clothes.

Cinching the girth of his saddle, Emin looked at her, then at Taunos, and then waggled his eyebrows at her, his black eyes sparking with laughter.

"You and Taunos, huh?" he asked in a low voice, leaning in.

Heat flooded her face. "What did he tell you?"

Emin hooted with laughter. "Nothing, but Amanah, have you seen your face? You look like you kissed the sun!"

She covered her face with her hands. "Is it that obvious?"

"Only because I clearly interrupted something last night. And you keep looking at him."

"I was trying *not to!*"

Emin chuckled. "Yeah, that was also apparent and another giveaway."

She buried her face more completely in her hands, until he nudged her again.

"For my part," he said, "I'm happy for you two."

"Good, now please keep it quiet so the nobles don't use it against us," Amanah hissed.

He nodded, squeezing her arm, and then led the way out of camp.

"Keep up slow poke—I mean, boss," he chided as he passed Taunos.

They made better time in the next days, especially as Rose recovered. They found freshwater and were able to replenish the water skins. Even the nobles waded in for a swim.

There was a feeling of joy, too, in stealing kisses with Taunos day after day. But even so, danger loomed, and not just because of the occasional sound of fists on flesh when Lamyi was in a sour mood. It turned her stomach, but she tried to shut the sounds out. She couldn't protect Taunos from Lamyi, and she couldn't protect him from himself.

But there were even worse things to worry about.

They were being followed.

Emin wasn't convinced of her conclusion, but the tight lines around his eyes and mouth betrayed that he was just as worried about the possibility as she was. For several days, they'd caught sight of other riders, singly or in pairs, always far enough out of sight that they couldn't see any distinguishing features. Sometimes they were behind them, other times far to the left or right. Once, a figure stood atop a tall spire and watched them approach and pass. It was as if the figure was a sentry, but they didn't respond to the banner dancing signals Amanah sent, as she'd have expected if they were from one of the nomadic clans.

It was impossible to tell if the figures were all different, or if some of them were actually the same people, maybe travellers from other groups crossing the wilderness. None responded to banner dances, and eventually Emin told her not to bother trying anymore. If they didn't want to communicate, what did they want? Had they stumbled on bandit territory —but if so, why weren't the watchers in larger groups?

She almost began to wish they'd attack, whoever they were, just to finish the awful suspense of waiting. Instead, it drew on, the tension ramping up when they spotted a dragon in the distance.

When her monthly bleeding came, the cramps doubled her over, worse than usual. She hobbled through the day, through her chores, and then laid down in a blanket near the fire, too tired and nauseous to eat though she knew she should. Emin was cooking something that smelled amazing but simultaneously made the nausea rise.

"You look terrible," he said.

She made a face at him. "Will you be useful and make hot water for tea?"

"I already have some going," he said, making a face in return.

"Good. Thank you." She pulled out her packet of special herb blend from her pack and then pulled her blanket further around her. Lying down with eyes half-open, she focused on outlasting the pain until she could steep the herbs that would help with the cramping.

Gurseh joined them, and then Taunos, who went right to the fire. Reaching forward with a stick, he rolled the stone that lay at the edge of the fire away from the flames.

Emin watched him. "I didn't touch it, I told you."

Taunos grinned. "You can actually follow directions? It's a wonder."

He rolled the squat, irregular stone, about the size of both his fists, in his blanket. And then, he came over and sat gingerly beside her with a suppressed grunt of pain, one hand on his stomach.

She frowned. "How bad is it?"

"I'll be fine. Here." He offered her the blanket roll.

She stared at him dumbly. "For me?"

He tilted his head. "Of course. Cramps, right?"

Readjusting her blanket, she accepted his gift with a nod, curling around the fire-warmed stone. "You sure you're all right?"

"I'm here."

She offered him a forced smile. She wouldn't make him talk about it, but she still hated seeing him in pain. She curled tighter around his blanket. "Thank you."

"Here." He stretched out his legs beside her, and weary and sore, she accepted, using his leg as a pillow. Everything hurt, her cramps causing all her muscles to clench.

She tried to get comfortable, but even though the stone loosened the pain in her stomach some, her back took over with the complaints.

Taunos rubbed her shoulder lightly, his voice a low murmur. "What can I do?"

She offered him her herb pouch. "When the water's ready, this is medicine. Can you steep it for me?"

"Consider it done. Anything else?"

"Can you... It might be silly," she said.

His eyes caught the firelight, one corner of his mouth curling in a crooked smile. "You don't need to ask for a hug anymore. I think we're beyond that."

"No," she said, face heating a little. "Could you rub my back?"

"Of course." The teasing left his voice, replaced with warmth.

"I don't want to be a bother."

"I'm happy to," he said. "Besides, if it was me hurting, you'd be trying to help. You tried to help the nobles and you don't even like them."

"How do you know I like you?" she teased, snuggling into him.

"One can hope," he murmured with a grin.

She smiled up at him, wrapping herself in his care like in her blanket. It eased her tension as well as the heated rock she curled around. "It appears there's a contagion, for I'm liking you more and more. Surely it can't end well."

"We never know how our stories will go," he said. "But I think we all deserve a good ending."

She snorted at him and his honeyed words, letting her eyes half close again, but this time in trust and comfort instead of in stubborn endurance.

Emin raised his eyebrows at her with a slight smile, before responding to something Gurseh was saying. He looked after her too, in his own way, just as she looked after him. Gurseh handed Taunos a mug of hot water, and Taunos shifted, dropping her tea bag into it to steep.

His hand made circles on her back through the blanket, until she picked up the blanket and put his hand on her shirt. She wanted his warmth as the evening cooled, and it bled through from his hand through her shirt and from his leg through his pants, just as the rock which warmed her center. So thoughtful of him.

He'd given her his blanket, leaving him with just his cloak against the evening chill. She tucked the corner of the blanket around his waist to help keep him warm, and sighed as the cramps began to fade away, replaced with the warmth of the stone she was curled around and good company.

"I'm pretty sure the watchers are getting closer," Emin said.

"They've been trying to disguise it, getting closer and then backing off and repeating, but yes, overall, I think a net is tightening around us," Taunos said.

"A net implies there are people ahead, too," Amanah said. "More than the one maybe-sentry we saw."

"And if no one's ahead, that raises the question: what are we being herded toward?" Emin asked.

"We're being herded toward Gahimbli, which is where we're going anyway," Gurseh said.

"But why?" Emin asked. "What do they want?"

"Why won't they just talk like normal bandits or nomads?" Amanah grumbled. "It's like I brought my banners for no reason. I can't believe I'm hoping for demands to be made—anything to break this looming silence."

"I don't know, but I don't like it," Emin said, his tone as sour as hers.

"So far, I don't expect there's more than five individuals, even though they shuffle themselves to keep their numbers hidden," Taunos said. "Though a larger group could, of course, be ahead."

"And there was that dragon in the distance today," Amanah said.

"We're getting close to the Hinanuri border," Gurseh said. "It makes sense to see the occasional dragon. I hear they have no respect for the border."

The border was a few days' hard ride away if they turned and rode directly for it, rather than not-quite parallel as they were doing. By the time they reached Gahimbli, it would be only two days away. She hoped they'd be spared any trouble, but Borlim had told them the tensions were rising.

Emin speared Amanah with a look. "And what are my orders for if the dragon comes close enough for us to see the rider?"

Run. The answer, of course, was to run and hope the dragon had recently fed, or at least didn't feel like roasting them that day. She really hated the idea of running.

"We toss Emin at it and hope it's hungry," Amanah said.

Emin snorted, but kept his eyes on her for an extra moment.

"Emin wouldn't be appetizing," Taunos joked. "He'd be as awful as the sandcat steaks, all tough and stringy."

Emin chuckled, shaking his head at them. "You two are trouble. You've both always been trouble, but teamed up? Jattanu help me."

"We knew there'd be trouble along the border," Taunos said, returning to serious conversation.

"I know, and the nobles are involved in something—whatever is bringing them to Gahimbli," Amanah said. "I just wish we knew what, if it affects us trying to protect them. It's hard to make a plan without knowing what's coming."

"We'll just have to be on our guard," Emin said. "Remember our jobs."

"Maybe the bandits are sea-wizards, here to curse us and the nobles," Gurseh said, his tone flippant.

Taunos leaned forward, posture eager. "What are the sea-wizards? I saw the area roped off in Ukish and I've heard of them, but what are they?"

"They're boogeyman tales mothers use to scare children into not straying far at night," Emin said.

"No, they're not," Gurseh countered. "I've seen them; they're real."

"Where do they come from?" Taunos asked. "What are they like? When did you see them?"

Amanah smiled into her blanket at his never-ending curiosity. She watched Gurseh, finding herself wanting to know more about sea-wizards instead of shivering at the thought. Especially if it helped in identifying if the bandits really were sea-wizards, somehow.

"They're not like Sea Peoples, who stay near the coast," Gurseh said. "Sea-wizards come from the sea, wander and trade and do their magic and such, and then return."

"Are they one people, or are they maybe samples of many various people?" Taunos asked.

That was an interesting thought. On the one hand, that would mean sea-wizards could come from anywhere, rather than being confined to one area as a home country. On the other, it could mean they'd be less likely to be loyal to each other or a sea-wizard country with its own agenda.

She wasn't sure how she felt about it.

"We were always taught they were one people," Emin said with a shrug. "But we were also taught that they'd steal us away if we didn't behave, so..."

Emin handed Taunos one bowl of stew and then another, and Taunos set one in front of her. Her stomach tightened, and she curled up tighter, blocking her face with her blanket.

"Maybe they're just people, like anyone else. Like traders," Taunos said as he removed the bowl before she could even ask, replacing it with the mug of tea he'd steeped for her. Again, without a word, without a production. As easily as breathing.

Yes, she was definitely falling in love with this man, for better or for worse.

"Thank you," she murmured. She didn't drink more than a few sips, but its scent was relaxing, like the circles Taunos was rubbing into her back.

Discomfort easing somewhat, her curiosity came alive from where she usually hid it deep within. She'd never encountered a sea-wizard. There was a lot she didn't know, and there was a thrill deep within her at the prospect of learning more. They still scared her, but Taunos's enthusiasm was catching—she found her curiosity warring with her fear. And maybe there wasn't actually anything to worry about with them. Maybe it was just that she didn't know enough. After all, she was far more daring these days than she'd been used to, and the moons hadn't fallen from the sky. Perhaps, one day, she would meet a sea-wizard and learn about them. Maybe even travel into the Hinanur Empire to see the dragons she'd heard whispered about—closer than a winged silhouette in the distance, but perhaps not *too* close at the same time.

"They probably are just people," Emin said. "If they exist."

"I'm telling you, they do exist," Gurseh said. "And when you say it like that, everyone's just people."

Taunos chuckled. "In my experience, people *are* just people. I want to know more, is all. So when did you see one? What happened?"

"I was a youth, and a sea-wizard came through Arruk. Haughty woman, but the power! She was amazing. You know the fountain by the fifth well? She shot the water from the fountain clear across the square to blast a merchant she figured was charging her too much. Then she stalked out, like anyone in her way would simply move for her."

Emin snorted. "After that show, I bet they did."

"All except one stunned idiot." Gurseh grinned sheepishly. "She stopped in front of me, scowled, and told me to move or she'd turn me into a fish and drop me in the fountain."

Emin laughed, flicking Gurseh's collar as if checking for gills.

Taunos chuckled, shaking his head. "It sounds like a pretty intimidating display. Why was she there?"

"Something about the library, I think. I stumbled over my feet to get out of her way, and she just... moved me to the side, as if the ground itself moved, but I swear it didn't. I swear it didn't, and neither did I, but still I was sliding out of her way. Then she headed for the library, and I counted myself lucky not to cross paths with her again."

Emin grunted. "I guess the library's famous enough to even attract sea-wizards."

Amanah shifted restlessly, pressure digging into her head. It tore Taunos's attention from the story, and his free hand came around, thumb caressing her cheek.

"What's wrong?" he asked.

"My braids are pulling at my scalp," she grumbled. "But I'm fine."

"If you want, I can undo them."

The ache of her cramps and her stitched-together leg were washed out by the comfort offered and the thrum of conversation around her, words she didn't need to add to, though she was included in the circle regardless. But she was particular about who she let touch her hair, and she wasn't yet ready to let down that wall.

She shook her head. "It's fine. It's just because there are only three, so less to distribute the tension."

His response was something between a hum and a growl. Somehow, she knew he was holding even this small discomfort of hers against the nobles, with their ridiculous requirement on three braids or less. That was fine, because she held it against them, too. But it was difficult to hold on to frustration when Taunos's hand skimmed up and down her spine, the sound of his voice doing as much as the warm rock to relax her and soothe her aches. She forced herself to finish her tea, then relaxed into him.

He, Emin, and Gurseh chatted easily, their voices entwined as they traded stories and jests, the sounds of their conversation washing over her, soothing. Taunos normally kept his hands busy with repairs and other small chores or projects in the evening, but he didn't seem to mind the change in routine, and she couldn't bring herself to feel guilty about it, either. Eventually, Amanah drifted to sleep with Taunos's hand absently rubbing circles on her back.

She jolted awake sometime later when Taunos tensed and sat up, eyes scanning the darkness. Gurseh was a few paces away, and her head was still pillowed on Taunos's leg. She eased up to sit, blinking.

"Your turn for watch, Taunos," Gurseh said, walking to his blankets to lay down.

She yawned, stretching stiff muscles, and looked at Taunos. He'd clearly been sleeping with his head against his pack as a pillow. Someone must have handed that to him.

"Why didn't you move to your bedroll to sleep?" she asked. "Aren't you stiff and sore now?"

"I'm fine. And you seemed comfortable at last, so I was happy to stay."

Heat rose to her cheeks. "Thank you."

He trailed his fingers down her arm. "How are you feeling now?"

Vulnerable. Embarrassed. Like she wanted to do the whole thing again but maybe without the cramps this time.

"Better," she settled on. "Are you going to take your nightly walk around?"

He nodded. "I can keep watch if you need to use the latrine first."

She smiled and kissed him briefly, then hurried away. Somehow, he could make everything seem like it'd be alright, even when unknown potential bandits were following them and the nobles were beating on him. Somehow, still, the troubles seemed a little lighter with him around, sharing the weight of them.

13

THE FIGURES WHO'D been following them grew closer and closer over the next several days. They never came near enough to see distinguishing features, and they never responded to any attempts to communicate. Even Inuwe and Lamyi became jumpy.

So when the day dawned and no riders appeared, Amanah shivered. That couldn't be a good thing.

They continued pushing on hard toward Gahimbli—with any luck, they'd arrive in a handful of days. As the morning wore on, the tension lessened into a vague strain weighing on her shoulders, one she tried to distract herself from by checking their pace and heading. There was nothing she could do about the riders, after all.

If their map was correct and they made good time, they could camp near a small lake tonight. The time of year was right to see miyo swarming, and the little insects would fascinate Taunos. She couldn't wait to see his face light up when seeing the shapes the swarm would create and hearing the music of their wings.

Even with everything going on—or maybe because of it all—she looked forward to the little moments with Taunos. In between spending evenings together laughing, they'd alternate with Emin and Gurseh in scouting around the camp, never leaving it unattended. And while they scouted, they would talk—and kiss. There was a way about him, an ease of being that he could craft when he wanted that she found herself appreciating more and more. Though they tried to be discreet while the nobles were in sight, she still often found him turned slightly toward her, as she found herself orienting toward him.

The other night, after she'd relieved Taunos on watch, she'd perched on a rock, worrying about what Lamyi would do to them when they got to Gahimbli, trying to think if there was anything she could do to prepare. She'd been winding herself up like one of the trinkets sold in the Arruk marketplace, all in vain, of course. Instead of going back to sleep, Taunos had sat by her feet and talked with her, one hand stroking her calf in long, soothing motions, and her futile worries had faded.

He'd been useless at the actual planning, of course. Every other suggestion he'd made had been something along the lines of "and then we see what happens." Some of those times, she'd sworn his eyes glimmered with mischief, as if he was teasing her. But his presence, the way he listened, it helped her sort out her own thoughts and form an outline of a plan as she spoke to him. And even more, his easy confidence that she would get through it all, and his resolution to be there with her, soothed her.

He'd eventually fallen asleep there, his head propped against her knee and his hand resting on her boot. It'd barely been sleep—more like a doze than anything—and she'd finally shooed him back to his bedroll a little before the end of her shift. But it made her heart swell, that little show of trust and affection, and how he so willingly gave up rest and comfort for her.

"Amanah!"

She snapped back to focus. Emin rode beside her, shaking his head.

"What?" she asked.

"I need your attention during the day, at least," Emin said, serious for once.

Her face and neck heated, blazing like the sun, she was sure. Then, anxiety washed over her in a cold wave. "Wait, was it that obvious? Have the nobles noticed?"

"No, you're safe. They're too busy pretending we're insects, and I only noticed because I know you."

She sagged a little in relief.

"But talking about my sister kissing one of my best friends is not why I called your name. Twice."

"You are so embarrassing."

He grinned, thoroughly unapologetic. "You were the one daydreaming about whatever instead of attending your work. That makes us even."

"All right, war-band leader." Amanah straightened. "What did you need?"

He wasn't actually leader of a war-band yet, but he'd get there—she had no doubt of it.

Emin puffed himself up, his voice serious again. "Check the horizon for me."

The land around them stretched flat, with dry, gold grasses stretching up amongst sparse, red shrubs as tall as the horses' knees. No riders still—at least, not that she could see. But the sky was hazy in the west, and Amanah rose, standing in her saddle as Nakii continued walking. Far ahead, the haze stretched down to the sandy ground.

"Windstorm," she breathed.

"That's what I thought," Emin said grimly. "We'll have to stop, but there's no cover for the horses."

"We can picket them on the lee side of the noble's tent and wrap their eyes. Then hope for the best." Too bad the tent wasn't big enough to keep the animals inside. Not that the nobles would allow it anyway.

"I'm not sure even Taunos can argue us into the tent," Emin said. "The nobles don't look on him anywhere near so kindly anymore. I don't think they expected him to defend us. Or to look at you the way he does."

"Embarrassing," she said, dropping back into the saddle and kicking his calf. "You're sure they—"

"I'm just teasing, Amanah!" Emin said. "Back to the windstorm, please."

She nodded, keeping one eye on the storm to track its speed while keeping her tone light for her brother. His favorite strategy to deal with danger was to distract himself and others with banter.

"Well, you don't have to worry about where we'll shelter," she said. "I, being the practical one—"

He snorted.

"—brought us a tarp, remember?"

"Good. I'll call a stop, and we can secure shelter before the storm hits."

She frowned, glancing at the sky. Still mid-morning. "It's moving fast —I'm betting it hits a little after midday. We'll have to bury the leading edge to avoid the tarp lifting."

"It'll be better than nothing." Emin turned away, nudging his horse to catch up to the head of the group, shouting for a halt. He paused by Taunos, dipping his head close to explain the situation.

Amanah collected the reins while Emin and Gurseh grabbed shovels. Taunos turned to the nobles.

"We need to stop and make shelter for that storm that's heading this way," Taunos said.

"That storm's still pretty far—we can keep going," Lamyi said. "Don't you want to get to Gahimbli before the rain of the gods? Actually, no, it doesn't matter what you want, and it doesn't matter that you've somehow got Lord Ifel's favor, Haari Taunos. He'll soon know how you let these people run all over you. Until then, you still do as we say. We don't have time to stop."

Amanah began unloading the pack animals, keeping her back to Lamyi as he ranted.

"Now, get back on those horses—stop it, what are you doing? Load them back up, now!"

She kept working. Her fingers were steady—she was nervous, yes, but not expecting an attack. Because Taunos was at her back, dealing with the situation. It was nice to trust someone besides her brother for the important things again. She'd almost forgotten how it felt.

And if Lamyi dared do anything to Taunos out here in the open, she'd rain down Jattanu's justice on him.

Taunos's voice continued behind her as he explained the dangers of windstorms in the barren landscape. Clearly, he'd been listening the times she and Emin had spoken of this possibility. Warmth spread in her chest.

"There's no way there's time for them to dig us shelter," Inuwe said. "Wouldn't it be wiser to continue on in hopes of finding a better place to wait out the storm?"

"Can you see any shelter?" Taunos swept his hand, indicating the flat land around them.

Heaving the bags onto the ground, she picketed the horses on short lines, and then glanced behind her. Inuwe was watching Emin and Gurseh dig, frowning with concern, while Lamyi argued with Taunos, poking his shoulder for emphasis, as if the spittle wasn't enough. How could Taunos be so calm in the face of all that? Maybe it was another type of combat: verbal instead of physical.

"Amanah, bring the tent over, will you?" Emin called. "I don't want this row to be too long. How big's the tarp?"

Giving the nobles and Taunos a wide berth, she spread the tarp and tent out. Gurseh marked the opposite end from Emin, lifting a shovel's worth of dirt from the ground, and began digging in a line toward Emin. They'd probably only get half a pace into the ground, if they were lucky, before the storm was on them, but at least the stakes could be driven in below the ground's surface, and lining the windward edge of the tarp and tent with packs would provide a little shelter from any debris that the storm might throw at them.

"We'll get as much done as we can, and more if you stop yelling. You can help by putting up your tent," Taunos said.

"It's not going to work. This is what happens when you have uneducated people thinking they're in charge." Lamyi scoffed.

"Are you an expert on these plains and the weather patterns here?" Taunos asked.

"Well, no," he admitted, "but there's no way your people can dig fast enough to shelter us fully."

"He's right," Gurseh told Amanah, breathing heavily as he stepped on the shovel and scooped up another shovelful of dirt. "And their tent, in the wind, it'll likely collapse, if it doesn't fly away."

"It probably needs to be collapsed from the start," she realized, biting her lip. "They'll have to lay on the ground like us, as if the tent is the tarp. And there'll be no shelter for the horses."

"Oh, they're going to love that," Gurseh said.

If only they had more than two shovels! She should have bought more. Amanah turned to Taunos and the nobles with a sigh, and went to deliver the bad news.

"They're doing everything they can to keep you safe. I'm not hearing any solutions, only complaints," Taunos was saying as she stepped up beside him.

"Speaking of," Amanah said, "I'm afraid we won't be able to set up your tent fully."

"Excuse me?" Lamyi asked. "That should be your highest priority."

"No, her priority is getting you safely to Gahimbli," Taunos said. "So I'd listen. What's the problem, Amanah?"

His deep brown eyes, softening when they met hers, sent a thrill through her, but she pushed it away, also ignoring the little curl at the edge of his mouth that told her he was suppressing a smile. "The tent, fully set up, will catch the wind. Like a sail on a boat."

Lamyi watched her with suspicion.

Amanah kept her gaze on Taunos's. "I have a tarp for us to lay underneath, and we should be able to dig deep enough to protect the leading edge of both shelters, anchoring them beneath the grass, but that's it. These fine lords will need to lay down to wait out the storm, just like us."

"Would you like to wait in the tent with us?" Lamyi asked.

Amanah blinked, her breath catching. Was he asking in earnest, or was this another trap? They had enough to worry about without that uncertainty. "Thank you, but I doubt the tent is big enough for all of us."

His lip curled at her. Offense at his offer being rejected, or annoyance at not being able to trick her in some way?

It didn't matter. There was work to do, and she needed to get back to it. "You should grab any valuables you can't part with and bring them in with you. Place your packs of sturdier things on the windward edge to provide extra protection from debris, just in case."

Amanah turned away, but Taunos followed her, his fingers catching hers briefly. "What about the horses?"

She bit her lip. "We'll have to hope Murihat has mercy. I'll wrap cloth over their eyes, but they won't have the shield of the tent. Of course, they also won't have the tent possibly bludgeoning them, either."

"I'll see if Emin or Gurseh want a break. I feel like shoveling right now. Is the tarp going to be enough?" he asked, eyeing it as they walked back to the others.

"We'll have a little protection, at least. It's not a lot, but the tarp's big enough to fit all of us, barely."

Taunos grimaced. "I'll stay with Lamyi and Inuwe, just in case. Communications will be cut off. Gurseh, Emin, either of you want a break?"

Emin tossed his shovel at Taunos, who caught it and immediately drove into the ground with a grunt.

"Will you be all right in there?" Amanah asked him.

"I'll be fine," Taunos said, driving the shovel into the ground again.

Emin stretched his back, then leaned down to whisper to Amanah, "He's claustrophobic."

"Taunos?" she whispered.

Her brother nodded.

Amanah frowned. That was a wrinkle they didn't have time to work around right now.

Still, she nodded as if Emin hadn't said anything—she'd keep his secret against anyone looking for a point of weakness to poke. "It'll be good to have someone with the nobles just to make sure they're safe."

"We'll need a rope for communication between the tarp and tent," Emin said. "Haari Taunos, you're about to be tested on how well you've learned the tapping language."

Keeping most of her weight off her healing leg, Amanah took the shovel from Gurseh so he could take a break. At least she'd been able to remove her stitches yesterday, though she still needed to be careful, or she'd aggravate the healing wound. She eyed the horizon. The storm was coming far too quickly.

While they traded off shoveling at a frantic pace, and the nobles griped and argued between themselves, Amanah and Emin also took turns testing Taunos on the tapping language, focusing on the most important words for him to know in this situation. When Taunos was shoveling, Amanah or Emin would tap him a message and have him interpret it, and when he was resting, he'd tap messages out, proving he could send as well as receive. By the time the wind began to pick up, they had a deep groove along the windward edge long enough for both the tent and the tarp. Amanah had dug another channel between the shelters for the rope, just in case, and covered it with a flat piece of rock they'd hit while digging, stamping it firmly into the ground. The last thing they needed was the wind catching the rope and tearing it from their grasp. She frowned, pressing her boot against the rock a final time.

Wind whipping around them, Taunos leaned in close as Amanah stood. His breath warmed her ear as he murmured, "How do you say beautiful in the tapping language?"

Amanah fought to keep the heat from rising to her cheeks. "Flirt."

He grinned. "Oh, that's another vital word. Best teach that one to me, too."

Amanah took a quick look around, but Lamyi and Inuwe faced away from them, squabbling about one of their packs. She turned to the side and bumped Taunos with her hip, setting him off balance. He laughed, and she couldn't help but smile.

His shoulder brushed hers as he stepped back to her, his voice just loud enough to be heard over the wind. "You were worrying again."

She nodded. "There's nothing else we can do, but I don't know that this will be enough."

He tangled his fingers in hers, hidden by their bodies. "We'll be all right. We'll take things as they come. Just like this storm that's coming—it surprised us, but you still formed a plan."

"But we don't know if it's good enough yet."

His thumb rubbed circles on the back of her hand. "Every single surprise this trip, you've faced with a calm competence that takes my breath away. I wish you could see it. I wish I could give you a glimpse of what I see when I look at you. I, for one, have no worries about getting through this storm."

She snorted. "That's because you never worry about anything."

"Not true. I'm concerned about after, instead. The bandits that disappeared—where did they go, and why?"

"They're probably sheltering from the storm, too," she said.

"But they disappeared before we saw the storm. So what motivated that?"

A sigh escaped her. "Yet another thing to think about."

The little curl at the edge of his mouth told her he was suppressing a smile. "I'm thinking it's extremely difficult to keep from kissing you right now."

A laugh broke out of her, the sound covered by the roaring wind, but there was an answering light in his eyes. She shook her head. "Are you distracting me again?"

His gaze softened, sending a thrill through her. "Is it working? I can't help by wrapping you in a hug, so yes, distraction is my tactic."

How many times had one of his jokes, his smiles, his stories, lightened the weight on her shoulders, just for a little while? She'd found comfort in the sound of his voice time and time again, in the little ways he tried to offer her a respite, like the night she'd spent with her head pillowed on his leg, talking of sea-wizards.

She gave his fingers a squeeze. "Thank you."

He inclined his head just a little, then stepped back, his fingers sliding from hers. "Also, it's true."

"Don't you have somewhere else to be?" she asked, narrowing her eyes at him.

He grinned, full of mischief.

At last, Emin straightened. "That's it. Stakes are in. Grab the packs and make sure the leading edge is secure. Then get inside!"

Amanah hurried to wrap the horses' eyes in cloth as the others gathered the last of the packs into the shelters. By the time she was done, the wind whipped around her in such force, she could barely see, each gust snatching the breath right out of her mouth. She shielded her face with her weary arms as she lifted up the edge of the tarp and crawled in.

It was quieter inside, though by no means silent. The tarp flapped on the leeward edge as Gurseh settled the last of the packs on the corners. Even then, the wind roared outside like a beast, punctuated by the occasional impact of dust and small rocks hurtling along. She hunkered down low behind the packs on the windward edge.

"Here." Emin handed her the rope. "Taunos wanted to know if you got in safe."

She tapped out her reply, keeping her tugs slow and clear. Receiving messages was harder than sending them, at least in the beginning. "I'm here. You three safe?"

"Good. We're safe." The taps came back a little muddled but clear enough.

She let out a weary breath. Closing her eyes, she lay in the dirt, Emin pressed next to her with Gurseh beside him. The storm raged over their heads, the tarp fluttering along her back, but the rope was like a lifeline, as Taunos's occasional check-ins reassured her. She hoped the claustrophobia Emin mentioned wasn't affecting him too badly, that the storm would be over soon, that the horses would be okay.

Eventually, the roar of the wind faded. Gurseh snored on the other side of Emin. Her brother chuckled next to her, peeking out of the tarp.

"He's out like a child," he whispered.

She smiled at him in the dim light, then tugged the rope to check on Taunos. "You all safe?"

"Good. All safe. Can I see you?"

She sent an affirmative and glanced at Emin. "I'm going to check on Taunos and the horses."

He nodded. "I'll get things packed up here and wake Gurseh."

She slithered out of the tarp, grabbing her pack and her bow as she went, just in case.

Outside, the land was even more desolate than it had been that morning. By the sun, it was very early afternoon, and the haze of the storm was receding. A few of the scrubby bushes were gone, and in some places the grass laid flat, as if some enormous giant had laid down to sleep. The horses stood clumped together, tails flicking, but at least they seemed fine. The nobles were wrestling with their tent, checking on their supplies with snappish voices.

Wandering to the other side of the horses, Amanah dusted off her clothes and sneezed.

"Amanah." Taunos's voice was warm behind her.

She spun around to him. "How did it go? It was tight in there."

"Emin told you, huh? I've been working on it." He touched her cheek, his thumb brushing over her cheekbone. "It was helpful to know you were there."

She leaned into the touch. "We all have things we dislike."

He turned, stifling a yawn. "Sorry. I'm a little tired. It was a long night last night."

The nobles had been restless, and every time they'd stepped out of their tent, Taunos had woken. On impulse, she tangled her fingers in his. "You know, you're not travelling alone, now. I know the jolting awake you do is likely reflex, but I just want to say, we're watching your back. I am."

His smile made his eyes crinkle, his hand warm around hers. "I know. I need to learn more of that tapping language, for next time. Will you keep teaching me?"

"Of course."

He stood there, as if he was drinking her in, when she knew she must look as much a disheveled mess as he did. Goddess Tenah, he needed to stop looking at her like that. It made it hard to breathe, to think.

She reached out, brushing a dusty lock of his hair away from his face. Her fingertips lingered on his skin, trailing to his temple, and she smiled as he closed his eyes and tilted his head, leaning into her touch.

Nakii stamped a hoof.

Letting her hand drop away, Amanah reined herself back to the things that needed to be done. "I need to check the horses."

Taunos stepped back and stooped, straightening with a torn strip of cloth pinched between his fingers. It wasn't theirs—it must have been blown by the wind, but from where?

He scanned the horizon, that intense focus he sometimes had back in full force. "I'll make a circuit of camp."

"We can see any danger coming, and we'll be heading out soon, I assume." Amanah scanned the empty land.

"I'll be right back." He turned, jogging away. As she checked the horses and removed the cloths from their eyes, she kept glancing out toward him, catching his figure wading through the wind-blown grasses, moving sure and steady in a wide circle around them.

She'd just finished when a shrill whistle split the air. Taunos. She spun in his direction. He crouched a short ride away, facing away from her, the tall grass nearly swallowing his form. What had he found?

"Camp alert!" she bellowed, blowing her whistle in reply. She ran for the tarp and her weapons.

Taunos's whistle abruptly cut off, and it was like someone punched her in the gut. A crowd of figures rose from the flattened grasses, surrounding Taunos. In a blink, he took two of them down, but there were still five on their feet—far too many to fight alone.

Amanah snatched up her pack and her bow and quiver as Emin and Gurseh came barreling out from under the tarp.

"Taunos went scouting and found trouble. Five bandits still engaged, two down," she reported, stringing her bow and checking her arrows.

"You're supposed to ride if we encounter trouble," Emin argued.

"It's Taunos." She strung her bow. He tried so hard to keep them safe, and she'd just told him they'd watch his back. She couldn't go back on that, even though he could take care of himself.

"And you're the practical one," Emin said. "Don't make me be."

She shook her head, sprinting back to Nakii and leaping onto his back.

Emin ran after her. "Fine, but only because you're good with those arrows."

Amanah urged Nakii into a gallop as Emin swung astride his horse, bareback as well.

Her brother's voice chased her as he spoke to Gurseh. "Get the nobles ready to ride, just in case. Nothing that isn't necessary, but they'll need their horses—"

"I know, I know. I'll take care of it. Go!" Gurseh said.

It'd only been a few moments before she'd thundered off toward Taunos, but it still felt like far, far too long. Outnumbered, Taunos danced, whirling among the bandits like the wind itself. Powerful, yet beautiful. As she and Emin galloped toward them, Taunos twisted, avoiding a staff blow to the back, and yanked the weapon forward and out of the bandit's hands, striking another on the head. One of those previously down rose, and another lunged to stab Taunos. He grabbed his attacker's arm and threw him into another bandit, taking out both of them before turning to deal with a third.

It was like the sandcat all over again. Taunos fought with breathtaking speed and precision, keeping his opponents stumbling into each other so he could deal with them one at a time, just as he'd once taught Emin to do.

Emin's mount raced right alongside hers, and he gave her a stern look. "If I tell you to go, no arguing, understand? You go, you warn the camp, and then you ride for help."

Ignoring that, Amanah glanced at her brother, grabbing an arrow. She could even the odds as they approached.

Emin nodded, raising a fist.

Three of them against seven bandits. They could do this. No need for her to ride back.

Amanah gripped Nakii securely with her knees, nocking the arrow as they galloped toward the fight. A little longer. Taunos only needed to hold out a little longer.

Taunos dodged sideways to avoid an attack, but two others tackled him.

Amanah flattened her lips, nostrils flaring as she prayed to Tenah, goddess of women, war, and death. She added prayers to Murihat, deity of deception, mischief, and mercy—no doubt they'd be Taunos's favorite deity—as well, just to be on the safe side, and to Hayzanu for his luck.

The bandits rose, leaving Taunos with his hands bound behind him, a gag stuffed in his mouth. Taunos rolled to sit up, but one of the bandits stood on a rope trailing from his wrists, preventing him from standing.

And finally, Amanah was in range.

Letting her fear and fury ride her shoulders, she stood on Nakii's back, crouching to even out her aim. One arrow, two, three, four. Shouts of pain rose into the air, and then she and Emin crashed into the bandits, Emin's sword flashing. She dropped back down to sit astride and spun Nakii around. Taunos had thrown himself backward into his captor, but now the bandit held a knife to his throat.

Taunos's boot tapped, and she narrowed her eyes. Now was not the time to pretend impatience. The arrows she'd shot at his captor had missed, but she'd taken two other bandits down, and Emin had cut down a third. She kicked her gelding back toward the bandits as Emin battled a fourth.

Seeming unconcerned by the knife threatening his neck, Taunos tapped his boot again, his eyes flickering to it, drawing her attention. Her gaze caught on the odd rhythm of his foot. A message—he was tapping—

The man behind him punched him in the temple. Taunos crumpled to the side, the message interrupted. Amanah's breath caught in her lungs. She aimed for the bandit, but Taunos rolled, sprang to his feet, staggered, then re-engaged, even bound as he was. It was too chaotic to shoot—she was as likely to hit Taunos as she was the bandit—so Amanah turned her arrow on another bandit approaching Emin, just as Emin took down his opponent. She shot the sixth as Nakii reached the battle.

Emin made it to Taunos about the same time she did, driving his sword into the bandit's side and kicking him away. Amanah pulled Nakii to a stop, a new arrow nocked, and watched the wounded bandits for anything resembling a renewed fight, while Emin helped Taunos to his feet and cut his bonds.

Taunos tore the gag from his mouth, blood trickling down the side of his face. "The nobles. This was to draw us away from the nobles."

Her chest tightened with dread. Of course—and she'd fallen right into the trap.

Jaw clenched, Emin grabbed Taunos's arm and hauled him onto his horse behind him. Taunos pointed to the ground here and there, places where the grass looked like it had been pulled back. The bandits had prepared this, forming shelters for themselves, camouflaged places they could wait and pounce from. How many bandits had watched them thunder by to rescue Taunos and then raced for the camp now guarded only by Gurseh? She avoided Emin's gaze, knowing he'd been right. She'd let fear overtake her sense. Guilt dug its claws deep into her.

Emin turned his horse to block hers. She glared at him.

"I know," she said before he could speak.

He blew out his breath. "No, you don't. I want you to ride a circle. Taunos and I will go in first, the triumphant return. You make sure there are no other surprises, then come back quietly to back us up."

She blinked. "Not ride for help?"

"If we're overwhelmed, yes, ride for help," he said.

"I don't think there are that many," Taunos said. "But they mentioned a sea-wizard."

She went cold. What could she do against a sea-wizard? What could any of them do? They didn't have magic.

"That's why I want your arrows," Emin said. "If someone's going to shoot at me, I want it to be you. That way, I know if I get hit, it was on purpose."

She snorted at his boast on her behalf, which was, of course, exactly the effect he wanted.

"Be careful," he said.

She shoved down the way her heart hammered against her ribs, forcing even breaths. "You be careful. If I have to patch up either of you, I'll make sure it hurts."

Of course it wasn't true, but it was hard to let them go do what they did so well while she was backup, even if it made sense.

Taunos smiled, all warmth and sunshine and easy confidence, and they were off, Taunos's grin becoming a grimace as he clutched for a hold on Emin's back as the horse surged forward.

How could the two of them set her heart at ease and also be a source of terror for the danger they'd be in? They were both so vibrant, so *alive*, and all she wanted was to keep them that way. Both of them.

But she had her own part to play, so she pushed away her emotions to focus on the task at hand.

Amanah urged Nakii into a gallop, riding in a long, sweeping arc as she scanned the ground for any more camouflaged hiding places, now that she knew what to look for. But she couldn't help but keep glancing at the flattened camp, especially as Taunos and Emin simply disappeared.

They disappeared.

Her heart hammered again, her breath stolen in ragged gasps. She should be able to see them, because nothing was in the way. The tent and tarp lay flat on the ground. But between one step and the next, they were stolen from her.

And yet she couldn't guarantee that while she couldn't see them, anyone else hidden wouldn't still be able to see her. She had to assume they could, that she couldn't sneak up on camp.

She swore. This was far too well set up. At least she had her bow and her pack with some supplies.

Tears sparked in her eyes as she finished her arc, then kicked Nakii into a gallop. They thundered toward Gahimbli, toward the last cliffs before the open plain of the city. Hopefully she didn't have to ride all the way there. Hopefully, she'd find help somewhere between.

14

AMANAH PUSHED NAKII as hard as she could without ruining him. She didn't know what the bandits wanted or what their sea-wizard could do— beyond apparently making people disappear. But she did know that if Emin and Taunos could fight their way through, they'd sound the whistle when all was clear, calling her back.

The sky darkened. No whistle had sounded, and she was far out of range now.

Focusing her thoughts only on her task, Amanah boxed up her worry, fear, and rage, and packed them away. She couldn't help the little tremor in her hands as she stopped to water herself and her gelding.

Ahunah, goddess of vengeance, would have nothing on her if she came back and they were …

No, she wouldn't even think it. They might be injured, but she could fix that. Maybe they'd be completely fine. Taunos did impossible things all the time, and Emin was always trying to one-up him. Between those two and Gurseh, no doubt the bandits were having massive regrets right now. She bared her teeth in some semblance of a smile. The bandits deserved every headache coming their way.

Except no whistle had sounded while she was in earshot.

She kept Nakii moving, alternately walking and trotting, through the rest of the day. She couldn't stay still, even when she finally needed to let Nakii rest. Even though she knew she should try to sleep. Amanah fed Nakii, fed herself, chewed and swallowed without tasting. She groomed the dust from her horse's coat, because it needed to be done. And then, there was nothing. Nothing but fidgeting under the weight of her worries.

Taunos's absence hit her keenly as the sun set, like a hole opening under her feet. Now that they were courting, he loved to touch her—just little things, like brushing his hand against hers when they exchanged items, or how he'd lounge, leaning back on his arms, shoulder to shoulder with her. When the nobles couldn't see, he often slung an arm around her shoulders or around her waist, and the clear enjoyment he got from her touching him in return was endearing—the way he leaned in and closed his eyes. She'd gotten used to it, had begun to relax in that casual contact as well as the sound of him, the way his voice took on a sort of measured cadence when he told stories that Emin and Gurseh teased him for. Just thinking of him calmed the wild thunder of her heart.

Being with him felt like coming home, his confidence and humor buffeting back the winds of her worries, sheltering her from them so she could rest until she had time to figure out the best course of action, then tackle the challenges refreshed and ready. He celebrated her for who she was, not for who he wished her to be.

The night seemed so much colder now, a gaping hole instead of the laughter around the fire to keep back the dark. She shivered and clenched her fists. In order to get that back, she had to leave them behind. In order to bring back help, she had to let Nakii rest. But it was impossible to sit still when tension hummed through her bones with the need to fix this.

Despair rose like a storm within her, the terror driven by the fear that she couldn't fix this. What if they were already dead? After all, why keep competent fighters as prisoners when you could kill them and remove the danger? There were no warm arms to wrap her up and ground her this time.

When she could no longer stand to wait, she clucked Nakii back to his feet. She led him along, walking him, and trying not to think about the way Taunos had carried her, how he possibly could match the horses for stamina, how he disliked riding. How Emin had looked after climbing up from the landslide, how cold and exhausted he'd been in the Lenuri camp, his grin of pride tinged with a hint of jealousy when he brought back the sandcat they'd killed. Between the two of them, they'd revived her hope— the belief that dreams were important and could be made real. It felt like she was living again. She wouldn't stop now, even if all she had going up against bandits and a sea-wizard were dreams and a wish for a plan.

Amanah swung back on Nakii and prodded him into a trot, but she couldn't leave her worries behind. All she could do was tamp her fears down tight and lock them away while she focused on the tasks she needed to complete. Later, she'd have time to unleash them. No doubt Emin and

Taunos were trading terrible jokes and Gurseh was rolling his eyes at them, pretending he wasn't amused.

No doubt.

The sides of a canyon rose before her, with caves dotting the cliff walls on either side, visible in the rising dawn. Hopefully, one of the caves was being used for shelter by a nomadic clan. Unless the caves were empty or sheltering bandits. A nomadic clan would be more likely to help than anyone in Gahimbli, and this would be faster than having to ride all the way to the city. She didn't know how long Emin, Taunos, and Gurseh had. The risk was worth it for them.

By early morning, Amanah made it to the base of the southern cliff wall. She left Nakii there with a quiet pat and his breakfast, and then, adjusting her pack on her back, began to climb.

Pulling from Emin and Taunos's brash courage, she shoved away her doubts. She hadn't planned for a bandit attack so tricky as this one had been, but next time she'd make certain to. Because there had to be a next time. Because they would get out of this, and Emin or Taunos would make trouble again in the future.

Amanah pulled out her whistle and blew hard, pitching it as low as it could go to carry farther in the curves of the canyon. She waited, pacing along the edge, then blew again. Turning to her pack, she opened it and withdrew the correct banners, as wide as her forearm and as tall as she was, dyed brilliant colors, just in case a nomadic clan heard her call. She blew the whistle one more time. If no one answered, she'd move on—she could simply carry the necessary banners. Maybe farther into the canyon...

The low hum of a horn answered her.

Eager anticipation gripped her. There, across the canyon, a woman stood, banners spilling out from her hands. Amanah's breath gusted out in relief, hope rising in her.

She began the dance, colors and pattern carrying the meaning across the distance. Red for danger, snapping the banners back in the direction she'd fled from, blue swirling among them for magic. Yellow for help, white for injury, twisted in the pattern for uncertainty. She repeated the patterns, and then stopped, turning back toward the other woman.

The stranger spun, indicating acceptance of the message, and then copied it out. Amanah spun her banners in return, indicating the message was correct.

The stranger's next banners signaled her to wait.

Amanah bit her lip. She couldn't just sit there. She needed help, either to bring back with her immediately, or to continue on in search of it. She replied with a flurry of banners, indicating her need to continue on soon, asking if she could speak with them face to face.

But the reply was adamant. Wait.

Frustration and desperation welled in her, and she sent up the flurry of banners for identification, indicating her clan as Kanhu and sending out the flutter pattern for her family. After all, her father's name had granted them shelter with the Lenuri in their caves. She wasn't above using her family to bring help back with her more quickly.

The answer identified the other banner dancer as from the Mahyami clan, and once again hope flared. Please, please, let her father's trade with the Mahyami tip this over the edge!

But then the banners fluttered, the same signal as before: Wait.

She hated that word, that fall of the fabric.

Grumbling to herself, she watched the other woman climb down, disappearing among the crags. But there was nothing to do. No embrace to support her. No jokes to distract her. She was alone.

No, she wouldn't let the terror or despair win. Steeling her heart, Amanah grabbed her pack and climbed down as well, to wait by Nakii.

It occurred to her after she drank and ate some nuts that she was doing just what the nobles did, using their family names and connections to open doors—or trying. It didn't work for her in Arruk, but here she had a chance.

But that meant she'd been right, that maybe she could do this in the city with Taunos's contacts, finding the doors that would open. It wasn't that she didn't know how to play the game—it was that the rules changed in the city. But she could find people who would play by rules she could play by, too.

She'd fallen into a restless doze when Nakii's snort and the stamp of his hoof woke her. She jolted to her feet so fast her name might have been Haari Taunos. In front of her stood fifteen strangers, all arrayed with weapons and supplies, leading horses.

"We are ready," the man in the lead said. "My name is Hemne, of the Mahyami. We ride to aid you."

She blinked, and then relief loosened her shoulders. "Thank you!"

"My daughter said you did not know how many enemies, only that there was possibly a sea-wizard?" the man asked.

Amanah nodded. "I'll tell you everything I know on the way."

They rode hard. Now that Amanah knew their destination was less than a day away, there was less danger of ruining the horses by pushing too hard for too long. As they rode, she told them of the storm and the bandits and the trap, how they had two nobles with them, how Emin and Taunos and Gurseh were competent fighters. How she had been assigned to ride for help if needed.

"It was a wise decision," Hemne said. "I have with me my cousin's son, our fastest rider. His job will be the same—to ride for help if we need it."

She inclined her head, accepting the words, but they didn't relieve the pit in her stomach.

"Do you know of this bandit group? Have you encountered them?"

Hemne shook his head. "I do not know of bandits who run with sea-wizards—not in this area. And I've heard of no one who can perform this vanishing magic you speak of. This is troubling news, and we intend to investigate as we aid you."

It wasn't long, and yet, it was far too long, before the land looked familiar. She slowed them, frowning, uncertain if she'd missed the place or if the entire camp had disappeared like Emin and Taunos had.

"It should be here, or near here. It's hard to tell, with the land all looking so similar, but we should have ridden far enough now," Amanah told Hemne.

She dropped down from Nakii, wading through the waist-high grasses, looking for signs of camp.

"Blood here," one of the Mahyami said.

Amanah jogged over, and let out a breath. She recognized these trampled, bloodstained grasses. "Taunos fought the bandits here. That means camp is just over here."

Except no one was there. All they found were trampled grasses, the tarp, and the nobles' empty tent, flattened in the dirt. No bandits or sea-wizards attacked them, nor were there any sign of hostages. Where were they? Her stomach twisted, and bile rose. It felt like a cold fist was squeezing her heart.

"They might not even be alive anymore. It's been an entire day," she whispered.

Hemne flicked his eyes at her. "Words of doubt. If they have fallen, embrace Ahunah and bring down vengeance on them. If they have not, show them Jattanu's justice."

She shivered, her stomach knotting, the crack of a whip in her memory.

Hemne frowned. "Jattanu's *real* justice, not whatever they call justice in the city. Besides, there are no bodies here."

Pushing aside her worries and vile memories once more, Amanah nodded. No bodies. That was a good thing, right? Although, they could be suffering, instead. She shoved that thought aside—it was not helpful.

There were tasks to do, to focus on instead.

"We need to track them. Surely they'll have left behind some sign," Amanah said.

Hemne nodded, and the Mahyami fanned out, alternating between scanning the grasses and the horizon—alert for more danger, but still looking for any clues. Before too long, a shout went up, and Amanah hurried to the scout who held up a braided and knotted cord—Taunos's handiwork. She recognized it as something he'd been working on whenever his hands needed something to do.

"Taunos," she breathed.

"They must be going this way. Keep alert for any more signs," Hemne said.

It was away from Gahimbli, and a chill ran down her back. The bandits had removed the nobles' guards from them, and now they were moving out of their way. Was this all to keep the nobles from their destination? Was it bandits, or were there Hinanuri forces, political forces, at work here?

They travelled slowly at first, but as they found more signs—a piece of Emin's shirt, a torn off strip of bandage, a bootlace—they increased their speed. As evening descended, a tent appeared in the distance on the desolate plain. It was much larger than the nobles' tent had been, a simple rectangle with a central pole.

"Attack at night?" Amanah asked Hemne. She did not want to wait long, but Nannil's blanket would help disguise their approach.

He nodded.

The Mahyami stationed their emergency rider well away, within hearing of a whistle, but not so close as to be anywhere near danger, and then Hemne sent scouts in either direction in a wide sweep around the camp. It looked deserted.

Amanah fidgeted.

She checked her bow, her arrows. She fed and watered Nakii and forced herself to eat and drink. The scouts returned, indicating all was clear, and they split into three groups—archers in the middle and two flanking groups with swords. Since none of them knew if the vanishing magic was still working, Hemne decided to err on the side of caution: assuming that fighters were ready for them and could see them coming.

And at last, the blanket of night covered them. It was time for action.

Once more, Amanah thundered forward, this time with several others riding beside her. She nocked an arrow, crouching on Nakii's back. Two bandits sprang up from the grass, whistles blowing, arrows drawn. She ducked low as an arrow flew by, narrowly missing her.

She shot one bandit in the heart, and the other dropped too, an arrow in his throat from one of the other archers. Amanah gave her ally a grim smile and set another arrow to her string.

"Attack!" Hemne shouted. Their surprise was gone—now it came down to speed.

Amanah headed for the tent. Hopefully that's where they were keeping prisoners. Taunos and Emin would surely be making a scene if they could.

Bandits emerged from the tent and engaged the Mahyami. She shot another before a third bandit pulled her off Nakii. She rolled into one of the tent poles, sending the structure shuddering. Dropping her pack, she leapt to her feet, dodging under the bandit's knife swipe, and burying her knife in the other woman's stomach. Sounds of clashes filled the air—grunts of effort, the ring of metal on metal, shouts, screams. Everyone around her was currently occupied. Amanah headed for the back of the tent to avoid the fighting in the front.

Flattening herself on her side, she carefully lifted the flap of fabric. Two guards charged out the front flap, and three more stood guard inside. Emin, Taunos, and Gurseh sat huddled together by the wall, Taunos slumped awkwardly between Gurseh and Emin. Blood crusted the side of his face still, but his eyes were open, and Emin and Gurseh looked well enough, though all three were tied with thick ropes at wrists and ankles. The nobles sat by the opposite wall, Inuwe shivering with fright next to Lamyi, who sat rigidly, half in front of him as if to shield him. The nobles, at least, were not tied.

Taunos's eyes caught hers, and he elbowed Emin, whose expression filled with satisfaction when he looked her way. Emin quickly let his gaze skim idly along the walls, no doubt to avoid drawing notice to her.

She tapped the ground, hoping Taunos, who was still watching her, could see the pattern. "Sea-wizard—which one?"

His eyes darted to the central bandit.

Amanah confirmed, and Taunos inclined his head just barely. Emin shifted his weight, coiling like a sandcat about to spring, and Gurseh rolled his shoulders.

Laying on the ground, half inside the tent with her bow arm holding up the fabric of the tent, Amanah took aim, and shot. The arrow slammed into the sea-wizard's back, and she rolled inside. Shouts of alarm rang out from the other guards. Coming to her feet, she buried a second arrow in the sea-wizard's chest as he whirled around.

A bandit swordsman lunged at her from the right. She blocked the strike with her bow, wincing, and then snapped it out to smack the bandit in the face. She reached for her knife, but her fingers froze, her arms failing to follow her directions. She couldn't dodge. She couldn't even suck in a breath. Her eyes darted to the sea-wizard, but he lay on the ground, unseeing eyes staring at the ceiling. Had she killed the wrong person? The bandit recovered and advanced at his leisure, sword glinting in the lantern light.

Like a spring being unleashed, Taunos tackled the third guard, who Emin disarmed and stabbed in the chest. She suddenly could move again and sagged to her knees, only to be forced to dive to the side to avoid a sword strike from the guard she'd been fighting before the strange paralysis. Gurseh snatched a knife from the guard and began sawing on the thick rope binding his feet.

The two guards who'd just exited the tent dashed back in, and the tent became chaos. As one of their captors went for Gurseh, Emin covered him, using Gurseh's shoulder to steady himself when his bound feet caused him to wobble. Also still bound, Taunos hopped nearby with uncanny balance, engaging them both himself despite his bindings, giving Gurseh time to saw through the ropes around his hands.

Amanah placed herself between the nobles and the sword-wielding bandit, dropping her bow in favor of her knife. Gurseh got free and began working on the thick rope binding Emin's feet. At the same time, Emin blocked a sword strike from another bandit with a borrowed sword, wobbling precariously. But Amanah's bandit closed in, and then it was all footwork and blocks and strikes, blades flashing in the lamplight of the tent. She stumbled on something at one point and fell. Inuwe shouted. The bandit's foot struck her hard in the stomach, slamming the air out of her. She coughed, trying to force herself to move, to breathe. It wasn't fast enough. The bandit loomed over her.

"Amanah!" Emin's voice was filled with terror.

"Get away from her! Don't you touch her!" Taunos snarled, desperation in his voice.

But both of them were across the tent, fighting their own battles. Gurseh finally made it through the thick ropes around Emin's ankles as Emin slammed his sword into his opponent's, blocking the blade before it could hit Gurseh's back.

Metal flashed at the edge of her vision. The bandit's sword, swinging for her neck. She twisted away just enough to take the cut on her shoulder, instead, as she rolled into him, slicing the back of his ankle with her own blade. Pain bit into her shoulder, down her arm, and she lost her grip on her knife.

Still bound, Taunos jumped up and kicked his opponent in the chin, flipping neatly around to land as she dropped. He lunged toward her, apparently heedless of leaving an enemy at his back, landing, rolling, and leaping again to smash into Amanah's attacker.

The bandit he'd been fighting chased after him, of course. Gripping her knife in her off-hand, Amanah whirled around, slamming the blade into the gut of the second bandit. She wrenched it free as he fell half onto the nobles, and then disarmed him.

The nobles kicked out wildly, Inuwe shouting with terror. Amanah staggered back from them, out of range. She turned, scanning for more trouble, but Emin and Gurseh had taken care of the remaining bandits in the tent.

Shoulders heaving, Taunos grabbed the bandit he'd fought and shoved him off the nobles with a grunt. "My lords."

Emin caught the wounded bandit and Gurseh bound him, hauling him out of the tent. Taunos slumped to the ground and snatched up a knife, finally able to work on the ropes binding him.

Amanah sucked in a deep breath. The first part was done—the one she'd worried most about. All three of the men were free, and none of them had been seriously injured. All the terror she'd been pushing back crashed down on her like a storm. She fought it back, pressing her hand against her shoulder, which was agony. She needed to see how the fighting was going outside.

One of the Mahyami spun toward her as she ducked out of the entrance, and she held up her hands, hissing as her shoulder protested. The woman halted, lowering her weapons.

"We have the tent secure," Amanah said.

The woman grinned. "And we have the ground secured. Well done."

"It couldn't have been done without your help," Amanah said, inclining her head in respect. "We'll bring the bandits out."

Emin shoved out of the tent, dragging a dead bandit by the foot in either hand. "Already ahead of you. Hello! Nice weather, isn't it?"

"Amanah." Taunos's voice sounded behind her, husky and strained with worry. His arms came around her waist, and he whirled her to the side of the tent. He inspected her shoulder critically, then stepped back, his gaze raking over her more thoroughly.

"I'm alright. Just my shoulder," she said. Relief lit in his eyes and he tightened his hold around her, and she locked her arms around him in return. The nobles were still inside the tent, given the sound of their voices. And they were all safe.

Letting out a breath, he held her face in his hands and brushed his thumbs across her cheekbones. "I thought I was going to lose you there, for a moment. I couldn't get there fast enough."

"I have two hands, you know." She leaned her head against his, voice wry.

"I know, but—"

"And you left your back unguarded."

He gave her a slow smile. "You were there, beloved."

Heat flushed through her at the endearment. Trying to shrug it away, she nodded. "Besides, I couldn't help you either. Until you decided to pretend you were a boulder rolling downhill."

He huffed a laugh, resting his forehead against hers. "You are formidable. Absolutely amazing."

She curled her fingers around the back of his neck. "We're both all right. We made it. And I didn't need you to put yourself in danger like that."

"You never need me," he murmured, trailing kisses down her neck. His lilting voice was calmer now, warm, without rancor. "But I'm glad to be at your side anyway."

"Me too," she said. She drew back reluctantly, taking a look at him. "Injuries?"

He shrugged, "Nothing major. You need stitches though. Sit down and I'll get your pack."

"It's there, beside the tent," she said.

He nodded, and headed off, among the flurry of activity the camp had become. Gurseh remained in the tent, but Emin and the Mahyami made sure prisoners were secure and piled the bandit dead—including one more sea-wizard—outside of the camp. Some of the Mahyami muttered to themselves about so many sea-wizards, and she shuddered in agreement. There was no way to tell a sea-wizard apart from anyone else—just through the effects of magic, like in the tent when something had held her after she'd killed the first sea-wizard.

It wasn't long before Taunos returned, handing her a water pouch while he dug into her medical supplies and copied the steps from stitching her up after the sandcat. Just as then, he spoke as he worked, distracting her with questions about her journey and catching her up.

"Emin and I were knocked unconscious right away upon getting back to camp, but we weren't injured, thanks to Gurseh's quick thinking. He managed to convince our lovely hosts that we could be ransomed, so long as we remained somewhat unharmed. He's better at bluffing than I imagined. But when Emin and I came to, we were tied up along with Gurseh. All we could do was work together, trading off distracting the guards or dropping another piece of a trail for you."

"It was a good thing you did," Amanah said. "I'm not sure what would have happened otherwise. I was worried about you all, but I tried convincing myself you were all too annoying to be too badly hurt."

A chuckle shook his shoulders, and Amanah smiled, relaxing under his gaze despite the final stitches. He tied it off and wound a bandage around her shoulder, his calloused fingers brushing her skin.

"I was worried about you, too," he murmured before kissing her.

"Let me take a look at your head. You still have blood all over."

"Can you believe they didn't let us wash up?" Taunos asked lightly, allowing her to angle his face so she could wipe away the blood.

"It's a good thing your head's so hard," she said. "You said you were worried about me? I wasn't held hostage by, not one, but *three* sea-wizards. You really do have to overdo everything, don't you?"

"I didn't realize there were multiple sea-wizards until you took out the first," he said. "And you're the one who rode off who knew where, through who knew what, only to return with an entire band of fighters. It would have been much harder to escape if you hadn't come to our rescue."

"Ah, so that's why the worry. You feared hard work," she teased.

He laughed, but his arms tightened so much around her it was hard to breathe for a moment.

Assured he was, in fact, more or less unharmed, she ducked her head to press her face against his neck and shoulder, filling her lungs with his scent as if she'd never get enough, letting the warm solidity of him convince every dark shadowy corner of her mind that this was real, that they were all safe, that it had all worked out.

She kissed him, all the desperation and fear of the last days pouring out of her. He crushed her against him, his fingers trailing down her back and then around to trace along her ribs, as if to reassure himself that she was all in one piece. His warmth surrounded her, the sense of peace and safety he exuded easing the ragged edges of the remains of her shoved-aside panic.

When she drew back, she was breathless and yet at the same time, more grounded than she had been since the attack.

He rested his forehead against hers once more. "I'm so glad you're safe."

She ran her fingers up the back of his neck again, smiling as his eyes closed, his features softening in relaxation. "Me too."

Emin cleared his throat behind her, making her startle. He grinned. "Not to interrupt this touching reunion, but I'm interrupting this touching reunion."

She scoffed, teasing. "This is very important."

He stepped up beside her, gripping her arm, serious for a moment. "I knew I wanted you shooting the arrows."

"Oh, sorry, I forgot to miss," she said, just to hear his laughter. The sound of it rumbled against her as she tugged him down so she could hug him, too.

He squeezed her, then drew back, patting her cheek in rough affection. "Come on, you need to hear this, and our new Mahyami friends might as well be included."

Amanah nodded, stepping into the tent with Taunos just behind her. Leaving the tied-up captives with a guard and another Mahyami tending their wounded, the rest of their allies crowded inside with them. Lamyi and Inuwe sat on chairs in the newly cleared tent, Lamyi's lips pressed together in a flat line. Even with their presence, Amanah was loathe to let Taunos go lest he vanish again. Bad enough she couldn't keep hold of Emin, too.

But Taunos stiffened, gritting his teeth, and she abruptly remembered his claustrophobia. Seven Mahyami along with the rest of them filled the large tent rather full.

Positioning them near the door, she tacked open the tent flap, then looped an arm around Taunos's waist and rested her head against his. "This okay?"

"Better. Thank you." His murmured reply and his arm tightening briefly around her stoked the fire within, burning away her worries. "Are you ok with being seen like this?"

She tightened her hold on him. "Better than letting you disappear again."

Emin folded his arms across his barrel chest. "Lords Lamyi and Inuwe, are you going to share what we overheard, or shall I?"

"Which part would you like us to repeat?" Lamyi's tone was cold and aloof, though he gripped Inuwe's hand.

"How are our rescuers?" Inuwe asked, swallowing hard.

Hemne grinned with pride. "I brought fourteen with me, leaving one behind for a scout. I'm bringing fourteen home, only five of which will need the healers' attentions."

Some of Emin's tension eased. "Glad to hear it."

"I can help," Amanah offered.

Hemne inclined his head. "My thanks, but none of the wounds are serious. They can wait, and you can be on your way."

"An excellently planned rescue," Taunos said, his expression soft as he looked at her. "Not that I'm surprised."

She could drown in those eyes, especially after her fears of never seeing him look at her like this again. She smiled, warmth filling her. Of course she'd done well, but it was also surprisingly nice to have that acknowledged somewhat publicly. At least here, in a tent mostly filled with allies.

"Yes. Quite the planner." Lamyi's flat praise sent chills down her spine.

"I thought I was dead," Inuwe said, his knuckles white as he squeezed Lamyi's hand. "I thought we were all going to die. After this, I am never leaving Arruk again. But these people came to save us, and they don't even know us. You each have my gratitude."

"And mine," Lamyi said stiffly, almost as if the words hurt coming out.

"In that case, why don't you try sharing?" Taunos asked. "Why were we taken prisoner?"

Inuwe took a cup from a side table that had somehow survived the fight and gulped at whatever it contained. Drawing in a deep breath, Inuwe leveled his shoulders. "As you know, tensions with the Hinanuri might break into war in the coming months. Lamyi and I have evidence that at least one of the Gahimbli nobles is working with the Hinanuri."

Hemne's expression was dark, and he traded troubled glances with Amanah and Emin. "Many of my clan and others in the area have sought refuge in Gahimbli from Hinanuri raiding parties."

Amanah's stomach tightened. All those people heading for safety, and instead, what should be a refuge could turn into a battleground?

"This attack was meant to prevent us from reaching our destination and delivering our evidence," Inuwe said.

"We were being taken to a sea-wizard who could take the information directly from our minds," Lamyi said, wrapping his arm around Inuwe's shoulders. "Afterward, we probably would have been ransomed and our evidence destroyed, but no doubt we and our guards would have suffered a tragic accident along the way to safety."

"These bandits and the sea-wizards were working with the Hinanuri?" Hemne asked.

"It seems likely," Emin said.

"And the Gahimbli nobles are working with the Hinanuri?" Hemne rubbed his chin, his brow knitted.

"At least one of them is. Very likely most are not," Inuwe said.

"So this all comes back to war," Hemne said. "Tenah help us."

Amanah agreed with him. The extent of Hinanuri meddling felt like a betrayal. Her family regularly traded with families over the border, but politics seemed to drive them apart regardless of other ties. Hinanuri against Dahuti, and the Hinanuri were clearly already employing strategies to win. She threaded her fingers through Taunos's. His fingers squeezed hers, and she breathed a little easier.

Inuwe took a deep breath. "We will present our evidence during the Festival of Dark Nights. All the nobles will be in one place until the end of the festival, so we can gauge reactions and get everything out into the open at once. This is why we wanted the famous Haari Taunos, as well, for protection during the festival."

"This all will be over soon—just as long as we reach Gahimbli," Lamyi said, frowning. "Now, I hate to be rude, but we need to leave. If you could dispose of those who attacked us, I would be grateful."

"We must hurry to Gahimbli," Inuwe said.

"We're going to have to leave things behind to make good time," Lamyi muttered.

Inuwe glanced at Hemne, inclining his head. "I think what we leave will make a good payment for our rescuers, no?"

Amanah's eyes widened. Maybe nobles weren't all pompous fools who couldn't learn to save their hides. It missed the spirit of her exchange with Hemne, reducing the Mahyami to a band of mercenaries, but at least he thought to pay his debts.

Hemne smiled, bowing his head slightly.

As Lamyi and Inuwe began discussing what to leave and what to take, the rest of them filed out.

Amanah turned to Hemne, letting warmth infuse her voice. "Mahyami Hemne, thank you for coming to our rescue. You and your people came together on short notice for people who you did not know. I promise I will never forget this. If the time comes when you need help, I hope you will call on me."

"Kanhu Amanah, I'm happy that when next I see your family, I will be able to speak of your bravery, competence, and, yes, manners. And, of course, how we were able to come to your aid." His eyes twinkled with mirth.

She couldn't help a small chuckle. No doubt he would use this story to get a good deal in trade. Still, she was grateful, and her family would certainly be happy to oblige them. While the politics of the situation had taken her by surprise, she'd proven she was anything but small and powerless here in the wilderness.

They'd saved the nobles, and more importantly, Gurseh, Emin, and Taunos. She couldn't help feeling a little optimistic, coming off that. If she could think of interacting with nobles the way she did the Lenuri or Mahyami, using Taunos's name instead of her family's, what else might she accomplish?

"That's one way to get them to unload the pack animals," Emin said, slinging an arm over her good shoulder.

Amanah reached up and held his wrist. "Are you truly ok?"

"Yes, I promise. Unfortunately, we were all helpless as babes too quickly to be hurt much. Then the fight... Well, you saw that."

She let out her breath, looking over each of them. "I was so worried."

"You did your job," Emin said.

"I hated it every step." She grimaced.

He laughed. "Yes, but you did it anyway. Thank you, again. Now, please stop rescuing me for half a breath so my ego can recover, hmm?"

She wrinkled her nose at him. "Stop needing rescuing then."

Emin smiled, embracing her tightly, and then stepped back. He grabbed Gurseh's hand. "We're going to scout. You two stay here—we'll be travelling most of the night to hopefully beat trouble to Gahimbli."

He paused, as if remembering that Taunos was supposed to at least appear as though he was in charge, and grinned. "Right, boss?"

Taunos snorted and waved him away. "I believe you have very important scouting to do."

Before long, they'd packed the horses, leaving a pile of nonessential items the nobles agreed to part with. As they rode out, escorting the nobles toward Gahimbli while the Mahyami picked through the leftover supplies, Hemne raised a hand in farewell, and Amanah answered likewise.

15

"WE SHOULD REACH Gahimbli the day after tomorrow," Amanah said, staring into the fire. Taunos was scouting, and Emin had handed her a plate of sandcat steak and beans that she hadn't touched. Her stomach churned too much to consider eating.

Inuwe remained himself—out of touch, a little aloof, but polite—but Lamyi had been bearable in the last couple days since they parted with the Mahyami. That seeming change of heart made her chest clench, and she wondered where the trap was. It'd close around them in Gahimbli, she was sure of that, but what form would that take, and how could they combat it?

"Don't look so glum," Emin said, kicking her boot lightly.

She scowled at him, but as she opened her mouth, he chided her. "There's nothing we can do about any surprises now. Why let it ruin your night?"

"I'm hardly *letting* it," she said.

"Amanah!" Taunos skidded down the hillside into camp, sending up a flurry of dust. As Emin waved it away from his face, Taunos gave him an apologetic glance before seizing Amanah's hand.

"What?"

"Come on, I have to show you something." She tensed, and he grinned. "Nothing bad."

"But... food..." She looked back at her untouched plate.

He narrowed his eyes. "Were you going to eat it?"

"Eventually."

"Well then, I can fill in the meantime. I need your opinion on something I found. You'll like it, I promise. Come on!"

Emin laughed. "Get out of here Amanah, before he completely reverts to a child."

"So then I'd be on your level?" Taunos asked.

Amanah couldn't help but smile at them, letting Taunos lead her out of the circle of firelight. He switched to a jog almost immediately, then sped up even faster, her hand tucked securely in his.

"Where are we going?" Her words came out in a gasp as she hurried to keep up with him.

"It's a surprise!" He looked back with a disarming grin.

His warm hand around hers sparked delicious shivers through her, and the weight of worries she could do nothing about flowed away. The silvery light from the moons glistened on the strips of sand between straggling grasses, and as they raced across them, laughter bubbled out from her. She gripped his hand tighter, curiosity filling her with questions he refused to answer.

Finally, he stopped by a tiny waterfall pouring out of a rock ledge at waist height. Puffing from the run, he indicated it as if he'd discovered great treasure.

"You found...water?" She raised her eyebrows.

"No, take a closer look. Inside the water. Do you know what that is, growing back there?"

She leaned forward, shooting him a look. The perfect innocence in his expression only made her more suspicious, but he didn't move as she peered into the water. In the crevice in which it flowed, behind the fall of water itself, moss grew, infusing the water with the sharp tang of citrus.

"It's called godstonic," she said, reaching in to pull free a patch of the soft, crumbling moss.

"Is it edible?" he asked. "The water's sour."

She burst out laughing. "You don't have to try *everything* in the world."

He looked all too satisfied with himself. "No, maybe not everything."

She shook her head at him, gesturing with the moss. "Don't tell me you ate this, too."

"Only a drop of the water. With the taste, I thought I'd get your opinion."

"Godstonic is a hallucinogen," she said. "Don't eat it."

"Good to know. Tonic?"

"This water will have traces of it in it. Enough of it will produce an effect—like being drunk, but with sparkly dreams."

"Interesting. How bad are the hallucinations? I owe your brother." A thread of mischief had entered his voice.

She snorted. Those two and their pranks. Sometimes she swore neither one of them would ever fully grow up—but then when things actually got serious, so did they. Just not for long. "It won't hurt him even if he drinks the whole water pouch, but I'm not saving you from his retribution. Besides, he'll taste it and know exactly what you did."

"This *is* retribution—but after this mission." His eyes carried a roguish glint. "And I can be clever with the taste, to disguise it."

"You'd want to make sure no one accidentally grabs the godstonic pouch, though," she said.

He nodded. "Maybe when we're on our way back, if I can find some again. Wouldn't want anyone unable to function out here."

"We might not camp here again."

"Maybe not, but even so, this is incredible."

"Is this really what made you come running into camp like that?" she asked, chuckling.

His fingers brushed hers as he took the moss to look more closely at it. "When there's a problem I can't solve, sometimes stepping away, taking my mind off it, helps me see the solution. I thought maybe it would work for you, too. And even if not, you deserve a little relaxation, a little fun."

A smile curved her lips, and she wrapped her arms around his waist. "Thank you."

"Anytime." He kissed her temple, holding her close with one arm, turning the moss over in his hand. "Same worries?"

She sighed. "Yes. Being late to Gahimbli, or what happens when we get there, or another attack, one where maybe they aren't so happy to leave us alive this time…"

"Do you want distraction, an ear, or solutions?" he asked.

"None of this is new. We've already talked about all of it."

He dropped the moss, holding her snug against him. "So we can talk about it again."

She tilted her head, watching him with a furrowed brow. "Why are you so patient with this? Why don't you get bored going around in circles with me?"

"Because you're important."

She huffed a laugh. "No, I'm just a nomadic havi." The words spilled from her without thought.

But he jerked backward, frowning at her. "You don't mean that."

He was scrutinizing her expression, and she sighed, deflating in his arms. "No, not really. It just… it all gets in my head. It's nicer out here, without the weight of it all, but I'm going back, and it'll all be there again."

"But you don't have to, if you truly don't want to."

She grimaced. "No, I'm not abandoning my plans."

A smile tugged the edges of his mouth, full of pride and confidence. He traced idle designs on her back with one finger as he held her. "So, will it help to go through the plan? When we get the nobles settled in Gahimbli, we find Yadi as quickly as possible. Hopefully he can help provide a buffer against any lashing out Lamyi wants to do, as well as providing us contacts. Then we just keep our heads down during the festival, right?"

"Are you even capable of keeping your head down?" she asked.

He chuckled. "Ah, so it's distraction then?"

She shook her head at him. "I'm surprised you even learned the plan. I'm certain you won't follow it."

"I can try. You know, it's like one of those structured dances you have, the ones where everyone follows certain steps," Taunos mused, his fingers trailing up and down her arm. "There's an elegance to those dances, a beauty. Like with your plans. It's different from the dances where everyone just expresses themselves."

She snorted. Somehow that was very Taunos, comparing his impulsivity and her planning to different kinds of dancing. She relaxed into him, resting her head on his shoulder. He held her in silence for a while, and the tension drained from her.

"You are so beautiful."

Amanah looked up at the breathy intensity of his voice, and the force of his gaze made heat rise to her cheeks. She smiled.

"And distracting," he continued, returning her smile.

"I'm distracting?" she teased. He was the distracting one, surely.

"Extremely." He nuzzled her. "Do you have any idea how hard it is to go through the day without making it completely apparent to Lamyi and Inuwe that you carry my heart, especially when you're being all capable and intelligent as you always are?"

She snorted, resting a hand on his chest. "I'm pretty sure they know, after the Mahyami came. They're just pretending not to see it."

"What they see or don't see has no effect on reality or how I feel," he said.

It was hard, keeping their relationship ignorable from the nobles' point of view. Her eyes seemed to keep searching him out, and whenever their gazes met, a little thrill zipped through her. She kept catching on his lips, his eyes, his hair, the ripple of his muscles through his shirt... She loved the hitch of his breathing when she surprised him, or even sometimes just when she met his eyes, followed by warmth suffusing his features, the joy that lit up his eyes. The heated intensity of his gaze when he was about to kiss her. The way he held her stole her breath along with her awareness of anything but how perfectly they fit together and how wonderful it felt to be in his arms.

She kissed him, melting into his embrace as his arms tightened around her. One of his hands rose, fingertips trailing up and down her neck, though they curled to avoid her hair. He'd done that ever since the night he'd heated the stone for her and rubbed her back—apparently, he'd taken her denial of him touching her braids to heart.

Finally they had to break apart, and he tipped his head down slightly, resting his forehead against hers, eyes searching hers. Their breaths came fast, hearts pounding in time with each other.

She traced her fingers down his chest and he let out a sharp exhale.

"You should know, I'm memorizing everything that makes you react like that," she teased.

His eyebrows raised, his hand drifting up and down the length of her good arm. "Brave of you to have barely begun playing this game with me and already turn to taunting."

"Well, I learned from the best," she said.

He laughed, and as he opened his mouth to reply, she cut in. "Emin, of course."

Shaking his head, he tugged her close, laughter running through him. "I think, for a little while, I don't want to talk about Emin."

She couldn't help but agree.

"I'm savoring this, too, getting to know you. What you like, what you don't." He grinned, leaning in to whisper across the curve of her ear. "The sounds you make, what makes your skin pebble."

She shivered, and he chuckled. "Point for me."

Amanah raised her eyebrows. "Like this is a game, hmm?"

"Only as far as you want to play. And only on the surface." Wariness was entering his eyes and she had pity on him.

"It was a bad joke, but I started it," she said, patting his chest. "Don't worry. I believe you."

He tightened his arms around her, resting his forehead to hers. "We're still learning each other. And it's just that you mean so much to me. I don't want to mess this up."

"Nor do I."

"How far do you want to go this time?" His voice was a murmur, thrumming through her.

She hmm'ed, trying to avoid the temptation to just kiss him again. He wouldn't do anything else until she answered. He always asked her this, and she'd gradually expanded their boundaries. Even though he was the impulsive one, this structure, these spoken limits, made her feel even safer, more secure, because she never had to question. Within those bounds he liked to surprise her, but no matter where she placed the line, he never, ever crossed it. He never pushed her, and he always made sure to check that she was enjoying whatever they were doing.

"Above the waist," she decided, her voice coming breathless as he trailed hot kisses down her neck to her collarbones. "But under shirts."

He grinned, and she leaned in, clutching him close to whisper in his ear, "And you can touch my hair if you want."

He pulled back to look at her, his thumb brushing across her lower lip. "Are you sure?"

"It's just hair."

"But it's important to you."

She slid her fingers up the nape of his neck and into his hair, and he leaned back into her touch, as she knew he would. "It's hardly fair if I touch yours and don't let you do the same."

His half-lidded eyes slid open again, and he shook his head. "I don't care about that. I don't want you to give anything you aren't comfortable with. I can wait. I will not rush you, no matter what."

"I know." She kissed his jaw. "My answer stands."

His voice dipped to a low rumble. "Tell me if you change your mind."

She nodded, and then he was kissing her again, his fingers sliding up between her braids. She melted into his hold, into his deepening kiss, running her hands up his back. He broke away and his muscles rolled under his tunic as he took it off in one smooth motion.

What a show-off. She snorted. "I didn't mean you had to take it off."

He threaded his sleeve between his belt and pants so his tunic hung from his side. "You can keep yours on. Whatever makes you more comfortable."

She was going to tease him, but her eyes caught on the still healing scratches the sandcat had left across his chest, no longer bandaged. There were other scattered bruises here and there that hadn't been there the night of the sandcat fight, but the worst was a large deep purple one, just below his rib cage.

She traced it gently with her fingertips, horrified. "Taunos."

He shrugged. "Lamyi's practicing precision."

She scowled at him. "It's not funny."

"Humor is my favorite weapon. It means this doesn't hold so much power." His fingers trailed across the back of her neck, soothing circles. "I'm all right. Truly."

He didn't look all right. Not at all. That bruise was ugly and full of menace, and she couldn't help but think of all the times in the sparring yard when he would laughingly correct the technique of his opponents, helping them get stronger, faster, more precise. And Lamyi was practicing on him, he said?

She met his gaze, worry spiking in her. "Please tell me you're not giving him pointers on how to hurt you more effectively."

He laughed, throwing back his head. "I may do stupid things but I'm not *that* foolish. Besides, he's stopped the last couple days."

"Thank Murihat for small mercies," she breathed.

He kissed her temple, his hands dropping to her waist, thumbs drawing tiny circles on her stomach. "I wouldn't let him seriously wound me. I promise."

Her gaze skirted over his myriad scars, marks of his hard life. The danger that still somehow never managed to keep him from laughing and joking at life. She had grown to love that about him, that he never lost his light.

His fingertips traced under the hem of her shirt, and she gasped with pleasure, her skin tingling at his touch. He ran his calloused hands up her bare back, freezing when he got to the scars.

"What are these?"

He'd been curious about every scar he found of hers, intent on learning the story behind each. There was no pity or disgust in his eyes, and maybe that made sense, with all the scars he bore. When she'd asked why he was so curious, he'd said, "You are my favorite adventure. I want to learn everything I can about you."

But now, his tone sounded almost angry instead of inquisitive.

"You have scars too," she pointed out.

"These aren't from fighting." There was a growl to his voice.

"No, they aren't." She pulled away from him. "Why are you angry?"

"This is from a punishment?"

She nodded.

He blew out a breath. "I know some lands have punishments like these, punishments that scar. I've heard Arruk sometimes ties people outside the temple, but it seems cruel to me. Mistakes shouldn't be permanent." His tone softened. "Do they hurt?"

She shook her head. Only the memories they bore hurt. "They're a few months old and fully healed. I was sent for Jattanu's justice."

"What does that mean?"

She swallowed hard. Gently, he tightened his arms around her, and she sank into his embrace, staring across the broken land. "Those people outside the temple sometimes? That was me. I was tied to one of the pillars in front of Jattanu's temple one morning and whipped, then left there until afternoon. It should have been all day, but Emin cut me down and carried me back to the guardhouse."

Taunos's grip tightened, his voice rumbling through her. "Sometimes I really hate your land." Then he drew back to look in her eyes. "Not the people, but the government."

She forced a smile. "This would be weird if you hated me."

"How could I hate you?" he murmured, trailing soft kisses across her cheeks. She shivered against him, relaxing into his hold while clinging to him like a lifeline. "I can't believe you'd ever deserve such a punishment. How could anyone?"

She shrugged. "It's not used very often. Seeing someone subjected to Jattanu's justice is enough to make most people determined not to let it happen to them. Borlim had to lock Emin up to keep him from doing something stupid and earning himself the same thing. More than cutting me down before my time was up, anyway."

"Borlim's a good man. I'm glad he watches out for you."

"As for why I was there, nobles get what they want, one way or another," she said. "At least out here, there are only two to worry about."

"What happened, beloved? What excuse did they use to do that to you? If you want to tell me." His hands stilled, resting on her hips.

She swallowed hard, tears pricking at her eyes just at the thought of sharing this story. But he was right—they were learning each other. For better or for worse, he deserved to know the heart of her pain. "I once got involved with a noble, soon after coming to Arruk. I didn't know the rules —neither did Emin. We got ourselves in trouble. Were suddenly, accidentally, indebted to others. The noble offered me a way out for both of us, paid off all our debts. And then there were kisses, honeyed words, empty promises. He gifted me small presents and invited me to a banquet, but of course that meant I needed a fancy dress. A tailored gown. He said it was fine, that I could have anything I wanted, and he would pay for it. I couldn't believe it. Shouldn't have believed him."

She waved aside her previous naïveté, and a bitter laugh broke from her. "He and his friends met me at the tailor's for measurements."

The silence from Taunos made her risk a glance. He watched her closely, full of compassion, anger, and sorrow, hands rubbing her back comfortingly instead of sensually now.

She took a deep breath. "When I entered the shop, they laughed at my clothes, critiquing them cruelly, including the one who I thought cared about me. The tailor came to take the measurements, but I wasn't about to stay, not when I had glimpsed who this nobleman was behind the mask. I tried to leave. He stopped me in the doorway. His eyes were... It was as if I were something that had crawled out of the foulest cesspit and attached itself to his shoe. He spewed poisonous words at me, said I never meant a thing to him and never would. I tried to slip past him, to leave. He grabbed my arm. I hit him to break his hold, and then I pushed him out of the way. He stumbled down a couple of stairs to the street, enough room to escape, so I ran. I thought I could hide for a while in the guardhouse. But all the things he'd given me, he said I stole, and he sent the guards to fetch his property."

Taunos became very still, his face tight with anger. "They believed him?"

She gave him a twisted smile. "Who would the courts believe? An upstanding nobleman honestly concerned about his property who had been violently assaulted—nearly trampled to death by a passing horse, to hear him tell it—on the street in broad daylight before witnesses? Or a poor girl from the wilderness who had just joined the guards, who they weren't sure they could trust? I'd already sold or traded most of the gifts, too, for things that were more useful, more necessary." She huffed a mirthless laugh. "That did not make me appear any more innocent. I couldn't pay the fine, so I paid in lashes."

"Who is he?" Rage was a thunder in his voice.

She scowled at him, placing her hands on his chest. "Taunos, I don't want to be saved, remember? Besides, you making him hurt isn't going to change anything. He has plenty of friends, the story is months old, and he'd probably just kill you."

"Are you safe? Do you need out of Arruk? Why have you never told me?" Taunos closed his eyes for a moment and breathed in deeply, mastering himself. He let his breath out in a rush, resting his forehead against hers. "Is there anything I can do?"

His roil of emotions stung her eyes with the promise of tears, especially as he tamed his impulses to try to fix things. She pushed both tears and emotions away and gave him a smirk. "Is this when you promise to burn the world for me?"

He scoffed. "Burning the world? Have you seen this land? I think it needs more water, less fire."

It drew a chuckle from her, and she wrapped her arms around his shoulders, careful of her stitches.

"Destroying things is easier than building them. I would much rather build a better world, a better future, with you." He sealed it with a kiss against her neck.

She curled her fingers into the hair at the back of his neck, nestling closer still to him. "I'm safe enough for now. Borlim wrote a sternly worded letter to the queen's council about how his guards couldn't do their jobs if they were going to be interfered with without an investigation. There'd only be chaos, and the guardhouse would be useless."

"And that worked?"

"The queen issued an order that guards on duty have all the same rights and duties, regardless of class, and that the area from the square including the guardhouse on down to the riverside havi market was safe for any guard, even off duty, regardless of background. Cases that go for any whipping or exposure—especially Jattanu's justice, being both—are now supposed to have a wealth of evidence that's not easy to collect. It's not a law yet, but it's helped."

"That's why you and Emin always hang out in that particular market, because it's safe?"

She nodded.

"It's horrible not everywhere is safe though." A muscle ticked in his jaw.

"Emin shielded you from a lot of it. We don't exactly enjoy would-be friends seeing our challenges."

"I still could have asked more questions. You wouldn't have had to face these things alone. You shouldn't have faced any of that."

"I told you, I'm not the only one with a story like that. Others still get caught in similar situations. They might not face Jattanu's justice anymore, but the fines can still be devastating. Or worse."

Taunos nodded. "Hopefully you can get into the bamimri and things will get better. I'll help however I can."

She drew in a steadying breath, opening up to him a little more. "I know you will. I try to help people where I can, but I'll have to step back from it when I get back to Arruk, lest they become a target. It makes me worry."

She rested her cheek against his shoulder again, and he kissed the top of her head.

"You know," he mumbled into her braids. "I wonder how many people you've inspired to change things. Borlim respects you. Lots of the people in the market do, too. Maybe that's just the beginning."

"Maybe. But it puts a target on me. And it's hard. To let go."

She could feel his cheek moving on her hair as he nodded. "I know. But you have people to help you when you need it. As you told me, you're not alone. And you deserve to be surrounded by people who see you for you. You are a wonder."

"You and your honeyed words." She tightened her hold on him.

"I'm serious. Listen, Amanah." He sighed, running his hand through his hair. "I'm not sure you realize how precious you and your brother are to me. You both have somehow slipped past my defenses. And every time you hit upon a vulnerability, a weakness of mine, you choose to do no harm, to offer safety. Neither of you has ever used a weakness against me."

Amanah frowned. "This is unusual for you."

"When travelling."

She grimaced. He offered her safety, too, but it shouldn't be such an unusual thing for him.

He sighed. "And yet, you always push me to be better, regardless. You don't cut me down, but encourage me to grow. I can't stand the thought of losing either of you. He's my best friend, and you… you're the partner I've been hoping to find."

"That's how it should be."

"Yes, but I want you to understand, I don't say this lightly. I don't love you lightly. I may enjoy games, but I will never play games with your heart. I said that before, and I want you to know it's true."

She swallowed hard, emotion clogging her throat. It was obvious how much this mattered to him, and therefore, how much she mattered to him.

He watched her intently, offering a slight smile. "I have a story for you, too."

"You're always telling stories." But she let him go, watching his face curiously.

"This one's more personal." He traced the deep gouge between his second and third ribs with his finger. It started horrifyingly deep and then curved sharply up toward his sternum.

"Someone tried to kill you," she whispered. It'd drawn her gaze before, the scar that spoke of death.

"Shh, you're skipping ahead," he teased.

But he nodded, darkness sliding back over his face. "I don't give my heart to many. You, and two previously. My first love, our community found us to be incompatible and we had to separate. My last love—well, that turned out to be one-sided. She gave me this. I was travelling with a people who live high in some mountains, learning to survive there. I thought I'd grown close to them, one in particular. A priestess. But I realize now that I was stupid and lonely, mourning the loss of my previous love."

He looked down, and she waited, just as he'd waited for her. He settled his hands around her again, moving in circles across her back, and she rubbed his shoulders wordlessly, offering him comfort for the memories he was facing.

He flashed a brief smile and cleared his throat. "It turned out they believed their god had singled me out to die. The priestess was tasked with getting close to me all through that winter, and I... I didn't see it. I didn't see the knife she had by the bed until just in time to keep her from literally carving my heart out of my chest."

Amanah kept her hands moving across his skin, as if his words didn't give her a chill. As if anger and fear for him weren't rising in her. She found herself rushing to put him at ease, to assure him he was safe now, with her. "I don't have a knife."

Amusement filled his voice. "Yes, you do. In your boot, as usual."

Her face heated. She'd forgotten that, but of course he hadn't missed it. "I mean, nothing I'm going to use on you. Do you want it, to be sure?"

"I'm already sure. I trust you." He met her gaze, eyes deep pools, intent on hers. "Since then, I've grown much more cautious, but I know you won't harm me, as surely as I breathe."

"Thank you." She ran her fingers over the scar in horrified fascination. They both bore scars, inside and out. "You shouldn't have survived. I mean, I'm glad you did, but... how?"

"It was a near thing. Mostly luck. I threw myself into a river."

"In winter?!" She gaped at him.

"It slowed things down. My own Borlim found me, brought me to healers. Saved my life. I don't remember any of it—I was unconscious." He chuckled. "What I do remember is when I woke up, he went on a tirade. I have never been lectured so thoroughly for my foolishness in my life."

He must have been unable to get justice for Taunos, if he was like her grumpy guardmaster, and set on avoiding those situations in the future, for Taunos's sake. At least he had someone to watch out for him sometimes. The Borlims of the world should be prized far more than they were.

"Your Borlim... was he with you in the mountains? How was he close enough to be able to find you and keep you alive?"

He tilted his head, a thoughtful look in his eyes. "You know... I'm not sure, but you'd probably call him a sea-wizard."

If magic had saved him, she could forgive it for a lot of harm. She ran her fingers over his skin thoughtfully, as high up as her wounded shoulder could reach without tugging at the stitches.

He took her hand and raised it to his lips. "This might be a stupid thing we're doing, you know. Borlim told you to be invisible. Mine would call me a fool. Reckless, even."

She frowned at him. "You're just now thinking of this? After all this?"

"No, but I thought it should be spoken. I didn't come here and intend to fall in love." He was solemn again.

Was he having doubts? She bit her lip. Well, she'd make her position clear, regardless of if he changed his mind. "Neither did I. But I'm not sad to have this, with you. I think it's worth the risk."

The light returned to his eyes, and he murmured. "Me too. You're worth being a little reckless for."

A weight lifted from her chest and she leaned into him.

"A little reckless? Coming from you?" she teased. "You'd be a little reckless for a new song to hear or a new fruit to try."

"I'd be a lot reckless for you, but then you'd scold me," he teased back.

She laughed. "You and your honeyed words."

"Ah." He swallowed hard, concern returning in the furrow of his brow. "Your story. He gave you honeyed words, you said. Sometimes I can't find plain words to express what I feel. That doesn't mean I mean them any less. Does it... would you like... I can try to stop. I don't always know exactly what's going to come out of my mouth until it does, but for you, I can try. I don't want to remind you of *him*."

She trailed her fingertips along the side of his face. "With you, it's not falsehoods or flattery; it's the poetry and stories in your heart coming out. You see me for me and don't want to change me, and I don't want to change you. And you've proved your honeyed words are harmless."

"Only harmless?" He smiled, tipping his forehead to hers as he tugged her close again.

"Sweet but overwhelming when there's too much at once, like honey." She wound her arms loosely around his neck.

"Ah so they work, then? I can come up with more."

"They do not." She laughed. "Actions do."

"They do, hmm?" Mischief danced in his eyes, in the quirk of his lips.

"Yes, actions are the important things." She raised her eyebrows in challenge, not at all surprised when he kissed her.

It was a deep kiss, the kind that left them breathless, and she drew him even closer, seeking respite in his arms from the dredged up memories. He held her tightly, as if he could shield her from all dangers, his hands smoothing their way up her back again. But he was still too far, too separate.

She took his hand from her waist and guided it down to her hip, her other hand curled around his neck, kissing him deeply, desperately.

He returned the kiss for a second, his fingers tightening on her hip, and then he broke away with a sharp breath. He stepped back from her, chest heaving.

She was panting too, she realized, but when she stepped forward, he held up his hand, his feet automatically setting in a stance she recognized from sparring. There was something shuttered about his expression.

"What's wrong?" She stepped back, giving him space the way he so often did her. Space to regain the self-control he so prized.

He turned shoulder to shoulder with her, but reached out and entwined his fingers in hers. "If we regret this and decide to go farther another time, that's easily remedied. But crossing a line we had and regretting that, that's a trust that's more difficult to mend. I don't want you to ever regret anything you do with me."

She squeezed his fingers. "You've already proven that, over and over again. But, you're right, we shouldn't go too far. I'm not trying to frustrate you."

"You don't. And you don't owe me anything."

"Regardless, I didn't expect this, so I didn't bring the herbs for a contraceptive tea."

He grinned, no doubt at her failing to plan for this, but his voice was still earnest. "I'm not in any rush. Besides, I want to be able to give you my undivided attention when we go much farther."

Heat flared in her cheeks and through her core at that. No doubt he wouldn't let his guard fully down even within Gahimbli, but not having to worry about bandits or creatures... that'd be smart.

"And as for herbs, I can't have children yet." He said it casually, but it snagged her attention.

"What do you mean, you can't have children yet?"

Taunos rubbed the back of his neck. "My Borlim... he's not a trusting person. I had a magical procedure, so I can't have children until it's reversed—also with magic. It was a condition for me to leave my land."

What kind of land required such measures? She frowned. "Are you all right?"

"I'm completely fine." He took her hands, kissing her fingers. "And I'm sure you'll feel more comfortable also taking preventative measures, but I thought you should know."

She stared at him. He'd offered personal information, thought ahead and spoken of it with her. And through all this, he'd thoroughly distracted her from her impotent worries of before. Her chest felt so full it might burst. "I was just surprised. Thank you for telling me."

She turned to face him, reaching out to see if he was ready. When he slid his hands onto her waist again, she brushed the hair back from his temple. "We'll find a pace that suits us. Both of us. Whatever you need, tell me, and I'll do the same with you."

He turned his head, kissing her palm, then swept her closer, burying his face in her neck. She ran her fingers through his thick hair again, delighting in its softness.

His fingertips brushed her scars again, and his eyes darted across her face. "Is this okay? These don't hurt?"

"It's fine," she said, trying not to squirm. "It just tickles."

Mischief flared in his eyes, and she began laughing, the darkness of their conversation eased as she realized she was suddenly in trouble, of a kind she wasn't sure she wanted out of.

16

GAHIMBLI'S STONE WALLS squatted ahead of them, a low grey-brown line among the red hills. Amanah patted Nakii, rubbing the salve further into his neck. The horses had made it through the windstorm with only minor abrasions, and now, they'd made it to Gahimbli in time, barely. The rain of the gods should start tomorrow night. Still, she found herself delaying, riding at the tail of the group. Once they were back among the crush of people, how could this bubble of happiness she'd found last? She wasn't the same as she'd been in Arruk, but it was all too easy for a familiar setting to shove a person into old habits. She didn't want that.

And then there was the question of what Lamyi would do once they were inside the city, where he'd be empowered by the presence of other nobles, without needing them to keep him safe from the wilderness. Would he take the risk of needing new guards just to spite them? She wouldn't put it past him.

The road led to the wide double gates, but a trail of people also trickled in single-file from a side gate, pulling along goats and horses laden with goods. Shadows packed against the walls, obscuring their lines. As they drew closer, the shapes were revealed as masses of huddled people and tents pressed against the city walls.

"Wait. Why are there people outside the walls?" Taunos asked the nobles. "Didn't Hemne say they came for protection?"

Lamyi waved a hand. "There's not enough room inside for all of them. Besides, how many of them are working with the Hinanuri?"

"If the Hinanuri attack, Gahimbli will be one of their first targets, being so close to the border," Gurseh said. "They need to be inside."

"I told you, there's no room," Lamyi said, far more patient than he'd been thus far. "You'll see. They say the slums go as far as you can see from the wall. We'll have to hurry through to where our lodgings are."

Taunos's jaw clenched as he stared at the city.

Amanah felt sick, cold spiking through her. How many of these people were Mahyami? How many had been driven to seek shelter here from threats of violence, unaware that at least one powerful family in the city was apparently working with the Hinanuri? Unaware that they would be viewed with suspicion because they needed help?

Anger and resignation warred within her, because this was the way of things, wasn't it? No matter what illusions she could cultivate with Taunos, this was what it always came down to. And yet, it was unacceptable. All these people would be smashed against the walls if they were still outside and the Hinanuri attacked. Maybe the army would have mercy on them, but she doubted it, and if they did, the Dahuti would make their lives even worse.

Taunos's hand brushed her shoulder. Straightening, she gave him a slight nod. She was fine—as much as she could be, seeing this. The fire in Taunos's eyes made her feel a little less alone though, against the cruelty— he really did hate it, too.

"What's the other gate?" Taunos asked.

"For the nomadic havi to bring goods to market and get back out quickly, disturbing the city folk as little as possible," Emin said, his broad shoulders slumped.

"It's just like the houses of the rich—the front door is for the rich, and the back door is for the servants and the poor," Amanah said.

Emin forced himself straight again. "Amanah and I should probably head to that one. We can meet up inside. The less trouble we raise, the better for the mission."

"Don't worry." Lamyi smiled, and Amanah shuddered. "We'll get you inside the main gates. We're not about to separate from our guard now. After all, how can you guard us if you aren't nearby?"

Taunos's gaze lingered on Lamyi, but he bowed his head. "Thank you, Lord Lamyi."

Steeling herself, Amanah stared straight ahead as they rode into the mass of people lining the road. The miserable poverty of the camps weighed on her as they rode past, following the nobles, joining the line that trickled through the entrance of the city.

She gritted her teeth as the gate guards eyed them, but after a quiet word from Inuwe, the guards waved them through. Relief filled her, chased by anger that she should feel such relief at all while other desperate souls pleaded to get in, only to be beaten back by the guards.

Gurseh patted Emin's back as he rode beside him, and Taunos placed Rose next to Nakii. They followed the nobles in silence as Amanah straightened her torn scarf binding back her braids. The press of people was even worse inside the walls, with the smoke from dozens of cook fires filling her lungs. The sun was hot on her shoulders, and she tried not to imagine it was oppressive. After all, it was the same sun outside the city.

This had to change. Lamyi certainly wouldn't speak for them, but Inuwe… might. Regardless, she wasn't going to let this beat her. She'd find Taunos's contacts and start the work needed. The bamimri waited for her, even though it didn't know it yet.

Taunos reached out to her, his fingers dancing across her arm in the tapping language, a message of sympathy. She gave him a small smile, but it was good to be mad *with* someone. It felt powerful, to be furious along with him, to be backed up by him yet again.

Shouts sliced through the noise of the square as they passed through. A market was always a hectic place no matter what city you were in, but this one was overcrowded, with families packed in tightly, tents set up wherever there was space. Amanah and Taunos nudged their horses forward, closer to Emin and Gurseh and the nobles. Rising to her feet on Nakii's back, Amanah stared over the sea of heads, ignoring the sneers of some of the city folk at her lack of manners. But if you couldn't use the tools at your disposal to see a greater distance, those who made their homes in the wilderness would never have survived. Horseback riding mastery was as important a skill as banner dancing.

Narrowing her eyes, Amanah scanned for whatever caused the shouting. Nothing stood out, but the flow of people heading out of the square was increasing.

"Trouble," Taunos said, his voice low and tense. "Get them to safety."

"What—"

"I'm going to figure out what it is and stop it."

And then he was off his horse, running through the crowd. Amanah peered after him, her gaze darting ahead of his path, trying to see what he'd seen, while Gurseh's hurried nagging of the nobles sounded behind her. Getting the nobles to safety. Of course. That's what she should be doing too. That was her job.

A pack of black-clad figures in a formation like a spear point sliced through the crowd, their faces wrapped with embroidered death masks. A Hinanuri death team, no doubt sent as a warning to the masters of the city.

A warning that would be written in the blood of their victims.

"Murihat save us," she whispered.

Beside her, Emin swore.

Where had they come from? How had they gotten in? Surely the guards at the gate would have stopped them.

"Gurseh, get the nobles out of here!" Emin ordered.

Inuwe's objection was cut off as Gurseh grabbed the reins of both nobles' horses and shoved through the crowd toward an exit.

Guards called out challenges from the entrances of the square, but the people in the square were packed in too tightly to move out of the way very quickly. Those who noticed the death team surged toward the gates in an attempt to flee, regardless of who was in their way. Taunos was racing toward the team, straight as an arrow, but he was still only a quarter of the way across the market.

One of the guards shouted, holding up a pile of empty robes for her fellows to see. Had the death team come in disguise, solidifying the gate guards' suspicion of the refugees outside the walls?

The guard's shout cut off in a gurgle, a crossbow bolt through her throat.

The crowd near the fallen guard surged, screams filling the air. They blocked the view of those farther back in the crowd, but panic was spreading.

"They're going to trample each other," Amanah said, snagging her brother's shoulder. "If we can keep them calm, split the streams of people to the other exits, too, more can get out."

Emin nodded and plowed his way forward.

The crowd jostled her, sweeping her nearly off her horse as she turned Nakii, fighting her way in the other direction. She called out, but no one was listening over their confusion and fear. How could the city folk stand it, hiding behind the bodies of these less-fortunate, hoping any attack wouldn't make it to them and their comfort? How many of these were Hemne's people, people he'd be hoping to see again, nomads who had sought refuge in the city from Hinanuri raiding parties?

Too many havi families had split over the war with Hinanuri, especially from clans like the Mahyami and the Kanhu. Trade ties and blood ties bound them to Dahuti and to Hinanuri both, and had done so for generations. But these people had come here for the chance of safety. She had to find a way to help.

Her banners. The banner dance would catch the eye of any nomadic havi. Perhaps if their panic was muted with the familiar banner messages from their youth, they could get out, and if they could get out, others could follow.

And just maybe, those in the death team would remember the ties and stop. Or at least delay.

It was a small chance, but it was a chance. Amanah leaned forward, urging Nakii toward the stairs. He snorted his objections but bounded upward, hooves clattering on the stones. A guard shouted at her, but she ignored him. Nakii would watch her back for a little while, at least—hopefully long enough. No one would want to risk being trampled atop the wall. The stairs ended in a wide expanse of stone with parapets on the far side only. Maybe they'd run out of stone for the interior side. No matter —it was wide enough for her mount, as she'd guessed.

She cast a quick glance around. Gurseh was out of the market with Inuwe and Lamyi, their horses racing up streets toward the middle of the city. People were fighting to leave each of the square's entrances, but it was still too slow. Guards were falling in the square below her—she gulped as a robed figure stepped up behind a guard doing his best to keep order and stabbed him in the back. As the guard fell, the figure turned, the black fabric of a death mask peeking out.

Definitely disguises, then. The death team was here to make a statement and take the threats out first, but at least they didn't seem to all be armed with crossbows. It gave her time—not much, but she'd work with what she had, as she always did.

She dropped down from Nakii's back and opened her pack. The wind was fierce up here, snatching at her braids, scarf, and clothes, helping to pull the banners free. Red for danger. Green for friendship. Black for choice. Her motions would carry the rest.

The wind snapped the banners out, ends whipping wildly. Amanah gulped as she stood at the edge of the wall. It was no different than sending a message across the badlands. This would make her a target, but she couldn't stand by. Anything less than everything she could think of to save lives didn't sit well with her.

So she danced, twirling the banners around each other in the strong wind, snapping them toward the directions of safety, spinning them to remind the death team that Hinanuri and nomadic Dahuti had faced danger in the past before, together in friendship. It wasn't likely to work, not on a death team, but she had to at least try. Nomadic havi or city havi, it didn't matter—they deserved to live, not be used. And if killing started, she'd exchange her banners for her bow.

A crossbow bolt whipped past her, tearing a hole in one of her banners.

"Hey, now!" the wall guard shouted at the same time. "You can't be up here!"

Nakii stamped his hooves in warning.

Chills crept up her spine, but she couldn't stop. Especially not now that the death team had targeted her. Amanah repeated the message, motions flowing, working with the wind, accounting for its strength. The square below began to thin as people pressed to the sides and streamed out the market's exits. People were now moving with purpose, no longer caught in the unthinking panic of before, and directing others. Hope swelled in her. Grounded in the banners and the wind, in the messages they'd grown up reading, from the littlest child to the oldest grandmother, they moved. At one end of the square, Emin waved his arms, ushering people through. Beyond, Gurseh and the nobles were far up one of the main roads, riding for the fancy estates at the city's center.

"You're not allowed up here," the guard said, and then "Whoa!" as Nakii neighed, hooves striking the stone again.

"Stop, or I'll—" The guard stopped, and fell backward, a crossbow bolt in his belly.

Nakii snorted, stamping nervously.

Crouching low, Amanah watched the square. It was emptying, yes, but there were still a lot of people in danger. The death team had dispersed into the crowd. Knives flashed, and people fell. One bent over a crossbow, resetting it for the next shot. Another crossbow was aimed at Taunos, who charged toward a black-clad man running for the center of the square, holding something that glinted in the sun.

Amanah's heart clenched. Of course Taunos had to be in the middle of it. She stuffed her banners in her pack and strung her bow. Below, the crossbow men aimed, one for her, one for Taunos.

"Down!" Amanah screamed, dropping to the stones.

A bolt skittered off the stone in front of her, and Nakii objected loudly. She peeked over the edge. A few of those nearest in the crowd had dropped in response to her scream—but not Taunos. Blood welled through his sleeve. A near miss. Her chest tightened.

Screams resounded from below. Taunos picked himself up and shouted, waving one arm. Urging people away. The exits were a mass of confusion, but people were now leaving in steady streams. Emin dragged a cart clear, creating more space for those fleeing.

The crossbow men reloaded, and several of the death team began to stab and slice their way through victims on their way to Taunos, who resumed his chase after the lone black-clad man. The man who held something that gleamed like metal.

Staying low, Amanah drew back an arrow, aiming at the man who'd shot at her. She loosed, but the wind took it and her arrow clattered harmlessly on the cobbles.

She grimaced as she met the eyes of the crossbowman, and slung her pack back onto her shoulders. The death team continued to efficiently murder anyone in their way, leaving bodies littering the cobblestones behind them. People huddled low, hoping to remain unnoticed or be taken for dead, while those on the edges scrambled to get farther out of the way. Several members of the death team headed toward Taunos, but he was closing in on the man with the metal.

"Taunos, down!" she shouted, nocking another arrow and ducking behind cover.

A bolt struck the stone a hands-breadth from her head. Her mouth was dry, but she pushed down the panic, peeking out over the market.

A new gash bloomed in Taunos's lower leg, where he lay on the ground. Had he heard her, or had he been knocked down by the force of the bolt? She didn't know, and it probably didn't matter. They were dead if this went on much longer. At least the wind was causing trouble for the crossbowmen, just as it was for her.

She aimed at her crossbowman and loosed, savage satisfaction taking her when her arrow plunged into the man's shoulder.

But she couldn't stay on the wall any longer, not while people were dying below, and Nakii could be shot at any moment. There was only one more crossbowman to worry about—it was difficult to use the weapon with a wounded shoulder, after all. Amanah mounted Nakii and guided her gelding in a tight circle with her knees. Down the stairs she rode, firing as fast as she could at any member of the death team she could get a clear sight on.

At the bottom of the stairs, people were packed in so tightly, there was no room to guide Nakii through without trampling them. Faces turned to her, scared and confused. And Taunos was still running, still being chased by four of the death team. She couldn't get to him to help. She stood, drawing her bow, and sighted on the last crossbowman. She loosed, but the man ducked, returning fire. A man next to her shouted in pain. She had to get clear of the crowd, but it was so densely packed. Amanah dropped from her horse to avoid trampling them.

She squirmed and drove in her elbows, desperate to make herself some room, shouting for them to get to the exits. The square wasn't emptying quickly enough. She kept catching glimpses of the scene as she worked her way forward, but she couldn't find a way through. Not in time to help Taunos or keep the death team from killing more people. Screams of pain and rising panic filled the air as the death team cut through bystanders. There was no more room to use her bow.

Taunos's hand snatched the shirt of the man he was chasing, but he ripped free. The man threw the metal he was carrying. It arced high, catching the sun as it fell, heading toward the edge of the square where the richer stalls were.

"Tena!" the man yelled. Death.

Every member of the death team turned and sprinted for the gate. If even *they* didn't want to be around, a lot of people were going to die.

"Move! Find cover!" Amanah shouted, shoving at the people nearest her, knowing there was no way it'd be enough.

Taunos was running again, and as the metal cylinder arced downward, he leapt into the air. In one motion, at the top of his arc, he snatched the container, twisted, and lobbed it into the well beneath him. Taunos fell after it, turning too slowly to make the landing. At least he would land to the side of the well, not in—

The world exploded.

A wave of sound and force battered her, and rubble quickly followed it.

She lay on the ground, her ears ringing, every limb proclaiming new bruises were forming. Dust coated her skin, filled her lungs. She coughed, convulsing as she struggled to take in enough air. Cautiously, Amanah pushed herself up, testing her limbs, and then turned, coughing with even that much effort.

The square was a disaster. Stalls were obliterated. Bodies littered the cobblestones, many moving slowly, but others still as death. Everywhere, people were bleeding, crying, staggering. Amanah's ears rang, the world blurring with every move she made. She couldn't hear anything above the ringing, couldn't feel anything beyond the blunted pain of her limbs, which made the grueling training sessions Borlim led seem like comfort. She'd probably feel even worse later.

Across the square, Emin staggered to his feet, looking dazed. Blood ran from a small cut on his cheek, and he was coated in dust, but he was standing. The death team was nowhere in sight.

But where was Taunos?

The well was missing. That didn't make sense. Where would it have gone? A familiar boot stuck out from under a pile of rocks that hadn't been there before.

Screaming, she lurched in a limping run over to him. Taunos lay face-down, rubble from the well half-covering him. She clawed at the rocks, pushing them off him as fast as she could, her throat raw. What had he done? The explosive, that must be why he changed course from the death team. And he'd caught the device, even though he must have seen the danger. Otherwise he wouldn't have been running toward the man.

And the death team. Rage reared up to meet her pain and terror. Whatever their mission had been, they were willing to kill and injure havi families to complete it.

Uncovering Taunos, she rolled him over. His head lolled to the side, his temple striking rubble she hadn't moved far enough away. Blood trickled down his face from that wound as well as from his nose and mouth. Cradling the side of his face to avoid accidentally hurting him again, she checked him for further injuries. The darker brown of his skin was coated with dust, as was hers, though bruises bloomed beneath. His chest rose and fell—he was still breathing, at least—but his shirt was damp with dark blood at his ribs.

Grit fell in her eyes, stinging them. Moans filled the air, reminding her of the full extent of this nightmare. The sheer number of people who needed help. All she had was the knowledge she'd been able to steal listening at the windows of the bamimri. What could she do? How could she help Taunos, much less all these people?

"Cleanliness first," she muttered, remembering the way the bimnas drilled that into their trainees. "Dirt is death."

She needed to get him clean and then deal with injuries.

"Amanah?" Emin's voice shook. When had he made his way over? He cleared his voice and then tried again. "We need to move the people… We need… We need to get them help. Is he…?"

She shook her head, avoiding her brother's gaze. She wasn't sure she could be strong for him right now, or for anyone. "He's alive. I don't know how bad it is."

"That was one of those new explosives." Awe tinged Emin's words. "I can't believe he caught it."

"Why would he throw it in the well? He was falling near it. What was he thinking?"

"Probably trying to contain the blast. We couldn't get them all to safety. He was trying to do what he could."

Get them to safety, Taunos had said. And he hadn't meant the nobles.

She leaned forward, touching her forehead to his. Tears burned in her eyes, blurring her vision. She'd have time later to shake him, to weep on his shoulder. She had to. He said he wanted to see where their relationship went, possibly share their lives together. What good was that if he went looking for ways to get himself killed?

She shoved down that rising storm, shoved it down deep in its own well and covered it with a capstone. Later, she could explode or shatter or both. Now, there was work that needed doing.

Taking a shuddering breath, and dashing away her tears, Amanah took stock of the square. "We need to see how bad the injuries are. Ask around. Surely the families have healers among them."

Emin straightened. "I'll ask those outside too, if I can get through the gates. Where should we put the injured? We'll need to clear an area."

"Ask for volunteers. I don't... The bimnas talk sometimes about injuries inside. Taunos was closest, and I don't know how... I don't want to move him yet. The less we move him the better, I think."

Emin nodded. "Most serious injuries over here. I'll get volunteers to grab rags and water."

"Boiling water," she said, standing beside him. "And alcohol for cleansing. Dirt is death. And bandages." Her gaze caught on the debris of the well. "We'll need clean water—this one's ruined. And the dead—they should be gathered together, away from the injured."

The necessities kept coming, but it felt good to have her focus on a problem to solve. Something she could possibly make a difference in.

"We'll place the less seriously injured closer to the city wall," Emin decided. "That way if healers come from the city, they'll come across those who need their help most first. The dead, we'll gather on the eastern edge of the market."

Amanah nodded. It was a good plan. She swept her gaze critically over her brother's dirt-stained clothing, stone-dust and mortar clinging to his skin, like hers. "Are you all right?"

He forced a grim smile. "Nothing a night of sleep and good food won't take care of. At least Gurseh got away with the nobles. You?"

She looked down at herself, as if that would tell her. "Just bruises, I think."

Emin clapped her on the shoulder and then swept her into a tight, fierce hug. She clutched him tight, the traitorous tears stinging her eyes and threatening to spill over. At least her brother was alive and uninjured. And Taunos would be too, or she would have words with him.

Emin stepped back and crouched by Taunos. Resting a hand on his shoulder, he spoke as if he could hear him. "Look, if you want to be the guest of honor at my next party, you're just going to have to do something truly spectacular. Lying on the ground? It's kind of underwhelming."

A laugh broke from her despite herself, and Emin flashed her a smile and then went to work.

17

THE PEOPLE MET the disaster with stoicism, coming together to do what they could. Those who were strong and healthy went to nearby wells for water, bringing it back in streams of buckets. Healers from various families put aside old feuds to stitch and bind the wounds of the injured, sending as many as they could out of the way to heal at home if they had one. Older healers—those whose experiences and knowledge would surely outweigh hers—found their way to Amanah with suggestions and questions, and somehow she found herself organizing them.

But Amanah had little knowledge and fewer tools. What they needed was a whole squad of bimnas. The bimnas were always talking about how important it was not to move people, to carefully categorize injuries before doing anything else, because the cure for one could exacerbate another. But there were no bimnas here—they were all in Arruk, because only Arruk held the bamimri. All that learning, so often boasted about, so desperately wanted, and it was no help here, to this multitude of suffering people.

Singly and in small groups, people came offering what they could spare: bottles of alcohol for sanitizing, strips of fabric for bandages, and needles and thread for stitches. Thankfully, Emin kept most of the volunteers busy, organizing and handing out supplies or clearing rubble so they had space to work, but the healers were all Amanah's. Even when they argued with her, they still came to her to settle disputes or to be assigned where their help was most needed. With their help, she was able to patch the worst wounds and triage injuries before going back and doing more thorough examinations. Otherwise, they'd have far more dead, with people bleeding out while waiting. Still, there were far too many people to see to. She hadn't even managed to do more than the bare minimum for Taunos yet, though it made her heart ache.

In mid-afternoon, Taunos woke, trying to sit up with a groan.

"Lie still." Fear and pain and exhaustion made her voice sharper than she meant it to be.

She was only several paces away, but the intervening space was filled with wounded people and she'd have to pick her way across to him. In the meantime, she didn't want him driving a splintered rib into his heart or something. The bimnas had once dealt with that, and even with their knowledge and tools, the person had died in agony.

The woman she was tending froze, eyes wide, and Amanah patted her shoulder, forcing a smile. "Not you. You're fine."

Amanah narrowed her eyes at Taunos, who was up on one elbow. "Haari Taunos, lie still."

He met her gaze with a grimace, then melted back down. Amanah finished stitching a large gash in the woman's side and bandaging it, then made her way over to Taunos.

She knelt beside him, taking his hand in hers. "I'm glad you're awake."

He forced a half-grin. "I'd make a joke, but I'm not sure it'd land even as well as I did."

Well, at least he was in good spirits, though knowing him, he'd joke with Tenah herself when she came to collect his soul. Amanah brushed her fingers across the small cut on his temple. "Stay still, please. I need to make sure you're not injured inside. How are you feeling?"

"Like I was blown up."

"You were. You seem to enjoy suffering a little bit." Exasperation crept into her tone, weaving its way through the fondness.

The corners of his mouth kicked up, even through the grimace of pain, and she shook her head at him, smoothing back his hair with gentle fingers.

An old man, one of the healers who'd given his expertise, stepped up beside her. She looked up at him, her fingers pausing in Taunos's hair.

The healer crouched, holding out a small pouch of pink powder. "I heard you ordering those we suspect have deep injuries not to move until we can give them a more complete check over—smart. We use this powder, you see. It'll paralyze them for a few marks. Usually they sleep through it, though it also gives vivid dreams."

Amanah nodded, pointing out those nearby who she suspected of injuries inside or to their backs or heads. "These ten. Can you dose each of them please?"

Hopefully this was the right thing. Doubt gnawed at her. She was making decisions as if she had knowledge she didn't have, but she didn't know what else to do.

With a dip of his head toward Taunos, he opened the bag to her. "I assume you'll take care of this one. Just a little under the tongue, one finger's worth."

She took the cap of powder he gave her, thanking him. Taunos was watching her, and she forced her worries away to smile at him.

Her vision went blurry, and she blinked back her tears, locking down her worry and fear tight again. "You were unconscious, covered in heavy stones. I need you still so you don't hurt yourself worse."

"I can help though." His eyes were on the powder, tension in his shoulders.

"Not if your back or ribs are damaged." She set the cap beside her.

"They might not be, though," he argued. His gaze roamed over the square, what he could see from his position flat on the ground, anyway. "How many injured? How many dead?"

"A lot." Her voice was hoarse, choked. "A lot are hurt. A lot more would have been without most of the blast going upward—but you destroyed the water source for this section of the city."

He winced. "I couldn't see where else to put it. I thought of throwing it in the sky, but I didn't know when it would explode."

"Well, it was a good thing anyway, because it threw sharp bits of metal everywhere. If you'd thrown it into the air, more people would have been injured. This way, we lost a water source, but most of the sharp pieces hit the well or the well's covering, instead of people."

"Where's Emin? Gurseh? Are they safe with the nobles?"

"Emin's here. He's fine. He's helping with organizing all of this." She waved her hand to indicate the square. "Gurseh and the nobles made it out —they're somewhere farther into the city—I haven't seen him since before the explosion."

"The attackers?"

"Disappeared."

His mouth firmed, his gaze roving his surroundings again.

She cut him off before he could ask another question. "I only quickly bandaged you, but you need a thorough checking over."

Hopefully late was better than not at all. Then, she could worry about potentially convincing him to... what? Put himself entirely in her hands? Let her make him utterly vulnerable among all these people, just after he fought a desperate battle?

One thing at a time. She closed her eyes, cleared her throat, and pushed her shoulders back. She eased his shirt up, but he was laying on it, and she stopped him from moving to help her pull his shirt up farther. That was too risky. Instead, she drew her knife.

"I hope you don't love this shirt."

"I don't love this shirt," he said, the corners of his mouth quirking.

"I'm going to cut it off you," she told him, all too aware of the story he'd told her, of the woman who'd tried to kill him.

He lay his hand on hers, over the knife. The warmth of his brown eyes drew her in. "I trust you."

Tearing her gaze away from his, back to her work, she cut the fabric away. Fresh bruises spread over the various scars scattered across his torso from his hard life. A bolt had ripped past his left calf, just missing piercing him, and his upper right arm also held the mark of his near-miss. The way he held his arm close to his side, he might have cracked a rib, too. And then there was the gash on his side, which she'd already hastily bandaged before checking others for the worst, most obvious injuries. It still bled, weeping like he had liquid to spare. She frowned at the bandage, soaked through again already.

His face had minor wounds. The blood that had come from his nose and mouth had leaked from shallow wounds rather than coming from deep inside. He didn't seem to have any trouble breathing, and she meant to keep it that way.

"Where do you hurt worst?"

"My side. I couldn't dodge everything. My rib hurts, too." He moved to indicate it, and she caught his hand, scowling at him.

"Here?" Gently, she prodded both sides of his ribs until she found the injury. A bruise was spreading over two ribs on his left side, but it didn't worry her as much as the blood loss.

"I said don't move and I mean it," she told him. "It's a miracle you're not dead, honestly. You must have Hayzanu's favor. That death team shot you. Multiple times."

"Good thing I have you." He winced. "Your warnings. They were helpful."

She swallowed hard. "And so easily, I could no longer have you."

He took her hand, threading his fingers in hers. "I'm here, Amanah. I couldn't leave those people to die. Not without trying to do something to save them."

Gods help her, she understood that all too well. It did nothing for the fear in her heart, however.

"I need to sew your side up. The bandage isn't working. I'm sorry. It'll hurt. I can give you the powder first, so you sleep through it."

He shook his head. "I don't need it. You can just sew me up. It's your turn, I suppose."

She reined in her exasperation, brushing dust from his cheeks. "You were buried under rubble, and I think your rib is broken. I shouldn't have moved you this much. If you move, you could injure yourself permanently. And gods know you can't help but move."

A wince crossed his face, a sudden vulnerability passing over his expression in a wave. "I'm tired. I might just sleep."

"Tired, like the night with the sandcat?" she asked. He'd gotten away with fewer injuries than he should have then, too. Of course, the way he leapt about, she'd also be weary.

He nodded, exhaustion softening the lines of his face and the curl at the corners of his mouth as he tried to smile at her.

She looked at the powder. "I'd rather be sure. There's so many people around, and I can't... I'm not leaving you alone, but if you startle because someone passes by and lurch your way to wakefulness, your rib could kill you if it's splintered."

He held her gaze for what felt like an eternity, and then he drew in a breath, like he was steadying his nerves. "I trust you."

Her mouth twisted. "I just hope I don't kill anyone."

He slid his hand up to clasp hers in both of his. "Amanah. I trust *you*. If people die, it's not on you, but on the people who attacked. You're doing everything you can to help."

Was it foolish of her for her heart to flutter at that statement? Perhaps, but her heart did so anyway. Her whole being warmed at those words, though she tried to keep her mind focused.

She put her hand on his cheek, then leaned forward, resting her forehead against his. She gazed into his eyes, bright with the pain he was trying to conceal. "Sleep, but come back to me, all right? I want you to come back to me."

He gave the barest nod. "There's nothing I want more in all the worlds."

She dipped her finger in the powder and placed it on the inside of his lower lip. Chewing on the inside of her cheek, she watched, holding his hand. In only a few breaths, far quicker than the others the healer was dosing, his eyelids fluttered shut and his grip on her loosened. She swallowed hard. Had she done it wrong? Had she harmed instead of helped him?

But his chest rose and fell steadily. After watching a few more breaths, she shook herself and went to work. With a freshly cleansed needle, she sewed up his wounds and bound them with clean bandages. Then, she folded his hands on his stomach in what she hoped would be a comfortable position.

She gave herself a moment to brush the backs of her fingers over his cheek, and then took a deep breath and stood. There was still a lot of work to be done, and it was time for her to get back to it.

18

HELP DIDN'T COME until the sun was halfway to the horizon. Once triage was complete and things were somewhat organized, she'd sent Emin to the city's center to get aid. And then, when no one came, she'd sent another, and another. There'd been at least five runners after Emin, but she'd lost count of how many.

When help did come, it was underwhelming. Two guards walked into the square, looking at the destruction with blank expressions.

Finally, there'd be someone who knew what they were doing, who could take control of this disaster. They'd want to show their authority right away, so Amanah kept her head down, training her eyes on the splint she was binding to a child's arm.

Relief and frustration warred in her. Twenty-five people had died while waiting for assistance. Amanah, bloody and weary, hadn't been able to keep them alive. Hadn't known how.

"Ah! There he is," one of the guards said. He was a thin man with a short, oiled beard and mustache. "Haari Taunos! I should have known. Trouble always rides with you."

Amanah's stomach dropped. Were they not here for all of the wounded? The man and the tall, stocky woman who must be his partner stepped over people, heading straight to Taunos. The man frowned, his steps quickening when Taunos didn't respond, speaking to his partner in words Amanah couldn't hear. She had to get to Taunos—it was up to her to keep him safe. His stillness, even more than his silence, was wrong. It reminded her of the sandcat aftermath, but this was so much more unnerving, even though she was the one who'd done it to him.

She tied the last knot and patted the girl on the shoulder. "You were very brave."

"It hurts," the girl said, looking down at the splint.

"I know." Amanah looked at her mother, cradling her daughter in her arms. "That's the best I can do, and I hope it's enough. Try to keep her arm still. If it heals crooked, it'll always be crooked."

"Thank you," the mother said. She rocked her daughter, then gathered them both to their feet. "Come, let's get something to eat."

Amanah's back ached as she stood, and her healing leg protested all the use. Her injured shoulder hurt, too, but she ignored it, hurrying toward where Taunos was still asleep by the well. She'd made him defenseless.

He had *let* her make him defenseless.

"Why is he over here?" the woman guard was asking. "Why didn't someone inform us right away that he was injured?"

Exhaustion and stress had eroded her self-control, and sarcasm burst out before Amanah could stop it. "Oh, well if we'd known you would come for *important* people, we would have sent runners to ask for help. Six times."

"That sharp tongue will get you in trouble. We were busy," the woman said.

"In that case, off you go to your important tasks," Amanah snapped.

"Not with Haari looking like death. He needs a healer," the man said.

Amanah flung her arms around at the square, filled with rubble and injured people. "All of these people do. But you've barely looked at them. You can't even give them comfort as they die."

Tears choked her snarl, the emotions she'd carefully bottled threatening to unleash themselves now that she was speaking of them.

"Healers are coming, don't worry. Come on, Hununu, help me pick him up." The man gestured at Taunos.

"Stop, you'll hurt him!" Amanah said, rushing to step between them.

"The healer has said to do this with injured people before. Are you saying you know better?" the man asked, stepping around her.

She didn't know better than a healer. She had no training. She was in over her head. A snakebite, an animal attack, those were things she could deal with. A market full of the dead and dying after a death team swept through… she shivered.

But as the man placed his hands under his shoulders, Taunos groaned and opened his eyes. "What's going on?"

"Be still, Haari." The man gently patted his shoulder. "We're bringing you to a healer."

"What about all these people?" Taunos winced as the man shifted his grip, jostling him.

"We won't trip, don't worry," the woman said.

Amanah gritted her teeth. They refused to see what he was saying.

But at the same time, Taunos was among the most wounded, at least of those still alive. And a healer would have more experience, more supplies. It was better than him staying here for help that wouldn't come. At least one of them would be tended by someone who knew what they were doing. She wouldn't have to worry about him anymore. She could focus solely on the others.

She blew out her breath, wiping the back of her grimy hand across her forehead. It felt like defeat.

"Relax," she told Taunos. "I didn't want to move you in case you had injuries inside that would get worse, but the healers won't come. They're bringing you to the healer instead."

"Just me? No." Taunos trembled, as if trying to struggle through the paralysis. That would be just like him.

"Down," the man said. "My grip's slipping. I'm going to drop him. Haari, why are you always so difficult?"

Amanah couldn't help a scoff of agreement, watching the two scowl at each other. Clearly they knew each other, but how?

"Leave me here, Yadi," Taunos growled. "If the healers are letting these people die, they can let me die, too."

This was Yadi? The guard he'd saved, the one he'd hoped would introduce Amanah to others who could help? So far, she wouldn't bet on his help. This was not what they had planned. They were not coming to Yadi well-composed, from a place of strength or even equals. Instead Taunos was immobile and wounded and she was exhausted and bloodstained. They were supposed to do this together. Now she had to readjust and she didn't find it nearly as easy as Taunos did.

"What did she do to you, Haari?" Yadi asked, his voice softening. "Are you unable to move?"

Amanah narrowed her eyes. "Where is Emin? Where are the runners I sent for help? Where are the healers?"

Yadi stepped forward, so close to her that she stepped back. He stepped forward again, gradually pushing her away from Taunos. Amanah gritted her teeth, hands curling into fists, and planted her feet, no matter how Yadi got in her face. She met his flat gaze, refusing to move any farther than the two paces from where she'd started.

She'd known help wouldn't come, deep inside. And Emin... what had they done to her brother to prevent him from returning? If she caused a disruption, they might arrest her, and then she wouldn't be able to do any good at all. But that didn't mean she was going to let herself be pushed around anymore. Her shield might be lying broken on the ground, but she was his too. She'd promised him she would watch his back. And all these other people made invisible by the city's lack of care needed her to advocate for them, too.

"Yadi," Taunos rumbled from the ground, his voice hard. "I am not leaving. If Amanah says I'm not to be moved, I'm not to be moved."

That was far too much faith for him to throw at her feet.

She swallowed hard, keeping her gaze on Yadi. "If you care about him, bring the healer here."

"You're havi, aren't you?" Yadi asked, his eye catching on the uneven cuffs of her sleeves, the way the sole of her right boot had begun to separate again, damaged by the blast, and on her three braids, no doubt disheveled. He turned back toward Taunos. "I'm certain she's done her best, but there's no way she's trained, Haari. Healers' education is expensive, lengthy, and exclusive. Normally I'd have this chat with you, but you need someone who knows what they're doing. The nobles have—"

"Yadi!" Taunos snapped. "I'm not joking. I'm tired and I'm in pain and I don't want to have to have this conversation right now. Amanah is my healer. Follow her orders. I'm supposed to be sleeping and not moving."

Hununu scowled. "Either his injuries have left him senseless—in which case, what he wants doesn't matter—or he never had sense to begin with. We should take him back with us anyway, Yadi. Bring him to the real healer."

"Leave," Taunos snarled.

Amanah knew he was paralyzed, but there was still a dangerous glint in his eyes. Hununu raised her chin and stood her ground though.

If they weren't going to respect even Haari Taunos… Her fists clenched. One thing first, then the next thing. She could still do this. She had to. It all started with the necessities, and right now, she had to get this man to listen for Taunos sake.

Sucking in a deep breath, Amanah stepped past Yadi to stand between the two guards and Taunos.

"This arguing is not helping anyone," Amanah said, making sure her voice was calm.

"Fine," Yadi said. "I'm bringing the healer here, but he's not going to be happy. Come on, Hununu."

"Yadi," Taunos said, stopping him in his tracks. "I get healed last."

"Taunos…" He dropped his head back with a sigh. "Do you realize I have orders? Do you enjoy making my life more difficult?"

"I mean it," Taunos said.

"Sometimes I really hate you," Yadi said.

One corner of his mouth quirked. "Happy to be of service."

Turning on their heels, the guards stalked away.

"We need more bandages, medicines, and thread for stitches. Also water, and something to sterilize wounds, too!" Amanah called after them.

None of the supplies would come, probably, but after everything, she wasn't going to not ask.

She knelt to check on Taunos, making sure the interaction hadn't caused any more damage. She avoided his gaze. How was she going to find a way out of this mess she'd entangled herself in? Their best shot at an ally in this city, and she'd angered him. He'd been an arrogant fool, but still.

"Anything hurt any worse than before?"

"There's a rock in my back. I think I'll live," he said. "And I'm a little cold."

"Well, if you can joke about it."

She couldn't fix the fact that he was cold, but she could at least remove the rock to make him a little more comfortable. Carefully, she eased her hand under him, sweeping away a bit of debris. She straightened his shoulders and his hips, since she'd paralyzed him so he couldn't get comfortable on his own, and then folded his hands back on his stomach, out of danger of being stepped on.

Hundreds of other things needed doing, as well. Suppressing a groan, she rose to her feet.

"Amanah." Taunos's gaze was fixed on her through the lines of fatigue and pain on his face. "Are you all right?"

She hadn't had a chance to think. Hadn't given herself a chance to think. When she eventually did, she'd break down, and when that happened, she wouldn't be able to help anyone else. So she locked her fatigue away with her emotions. Catching her shoulders slumping, she pushed them back, wishing Emin was here.

"I don't know. Go to sleep." She stooped, brushing her fingers across his. "I'll find you a blanket if I can."

"Wake me if someone tries to steal me away."

"No promises." She fell back on teasing to reassure him. "I might get distracted. Or it might be a sea-wizard, come to show you magic."

He chuckled, and for a breath, all the weight on her was a little lighter.

His confidence in her was a precious thing, and it bolstered her courage. She turned and got back to work.

The sun sank below the wall and the air cooled, but no healers from the city came, nor did Emin or any of the runners return. With the help of so many volunteers pitching together in the emergency, they'd managed to at least minimally treat all the wounded. Most of the less-injured people had left, but some had stayed, clearing room among the rubble to move those who could be moved to slightly more comfortable ground. Others wandered among the injured with cups of bone broth that boiled in the pots over fires that had been restarted. Someone had even tended to Nakii, unsaddling him and giving him water and grain, tied out of the way.

Amanah kept her focus on single tasks that she knew how to deal with. Otherwise, the sheer magnitude would overwhelm her more than it already did. But mistakes built up, as did decisions made with little to no planning. They ran out of bandaging, and more people were bleeding. Some of the healers turned to cauterizing wounds. If she'd been more conservative with bandages, could she have stretched them farther? Should she have? She had no idea. She'd never prepared for something so catastrophic, and she had no idea how best to handle many of the wounds. Every slightly clean piece of fabric had been shredded and turned into bandages, leaving nothing to stave off the chill. She'd had to weigh the bimna's "dirt means death" against the knowledge that blood loss also meant death. How did the bimnas even begin to calculate those decisions?

Injured people shivered on the cobbles, including Taunos. That couldn't be good for them either. She should have kept behind some blankets. The pile of the dead would have been so much higher without Taunos's heroism, and now he was lying on hard stone without even a blanket. She didn't know how to help him. She couldn't even keep him warm.

And the city healers wouldn't come, even for him.

But now there was nothing to do. She'd done everything she knew how and everything the more experienced healers thought of, too. They were incredible, both in their wealth of knowledge and at making do with what they had. There were fifteen people left that she didn't have the first idea on how to help, besides keeping them still, and about twenty more who she had helped but now could do nothing else for.

The mourning songs rose into the night as funeral rites for those who had passed were performed. At least the guards, standing uselessly at the entrances of the square, had allowed that much. Every time she saw the guards, she wondered where Emin was. How he was.

Someone passed her a cup and Amanah numbly took it, draining the liquid within mechanically. She was so tired, and yet, it wasn't enough. She hadn't done enough.

"Go and get some rest." The healer who'd brought her the paralyzing powder was standing beside her. Patting her shoulder, he took the empty cup. "It's all up to the gods now."

She nodded, too tired even to pray. If the gods could see, they would care or not, she supposed. Her feet carried her to Taunos without conscious thought, and she sank down beside him, taking his hand in hers. His hand was chilled instead of its usual heat, but he squeezed her hand right away. She tilted her head, clasping his hand in both of hers to warm it, even though he always teased her for being cold. The others that had been dosed were still sluggish, but Taunos's reactions were once again just as fast, just as strong, as they normally were. And yet she knew the powder had worked. Maybe she'd given him too little. She rubbed her eyes with her free hand.

He was watching her, eyes bright in the dusk.

"I wish I could do more," she whispered. "If there was a bimna here..."

"They have you," he said, squeezing her hand again. His thumb rubbed across her knuckles. "You've worn yourself out for them."

"You broke yourself for them," she pointed out.

He grinned. "Ah, it's a contest? Excellent. I win."

She snorted, going to shove his shoulder but thinking better of it just in time. What was this magic of his, that he could lift her spirits so easily?

"Why don't you go find something to do?" Hununu's voice sounded behind her.

Just like that, the tension returned.

The guard was a little way across the square, making her way toward them, trailed by Yadi and an unfamiliar man with a salt-and-pepper beard and spectacles balanced on the end of his nose. He wore rich purple robes and a white wrap on his head, pinned with a clasp in the shape of the sigil of Hayzanu, the god of sailing, exploration, and pleasure. Hayzanu oversaw healers, as well—the bamimri burned incense and raised prayer flags for him at dusk and dawn every day, during the times of transition.

Amanah tugged her headwrap lower over her braids, but she was too angry to bow her head in the proper show of respect for one so learned. She shifted to rise, but Taunos's hand tightened on hers.

"Stay. Please." Vulnerability flickered just for a moment behind the pain in his eyes.

251

She'd told him he wasn't alone, that she'd watch his back. She squeezed his fingers and nodded. "I'm here."

Behind Yadi and the healer came Emin and Gurseh. Her heart leapt after so long fearing for them, wondering what had happened to them.

"Emin! Are you two alright?" she asked. "Wait, where are the nobles? Who's with them?"

"They're with supplemental guards at a fancy manor. They're fine and we're fine. Are you fine?" Emin asked.

She couldn't answer that. She didn't even want to consider how not ok she was.

"Here is the healer, Haari," Yadi said. "Are you still insisting the others be healed first?"

"Yes." Taunos's voice was firm.

The healer shook his head, scowling at his surroundings.

Hununu snorted. "Folly."

Yadi stabbed a finger at the far end of the square, his voice taking on an edge. "Hununu, take the healer to that end and help him in whatever he needs to work."

"The worst wounds are all gathered here," Amanah said, indicating them with a sweep of her arm.

Yadi pressed his lips together, then inclined his head to the other end of the row of critically injured patients, talking to his partner. "Go on."

"You can't possibly expect me to work like this," the robed man complained, following Hununu to where Amanah had gestured. "There's not enough light!"

Emin clasped hands with Taunos's free hand, bending low so Taunos didn't have to reach up. "You going to be all right?"

"Don't worry, I'll still beat you in the wrestling match when we get back to Arruk," Taunos said.

Emin snorted. "So you're delusional. It's worse than we thought!"

Amanah wrapped her free arm around Emin's shoulders, burying her face in his bulk for a moment. Her brother was back, unharmed. He squeezed her tightly, clapping her shoulder when she let go. She desperately wanted to scream, to rage, to weep, but not yet. Not yet.

Not until every last person had been seen to.

"I'm sorry for the wait. I had to get your friends out of holding first." Yadi squatted down by Taunos. "Glad to see you're still with us."

"Holding?" Taunos frowned.

"You arrested them?" Amanah asked. How she could still be shocked, she didn't know. "What about the threat to Lamyi and Inuwe here in the city?"

Emin shrugged. "Lamyi apparently hired extra guards here, and you know how they feel about havi and horses."

She turned to face Yadi, her voice rising despite herself. "They were warning you of danger and protecting people. They were *doing their jobs*—in fact, they were doing *your* job!"

Yadi narrowed his eyes at her at the last comment, but his expression looked troubled. Good, he should be.

"I am not the entire guard of Gahimbli, nor am I in charge. Fortunately, Lord Inuwe spoke up on your behalf," Yadi said. "Once I tracked him down, Lord Lamyi also stated you were in his employ, though he said you were terrible at taking orders. That's how I knew he was telling the truth, about Haari, at least."

Taunos chuckled.

"I am under orders, though. I need to go ask questions," Yadi said, standing. "All four of you, stay here. Once the healer completes his business, we'll escort you."

"To jail or to a bed?" Amanah asked.

He sighed. "To a bed. Probably. Unless I get very different answers than I expect to get."

She scowled at him as he walked away.

"What happened to keeping your head down?" Gurseh asked. "You're drawing a lot of attention to yourself right now. Possibly deadly attention."

"Keeping my head down didn't help any of these people," Amanah shot back, her eyes hot with unshed tears. "So why should I continue?"

"You did good work while we lazed about," Emin said.

She leveled a flat look at him. "You were in jail. They threw you in jail!"

He met her gaze calmly. "I know. I was there."

She pressed her lips together, struggling for control of her temper. Only a little longer, and the healer would finish his examination and the worst of the wounds could be fixed with knowledge she didn't have yet and—

On the other side of the line of wounded, the healer stood up. "No, no, no. This is simply unworkable. I cannot do this any longer. There's no lights, everything's dirty, and it's cold out here. I will finish my examinations in my office."

"And how far is that?" Yadi asked, coming back over.

"Only two wells over. You two guards can round up some people to carry them."

Yadi frowned.

Two sections of the city? Amanah shook her head. Where had they found this man? He expected severely wounded people to walk across two districts supplied by different wells?

"No," Amanah said.

This would surely land her in more trouble, but she couldn't let them move these people without even examining them. The healer hadn't checked for all the things she might have missed. She'd seen too many people carrying injuries for life because they'd used broken limbs too long.

But the healer either didn't notice or didn't care. He clapped his hands and nodded. "If we've had enough of outbursts—"

"Lie still, Haari Taunos. All of you, lie still." Amanah wasn't quite sure where that tone of command had come from, though it was her voice speaking. Maybe she'd listened a little too long at the bamimri windows.

Every eye turned on her and she flushed, but she didn't back down. "If you want to work again, or wrestle again, or fight again, you need to lie still until your wounds are tended."

"I wasn't planning on doing anything else," Taunos said.

"Now listen here, young woman," the healer began.

This time, Taunos cut him off. "Her name is Amanah."

The healer scowled, and Hununu pushed her way forward, standing toe-to-toe with Amanah. "You are impeding a guard's work. I will not warn you again. I happen to know we have a jail cell free."

"Step back, Hununu," Yadi said.

"This is foolish, to listen to her over an esteemed member of the healer's guild," Hununu said, rounding on Yadi. "You can hear the wilderness in her voice. For all we know, she was in league with the death team. The reports say they took out guards first, but left her alive."

"I have tended the very lord of the city!" the healer said, puffing out his chest. "I will not work in such conditions!"

"I will," Amanah said. "Just tell me what to do."

"Most certainly not! There are proper ways of getting this schooling for a reason," he said.

Amanah glared at him. "I'm willing to do the work you aren't willing to do. You have the knowledge and training I lack. Why—"

"And I will not give them away to some degenerate!"

"Help me help these people! I can't do it on my own and they should not suffer for my ignorance!" Her voice cracked, and angry tears glittered in her eyes, breaking up her vision.

"Stop!" Yadi snapped.

Silence fell. Taunos rubbed his thumb gently over her knuckles, battered and bruised from fighting the rubble. She curled her fingers around his, glaring at the healer.

"I will not work like this. I will not tolerate such wanton disrespect," the healer said, clipping the edges of his words.

Yadi rubbed his forehead and let out a long sigh.

"We wouldn't dream of asking you to," Hununu assured him. She turned to Yadi. "He is the most highly esteemed—"

"You can go," Yadi said to the healer. "Thank you for your time. Hununu will escort you should you require it."

"What?" squawked the healer, sounding remarkably like a startled bird.

"What are you doing?" Hununu demanded.

Yadi rounded on her. "You may dismiss them, but I have seen nothing but bravery and devotion from these people. Every story I've heard has been the same. Haari, yet again, put himself in harm's way, and this young woman—Amanah, yes?—has worked tirelessly all day, saving lives. Apparently this square was filled with bodies, and without her and the mercy of the gods, more funeral pyres would be burning. I will not undo such work so a man who's spent all day in rooms prepared for healing, with water and shade and food and comfort, can continue to practice his craft without a modicum of discomfort."

"The guardmaster—" Hununu began.

Yadi interrupted her. "—is friends with Borlim of Arruk, did you know that? And these two—" he indicated Emin and Gurseh— "mentioned Borlim with familiarity. Did you see their hands? Did you even look? Look at this!"

He seized Amanah's hand before she could flinch away, thrusting it into Hununu's face. "This hand tells the same story. Look at the scrapes and bruises. Same as on his."

He pointed at Emin's hands. Ever the show-off, Emin raised his arms to display the battered backs of his hands better.

But Amanah wrenched her hand free of Yadi's grip, shuffling away from him with a glare he was facing the wrong direction to see. She wasn't a piece of evidence to be held up for inspection.

Yadi was continuing regardless, his focus apparently solely on his fellow guard. "Those are hands who have worked hard to save lives. And we need all the lives saved we can get, especially when, with the war, we may yet need people who rush headlong into danger. A Hinanuri death team walked into this city and all these people lived to tell the tale,

Hununu. We should be celebrating, not trying to point fingers at the ones who saved our city. We can't win every day, but when people have worked so hard to scratch even the smallest win out of defeat, we do not throw them away."

Amanah pressed her lips together. It shouldn't take a tragedy to make people remember those they'd forced to the edges, the ones desperately trying to scrape by. If this sentiment got these people the medical care they needed, she was thankful for it, but how long would it last?

Hununu glared at Yadi, and then turned to the healer. "Come on. Let's get you home."

Amanah stared, not surprised but still unable to tear herself from watching as the healer and Hununu turned their backs on them, walking away. They had the power to make things better, and they chose not to use it.

"You really believe in her?" Yadi asked.

She glanced at the guard, who was looking at Taunos.

"Whole-heartedly," Taunos said.

"She's what you've got." Yadi folded his arms, shooting a sour look at Hununu's back.

Amanah's stomach knotted. "I...I don't know what else to do. I've done everything I know to, all of the wisdom the older healers had. I haven't studied in the bamimri. They need more help than I can give."

"Can you prepare them for transport?" Yadi asked. "I know someone who might be able to help, but she cannot travel far, so we would need to bring these people to her."

"Cannot or will not?" This wasn't any better than the healer's plan, and she'd rejected that.

"Cannot. Truly."

She watched his face and then nodded. It was better than leaving them to shiver on the ground, probably. Had her pride gotten in the way? Should she have sent them with the healer, instead? Especially since they had to move the people anyway. Had she only caused these people more suffering because she was angry at the person who knew how to help them?

"I'll do my best," she whispered.

Her hands shook, and Taunos pulled the one he held gently over his chest so he could place his palm over top. She stared down at their hands, at the rise and fall of his chest. She took three breaths in time with his, instead of the quick shaky inhalations that wanted to come. The panic took two steps back, enough for her to think, to deal with it.

She squeezed his hand in thanks and looked back at Yadi. "We need blankets, water, and stretchers. Can you get these things?"

He nodded. "I'll see what I can do. Emin, Gurseh, I need you with me. After all, I swore not to let you out of my sight, and you can help carry things."

Emin clapped her on the shoulder and Gurseh clasped her arm, and she returned the gestures, though her stomach twisted as she watched them follow Yadi across the square and out of sight. Not to jail though, not if Yadi could be trusted. Except she didn't know if Yadi *could* be trusted.

Once she found her calm, she wrestled it with both hands as if it were a wild stallion, pouring her focus into each person, one at a time. She hardly even remembered faces, only each wound she found, each problem to solve. People asked her questions that she responded to, steadying possibly broken bones for transport, arranging limbs to keep ribs and spines straight, moving people onto blankets that appeared from somewhere. She was too busy to wonder from where, instead dredging her memories for each scrap she'd gleaned from the bimnas, each nugget of forbidden knowledge. Knowledge that she hoped was enough to keep these people alive and able to recover, every one of them that remained.

Finally, there was nothing else to do. Everyone was as ready as she could make them—she just hoped they didn't have to travel far.

There was a murmur of voices around her, one she'd been blocking out, but now she returned to it. Emin, Gurseh, and Yadi stood beside Taunos, chatting quietly.

"Are you all right?" Taunos asked.

She frowned at him. "I should be asking you. I didn't get blown up."

He laughed, then winced and held his ribs, his laughter fading to a rueful smile.

"You were pretty far gone there," Emin said, watching her with concern.

"I was concentrating," she said, bristling though she wasn't really sure why.

He raised his eyebrows, pride shining in his eyes. "Well, healer? Are we ready to move them now?"

She flushed. But there was a crowd of people around her, waiting for her word. Where had they come from?

"Yes," Amanah said, clearing her throat. "It should be fine now. As well as can be, anyway."

"Good," Yadi said. "We'll get people patched up and you can check in with your employers."

Between her brother and Taunos, there was a little too much chaos in her life, it felt at times. And yet, they supported her, even when she stood up to a trained healer, for better or for worse.

And this... this work was needed. No one was going to stop her from standing here, between injury and illness and those who needed her help, whenever they needed her.

19

THE REST OF the night passed in a blur. Yadi brought them to an enormous house owned by some noble. Someone took Nakii while Yadi ushered them inside, where low tables had been shoved together in the middle of a dance hall. The wounded were laid carefully on the tables, and the healer—a grey-haired woman with light brown eyes and jewels in her ears and around her neck—rolled in on a chair with wheels.

Amanah tried to pay attention, following the orders the woman gave her, but the details slipped out of her mind as soon as she completed them. Exhaustion weighed heavily on her, and all she could understand was that the people she'd brought here were going to live. More than that, most would recover well. She'd made many, many mistakes, but most could be corrected, and the healer's brisk tone held no condemnation as she rolled from one patient to the next, pointing out observations and fixing the wrongs, sometimes instructing Amanah in how to do so when it involved something she couldn't do, confined to her chair as she was.

One by one, the injured's wounds were washed, dried, and bandaged, and they were sent to bed—real beds in guest rooms in the house. Amanah barely had the energy to wonder at it, near crumpling with relief when the healer pronounced Taunos—the last of the patients, true to his word—to be well enough to walk to his room with help, provided he was careful. He would be fine.

Taunos's movements were stiff as he got up from the table, and he needed support at first. Guilt twisted her stomach. She'd needlessly made him lay so long on the cold stones of the square. All his bruises looked angry. He hadn't deserved such pain as she'd helped bring on him.

"I'm sorry. I worried for nothing," she said. "I shouldn't have given you the powder. You didn't need it."

"Nonsense," the healer interrupted. "I'm going to assume that's the fatigue talking, because I hear you patched up most of these people, and your care saved lives. That's the work of a wise woman, not a foolish woman thinking just because something turned out to be unnecessary means that taking care to prevent further injury was wrong."

Amanah flushed, bowing her head. Then a thought struck her, one she should have had before. "Please, where are Lords Inuwe and Lamyi? Are —"

The woman snorted. "Those two are at Lord Biryewi's house, closer to the center of the city. They're both fine, and have ordered you to join them tomorrow for the Festival of Dark Nights."

She pressed her lips together.

"I'll take care of the wounded for as long as they need, and I've sent supplies to the people in the square, so there's nothing more to worry about tonight."

Amanah swallowed hard and nodded. "Where's my brother and Gurseh?"

"They have a guest room here in my house. Now, off you go. Follow Sadi, here." She indicated a plump servant standing by the door. "She'll take you to your rooms. Get some sleep. I don't want to see you again until you have life back in your eyes."

Taking Taunos's arm across her shoulder, she braced him against her with her hand on his hip to avoid his wounded side and helped him limp after Sadi.

"Thank you," Taunos said, tilting his head to whisper across her ear.

She forced a small smile at him, still battling away the emotions she'd kept at bay all day. She wasn't ready to deal with them yet.

Sadi took them down a long hallway and stopped at a paneled door about halfway down. "This and the next room are both still open. You may take which you prefer."

"Thank you," Taunos said, and Amanah mumbled the same.

With a bow, the servant turned and walked away.

"Come on, you need to get to bed," Amanah said, shouldering open the door.

"You need rest, too."

She helped him across thick rugs to the large bed at the center, piled with pillows and soft blankets. Easing him down to sit on the bed, she knelt to undo his boots, pulling them and his socks off.

"Amanah, you don't have to—"

"You don't want to sleep with your boots on," she said. She had to keep moving, because once she stopped, there would be nothing to hold back her feelings and the memories of the day. Even though she was exhausted, she couldn't stop. She'd shatter into a million pieces, unable to ever be put back together.

"You're welcome to stay, if you want," Taunos said.

Amanah narrowed her eyes at him. "You're injured."

He chuckled. "I am well aware of that, thank you. What about your leg? Your shoulder? Did you hurt yourself worse saving lives?"

Even though Taunos was so battered, he was still worried about her? She shook her head. "I'm a little sore, but I'm not as injured as you. I'll be fine."

Pulling back the blankets, he swung his legs onto the bed, his arm clamped against his side. He sank back against the pillow with a pained grimace, then offered one hand to her.

"Today was a long, difficult day," he said. "You're trembling again. If it will help, I'm here. Just a hug, nothing else, if you wish it."

She *was* trembling, and the realization made all the emotions she'd pushed back all day flood across her, abrading her soul. She didn't want to be alone. She turned away from him and went to the door. Shutting it firmly, she turned back to him.

"You're injured," she said, making her way back and taking off her boots. "So we're not doing anything. I don't want to hurt you more. But a hug would be nice."

He raised himself on his elbow as if to sit, wincing at the movement. "I can do a hug."

The wave of grief and fatigue eased a little, drawing out a smile. She touched his shoulder, pushing him gently back down. "A laying down hug is fine."

"Oh, that, I can definitely do," Taunos said, settling back with a sigh. His hair was a wild cloud on the pillow, his face lined with pain and fatigue, but his eyes were calm and warm and fixed on her.

She took off her boots and then her socks. Blood spattered her clothes, and she grimaced, glancing at the clean sheets on the bed. Wrinkling her nose, she took off her shirt and pants, leaving her undershirt and leggings. There was a washcloth on the table with a bowl of water, still warm, and she washed her face and arms, then turned to Taunos.

His eyes were half-closed, but he was still watching her with soft concern. He drew back the covers beside him.

Enough delays. She shook like the last leaf on a tree as she went to him, blowing out the lamp. She lay down, nestling gingerly against his chest, shifting until she was sure she wasn't going to hurt him and her own wounds didn't complain. He wrapped his arms around her, one hand rubbing her back silently. The tears came, and she tried to hide them in her hands, but he stroked his thumb across her cheek.

"I've got you," Taunos murmured. "You're safe. You can let go."

"I don't want to be a bother," she said, pulling away. This had been a bad idea. She felt so knotted up inside, bursting with all the emotions she'd pushed away to deal with later, that now, she felt like if she did unleash them, she'd never stop.

"Ah, yes." He kissed her fingers, muddling his next word, though the endearment and teasing chiding came through. "Holding you is so arduous, such a chore."

A half laugh broke from her, combined with a sob that sparked tears in her eyes, so tightly were her emotions bound up in themselves.

"Tears aren't weakness. If you deny yourself this, your emotions, acknowledging your pain, it can become sickness, like rot." He tightened his arms around her, repeating himself as he kissed her braids. "I've got you, beloved. It's safe here to fall apart for a little bit."

"You say that like it's easy, but you never fall apart."

His fingers brushed her braids back from her face, his voice a quiet rumble in his chest. "I do. And when next I do, I want it to be here, in your arms, where the ragged pieces of me will be safe. I just hope you know the same, that you're safe with me. Every part of you."

Like the rain washing away the mud, nearly washing away her brother in the mudslide, his words washed away her attempts at composure. Sobs clawed their way up her throat. She wept into his chest, holding onto him like a lifeline. Tears flowed for all those she couldn't save, for the anger and the fear, for the suffering that had filled the square which had so easily been ignored by those who should have helped. For the battle she'd face tomorrow and in the future, to make sure such things didn't happen again.

But she'd found someone else who could possibly be an ally—the noble healer in the wheelchair. And maybe, eventually, the days like this wouldn't turn out the same way. Maybe more would live. At least, they would if she had anything to say about it.

In the meantime, she had safe arms to fall apart in, an embrace that still somehow managed to beat back the fears and pain that ate at her, a peace that would help her put herself back together again afterward. Taunos hummed a low tune to her, his fingers brushing back her messy braids, soothing her until her shaking quieted. She shifted closer to him, letting his wordless humming, his heart beating, his warm arms around her, carry her off to sleep.

Sunlight streamed onto her face from the large window near the bed, awakening her. It took her a moment to remember where she was, why she was lying in this soft bed, a blanket over her shoulders as if someone had tucked her in. Arms loosely encircled her waist, a warm, broad chest at her back. Taunos.

She sighed as contentment draped her like the blanket, and she shifted backward, closer to him. His arms tightened around her, a slight, sharp movement behind her attesting that she'd woken him. But, almost immediately, he took a deep breath and sighed it out, pulling her more closely against him. Snuggling into her as she had him.

She peeked at him over her shoulder. "Sorry. Go back to sleep."

His lips curved into a smile as slow and sweet as honey, his eyes already drifting closed once more. He rested his head against hers, his nose a line down her neck, nestled close. Enveloped by the safety of him, she let sleep carry her off again.

The next time she woke, the bed behind her was cold. The door clicked shut, and she sat up, blinking bleary eyes. Taunos limped over with a tray of fruits, pastries, and tea. He set it on a table against the wall and sank into a chair beside it with a stifled groan, checking his bandages.

"Are you all right?" she asked, getting up.

"Fine. You looked so beautiful, so peaceful, I didn't want to disturb you. Thought I'd retrieve breakfast. You're probably hungry."

"I could have done that. You need to rest," Amanah said, heading behind the screen for the waste chute.

"I enjoyed the walk," he said. "And I wanted to do something nice for you. You took care of everyone yesterday. It's far past your turn to be taken care of. How are you feeling?"

"Fine." She finished, wishing she had fresh clothes to put on, but she'd already slept next to him like this, so she supposed what she looked like didn't matter. She washed her face and hands with the pitcher, bowl, and cloth provided, then stepped back into the room, undoing her mostly unravelled braids.

His eyes landed on her, first a quick sweep, assessing her for injuries, then softening, warming, contemplating her as he munched leisurely on one of the pieces of bread.

The memory of those eyes on her last night, the way he'd held her as she wept, crashed over her. Her cheeks heated, though she tried to ignore it, answering his question more fully as she considered the pastries. "I feel better. Thank you. For last night."

"Anytime," he murmured.

She looked at the teabag options: a sparkberry blend that he must have noticed her preference for, and a contraceptive blend.

She held up the second option. "You, Haari Taunos, are injured."

"And you are a healer." Mischief sparked in his eyes. "And in my defense, you are incredible. Exquisite. I don't know enough words to describe you, but if I could wake up every morning with you in my arms, I would be happy."

She hmm'ed to cover the lightness his compliments filled her with. "Didn't you say you can't have children right now anyway?"

He gave her a flat look still filled with fondness. "I know you well enough to know you prefer to take things into your own hands. And I'm not pressuring—it's all up to you. Brew whatever you'd like."

"You didn't get a strainer for separate cups?"

"I'll drink whatever you're drinking," he said, leaning back. "Why should you have to drink alone?"

She smiled at that, cheeks heating again, and steeped the contraceptive blend, just in case. They ate quietly for a bit, until she poured tea and handed him the cup so he wouldn't have to get up again, then took one for herself. Leaning against the wall, she watched him in return, sipping her tea. She smiled softly.

She loved him, loved loving him, even when they weren't doing anything. That morning with the sun shining on her and Taunos's arms around her, she didn't know how long it'd been since she'd felt such love, comfort, and ease. The utter comfort of it was unexpectedly refreshing. She wished it would never end, but she supposed looking forward to the next time would have to do instead.

"What?" he asked.

Was that a hint of red under the brown of his skin? She grinned. "What, does Haari Taunos get embarrassed?"

He groaned, something flashing across his face too quickly for her to read clearly. Annoyance? Hurt? Grief? "Please don't start *that*. Of course I do."

She raised her eyebrows, grabbing a pastry. "What's wrong?"

"I'm just a man," he said. "All I do is the best I can. It doesn't mean I don't have faults, don't have wounds."

"Of course not." She knew that well. What had she said to set this off? "Oh. The stories bother you? The fame? The bigger-than-life, can-fight-off-ten-warriors perception of Haari Taunos? Why do you reach for it then?"

"I don't reach for it," he said. "It's like yesterday. I see a problem, I try to fix it."

"And you get blown up."

A chuckle burst from him. "Sometimes, on the really exciting days."

But the humor faded quickly from his eyes, leaving behind... worry?

"You didn't care when Inuwe used the stories to threaten the Lenuri. Though I'm glad he didn't get you killed."

He took a sip of his tea. "Sometimes it's fun, the challenge of it. And it's always worthwhile, trying to help people. But when people see only the stories, they stop seeing *me*. I don't care usually, especially with people like Inuwe, using the stories to try to stay alive. But it hurts when it's people I love."

His mouth tightened, and he stared down at the cup in his hands.

Ah. There it was. She swallowed the rest of her pastry and set down her tea, going to him. Her fingers found the unruly lock of his hair, brushing it back from his face as she stared down at him. She cupped her fingers under his jawline, drawing his gaze up to her.

"I see you."

His mouth parted, his features relaxing. "And I see you. Amanah, I love you."

She smiled, taking the tea from him and placing it on the tray. Moving slowly, gingerly, she perched on his lap, needing to be closer to him. She brushed her fingers over his cheek, curling around to the hair at the back of his neck.

"I love you, too. I thought I was going to lose you," she whispered. She pressed her forehead to his, her nose to his. "I want this, between us."

His hands settled on her waist, sliding around to her back, his eyes drinking hers in. "I want to show you just how much you mean to me every day of my life."

"That's what I'm afraid of." She kissed his forehead, blinking back tears. "Taunos, you went and got yourself blown up. How am I going to love you if you're in pieces?"

His voice tightened. "I didn't mean to frighten you. Someone needed to help those people though. I was there."

"I know. I know. And I love that about you. I just don't want to let go of this."

He tightened his hold around her. "Nor do I. You were there, too. I knew you would be. I love that about you."

She traced his face with her hands, echoing his words. "Someone needed to help."

The slow curve of his lips drew an answering smile from her. He raised a hand, bushing back a lock of her hair, running it through his fingers. "There was a message on the breakfast tray from someone I know in Arruk. I had one of the merchants in the market watch for Gitu and his family, and then send me a message here in code. I knew Yadi would hold a message for me. I had Gurseh read it for me: Gitu and his family all got out safely."

She blinked, then smiled. Good, that plan had gone as intended, then, even though she hadn't been there to oversee it. Gitu, Anila, little Aaya— all of them would be ok. Her heart lifted with the news. The Hand hadn't needed her. Probably wouldn't in the future, either.

Taunos's eyes were intent on her as he rested his forehead against hers. She closed her eyes, relaxing into him. He knew she'd care, and he'd made sure to find out, even before all this. A well of gratitude filled her.

Worry threaded through his voice when he spoke. "If the nobles knew you were smuggling people out of harm's way in the city, out of reach of their wrath, we both know they'd turn the full force of that wrath on you."

She drew back, mouth flattening into a hard line. He wouldn't try to forbid her from her work, would he?

"We both choose to do dangerous work. We both run into danger to save others." His voice thickened with feeling, and he slid his hands up her back to her shoulders. "When Emin was climbing that rope and you were in so much pain, and all I could do was hold you and keep you there, in that agony... I *hated* that. I hated that I couldn't end your pain. And the sandcat, when it sprang at you, all I could see for a moment was it tearing you to shreds. And it's only gotten worse since: when you rode through the night for help, and then up there on the wall yesterday, banner dancing. They shot at you. If they'd hit you..."

He sighed against her, and his eyelashes brushed her cheek. She nuzzled into him in return, grateful for his understanding. They were together, alive, and with injuries that would heal.

His arms tightened around her. "But if all I can do is comfort you when you're in pain, or watch your back when you're in danger, or hold you when you need it once you come back to me, then that's what I want to do. All of me that's free, it's yours."

She rested her head on his shoulder, tucking her face into his neck, relishing his closeness. "Whatever happens next, I want you at my side."

He ran his fingers down a lock of her hair, twisting it gently around his finger as he brushed it back from her shoulder. "It's nice to have someone I can trust. To know I can rest for a bit, that you're watching my back."

"It's the same for me." She pulled back to look at him. "So we'll have to find a way to live with this fear."

There was no levity, no jokes this time. His words had the quality of an oath. "I hope so, for a long, long time. Because I would never even try to stop you from being a hero."

"Me either," she whispered. "I just wish I could *know* you'll always come back to me from whatever heroics you run off to do."

His other hand came up to cup her face, thumb brushing her cheekbone. "I will always come back to you, as long as it's in my power."

"And please remember that you're not alone anymore."

"I know."

"And would it kill you to plan once in a while?"

A laugh burst out of him. "Well, clearly more of our heroics should be together. Perhaps your planning will rub off on me. One can hope."

"I suppose I'll save you, if I have to," she returned.

The laughter dancing in his eyes flared at those words, then faded slowly to leave behind that earnest intensity she was coming to know so well. His arms wrapped more snugly around her. "You should never have to hide how brightly you shine, and you shine brighter than the sun, beretabeiur."

She tilted her head at the murmur of syllables. "What was that?"

A hint of red flushed under the brown of his skin. "Ah."

"Bere... something?"

"That requires a story."

"I hear you're good at stories," she teased.

A breath of laughter escaped him as his hand found a lock of her hair again, running it through his fingers. The pure distraction her loose hair gave him made her smile.

"You're going to have trouble with that when I rebraid my hair," she warned him lightly.

"Your hair's so pretty no matter what you do with it." He smiled at her. "Does this bother you?"

"No, it's relaxing, actually."

He made a pleased noise deep in his throat, repeating the motion as he began his story. "Songs are important to my people, and drums keep the beat of songs. Without the drums, without a beat, the music devolves into chaos."

She raised her eyebrows but kept silent.

His fingers trailed down to her wrist, and he took her hand. "It means 'drumbeat of my heart.'"

"I'm keeping you from chaos?" she asked. "I'm not sure how to interpret that."

He pressed her hand to his heart. "I lose my way sometimes, get distracted. You're steady. You help keep *me* steady. You help me be a better person. So it's meant to be a compliment."

"Well, I do like your heart beating," she said, kissing him. "It's a bit long though, isn't it?"

"I'd probably shorten it to Tabei. If you don't mind it."

"You can't have *all* the nicknames. I kind of like having one just from you." She squeezed his hand. "You trust me, which means more than I can say, even if you also throw things into chaos. You inspire me to take risks, you help me be braver. You make it seem possible that it might not all end in disaster."

"You deserve to have the things you want. Don't crush the life out of yourself to give to others," he said. "Your life, actually living it, is important too."

"Why aren't you ever worried about what others think of you? You've never cared about being seen with me."

He shrugged. "Many of these nobles view me as a diversion or an ornament. They use me—my attendance, knowing I'll tell stories and mingle—and in the meantime I learn things. We're just using each other. It's not real like it is with Emin, with you."

That was incredibly… sad.

"And as for you," he peppered kisses along her jawline. "I don't like letting other people into our relationship where they don't belong. I just want you comfortable and happy."

She kissed him gently, and then urgently, until he groaned in pain. They broke apart, and he clutched his wounded side with a rueful grin.

"We'll just have to be careful," she said, once she was sure they hadn't reopened any wounds.

"If you can handle it, I can handle it," he said, his grin a challenge, his fingers tracing over her jawline.

She leaned closer, kissing him tenderly, keeping space between them so she could run her hands along his skin with all the gentleness he'd ever shown her, now returned to him. His fingers clung to her back, gliding over the bandages on her waist to clutch instead at her hips, as if she were a treasure beyond measure. He was right, she realized. This thing between them was precious, and hearts were easily hurt.

But that meant that love and laughter were even more important. She would gather all of it that came her way, armoring herself in that brightness to guard against the darkness and despair that life could bring. And perhaps the joy could buoy them through the storms, safe through to the other side.

20

A KNOCK ON the door sounded, and Sadi's voice came through the wood. "Lady Rebaya would like to see you for a simple lunch and to discuss arrangements for the rain of the gods. Please dress in anything you would like in the wardrobe, and leave soiled laundry by the door for washing. Feel free to choose clothing for the Festival of Dark Nights tonight as well, and lay them out on the bed if any alterations need to be made over lunch—our seamstress will come by if needed."

That was right—they were supposed to meet Lamyi and Inuwe at the Festival of Dark Nights. Amanah looked over at her dirty clothes from last night, wrinkling her nose at all the blood, dirt, and other bits she didn't care to identify. "Well, that answers that question, anyway."

Taunos glided his fingers over her shoulders. "What's wrong? You've got your worried voice on."

She headed over to the enormous wooden contraption lurking in the corner. She'd been wondering what kind of clothes nobles kept in wardrobes in spare rooms, anyway. The space was full of colors. Loose, flowing gowns of the entire rainbow pressed against matching robes and shirt-trouser combinations.

Her worries sharpened. While she was glad she wouldn't have to wear her bloody clothes again, generosity of this magnitude was not something she was used to seeing from nobles. What would it cost? Maybe there was still time to flee. Except how could they hope to find somewhere to hole up for the rain of the gods without being found right away?

"What's wrong?" Taunos asked again. He'd stepped up behind her, and now leaned around her to look into the corners of the baited wooden trap.

She gestured expansively. "Who keeps clothes like this? For guests? Does every guest room have clothing like this? Why waste the money?"

"Maybe they're being good hosts. Maybe they knew one day an exhausted healer would need to stay the night and would appreciate non-bloody clothes in the morning."

"So long as what they want in return doesn't cost too much," she muttered.

He squeezed her hand gently. "This is Yadi's mother's house. The healer you worked with yesterday is his mother."

"Oh." She pressed her lips together, still uncertain on how she felt about Yadi, not to mention his mother. The room had been generous—so far. She could have kicked them all out. She didn't have to work on anyone at all.

But how far could she trust the generosity of a noble? Was she being reduced to fleeting entertainment again?

She hmm'ed. At least they had shelter for the rain of the gods. "So, clothes? Is this provided freely?"

"I think so."

Amanah pulled in a breath, steeling herself, and turned back to the wardrobe. "I suppose we need to choose."

The problem was that the choices were overwhelming. Every dress was beautiful, far too expensive, and they seemed so delicate. With hems and necklines and sleeves of all sizes, it was too much. Whatever she chose, she'd stand out, because she didn't belong.

When she was on her fourth increasingly frantic search through the wardrobe, Taunos took her hand and turned her gently to face him. She leaned against him, and he stroked her hair, which fell in loose waves down her back, since she hadn't yet rebraided it. When she was calmer, he spoke, his voice rumbling through her.

"If you could wear anything, what would it look like? What would it feel like? What would you be able to do in it?"

"Something I can run in." Utility first. But... she also wanted a dress. She might never again have the chance to wear a dress so fine, after all. So, a dress she could run in. That would narrow the options. She took a deep breath, steadier now, and turned back to the wardrobe.

More methodically now, she sorted through the dresses, only taking out those that wouldn't hinder her movement too much. She measured them against herself. Although she was used to wearing what was available regardless of how well it fit, anything too small or too large wouldn't be helpful. She handed those that might work to Taunos, who laid them out on the bed. When she was done and turned to view the smaller pool of clothing, she sighed. There were still too many choices.

"What else?" he asked. "Favorite color? Favorite feel? What would be part of your perfect dress?"

"Nothing too flashy, but still pretty. Something that flows like a cool night's breeze."

One by one, she handed rejected gowns back to him, which he returned to the wardrobe, until only four remained. That was manageable, and she chose a deep blue dress patterned with flowers falling in a diagonal from shoulder to hem. Slits in the skirt allowed for movement, paired with black leggings so she'd easily be able to fight or ride if needed.

"This feels nice," Taunos said, running his fingers along the cloth. "Silk, is that what it's called?"

His never-ending curiosity made her snort, but she nodded. "Look, there are silk suits here, too."

"Let's see," he mused. "Something that will complement yours."

Of course, among the overwhelming options, there was a deep blue tunic and trousers with flowers on the back and cuffs to match hers. They quickly changed into the formal wear, and she tucked herself into his arms and smiled to see how well they matched. The desire to do this through the festival, too, rose in her. Could she? Without bringing down ruin on herself or others?

With a sigh, she withdrew, and they switched to loose-fitting robes with cloth belts for lunch with their host. Both opted for their boots instead of the slippers at the bottom of the wardrobe, and then they headed out the door, asking the first person they met in the hallway where they were supposed to go for lunch.

They were led to a sitting room just as Emin and Gurseh came down the hallway, led by another servant. Both looked clean and refreshed in borrowed clothes, as if they hadn't spent all day yesterday working to clean up a disaster.

"Did you get fancy new clothes too?" Emin asked with a grin.

"On loan, I'm sure," Amanah said. "I hope I don't damage it with my boots. I intend to wear them to the festival, too, just in case."

"No one will be looking at your feet anyway," Emin said.

They entered the sitting room, where couches were clustered together among little tables, lamps gleaming in the walls. Lines of pain were beginning to tighten Taunos's expression, so Amanah pointed him to a couch while Emin wandered the room, inspecting the furnishings and looking out the windows. Sadi came in carrying a tray laden with glasses with ice, a pitcher of water with fruit in it, and assorted tiny sandwiches.

It all served to underline how out of her depth they were now. Too much could go wrong. Surely there was a trap here and she couldn't see it. It knotted her stomach.

Biting her lip, Amanah murmured a thank you to Sadi and retreated to settle beside Taunos.

"I'm interested in how the nobles pass the time during the rain of the gods," Emin said, plopping down on her other side on the couch. Taunos winced, and Emin slapped his back. "Do you think there'll be much singing?"

"Don't make me redo his stitches," Amanah chided.

"As long as they feed me, I'm good," Gurseh said, perching on the next chair over.

"What's the plan? We stay there for the entire time?" Amanah asked. "If we're expected at the Festival tonight, we won't have time to find another place to stay."

"How's the hero of the square?" Lady Rebaya wheeled herself through the doorway, splendid in another set of jewels, this time dotting her hair. Her clothes were simple, serviceable wear, however, and from the stains, Amanah wondered if she had just come from the injured.

"He's fine," Amanah said, darting a look at Taunos. "So long as he tries to avoid further heroics for a bit."

Rebaya laughed. "Not him, silly. I mean you."

Her face burned with heat. "The—what? I'm not—"

Emin laughed, nudging her before he switched couches to sit with Gurseh. "I haven't seen her at such a loss for words in a long time."

Taunos bumped her knee with his. "Took them long enough to notice the true hero."

"How are they?" she asked, wrenching her mind away from that frightening thought. She clasped her hands together as if she could hold on to sanity, but also to avoid trying to hide behind her palms. "The people we brought? Thank you, again, for helping them."

"Most have returned to their families now," Rebaya said. "I think my home makes them uncomfortable. I have healers going out now, to check on them before the rain of the gods."

"Thank you." Amanah's gaze dropped to the thick carpet. Perhaps she'd misjudged this woman.

"Now, let me tell you what's going to happen," Rebaya said. "I'm not sure how much you heard from last night—you were exhausted. All the nobles of Gahimbli spend the rain of the gods together. Each household takes turns hosting the others, and this time is Lord Biryewi's turn. Lords Inuwe and Lamyi are already there. Yadi tells me Lamyi's already hired extra guards for his and Inuwe's protection. You four are still going as well, but are not quite as necessary to Lamyi and Inuwe as before."

Amanah exchanged looks with Emin. They were being replaced. Was this in preparation for an accident to befall them? She shuddered.

Taunos took her hand, threading their fingers together, and pulled it into his lap, covering their twined hands with his free one. Amanah took a deep breath, resting her good shoulder against his.

"Therefore," Rebaya continued, "you four are also my personal guests."

"What?" Amanah's throat went dry. She took a sip of water, wrinkling her nose at the fruit bumping against her lip in the glass.

"You will arrive with myself and my son. You can trade off mingling around your guarding duties." She looked quite satisfied with herself, and Amanah blinked at her.

"No doubt Inuwe and Lamyi will take care of their business during the festival, still?" Emin said.

"No doubt," Rebaya said. "Most of the nobles do, after all, since they're all together anyway. Then afterward, you'll be taking them back to Arruk, I hear."

"But… we're guests? We're staying in a noble's house for all of the rain of the gods? Wearing your clothes?" Amanah's voice was strained. Taunos squeezed her hand, and she reminded herself to breathe. "What will all this cost us? What do you want from us?"

"What was your name again?" Rebaya asked, turning her chair a bit to face her directly. "Please forgive me, but it was late and there was a lot going on. 'Hero of the square' is a bit of a mouthful for casual conversation."

"Amanah," she said, swallowing hard. She took another sip of fruity water.

"Amanah, thank you. Would you like to train as a healer?"

Her mouth fell open, her eyes staring at Rebaya only to find the noble's expression serious. This lure, dropped in her lap like this, it had to be a trap. A test. "I—the bamimri doesn't allow havi—I can't pay—"

Lady Rebaya flicked her hand as if swatting away her words. "I didn't ask what you can or can't do, or about silly old rules that have stayed alive far too long. I'm asking what you want."

"I helped those people because they needed it. No one else was organizing things."

Rebaya frowned. "That was still not the question. It's very simple. Do you want to learn healing as they teach in the bamimri?"

Dreams spoken died. Except she had spoken of dreams, and some of them had come true. She clutched Taunos's hand.

Amanah's gaze flickered to the door—shut—to the windows—curtains drifting in the wind—to Emin—nodding at her with bright eyes—to Gurseh—rolling his hand for her to get on with it—to Taunos beside her, his thumb stroking the back of her hand. His knee bumped hers, and he gave her an encouraging smile.

Nobles didn't give people like her what they wanted without massive strings attached. But nobles also didn't do anything Rebaya seemed to have done so far. Amanah had watched her work on the injured late into the night until her eyes were dull with weariness. It was far more than the healer Yadi had brought had done. It was far more than she'd ever have guessed a healer would do.

And then, Rebaya had given them real rooms instead of tossing them onto the street as she so easily could have done. If she was truthful, she was even having healers check in on them. Could Amanah judge her the same way she did Inuwe and Lamyi?

Drawing in a shaky breath, Amanah returned her gaze to Rebaya. "Yes."

Rebaya smiled. "You showed enormous dedication and the heart of a true healer, Amanah. You would be an asset as a bimna, or apprenticed to any healer, though I'm guessing you've already learned some from healers you have access to? Some of your techniques were interesting, to say the least, and your work in the square was resourceful."

She nodded, unsure she'd ever find her voice again. How much longer could this benevolent facade last? In Arruk, healers that weren't bimnas were rare because of the bamimri. But she'd learned what she could from the healers at home before coming to Arruk and stealing what secrets she could from the bamimri, and she'd enjoyed her talk with the healers of the Lenuri.

Rebaya continued. "I'm going to pressure Lords Lamyi and Inuwe to sponsor your entry into the bamimri. If they do so, they'll have to support you publicly, which I imagine would be a breath of fresh air. But if that doesn't work, I want you to know, I will sponsor you myself, should you wish it."

Amanah gaped at her. "But, the bimna's residence must be in Arruk."

Rebaya's smile remained. "I share a small home with other nobles there on a rotating basis. You can use that address."

Anger crawled its way up Amanah's throat to pour out her mouth. "Why now? Why do you want to help now and not help the people crowded in that square earlier, or the people huddled against the city walls? Why was this all allowed to happen in the first place?"

"Amanah!" Gurseh scolded.

Emin crossed his arms over his chest, watching intently.

Only Taunos didn't move, his shoulder secure against hers, his fingers curled around hers.

Rebaya winced. "That's fair. From where you're sitting... Yes, I can see how it would look."

"I just want an answer," Amanah bit out.

"Various clans have been coming here for months, driven from their lands by Hinanuri raiding parties. Troublemakers here have convinced the guard that these are not refugees, but spies, but even more than that, there's not enough space to house everyone. When you have nobles working together for various reasons to shove the newcomers to the side... Well, I have been outvoted. Even being rich and of a clan currently enjoying power, I do not get everything I want, my dear. Especially when the queen and council—and clan leaders—disagree with me.

"I thought I would have more time to help, and, in the interest of honesty, I didn't go there to see the conditions myself. I thought I was helping where I could. Last night showed me it wasn't enough. When Yadi told me what had happened, described what you'd done and with what resources, well. You woke this old woman up."

"So all this... the rooms, the clothing, this lunch," Amanah said, indicating the room with a wave of her hand. "When do we get the bill, and how long before we must pay it?"

Rebaya gave her a flat look. "My conscience is paying the bill, if you must look at it that way. I give you my word, I will not ask you for coin."

Taunos's thumb stroked across her knuckles, soothing. If Taunos trusted Rebaya, she wouldn't ask for blood and pain either, would she?

Her voice was quieter when she asked, "What *will* you ask for?"

"More than you will want to pay, I'm guessing." Rebaya sipped from her glass. "I ask that you shake up the complacency of the nobles. I ask that you show them the determined young woman I met last night, and confront them with their errors just as you have done for me."

Amanah bit her lip. She'd known this was coming, that shaking up the system would be risky, but now that she was on the precipice, the drop looked far too high. "People won't be happy with me. They'll come after us."

"You are the hero of the square, Amanah, and you will be my personal guest. And we will be at Lord Biryewi's house. I promise you, they will not be able to touch you for the rain of the gods, and then you'll be on to Arruk."

"And then they will take their revenge," Amanah said.

Rebaya wheeled her chair closer. "Listen, Amanah. Will I get something out of this? Yes. Does what I want put you in some danger? I won't deny it. But you're not getting out of here without danger anyway, not with what you did. You can't hide from who you are. I think you can handle it, and I think I can shield you. I'll send Yadi to Arruk with you if need be. Jattanu knows he needs to get out of Gahimbli from time to time. And I think it might just be the slap in the face some of these nobles need so we can make some changes. Will you help me?"

Still, the feeling of being trapped hovered over her. She hated it. "Do I have a choice?"

A sad smile curved the noble's lips as she reversed, the wheels of her chair narrowly missing one of the tables. "I can't send you somewhere else for the rain of the gods. I need you with me to protect you. But I will write my letters for you now, before the carriage comes. You'll have them regardless of what you decide. It's not a lot, but it's what I can offer."

"What exactly do you want us to do?" Emin asked. "I assume you don't want us actually slapping nobles in the faces, though if you do, I have some names—"

He cut off as Gurseh elbowed him.

Rebaya shook her head. "Nothing so crude. And I don't necessarily want *you* to do anything. It won't be as powerful coming from you."

"I'm not letting you use my sister alone. She has backup," Emin said.

Rebaya's gaze went back to Amanah. "You don't have to give me an answer right now. The carriage will be ready for us in a few marks. Don't eat too much before—there'll be plenty of food there and it'll be an insult if you don't eat."

"We're going in one single carriage?" Gurseh asked, surprise and awe filling his expression.

A slow smile spread across Rebaya's face. "Yes."

"But.. With you?" he pressed.

"And Yadi, my son."

Gurseh stared at her. "In your carriage. Us."

"Indeed. Won't that make a statement." Rebaya beamed.

Amanah glanced at Taunos. She didn't want to be a statement. She just wanted to be able to help people. But maybe there was no meeting her goals without stepping up, no making people hear her without also being seen.

She tried to hide her grimace, but her hand tightened on Taunos's. He tapped her wrist with his thumb, and it took her a moment to realize it was a message of support.

At least Rebaya was helping them. And she wasn't alone. She tapped back to Taunos her gratitude.

"Well," Emin said once Rebaya and the servants left, leaving them in the sitting room. "We need a contingency plan. Amanah?"

She let the grimace out now. "Sorry, I didn't have a plan in case a death-squad found us and we got nearly blown up."

"What?" Emin gasped in mock horror.

Taunos chuckled, and Amanah couldn't help but smile. "All right, what contingency do we need to plan for?"

"Well, overnight and in the jail, Gurseh and I were talking with various people."

"You were talking?" Amanah asked, mocking his pose from before.

"Awww, imitation. So cute," Emin made a face at her and she returned it with one of her own.

Her brother continued, snapping back to war-band leader mode. "The attack with the sea-wizards that was meant to stop Inuwe and Lamyi? Well, there's also rumors of Hinanuri spies in the city. And there was the death team. The guards were afraid the attack in the square was a diversion. Afraid more is coming. And their numbers are now lessened, because the death team targeted so many of them in the square."

"They'll attack during the rain of the gods. They'll attack Inuwe and Lamyi again, at least," Amanah guessed.

Emin nodded. "I think so. Even if our favorite noble lords complete their business, if another death team makes it inside and steals the evidence or kills them, others can be threatened into submission."

Taunos tilted his head. "The Hinanuri don't view the rain of the gods the same as you do, I'm guessing, or they wouldn't be outside to carry out an attack with a death team."

"They believe similarly, but they believe in wind spirits," Emin said. "Some of the Dahuti nomadic clans do as well, but the Hinanuri believe wind spirits take messages to the gods. So they spend the rain of the gods as close to the wind as they can get, so the spirits can take their breath to the gods as proof that life is still being lived."

"So it's a quieter thing for them," Taunos said.

Emin shrugged. "It's a more flexible thing. We stay inside day and night, or Jattanu's judgement may come down on us for viewing that which is of the gods. The Hinanuri don't, because they trust their wind spirits."

"So all the Dahuti will be inside—"

"—as many as possible," Amanah amended. "For as much time as possible."

"—but the Hinanuri won't, necessarily," Taunos finished.

Emin nodded. "And if I were them, that's when I would attack. Part of it depends on Lamyi and Inuwe's timing for whatever they have planned. I'd say probably near the end when everyone's tired, but I'm not betting against impatience, either."

"Ah, that's the other thing," Amanah turned to Taunos. "Little sleeping is done during the rain of the gods."

"Except for us," Emin interrupted. "I know it's tradition and all, but the gods are just going to have to forgive us, because we're not patrolling while half-dead on our feet and too exhausted to see more than the next step. We should stay alert, patrol the house, as much as we can. Stay in pairs, just like in Arruk: Gurseh and me, Amanah and Taunos. If you see anything suspicious, one delays and the other gets help. We sleep in shifts, before you're exhausted."

"Are you going to do it, Amanah?" Gurseh asked. "Are you going to talk to the nobles and take Lady Rebaya up on her offer of getting you into the bamimri? This is your chance to climb higher."

Taunos had spoken of the nobles using him just as he used them. And with the support of Taunos, Emin, and Gurseh there... maybe she could do this.

She drew in a bracing breath. "She wants to use me. I can use her offer in return. There's no going back from this, but maybe we've already crossed that point. Borlim's already going to be angry I've ignored his orders."

Emin nudged her. "Not on purpose. And besides, think of it as an alliance, perhaps. Just like with the Lenuri and the Mahyami. You already know how to do this."

She forced a brave smile. "I suppose I might as well stir up trouble while I have some defense, because I'm not sure an opportunity like this will ever come again."

"I have complete faith in your ability to do what you set your mind to," Taunos said. "Now it's time to show them what you're capable of, even if they pluck their own eyes out to avoid seeing your brilliance."

She leaned into him. The burden of worry seemed not so heavy when he was with her. "I just hope we can deal with the trouble it'll draw."

"I think trouble finds us anywhere," he murmured. "So I try to snatch every bit of happiness I can. And if there's danger, I'll meet it with you, at your side."

Emin nodded, snagging two sandwiches. "Now that you're all puffed up with hero monikers, I really can't let something happen to you, I guess."

Amanah leaned forward and flicked his shoulder before he could dodge. His laughter brought a smile to her face.

Emin stood. "I'm going to find Yadi, make sure we won't have trouble doing our jobs. Guarding, that is, not picking on big brothers."

She grinned. "I never have trouble with the last one. You make it so easy."

21

"I CAN'T BELIEVE we're going to a nobles' celebration," Gurseh said.

They were in Emin and Gurseh's room. Amanah had checked Taunos's bandage, but the wound hadn't re-opened, and she'd bound his bruised ribs for support. Taunos had taken some concoction Rebaya had given him for pain and was able to walk longer without help. They'd just have to find places for him to rest during the party occasionally.

But Taunos still needed help with things like boots, and none of them were used to these fancy clothes, so they'd decided to make it a group project. The men were working their way through buttons and belts while Amanah changed into the dress behind the screen.

"I can't believe we're riding there in the company of a noble, as her guests," Emin said.

"Me neither," Amanah said.

"I'm looking forward to it," Gurseh said. "A little taste of leisure."

"We'll still be working," Emin said. "We still need to guard Lamyi and Inuwe."

"I wish I knew what to expect," Amanah said, stepping out from behind the screen. "I know what to expect in Arruk and in the wilderness, but not here."

She paused, suddenly aware of the way Taunos was staring at her. He seemed like he was barely breathing, but then he was out of his seat and taking her hand. "You're so beautiful, beloved."

Her cheeks heated. "You look quite handsome yourself."

"Oooh, do I get to be embarrassing?" Emin asked, leaning forward with a huge grin.

She cleared her throat. "You each look nice."

"Oh, well if I look *handsome*…" Emin tossed her a grin. "You do look beautiful. I'd hardly know you for my sister, if it weren't for Taunos's eyes glued to you."

"Well, if you're going to be embarrassing," Taunos said, then leaned forward to kiss her cheek. She turned to catch his mouth with hers instead, just for a breath or two.

Amanah smiled, stepping past him. "I need to do my braids."

"Mirror's over here," Emin said, nodding to it. "Is this button supposed to do this?"

"You had trouble with your belt, and now you can't do a button?" Taunos teased.

Gurseh was already helping, his fingers quickly pulling the button into position, while Emin spouted back at Taunos. "I'd be careful who you tease, man-who-can't-put-on-his-own-boots."

Gurseh patted Emin's cheek, and Emin squeezed his hand.

"I was blown up yesterday." Taunos chuckled.

"Alas, you're still able to run your mouth," Emin said.

"You both are," Amanah said. "Too bad for Gurseh and me."

"If we feed them, they shut up for a moment," Gurseh said. "Good thing there'll be food there."

"Too bad they have big mouths."

Laughter belted from Gurseh, and she grinned.

Amanah laced up her boots, then stood in front of the mirror to begin her braids. It was all going to be fine. It had to be. And anyway, it wasn't like they had much of a choice. They had to be there anyway, so she might as well get something she wanted out of it at the same time.

Emin shouldered into her, oiling his ridiculous mustaches, and she bumped him back, jostling for room in front of the glass. She snickered at him as he twirled the thin strands around his finger and gave her a ridiculously extravagant bow. With him out of the way, she began the next braid, partitioning her wavy black hair.

Emin raised his eyebrows. "Nine braids?"

Her hands froze. "Why, do you think it's too many? I was going to make them messy."

Concern lurked in his eyes, shooting ice through her. "You'd have to make a lot of mistakes. We already know what happens when you forget to do that."

She pressed her lips together. He was right. Fewer was safer, but nine was the number of luck, the number of the gods.

Taunos frowned. "It's your hair. Would it really be that bad, since we're already coming with Lady Rebaya?"

"If she were to do it the way she wants to, every noblewoman would see a pattern nearly as intricate as their multiple maids worked to get their hair," Emin said.

Taunos made eye contact with her through the mirror, shrugging into the long jacket of his suit. "I wish you didn't have to make yourself smaller to avoid the notice of the petty and small-minded. They should see how stunning you are."

Amanah flushed, losing her words in the sudden rush of heat through her core.

"It'd be a big statement," Emin said. "One you can't take back."

"So is riding in Rebaya's carriage," Gurseh said.

"And if they try something this time, we're there to back you up, and so are Rebaya and Yadi." Taunos's eyes were deep and fervent, and if she turned, his lips would be a feather width from hers.

Amanah kept her gaze fixed on his through the cool distance of the mirror, ignoring the blush of the woman reflected back at her.

"You're apparently the hero of the square, too," Emin mused. "So if you want to take the risk, now's probably the smartest time. I know you'd rather do the proper nine."

That was true. Nine was the number for important nights, and this night, the beginning of the rain of the gods, was important.

"Fine. I'm doing nine." She might as well do things the way she wanted, since she was apparently stepping fully into view of the nobles she'd tried so hard to avoid. If she was doing this, she'd do it on her terms.

Taunos smiled, and she couldn't help but return it.

She cleared her throat, forcing her fingers to continue their weave. "Stunning, you said?" she asked, and was pleased to discover that she could keep her voice steady. "You're laying it on a bit thick."

His smile widened, and she cursed the heat in her cheeks betraying how he affected her. And yet, his distraction kept her from worrying, between his light bickering with her brother and his flirting with her. She didn't have time to overthink things, to lose her nerve.

Maybe that's why he threw himself into things.

She finished her braids and then began to weave them together in a nine-stranded weave crossing her head, the pattern meant to entice Hayzanu to give them luck. The impulse arose to pull each strand firmly and lay it neatly, just as her mothers had taught her, but she forced the mistakes, just enough to keep her from giving too much offense to "the petty and small-minded."

She added a couple luck twists on either side, then tied off the weave of the braids and turned to Taunos. "What do you think?"

His eyes darted over her, his smile growing. "As lovely as the star-studded sky."

Wrinkling her nose, she raised her hands to her head. "I'll have to pull out some braids and skip more stitches then."

"No!" Gurseh snatched her by the wrist, as if to stop her from destroying a piece of art.

"It's fine," Emin said.

"Are you sure?" Amanah asked her brother.

"You should have what you want in life sometimes, too," he said. "And I think you made enough mistakes not to draw too much ire."

"I wish you didn't have to worry about that," Taunos said.

"Can you do my braids next?" Gurseh said. "We might as all make a statement, hm? Spread out the jealousy among all four of us?"

Taunos grinned. "Brilliant idea."

"I agree—less work for me," Emin said.

"Oh, good plan, irritate the person in a position to tug on your hair. You're so smart, Emin," Amanah said, laughing.

She started on Gurseh's hair, braiding quickly in the nine braids he requested, wound in a pattern for luck and glory. "Do you think we can trust Rebaya's offer?"

"I think she's been honest about admitting we don't have a lot of choice," Emin said. "Not that I love that."

"I meant about the bamimri."

"You should take it," Emin said.

Taunos nodded. "I think you belong there. You've wanted this and the door is open. Why not step through?"

"Do you really think I could ever belong there?" she asked.

"Nope—you're too good," Emin said with a grin. He ruffled her braids, and she made a face at him, tying off Gurseh's hair. He leaned in to whisper in Gurseh's ear something that made him grin.

Taunos stood at her side, watching her work. "I don't know about the people, but you deserve to learn whatever you want. You're more of a healer than that man Yadi brought to the square."

She smiled at him. Grabbing her brother's shoulder, Amanah plunked Emin down in the chair next, portioning his hair out as well.

"Why is it the Festival of Dark Nights anyway?" Taunos asked. "It's actually brighter outside with the stars falling."

"Because if the stars continue to fall and die, the nights will always be dark," Emin said.

"Also it sounds poetic," Gurseh said. "Don't forget that."

The conversation turned to lighter things, and after tying off Emin's braids—also nine, in a complex pattern for health, luck, and vigilance—Taunos took his place in the chair.

She ran her hands lightly through his thick hair, which fell to his cheekbones in front. "Your hair's too short for this to be easy. Any requests?"

He shook his head, the barest movement. She could feel him resisting leaning into her touch, and she smiled.

"Do what you think best, Tabei," he said.

"It's your message to the gods," she said.

He shrugged. "They aren't my gods, so I don't know why they'd listen to me."

Emin and Gurseh had plenty of laughing suggestions as they took care of last-minute details including head scarves, but Amanah dismissed them, weaving nine tight braids in a semblance of the pattern for health and safety, because that's what she wanted more than anything else for him. He didn't need it, but she added luck twists to his hair too, just in case. As she braided, Emin and Gurseh worked around her with final touches to Taunos's suit. Emin delicately tied her scarf on over her braids next, so they'd all be ready once she finished.

Taunos grinned at his reflection. "That looks interesting."

"You think everything's interesting," Emin said, tossing him a scarf.

Amanah tied it on for him so it'd lay properly. Everyone needed headscarves while the stars died, and Rebaya had provided them each with scarves to match their clothing.

"There. We're ready," Emin said.

Amanah winced. Just like that, the distraction was whipped away, leaving her staring at the cold reality of what was coming. She didn't feel ready at all. But at least she wasn't doing this alone.

"We're waiting!" Emin sang, swinging open the door. He immediately gave lie to his words by wrapping his arm around Gurseh's waist and tugging him out of the room.

"Are you ready?" Taunos extended a palm to her, as if she were a noble.

She let him take her hand, and he spun her with dancing steps toward the door. The anxiety faded as humor rose in her once more, and she let herself imagine a world in which she could weave her hair in however many braids she wanted, in whatever pattern she could manage without worrying.

They followed Emin and Gurseh down the hallway. Taunos's fingers continued clasping hers gently, his steps quick, enticing her to match her pace to his, except then would they end up racing each other like children? Perhaps, if he wasn't injured.

The image was so outlandish she couldn't help but laugh, and he looked at her with a question in his eyes and a smile on his lips, as if her mirth brought him true enjoyment. But the sand timer in the hall said they had no time. They had to be inside before dusk, before the stars fell.

The carriage was full, with Emin, Gurseh, Amanah, Taunos, Rebaya, and Yadi. Rebaya's dress shimmered, flowing from one shoulder, and her elaborate braids were coiled and studded with jewels woven among the strands. Yadi wore a fitted suit, highlighting his broad shoulders. His braids were simpler, but gold and silver threads wove through each plait.

"You each look so handsome, so beautiful," Rebaya said. "And your braids! Incredible work. You'll stand out for sure with such elegance. Who managed these designs?"

"Amanah's quite talented," Emin said.

"You would be too if you practiced," she said. He shot her a rude gesture, and she responded in kind.

Rebaya chuckled. "If you two behaved like nobles, I doubt anyone would be able to tell the difference, with you each looking so nice. Good thing I intend to make sure everyone knows exactly who you are."

Amanah bit her lip, but Emin jostled her. This was, after all, what she'd signed up for.

"Here," Yadi said, leaning forward. "Let me fix your collar. It should lay like this."

He and Rebaya quickly fixed snaps, ties, collars, and sleeves so they looked like they'd known how to put fancy clothes on in the first place.

As Yadi sat back, he tilted his head at their feet, brow furrowed. "You are all wearing boots?"

"Oh, did you not see there were slippers in the wardrobe?" Rebaya asked.

"Boots don't go with these clothes," Yadi said.

Heat rushed to Amanah's face, but Emin shrugged next to her, as casual as if he were at one of his parties, rather than walking into the nobles' world and already being found out as a fraud.

"I know, I know, they're the wrong footwear," Gurseh said. "But Emin insisted on boots."

"Boots go better with fighting," Emin said. "Just in case."

Rebaya smiled at Emin, patting her son's arm. "Take notes, Yadi. Guard duty's not always fashionable. And I rather like the combination. It makes a statement."

"I have my sword," Yadi said stiffly. "Just like they do."

Amanah resisted the urge to fidget, bracing herself for the evening to come. Actually, it'd be the entire rain of the gods, and it weighed on her. But first, they just had to get through one evening. Then, the next. She could do that.

Throughout the ride, conversation was light, but Taunos sat stiffly, staring out the window. That's right—he didn't like closed spaces.

"Are you all right?" she murmured to him.

"It's nothing," Taunos said, gently squeezing her hand. He tapped on her knee, taking a slow deep breath. *I can handle it for a little while.*

"We'll be there soon, right?" she asked Yadi.

Yadi nodded. "Lord Biryewi is always a good host."

Not what she was asking, but that was fine. Amanah gripped Taunos's hand for the rest of the ride, trying to avoid the anxious thoughts fluttering through her.

The carriage stopped, and the driver unfolded a ramp and helped Yadi wheel Rebaya out. A large crowd stood in front of yet another enormous house. Waiting. Amanah gulped. The magistrate's sneer caught her memory, along with the dozens of other nobility she'd had passing interactions with in Arruk. She would almost rather face a death team than more nobles, even though they were in a new city.

Emin and Gurseh got out next, and then there was no more delaying. She forced the wrestling vipers of her worries down. These nobles might eat her alive, but it'd be worse if they saw her fear.

Taunos held his hand out to her as she exited the carriage, and every eye in the crowd turned to them. Amanah balked, but Taunos's warm fingers entwined in hers. She forced herself to move forward with him, clinging to his arm like a rope over heights, because without that contact, she would turn and run.

Lamyi stood near the front, the edge of his lip lifting briefly when he looked at her, and then he trained his gaze on Taunos. "Hurry up. Let's go. We want to introduce the hero."

"Don't you know?" Taunos asked with a slow grin. "I'm not the hero of the square."

Lamyi frowned. "If you aren't, who is?"

"That would be Amanah here," Rebaya said, gesturing to her. She waved her forward, giving Amanah no option but to walk toward her. Hopefully they couldn't see all the tightness in her shoulders and back. She consciously loosened her fingers on Taunos's arm, lest she give him bruises.

Rebaya continued through the crowd, passing Lamyi without pausing. "Lovely to see you, Inuwe. Lamyi, shut your mouth; you're not a fish. And aren't you glad you didn't go introducing the wrong hero and looking like a fool?"

Lamyi stammered for a moment, and then his hand snaked out, grabbing Amanah's free arm. "Well, come on then, hero. Let's go, shall we? Smile."

Everything in her balked at his hands on her, especially after everything he'd done on the journey to Gahimbli. And tonight, she had an alliance with Rebaya, which meant it would be best to do this near the noblewoman, where her protection might stand.

"Lord Lamyi, you seem to be under the mistaken impression that I gave you permission to touch me." Amanah wrenched her arm out of his grasp.

He turned to face her, hissing, "You work for me."

"I work for the guardhouse of Arruk. You are the job, nothing more. Besides, working for you still wouldn't give you the right to touch me."

"How dare you," he started, but Taunos stepped between them.

"Why don't you take a moment to remember your manners."

Amanah took the moment to check her arm, but though it was a little sore, it didn't seem like it would bruise. Emin was at the top of the stairs already, watching with a stony face, too far to help, with too many people between them.

She was surrounded by a sea of faces and eyes, and Lamyi was going to make a spectacle of her, to use the heartbreak of yesterday to fuel some gain for himself. She had agreed to let herself be a spectacle—but for Rebaya, not for Lamyi.

She shot a glance at Rebaya. Servants fit poles into slots in her wheeled chair, converting it temporarily into one of the carrying chairs nobles sometimes used in Arruk. The noblewoman inclined her head toward the stairs.

But what was she supposed to do? If she tried to pass Lamyi, he'd grab her again. She couldn't use violence—nobles would never allow a lower-class person to get away with violence against a noble. They'd close ranks against her. But she wasn't about to let Lamyi haul her up the stairs like a doll.

She sucked in her breath. "Taunos."

Her voice was quiet, but Taunos glanced at her, his eyes quickly returning to Lamyi, to the danger.

"Come on, Taunos," she said, letting her voice carry. "Let's see if there are better manners inside. I believe Lady Rebaya is ready to go."

The noblewoman smiled, revealing white teeth. "I am, indeed. Please join me, my guests. I was going to let Lamyi introduce you, but as he's acting like a petulant child, it will be my honor."

Amanah stepped past Taunos, who angled himself between herself and Lamyi.

Still Lamyi scowled at her. "You're my guards."

"You can still retain them if you find where you hid your manners, Lamyi. But first, they are my guests," Rebaya said.

Lamyi grabbed for Amanah's arm again, but Taunos blocked him, and she dodged away. She carefully ascended the steps ahead of Rebaya, hoping she would be allowed this. Servants were supposed to stay behind the important people, though guards got a little more leeway. But if she didn't move toward a goal, she'd flee, away from the eyes, away from the public humiliation Lamyi was putting himself through. Humiliation he'd no doubt blame on her.

Taunos followed at her back, a safe place in the crowd. A few more steps. Amanah kept her head high. His arm guided her hooked in hers as he came forward to her side when her feet took the steps slowly. Slowly, lest she run.

At the top of the stairs, Rebaya murmured, "Stop there."

Amanah froze, forcing herself blank. Forcing herself not to tremble. Rebaya sat on one side, and Taunos stood on her other side, with Emin and Gurseh next to him. She hated all these eyes on her. All she could think of was waking up that morning with sunlight on her face and Taunos's arms around her, snuggling into her. She drew in a deep breath, as if she could inhale the peace of that moment.

There were too many people. Danger lay cloaked in smiles, which was not the kind she could handle. She had no doubt about it now—she'd absolutely rather face another death team than walk into this building and be trapped here for days. But the stars would fall soon. Amanah clasped her hands tightly together, trying to regain her composure.

Rebaya's speech was short, at least. Something about heroes being found where you least expect them, about rewarding those who sacrificed for the good of the city, about celebrating hard work and resourcefulness. Amanah kept her eyes on the darkening sky, as if she could ignore all the nobles looking at her.

A hand touched hers, and Taunos gently squeezed her arm. She looked down.

"Come on," Rebaya said. "We're done for now. Go inside. Regain your composure, but then don't forget to present yourself to Lord Biryewi."

She nodded mutely. Rebaya rolled inside.

Amanah followed—she had to. Inside the entrance hall, there were still more people. Some were staring, others dashing about. With every step she took, more people stared. She tensed to avoid shuddering, cursing herself for ever agreeing to this. Her? In the spotlight? Her worst nightmare.

Taunos slipped an arm around her back, supporting her, guiding her, embracing her, all at once as he murmured in her ear. And then, she was standing at a window overlooking a garden. Blooming flowers spilled over a bed of soil beneath the window, filling her nostrils, and the wind whispered secrets through the leaves of the trees. Taunos stood behind her, back to back, shoulders touching hers. Then Emin was there too, standing shoulder to shoulder with Taunos. Blocking her further.

Hidden from view for a moment, Amanah took deep breaths, trying to quell the trembling. She hated the thought of anyone else catching her so undone, but somehow it was different with them. Her stomach was still a snarl of snakes, but she was safe. Taunos chatted amiably with Emin, while she gripped the windowsill as if she could wrestle her emotions.

Tears pricked her eyes, and she scrubbed them away. She wasn't trapped. She'd chosen this. She would use this, because she would not let the Lamyis of the world beat her. The petty and small-minded, as Taunos said.

He was humming softly now, the tune he'd played that night in the Gods' Tree reverberating through her. The peace he could create flooded her, loosening some of her fear so she could hold on to her goal.

She heaved in a deep breath and turned.

Taunos glanced back at her, then turned, his thumb brushing her cheek. "Better?"

"I think so." She had to clear her throat to get the words out.

"It was past time they heard from us," Emin said. "And Lamyi being rough with you like that? Everyone saw you gave him no cause for that."

"Rebaya humiliated him," she said, but her stomach knotted.

"Maybe. You all right now?" Emin asked.

She nodded. "You can patrol."

"Every two marks, we trade off," Emin reminded them. He smacked Taunos's shoulder lightly. "Take care of her."

He chuckled. "She takes care of me."

"Yeah, but she doesn't need reminding." Emin sauntered off as a smile found its way to Amanah's lips.

Taunos rubbed her shoulders lightly. "Are you really all right?"

She swallowed hard. "I hate this. All the eyes on me. You love it, but for me…"

"For you, it's danger."

"I said I'd do this, so I will. It's only a week." Seven days of people staring at her. "Will I ever be able to go back after this?"

Tears sparked in her eyes. She wouldn't. She knew that. This was an ending.

Familiar, warm arms held her tight, the rumble coming from Taunos's chest vibrating through her as he spoke. "All we can do is our best. We can't go backward. Only forward. What they decide to do or not is up to them. It only says anything about them, not you. But maybe someone will surprise you."

"In my experience, it's always a bad surprise."

"Always?" He pulled back to look at her.

She smiled, winding her arms around his waist. "Maybe not *always*. More than that though, I've never cared for being the center of attention. I prefer our agreement—you keep everyone distracted so I can get things done."

He smiled at her, fingers caressing her skin, though a troubled look stole over his face as he looked down the hall. "I'll see what I can do to get enough focus off you that you're not overwhelmed. I have some friends here, I think, for now."

"For now?"

"Depending on how they react, they may not be my friends any longer." His face was grim.

She sucked in a deep breath, as if she could breathe in the confidence that always cloaked him.

He leaned toward her, murmuring, "If it goes *really* badly, we could escape into the garden. Maybe there's another tree to climb."

Amanah snorted, surprised out of her apprehension. That would be outside though, and—

His eyes danced. He'd done that on purpose, and it'd worked. The panic was easing, little by little.

Taunos leaned in, his lips by her ear sending a flush of warmth through her, distracting her. "How public do you want to be here, beloved? I don't want to lose you in the crowd, and I would love to dance with you, but—"

She snorted, happy to continue the distraction against her nerves. "And the fear of being separated is the main reason for this question, I'm sure."

He smiled, but worry lurked in his eyes as he stopped, coaxing her to face him. "You deserve acclaim and appreciation, and I'm glad to see you get it. But you deserve it in a way that you can enjoy, not one that makes you so deeply uncomfortable. I don't want to add to that discomfort."

She tangled her fingers in his. "Thank you. But you should know, you have a way of making me feel better."

"Ah, it's working." He flashed a grin at her, and she let her head rest against his.

"I'm not hiding anymore. I can't go back."

"So, will you dance with me?" His fingers gently cupped her neck. "Before you object, I've had my pain medicine, and I have plenty more for the next few days."

She couldn't help but laugh and tug him closer. "I want to dance with you. I just don't know if I want to deal with the consequences."

He kissed her eyebrows. "Let me know when you decide what you need. I am, as always, ready to jump in."

"No, I'm apparently throwing caution to the wind, so why should I deny myself? I want to dance with my iayu, my poet-warrior, with his honeyed words and ridiculous lack of self-preservation. Even if it's in a corner."

He hmm'ed against her throat. "I like being yours."

She wrapped her arms around his neck in return. "So, yes. We are dancing, and we are eating these nobles' food, and I am kissing you. And they'll have to deal with it, because I have to be here and making a spectacle anyway, so I might as well do some things I want while I'm at it."

His eyes sparked with humor. "And you want to kiss me?"

"And just like that, I'm cured," she drawled, and he laughed.

As she followed him into the swell of music and conversation, she tapped a message on his inner arm. "Thank you for being there for me. Again."

His gaze was warm as he squeezed her hand. "Always."

22

SHE WAS STILL coasting on the wave of Taunos's support when Yadi stepped out of the crowd and beckoned them into the main hall. The huge space was alive with the festival. Music filled the room, and the tables on one end of the room creaked under the weight of breads, jams, honey, and sizzling meat. Nobles danced in the cleared space in the center, while around the edges, others mingled and exchanged courtesies, some filling the small seating areas scattered along the edges. Inuwe and Lamyi were among the crowd, and Inuwe's expression filled with relief when he saw them, while Lamyi said something to the crowd he was with, sparking several sneers in their direction. Guards for other noble guests loitered on the edges, scanning the room for trouble, while at the doors, more guards stood stiffly at attention, each wearing the sashes of Biryewi's household.

A glance at Taunos revealed his eyes darting to every entrance and exit, every weapon, just as he'd never stopped assessing threats out in the wilderness. Her heart warmed at the reminder that she wasn't alone.

Inuwe intercepted them before they got very far into the room. "Haari Taunos, Amanah! I'm glad you and Emin and Gurseh came."

Amanah eyed him warily, unsure how to interpret his greeting. Yadi stepped to the side, as if to give them at least the illusion of privacy.

"We've already hired extra guards, but we'd like you to also guard us for the duration of the feast." Inuwe cleared his throat. "I would feel much more comfortable knowing you're watching out for us."

The glare Lamyi was sending across the room could murder someone, but in a blink, it became a smile toward his conversation partner, so smoothly she could almost believe she'd imagined it.

She'd prefer not to work for Lamyi again, but if Emin was right and another Hinanuri death team did attack, she wasn't sure she could look herself in the eye if she didn't try to keep people safe. Even those she didn't like very much.

A squeeze of her hand made her look at Taunos, who raised his eyebrows. She gave him a slight nod.

Taunos finally returned his attention to Inuwe. "Plans are already in effect to keep you safe, Lord Inuwe. We'll be guarding you and Lamyi through the Festival."

Inuwe nodded and clasped Taunos's free hand, then hers. "Thank you."

As Inuwe headed back into the crowd, Yadi returned to them. He led them to the side of the room where a tall, thin man reclined on a low couch with a book. All other seating was claimed, but there was a circle of empty space around this one. Two guards stood nearby, their boots just off the large rug that ran under the couch and the little table beside it. Yadi bowed low and Amanah stiffened. This must be the host, Lord Biryewi.

She bowed, as did Taunos, though not as low as he probably should have, and Amanah prayed to Hayzanu that his injured ribs would not be marked against them.

"Here they are, Lord Biryewi," Yadi said. "The one we call Haari and Amanah, the hero of the square, who organized the rescue efforts. Without her tireless work, many more lives would have been lost."

After setting his book aside with precise movements, Biryewi watched them over steepled fingers. Sand trickled through the glass of an intricately wrought timer on a shelf behind him, and Amanah imagined she could hear the movement of the tiny grains as time dragged on. Her spirits drifted lower. He was staring too long at her. Had he heard about the altercation on the stairs? Had she made a mistake in trusting Rebaya? Would this man see only trouble when he looked at her, or something else?

Taunos seemed completely at his ease, his stance falling naturally into one that conveyed just enough respect, while also seeming almost like he was lounging. Except she knew he'd need to rest soon—most of his weight was off his injured leg.

The noble's gaze flicked down to their joined hands, and Amanah snatched hers back without thinking. That reflex to hide, to draw no attention, reared up in her with suffocating intensity. Danger stalked her here, and once again she asked herself why she'd agreed to this. It took no more than a pointed glance for her nerves to fail her.

She folded her hands in front of her, palms flat. It was a pose that she could easily defend herself from, but Arruk society seemed to think it meant she was weaponless, and that put them at ease.

"My lord," Taunos said smoothly. "We don't wish to take up much of your time. We're sure you're very busy."

Finally, Biryewi rose, prowling past them, circling them like a predator. Looking for weakness. Amanah made sure her shoulders were back, her spine straight, her expression composed.

"Haari, you make a commotion, that's for sure. And now you have as well, Amanah." Biryewi flicked his glance at her as he stooped, picking up a cup of fruit water from the table. A jug sat beside it, beads of condensation on its porcelain surface. "I have need of such skills as I've heard from you, Haari. I'll pay quite handsomely, of course. Perhaps there will be jobs for you too, hero of the square."

Her stomach tightened more, painfully, and she pressed her lips together against the rise of nausea. How many lords would try to catch them up in their talons? To use them. Would they shred them apart while fighting over them? Anger rose up, battling the fear back.

Taunos's sleeve brushed hers, and she focused on breathing, trying to remain composed. She did not trust this man, their host, but did she need to?

"I'm afraid I'm not in as good a shape as I may appear," Taunos said. "I was blown up, after all, as I'm sure Yadi told you."

Yadi flashed a slight smile, but stepped away to the edge of the carpet, leaving them their privacy for the second time since their entrance. She wasn't sure how she felt about that.

Biryewi's eyes flickered over Taunos's plaits, and his voice filled with amusement. "I thought I saw a number of luck twists in your hair. Who is so concerned for your safety, I wonder?"

His gaze landed on Amanah, pinning her as he took a sip from his glass.

"Danger might come." Amanah's voice was stiff, but at least it didn't waver. "And when it does, Taunos runs into it. Even when he's injured." She shifted her weight, brushing her arm against Taunos's. "I figured asking for a measure of luck would be practical."

Biryewi was watching her, and she felt like a rodent caught in a viper's jaws. "I've heard many stories from the square. You moved people away from danger even before the explosion. How did you know what would happen?"

"Taunos saw the death team and the explosive," Amanah said.

"How is it that Haari Taunos saw the death team and the city guard did not?"

The noble's cool, smooth tone was grating on her. Her eyes narrowed. "You would have to ask them."

Biryewi waited, as impassive as the statues in the entry hall, and she went on cautiously. Trying to avoid further trouble. "Taunos went running toward the death team, so Gurseh got Lord Inuwe and Lord Lamyi to safety, and Emin and I worked to get as many others safe as we could."

The faintest of twitches at the corners of his mouth might have been a smile—or perhaps something he'd eaten disagreed with him. "And did you really ride a horse up the city wall?"

A bit of defensiveness crept into her tone. "I needed to get up high fast, for the banners."

"Why?"

"The people needed help. Yelling wasn't working. I hoped the banners would catch enough attention from people who could read the messages to help."

Biryewi smiled behind his glass as he took another drink. "Why did you really do it? Most of the guards on duty in that square are dead now."

The suspicion stung more than it should have, and Amanah scowled, anger keeping her tone from wavering. She hadn't even noticed guard uniforms last night—she'd been too focused on trying to keep everyone alive. "If you can't see that helping people in need is worthwhile, I'm not sure this conversation will go anywhere. I tried to help as many people as I could."

Then she bit her tongue. This man was not her brother, Taunos, or Gurseh. This man had the power to toss them out of his house.

Taunos tucked her arm in his uninjured one, using the motion to disguise tapping a message to her. *Breathe.*

She tapped back. *I can't believe they suspect me of working with the enemy. But I said too much. I should have been more respectful.*

He needed to hear it. And not from me.

I shouldn't have snapped. Now we'll be thrown out. We'll be—

Lord Biryewi was watching her fingertips on Taunos's arm. She clutched Taunos's elbow, message aborted, and braced for the derision, the loss of any hope of help.

Birywei paced around them again. "There have been rumors of Hinanuri threats, but then again, there have been rumors that she's caught you up in sea-wizardry, Haari, and is the source of those threats."

A muscle in Taunos's jaw feathered, a flash of something dark passing over his features. There was a warning in his voice when he spoke. "I can assure you, she is not a sea-wizard, nor is she a threat to you."

Biryewi stopped in front of them. "Yadi said there were two other guards with you, one of them also a havi, the other middling class? Why so many havi, Haari, and both from the wilderness? Lamyi told me you were allowed to choose your team."

Taunos stiffened further. Amanah tapped on his arm. *Relax or you'll pull your stitches.*

He glanced at her, still covering her hand with his, but he drew in a deep breath, his tone calm when he answered Biryewi. "Amanah is the best rider and archer I've ever seen, and Emin is a phenomenal leader and fighter. Gurseh can read, is capable with a variety of weapons, and has worked well with the nobles on the journey here. They are all admirable people."

"And where are the other two?"

"Emin and Gurseh are patrolling the perimeter to be sure of security. I trust we'll have no trouble with your guards in the completion of our duties?" That hint of warning crept back into his voice.

Their host's eyes weighed them, narrow, hard, unyielding. And then, the predatory sharpness eased away and he nodded. He turned to Yadi. "The guards have their description, correct, Yadi? They know this team is to be undisturbed in their work."

"Yes, my lord," Yadi replied. "I've introduced your house guards to Emin and Gurseh, and I doubt anyone missed Amanah and Taunos."

Biryewi smiled, this one warmer and truer than his previous ones. Amanah still didn't trust it. "Lady Rebaya knows how to make an entrance. Forgive me the theatrics. Lady Rebaya spoke quite highly of you, Amanah, and it's not often that she brings a guest. I needed to know what type of person you were, as you are in my house and therefore under my protection, and yet, you are here to place a target on your own back."

"One would think standing up to a death team would be enough to prove who I am," Amanah said. All was *not* forgiven.

He flicked his fingers at the two of them. "Are you certain about this? Do you realize what you're inviting down on your heads with Rebaya's scheme? People aren't going to be pleased."

Taunos scowled. "I don't seek public approval for my choices."

Amanah drew herself up. How dare this man toy with her simply to satisfy his curiosity, and then question *her* judgement! The coming week was going to be a trial. At least Taunos brought light with him, making it easier to face the darkness with him.

"Lord Biryewi," she said, trying to keep her tone calm and even. "If people choose to be angry with me because Taunos is at my side, there's nothing I can do about that. Even if he wasn't there, they'd find fault with my very presence. Lady Rebaya said you take your hosting duties seriously. Was she wrong?"

The nobleman gave her a thin smile. "She is not wrong. Which brings me to Lord Lamyi. Will I have trouble between you and him?"

"Not from me. It's my duty to keep him safe, and I take my duties seriously as well." Lord Lamyi and Inuwe had that message to deliver, too. That would cause a bunch of trouble—but she didn't trust this man enough to warn him.

Biryewi nodded. "I do agree with you, for what it's worth. I'm glad you're here, in my home for this Festival of Dark Nights. Rebaya vouches for you. Yadi admires Haari. And the havi love you, Amanah. This is something I agree we need to recognize."

Amanah narrowed her eyes.

"But I do not want a revolution, because I don't want any more people to die," he said. "I want to get through the next few days with minimum disturbance. Then we can continue working toward a better solution, beginning with finding somewhere safer for the camps outside the walls."

"You're waiting for a convenient time to help, while out there people have been suffering and dying," Amanah said.

Biryewi raised an eyebrow. Amanah stiffened. It wasn't wise to annoy the powerful, in any case.

But no one came to drag her away.

Biryewi drew in a deep breath. "Perhaps you're right. But I do want to help, without cultivating more pain and division."

Perhaps Taunos was right, and this wasn't so different than speaking with the Lenuri and Mahyami clan heads, after all. Perhaps she could stand her ground and keep hold of who she was without bringing down trouble on her head, given the right circumstances.

Taunos slid past consequences that would apply to others all the time, as if Hayzanu greased his way through the wheels of life. Perhaps some of that was rubbing off on her.

She bowed her head as a peace offering. "I want the same."

He returned it with a nod. "All right, then. Be aware, I have my guards throughout the house, but other nobles have theirs as well. I can't guarantee how others will receive you, but my guards know how I prize my guests' safety, and that includes you. If you are in trouble or need anything, call my master of servants."

Biryewi extended a hand, and an older man stepped forward from the background, nodding to her. The man wore silk robes like Biryewi, but the simple embroidery contained patterns she'd seen among the Lenuri when they sheltered in their cave.

"I am Havi Esem Bayi of the Lenuri, master of servants here. I am here if you need anything."

Biryewi snorted. "Come now, Esem, you're not havi anymore. Don't slight my honor like that."

But Amanah stared at Esem, her heart hammering in her chest. A man who had once been havi from the almost-entirely nomadic Lenuri clan had been made master of servants here? She'd never heard of that happening before—such a position was considered honorable and brought with it great pay. Nearly always, it went to someone from the middle classes. And the nomadic clans rarely settled down so long in the cities before returning to the wilderness, much less out-competing middle class city-dwellers for such a position.

The master of servants met Biryewi's gaze with an easy smile. There was no tension there, no anxiety. No fear of reprimand or punishment. Instead, there was a hint of teasing to his tone. "Ah, but you wish to be welcoming. And for a havi guard who spent yesterday saving lives in the poorest area of the city, well, could there be any greater honor than reclaiming the status I began with?"

Amanah stared at Biryewi, trying to figure out what angle he was pursuing, and then at Esem. The back of her neck prickled. First the threatening demeanor, now this? What new trick was this? "I do not enjoy being toyed with."

"I told you," Esem murmured, loud enough for her to hear, but not so loud as to carry beyond this pseudo-private space.

Biryewi looked at the ceiling in exasperation, but he smiled at the same time. "Please, Esem, once again, clean up my mistake."

Turning to her, Esem gave a slight bow. "No games, not anymore. You are welcome here, and it is truly an honor for me to introduce myself to you as the havi I once was."

Amanah bowed in return. "Thank you, though I don't know that I deserve such words." She hadn't done that much, after all. Hadn't done enough. At best, it was the possibility for a beginning. "As for our welcome, well. Actions are what matters most."

"I've offended you," Biryewi said, sinking back onto the couch. "I do apologize."

"Once again, actions." Amanah made herself smile slightly. He'd made her feel threatened, all to test her. It reeked of other nobles intimidating lower ranks to get what they wanted. It'd take more than a 'sorry' to fix that, but at the same time, it was dangerous to needle nobles.

"You said we are welcome. No ceremony with the bread?" Taunos asked, stepping forward half a step.

Esem's eyes lit up, but Biryewi looked curious.

"You've had the peace ceremony?" the master of servants said.

Amanah nodded. "We sheltered with the Lenuri briefly on our way here."

Esem beamed at them. "Wonderful. Alas, nobles in the past violated the rules too many times. The clans here no longer use the peace ceremony, as it's no longer considered a safeguard. But I will personally look out for you."

"I know you're working as his guards, but try to stay away from Lord Lamyi," Biryewi said. "I fear I will have to publicly humiliate him and that will not endear him to you. But what is one to do with a second-nephew?"

Of course. Many nobles across the cities were related. It shouldn't make ice crawl up her back.

Taunos spoke up stiffly. "I had to humiliate him semi-privately already, on the way here. He took exception to Amanah saving the life of Lord Inuwe."

Biryewi frowned. "What? He and Inuwe have been partners for years. Inuwe brings out Lamyi's kinder side, thank all the gods."

Amanah bit back a snort. Lamyi had a kinder side? That also meant Inuwe accepted Lamyi being rude to everyone else so long as he wasn't mean to him—which, honestly, tracked with their trip here.

"Yes, but that doesn't mean he wanted Amanah treating him for a snakebite," Taunos said.

Amanah met Biryewi's gaze, refusing to shy away.

"Well. That's disappointing." Biryewi sighed. Then he beckoned to Esem, who handed him a bulky bag that jingled. "Here, I have something for you and your team, for the square. You did our people a service and two of your team were jailed for it. Disgraceful."

Taunos took it but passed it to her. "Actually, maybe you should hold this."

The quirk of his lips made her smile as she took the coin purse and tucked it into the wide fabric belt around her waist. "Yes, I've seen you handle money."

Biryewi watched them, the corners of his eyes crinkling. When he spoke next, he raised his voice to a regular volume, easily overheard now. "Now. I know you're also working, but every guest is to contribute to the entertainment. What would you like to do? A banner dance seems fitting, hmmm? Banners will be provided."

Of course that's what they'd want. She should have guessed. "Yes, my lord."

Do you want to? Taunos tapped on her arm.

Rebaya wants a spectacle. Banner dances are certainly eye-catching. She stifled a sigh.

But do you want to?

"If you'd rather something else," Biryewi said, his voice lower in volume now, "that will be acceptable."

Her eyes widened, and he smiled. "Esem taught me the tapping language too."

Amanah bit her lip, trying not to flush. She cleared her throat, straightening. "A banner dance will be fine, my lord. Given I'm here because of a banner dance, in part…"

Biryewi nodded, rubbing his hands together. "Wonderful. And Haari? Stories?"

"I can do that," Taunos said with a smile.

Their host gave them a slight bow, his voice carrying in the room. "I do need to welcome my other guests now, but Haari, it is good to meet you, and I'm honored to meet you as well, Amanah. We could use heroes as valuable as either of you, much less both, and I'm honored you're staying with me for the rain of the gods. Please, enjoy the festival."

A performance, but one for their benefit, perhaps. She closed her eyes and wished for the wind in her hair, the freedom of a horse beneath her, the security of a bow in her hands. Calming things.

As they stepped away, back into the churn of the crowd, Esem stopped them with a light hand on their arms. "Please, I just want to say, it brings me pride that you'll be banner dancing. I heard all about it on the wall. I'm eager to see a banner dance once again with my own eyes, and for everyone to remember all you did after, as well. I hope tonight is the beginning of a turning point."

Amanah smiled, though her face burned. It was all far too much attention. Esem bowed and left them, and they continued through the crowd.

"Why did you agree to the banner dance?" Taunos murmured. "You seemed uncertain."

"Why did you agree?"

"I like telling stories. But you don't like performing."

"No, I don't. But everyone else will be giving some sort of

performance, it seems, so that's better."

She had grown since leaving Arruk, and that shell was too small for her now. But there had to be some room between all eyes on her and sneaking past unnoticed, didn't there? At least she wasn't in front of a crowd now, but simply in it. And if she was going to play this game of favors, she was going to be herself as she did so.

There it was, the core of it. "I did it for me," she answered in a low voice, her eyes skimming over the crowd, the sea of jewels and silks and eyes. "It's part of me, the banner dance. It might be too low class for the nobles, but I... they'll just have to deal with it. And I'm afraid with all this game playing... I don't want to lose myself."

23

AFTER AMANAH AND Taunos had completed a circuit of the hall, mingling with others as Rebaya had suggested, they found a chair, giving Taunos's injuries a much needed rest. Her leg and shoulder ached a bit, but she'd be fine for a little longer. Emin and Gurseh came back into the hall after a circuit on patrol. Several guards stared at them as they entered, but Biryewi's household guards merely gave them a nod and waved them through.

"How'd patrol go?" Taunos asked as Emin and Gurseh wandered over. His voice was quiet and he tugged at the side of his scarf idly.

"If some of these guards were on my squad, they'd be wrestling for their honor back, I swear to Jattanu," Emin murmured, barely audibly. "Nothing out of place though."

"Biryewi's master servant is here for us in case of emergencies, it seems," Taunos said.

"Yes, everyone's being oddly nice. It's kind of disconcerting," Emin said, his voice returning more to normal volume, though not quite as booming.

"You'll have to get used to it," Gurseh said. "It's no less than you deserve."

"Next patrol is yours." Emin pointed to a huge, intricate sand timer near the entrance, marked at regular intervals with gold stars. Colored sands flowed through it—according to Yadi, the sands were from every part of Far Dahutad and represented their unity as one people. "I've been using that to keep time. Make your patrol before it hits the sixth star."

Amanah nodded.

"Inuwe and Lamyi are in that crowd by the wall," she said, tilting her head. "They have two of their new guards beside them."

"We've been keeping an eye while mingling," Taunos said.

Amanah stifled a groan. "Far too much mingling."

"What, is your hero career already weighing on you?" Emin nudged her with his elbow.

Gurseh clapped them on the shoulders. "Let's find something to eat before you two have to patrol."

They went forward together to investigate the overladen banquet tables along one wall. The food and drinks were like nothing she'd ever seen before. Some drinks were even on fire, while food was twisted in fantastical shapes. There were spears of exotic meats coated in sauces, salads arranged in intricate, artistic patterns, vegetables cut into whimsical designs, bowls of fruits—frozen, smoked, dried, fresh, grilled, and candied—and fried or baked breads of every form she could think of: circular loaves, enormous flatbreads, braided breads, breads puffed at the top, breads without yeast but filled with fruits, and tiny mounds of fried bread dusted with sugar. Flavored yogurts of five different varieties were on offer, as well as tiny bite-sized cakes of more kinds than she'd ever thought existed. Hollow balls of chocolate the size of her fingertips, dusted on the outside with gold, sat at one end, next to a spread of finger bowls of honey—twelve different varieties.

She loaded up one of the small plates available with as many options as possible, but when she got to the table of honeys, she traded a look with Emin. His pleading eyes worked just as well now as when they'd been children, even though he was the older one.

And she had decided to enjoy herself, to be among these nobles without losing herself at the same time.

With a sharp nod, she handed her food to Taunos and held out her arms. "All right, load me up."

"Yes!" Emin wasted no time handing his food off to Gurseh. He set bowls of each type of honey in her hands and along her arms, keeping two to hold himself.

She walked carefully, balancing the ten small bowls, while Taunos watched her with amusement and pride.

Gurseh scoffed playfully. "Show off."

Some people sniffed or looked on with censure as they headed toward the stairs leading to the balcony overlooking the main floor, but many ignored them. A few smiled or nodded at them. There was a thrill in her stomach at that. Would she one day get used to such treatment from nobles? Would casual respect be in her future somehow?

It took Amanah and Taunos a bit to climb the steps, but it was easier to breathe up there, where there were fewer eyes on them. They stood in the lantern light around the small ebony circle of their waist-high table, perched on stools overlooking a room ablaze with lights and color. The food was delicious, and Taunos and Emin were soon offering bites of exotic meats and strange grains around their tiny table. She grinned at how this communal food exploration of Taunos's had somehow been incorporated into their group. So many new foods to try, and between them, they could all get little bites of almost everything.

Of course, Emin's plate ran out first. He practically pouted when he saw it empty. "Gurseh, there were Hinanuri starfruits down there, right? Come get some with me."

As they headed off to load up their plates again, Amanah checked the sand timer down in the main room. Still plenty of time.

"Here, try this," she said, offering Taunos one of the hot peppers she'd found.

He bit it in half, eyes alight with eagerness.

And then his face went red as he spluttered and coughed. Amanah couldn't help but laugh as he gulped water, patting his back until the coughing fit passed. When he straightened, mischief danced in his eyes. She backed away, laughing, but he caught her, pulling her close and kissing her deeply. She wrapped her arms around his neck, drawing him in. He tasted spicy, the heat of the pepper on his tongue.

He grinned as he let her go. "Had to share, after something like that."

And then, he took the rest of the pepper in his teeth from her hand. She shook her head at him, chuckling. He'd taken another bite, even after knowing how spicy it was? Of course, this was Taunos, so she should've expected it. Again, he coughed and sputtered, his eyes watering.

Amanah had pity on him, coating a handful of flatbread with yogurt and the ruwuberry honey he'd enjoyed. "Here. This should cool the fire."

"It's good. Burns. But good." Taunos's voice was hoarse. He shoved the bread in his mouth as Emin and Gurseh returned, carrying plates laden once more with food.

Emin looked from Taunos to the stem on Amanah's plate and whistled. "Amanah, coal peppers, really? I thought you liked the man!"

She giggled. "It was funny."

"It was tasty," Taunos mumbled through the bread.

"It nearly choked you," she said.

He shrugged. "I'd do it again."

"Then I'd better save you from your folly." She picked up the other coal pepper on her plate. He leaned forward, his eyes dancing with challenge, and she laughed, coating it in sparkberry honey and popping it in her mouth.

Making a show of disappointment, Taunos swiped a random colorful tidbit from Emin's plate instead.

"I swear, I leave for two moments, and my sister tries to kill my friend. Can you believe it?" Emin asked Gurseh.

Chuckling, she shoved Emin's shoulder.

"Don't push me off the edge," he yelped, even though there was a balcony and two paces between him and said edge.

All at once, the reality of where they were crashed down on her. They weren't around the fire or in the market at Arruk, joking around. They were at a nobles' party where at least one powerful man already had it out for her. Where apparently some suspected her of collaborating with a death team to kill guards.

Ice ran along her spine. How many people had heard Emin's jests and wouldn't take it for humor? And if they could make her out to be dangerous, what would they do? What would they entice others to do? At best, she would lose her chance at the bamimri. At worst... She gulped in a breath.

"Emin, quieter," Taunos murmured. He wrapped his arm around Amanah's waist as if he could shield her from noble feelings or her own anxiety.

Emin raised his eyebrows, then glanced around. In the next breath, he cracked a joke to Gurseh, as if nothing had happened, but he also reached out and squeezed her uninjured shoulder.

Slowly, her shoulders loosened, and she leaned into Taunos, resting her head against his. They were just jokes, any of them could explain that. Why should she allow the nobles to use her without having fun of her own? She caught Esem's eye, the master servant carrying a tray of colorful candies through the crowd, and he nodded at her. At either end of the balcony, Biryewi's guards stood at attention.

And more importantly, right beside her were three warriors—even if one was injured—all watching each others' backs. She may not know how much she could trust the nobles, but she could trust Gurseh, Emin, and Taunos. That wouldn't end now.

So when Taunos asked if she wanted to dance, Amanah agreed. The music swelled as they twirled and dipped along the side of the main dance floor. Taunos's ribs stopped him halfway through a song with a swift beat, and in the midst of nobles all around them leaping and skipping across the floor, he instead held her close.

"This isn't a slow dance," she murmured to him.

"It is now."

"Maybe for you," she said, his good humor infectious as always. She spun away and danced around him, always coming back to him so that he didn't have to move much.

When the song ended, he tugged her back into his arms with a laugh, murmuring into her ear. "I still need to give you a real dance."

As the marks wore on and the rain of the gods fell outside, they carved out their peace, their happiness, among the festivities. They danced, they patrolled, they mingled, they ate, they drank, they patrolled again, and they met even more people. Eventually, Emin and Gurseh headed off to a pillow-filled corner to catch some sleep—after all, as Emin said, they couldn't crash at the same time.

Taunos had a power here, even wounded as he was. It was only because the nobles allowed him this power, and yet he wasn't afraid to use it. His wounds limited him, even with the light exercise of the party, and as the night wore on, he murmured in her ear when he needed a break. As she helped him find a place to rest without straining his ribs or stitches, she glanced at his carefully blank expression, reading the weariness and pain he tried to hide. It was sad, that even here among the nobles he seemed to like—at least at times—he didn't trust them to know he was in pain. But he trusted her. After a short rest or a dose of pain medicine, he'd make a joke and they'd head back into the fray.

Lamyi kept shooing them away whenever they got close to whatever group he was with, sending them to patrol for danger, as if danger couldn't be in the crowd, especially with at least one noble apparently working with the Hinanuri.

Amanah walked with Taunos through the crowd after one such interaction, nodding politely as Rebaya introduced her to one noble after another. Some remained distantly polite at best, though others seemed to actually care. She told the story of the square over and over, and it was exhausting, living through it as she told it again and again. Worse was when some nobles clearly saw her tales of the horrors and suffering as entertainment. It turned her stomach, and she clenched her fists, but there was nothing she could do about them. She had to take the risk and stand up for her voice to be heard and for aid to be collected for the families in the square.

She could handle large crowds of friends, but even then, they wearied her. This, being surrounded by enemies all looking to taste her pain, to chew her up and spit her back out, was too much. Her nails dug into Taunos's arm.

She didn't know exactly how Taunos wielded his charm to get them out, but the next thing she knew, her back was against one of the pillars lining the hall, with Taunos pressed against her. His hands framed her face, his forehead resting against hers, and beyond him, the walls of the hall. No one was watching them, and she breathed a sigh of relief.

"I'll keep the groups smaller. Half? A third?" His voice vibrated through her.

She nodded. "Thank you."

"No need to thank me, Tabei. I'm sorry, I miscalculated."

She shook her head. "It's not you. How did you get us out?"

"I told them I needed to whisk you away for some very urgent kissing." He grinned, but surprise still lit in his eyes when she leaned forward and kissed him.

She'd be a spectacle, but she could do it on her terms and perhaps even create something good out of it by the end.

But as the night went on, it seemed more and more nobles looked at her with suspicion or amusement, instead.

One nobleman scoffed when Rebaya introduced her before being called away. After Rebaya was out of earshot, the man narrowed his eyes at Taunos. "How could you associate with someone like her, Haari?"

"Lord Saawe," Taunos said, a thread of danger in his voice. "What do you mean?"

"I know you," another noble said, considering her over the rim of his glass. "Lamyi's warned us about you already. Your lies won't go far here, though I am curious. What do you have over Rebaya to get her help?"

"Lies?" she choked out.

Saawe nodded. "Lamyi told us all about your trip here, you know. About your unprofessional attitude and how you tried to get him killed by working with the Hinanuri. And then, when he brought you through the front gates of our city so the guards would have an easier time capturing you, you blew up the whole area? Ruthless."

Amanah's hand clenched around Taunos's. "I did no such thing."

"My favorite part is her making herself out to be the hero for that disaster. Quite ingenious, actually," said another.

Amanah gaped at them, her cheeks burning with outrage. A new city, and she'd fallen to the same old tricks. Would Rebaya also turn out to be false? She'd let down her guard a little for her, and the thought that she might have tricked her too made tears spark in her eyes.

Saawe swirled his glass. "I'm interested to see Lamyi sort you out. Although you get points in my book for arrogance, coming here to pull scams right under the noses of those who will arrest you. Shouldn't be long now. I doubt even other havi will want to be around you afterward—and that's assuming you keep your life."

"Watch how you speak, Lord Saawe," Taunos growled. "You can ask Yadi if my word isn't enough. Lamyi may be spreading stories, but it doesn't change the truth. Amanah truly did save lives, including Lord Lamyi's."

"Consider your favor nullified, Haari Taunos." Lord Saawe's lip curled, and he stalked off, the rest of the group quickly trailing him.

She'd never win at this. Why had she thought she could win at a game where the nobles supported each other against havi, regardless of clear lies?

Amanah bit her lip. "Were they friends?"

"No," Taunos said, staring after him. He looked disappointed in the man.

"You'll lose contacts, people who might help you in other ways," Amanah said.

Taunos turned to face her, tugging her close. "I don't care. Even if they all turn on me, I won't care. I can't call someone a friend who can't accept you or Emin based simply on your station. But I do mind your name being dragged through the mud, so let's find Lamyi. I have questions for him."

That was what she was afraid of.

But Amanah weaved through the crowd after Taunos and tugged him to a halt. "Are you sure you don't mind?"

He stepped into her, wrapping his arms around her and resting his cheek against her braids. "I'm in this with you, the two of us together. I am on your side, always."

It put a smile on her face, and she breathed easier. The sound of Rebaya's voice as she spoke to someone caught her attention, and as she scanned the room, Yadi caught her eye and gave her a nod. She straightened her shoulders. She couldn't do this alone, but she also didn't have to. Perhaps some of these people would never accept her, but there were others she could trust. She could trust Taunos, and so far Rebaya had been honest to the point of bluntness with her. Maybe others doubted her integrity, but why should she care what they thought? Taunos didn't, and he'd known them longer. As far as retaliation, well, she had protection of her own for the first time.

When they found Lamyi, he was telling a story—thankfully not about her this time.

"Lamyi, a word please," Taunos said.

"I'm busy, and you should be, too," Lamyi said.

"Do you want to do this here?" Taunos asked.

Straightening, Lamyi set his drink down on a side table nearby. "Do you?"

"Last chance," Taunos said.

Lamyi scoffed and turned to his friends. "Excuse me. Servants are so troublesome sometimes, are they not?"

As soon as the crowd had drifted away, Lamyi turned to them, eyebrows raised.

"You know full well the stories you're spreading about me are false," Amanah said. "I know you don't like me, but why? Why spread these tales?"

Lamyi clasped his hands behind his back. His voice dropped to a low murmur. "Are you not responsible for my safety?"

She frowned. "Yes."

"Inuwe and I need to make sure we have enough support to combat those who will remain loyal to the traitor even after we unveil the evidence we gathered. That means knowing their names."

Taunos frowned. "And so you're setting up Amanah as a sympathizer to see who reaches out to her?"

The smile Lamyi gave him was cold.

"They don't know me. Don't you think that might look a little blatantly like a trap?" Amanah asked.

Lamyi flicked his fingers at her. "Not everyone is so paranoid as you, and this sort of thing is done every Feast of Dark Nights. Please trust me to know my society better than you do."

Amanah hmm'ed. "And yet, you're using me to fish for traitors."

"All you need to do is keep being yourself. I trust that won't be too difficult for you to manage."

Amanah narrowed her eyes and was about to turn and go, but Lamyi took her arm, murmuring. "One more thing."

She shook him off, exchanging a troubled look with Taunos, and walked with him past party-goers until he stopped by presumably the next group of people he intended to chat with.

"Let me offer you some advice," he said, his voice overly loud. She eyed him. "Stay away from Lady Adinna."

Amanah frowned at his back as he sauntered away. He was anything but a friend. But going against his orders now would be very public. She exchanged a look with Taunos. Rebaya had indicated her chances would be slim without Adinna's support.

When Emin and Gurseh finished their nap and completed a patrol, Taunos took them aside and explained what was happening.

"I think there's more here. It's bad enough he's using Amanah as bait, but that last interaction…"

"It was very strange," Amanah agreed. "The only thing I can think of is he knows I have to talk to her and hope to gain her favor, and he's setting it up for me to disobey orders. Except he didn't give it as an order."

"I don't like it," Emin said. "Keep on your guard. But first, you two need to rest. Four marks, and then report back in."

Everyone tried to stay awake as long as they could during the rain of the gods, except for the other guards, who also caught snatches of sleep in shifts. It was a great equalizer—everyone looked equally undignified in sleep, even Lord Biryewi. But it meant that the corners and edges of the room were filled with exhausted people.

But there was no way Taunos would be able to sleep with people he didn't trust walking past him. They eventually found a space beneath a window—most people avoided the windows, even heavily draped as they were, between the stars falling and the rumors of threats of more Hinanuri death teams.

"Here. You were my pillow for a little bit one night," she said, taking off her sword belt so she could rest her back against the stone beneath the window. There were patrols and sentries to guard against an attack, and she was inside, so that shouldn't invite too much bad luck, right? Especially with the drape closed. "Time for me to return the favor."

The stars had been falling for marks and marks, and the night was old. Taunos's shoulders were slumping, his natural speed muted, and exhaustion and pain were marked in the lines of his face. Still, he raised his eyebrows at her.

"I can take first watch," he said.

"No. Come on. I'll watch out for you."

"I'm supposed to watch out for you."

"We watch out for each other. Right now's my turn," she said.

He set aside his sword belt and sank onto the ground beside her, one arm clasped to his side.

"Let me check your bandages," she said.

"I think it's fine," he said. "Just tired."

She brushed his hair back from his face. "Time to sleep then."

He lay down, head pillowed on her lap. With one hand, he pulled aside the heavy drapes. "What's it like at your home, this festival? When you aren't partying with nobles?"

"Simpler than this, but not that different. We line the tents all up together so we can go from one to another without stepping outside, and we fill the space with music and laughter and life, like this. We take turns entertaining each other, like this, but not so formally." She raised her eyebrows at him. "You mentioned other people have other celebrations. What about yours?"

"We celebrate outside, with songs and games and fires. My sister loves it."

She'd never heard him mention a sister, or any family at all, but the affection in his voice was clear. She brushed her fingers along his forehead, as if his hair wasn't braided back, and instead falling into his eyes. "You miss her, your sister?"

He gave her a ghost of a smile for a response, then let go of the drape and hooked his arm around her back. "But I like being here, too."

He closed his eyes, still holding her in one arm as if afraid she'd disappear. Her fingertips ran over all the little scars and more recent cuts and bruises on his face.

His lips quirked in a smile. "That tickles."

"Hmmm," she murmured. "I'll have to remember that."

As she hoped, it sparked a wider smile from him. She smoothed his eyebrows, thumbs brushing his temples, and felt him relax, little by little, until his breathing deepened and evened. The peace of the moment lay thick and warm on her, and she wished it would never end. She didn't want to go back into the maze of traps of the nobles.

What an adventure it would be, to join him on his travels. He could learn all the stories, songs, and games like he wanted, and she could learn different ways of healing, sharing what she learned from the bamimri. They couldn't keep their knowledge hoarded if she learned, left them, and gave it away. And she could see the places and people she dreamed of, all while doing the work she wanted to do. They'd keep watch over each other, just as they did now.

She would have to work toward making it possible.

~

Everyone took their turn to entertain, so the days were filled with readings, music, performances, and celebration. Somehow, between the tension of talking with nobles until her throat went dry, the danger of a potential attack, and the need to keep far from Lord Lamyi, she found moments in which she enjoyed herself.

After talking to yet another group Rebaya introduced her to, Amanah turned her thoughts to the upcoming entertainment slots assigned to them. "What story are you going to tell, Haari Taunos?"

"I haven't decided yet. The right one will come to me."

"I have an idea about that." He quirked his eyebrows, and she continued slowly. "What about telling my story, the story of the square? I've already been telling it, but you've heard it enough times by now to do it justice, and you're good at telling stories."

He grinned. "I can do that. If you're sure? This is your story."

She nodded. She didn't enjoy standing in the light, didn't crave the weight of a crowd's attentions like Emin and Taunos."Perhaps some people will listen to you who won't listen to me. We can use your charm to our advantage."

He pressed a kiss to her temple. "Then I'd be honored to."

When it was her turn, she danced a message of unity and care with borrowed banners. Biryewi's master servant nodded along, eyes shining with pride. Right after, Taunos told her story of the square for everyone to hear, his lyrical voice spinning the words so the hair on the back of her neck stood up. It was both thrilling and freeing, working with him in such a way, using his strengths to support her goals.

Emin taught the nobles a Kanhu song from their family for his entertainment. She couldn't help but smile with pride at the way who they were was being incorporated into this event. Gurseh, and Taunos joined her in stomping and clapping along, and soon several others joined in, no doubt aided in loosening their inhibitions by fatigue and drink. Maybe nobles weren't *all* bad all the time. Maybe things could change.

Biryewi's guards were attentive and polite, and occasionally other guards would step up to them for a quick, polite word of support or question about the square and their journey to Gahimbli. A few times, nobles and their guards squared off, with one dispute or another, but Biryewi's guards quickly broke them up.

The cluster of guards that joined them after yet another skirmish was cut short included a grizzled man with a perpetual frown.

"Make sure you run through the current state of alliances with the nobles you serve," he said to the younger guards in the group, "and stay close to them. Nobles are getting tense. If a fight breaks out, Biryewi's going to come down hard on everyone."

"Easier said than done," said another. "Especially since some of them *want* fights."

"They won't be doing the fighting," said the older guard. "It's easier to needle someone when you won't be paying the price."

The young one looked back at Amanah and Taunos, shifting his weight. "Be careful. Everyone knows the accusations by now, that you're plotting to steal bamimri secrets and sell them."

That was true, except for the selling part. Amanah scowled. "Lamyi's telling his stories again?"

"No, not Lamyi. Several of the other nobles are saying these things."

"That and that you're working with the Hinanuri. Working with that death team that hit the square," said the frowny guard.

"The death team killed mostly havi, many from the wilderness. None of those people should have died at all. Why would I be working with them? Why would any of us be?" Amanah asked.

Frowny guard folded his arms. "Perhaps to get an invitation here..."

She scowled.

"Rebaya's influence won't protect you for long if you keep shaking things up," said the first one.

Amanah rolled her shoulders, loosening them as if a fight might be imminent. "We'll be as careful as we can be. You as well."

The young one winced, looking up at the oldest one. "If there is a fight..."

"Don't say it," the older one said. "We might enjoy each others' company off the clock but the job's the job. If I have to hit you, I won't like it, but I'll do it."

The youngest guard quailed, and Taunos stepped forward, clapping him on the shoulder. "Remind your nobles of Biryewi's requirements, and if it comes down to it, I don't intend to fight any of you. I plan to save my efforts for a real enemy."

"You really think the Hinanuri might send a death team?" the youngest asked.

"They sent one already," Amanah pointed out. "And Lamyi and Inuwe were captured on the way here."

"They were only held briefly, thanks to your rescue," Taunos said.

The older guard stepped forward, pointing a finger at the two of them, and Taunos placed himself between her and him. "You two need to be careful. Lamyi is not happy with you two enjoying yourselves. Unhappy nobles make things difficult for those they employ."

"I already know that," Amanah said.

Taunos stood tensed and watchful in front of her, as if she were a noble and he was her bodyguard. Yet he was the one who rubbed shoulders with the nobles. It was odd, but she wasn't complaining. It helped her keep hold of her confidence, even in this situation so far out of her depth.

"Then you might start acting like it," the guard grated.

"We have our orders, just as you do yours," Amanah said, eyeing the vaguely threatening guard. "We're doing as Rebaya ordered, and displeasing her would be just as foolish, would it not?"

The guard stepped back, eyeing Taunos, and then flicking his gaze back to Amanah. "Hopefully it's worth it, this commotion you're causing."

"It is." Her voice was hard, final.

"Come on, Emin's waiting," Taunos said, deftly intervening.

She turned, letting him guide her away with his hand at the small of her back. Emin was in the other direction, standing near Lord Lamyi, looking bored.

"If he knows who Emin is, he knows that was an excuse," she said.

Taunos flashed a small smile at her. "The important thing is, it got us out of there."

Her mouth tightened in a grimace. "Do you think it'll come to fights between the nobles?"

"I hope not."

"Which noble does that older guard work for?"

"I don't know, but I intend to find out," Taunos said. "That warning sounded a little too strong, and I didn't like his willingness to just follow whatever orders he's given."

"These people should be working together, not fighting, especially with the threats."

Taunos tugged her closer with a sigh. "That's not how they think of it. Old rivalries seem stronger, more immediate, when your rival is in front of you, and they may not believe the threat of a death team."

Amanah shook her head. She wanted to protest, but no, she could absolutely see it.

"Amanah, there you are!" Lady Rebaya's voice cut through her thoughts as the woman's wheeled chair cut through the crowd. "Come, dear, I have more people for you to meet."

The noblewoman's voice lowered, just for them. "This one will be hard, but you can handle it. We're struggling to find allies for you, my dear. But we're not giving up. Time to go after perhaps the most influential voice—Lady Adinna. Smile."

Lady Adinna. The one Lamyi told her to stay away from. Amanah swallowed hard, glancing at Taunos. He nodded, stepping into position as her own personal guard, and she followed Rebaya to a group of women including Adinna.

"These are some of the biggest patrons of the bamimri," Rebaya said, introducing each woman one by one. The introductions slid over Amanah, exhaustion making it hard to remember names when she'd met so many already. She gave them a polite bow, however, keeping her expression carefully blank as Rebaya introduced her as the hero of the square.

Adinna raised an eyebrow, swirling her blue drink. "This is the little thief coming to steal our secrets, who experimented on poor little Inuwe and Lamyi?"

"I never experimented on them," Amanah said.

"Everyone's heard about you by now, enough that I cannot fathom why you're here or why Lady Rebaya is introducing you to us," said another.

"If it was just Lamyi, that would be one thing, but some of these stories are coming from people who don't even like Lamyi," said another.

"But where did they hear these things from?" Rebaya asked. "I would bet that if you trace these back, it would all be rooted back with Lamyi."

"You can believe what you like, Rebaya," Adinna said, flicking her fingers in dismissal.

"The same goes for you," Rebaya said. "Use some common sense. Amanah's never been to this city before. How would all these people suddenly know her?"

"What about the rumors that you worked with the death team?" asked another. "Have anything to say about that?"

"Was it really a death team? Or a fake?" asked Adinna.

"Of course it was real!" Amanah said. "And I shot two of them."

"If it were real, they'd be dead," said another.

Taunos's voice was light. "Or, perhaps, they made mistakes. No one's perfect, and in battle, all it takes sometimes is one slip."

"I treated some of the wounded," Rebaya said. "I assure you, the attack was real, and Amanah worked herself to exhaustion to help those people."

"And how will you be paying for the damage to the square?" Adinna asked. Then she waved a hand. "Nevermind, I suppose it should come out of the coffers of whoever put you up to it. All a wonderful story, I'm sure."

"I don't count bleeding children with broken arms screaming for their parents as a wonderful story," Amanah snapped.

"And we're supposed to accept that you organized the efforts, all without training? Who really did it? Whose credit are you taking?" Adinna asked.

"I did it," Amanah said. "Someone had to. I was there."

"Well," said another woman, reaching out to pat her arm. "That's all in the past now. You can go back to your place in things and let the rest of us deal with the mess."

A chill shot through her at the casual condescension. It was the same as the magistrate's wife at the horse race. She'd already seen what came of her staying out of the way of nobles. They might complain about her not staying in her place, but they never stayed in theirs.

"I cannot," Amanah said. "If I did, people would still suffer, unseen by those who wish not to see."

Adinna narrowed her eyes at her. "I don't see you there now. If I'm not mistaken, you're at a party."

She was, and she couldn't express how much she'd rather be elsewhere. Not without shaming Rebaya, who brought her. "I plan to get into the bamimri, as no doubt you've already heard. I didn't know enough to help everyone, and if I can learn more, I can help more people. That's better for everyone."

Adinna smiled. "A nice sentiment, yes, but it's very difficult work. Do you even know how to read?"

Her face burned. "No."

"Well, then. You should consider accepting your limitations. How are you supposed to study the texts without even being literate? Others better suited to the work will take care of the rest."

Anger roiled in her stomach, tightening her sweating hands into fists. As if she couldn't learn to read, if she could find someone willing to teach her!

"Besides," another said, "You already mentioned you're not cut out for it, that you weren't good enough. Why bet on a losing horse? I'll be advising the bamimri specifically not to accept you. You should return to patrolling streets or whatever you do."

"What if it was your father whose leg was nearly blown off?" Amanah burst out. "What if it was your sister who was hit in the head with rubble? The healer that was finally cajoled into coming to help barely looked at them before turning away. And you think I'm not cut out for it, when I spent all day fighting Tenah herself for each and every life?"

"Don't be dramatic," Adinna said. "You weren't alone."

"No, I wasn't. I was aided by havi healers who also fought death with me. They and their experience is why so few died. But the healer that came, he tossed away their knowledge as if it were horse dung. Like you're doing right now."

Adinna waved her words away. "Maybe we should give these other healers a chance to get into the bamimri, then. I'm still not hearing a good argument for you."

"You didn't see her work," Rebaya said.

Adinna gave her a flat look. "We could discuss your lack of skepticism, I suppose, Lady Rebaya, but I was being polite."

Amanah shook her head. She could feel Taunos's presence just behind her shoulder, but this wasn't a fight he could help her with. "You're right that I'm at a party. Obviously. But why are the requirements so strict? Just because someone is havi or from the wilderness doesn't mean they can't become bimnas with equal knowledge to anyone else. Why require such an exorbitant sum simply to test for entrance, and why require a permanent residence, an address in a section of the city so many people can't afford? What does that do except exclude people?"

"This argument right here is why you can't be a bimna," said another bejeweled lady. "You're proving my points for me, thank you."

Her fists clenched. "I've lived six months in Arruk trying to keep my head down and trying to help people. And even on the way here, repeatedly, when I try to help people, I'm threatened."

"One would think you would learn," Adinna murmured. "Alas, I suspect you're no brighter than you look."

"If you don't have a problem with people being smashed against the wall, used as human shields, and then left to suffer because you can't be bothered to help them, then you're no different than the worst scoundrel in the worst part of town. All that separates your lack of empathy is that you have more power, more reach. You could do good if you just chose to. Some of the people here have seemed friendly, but I don't know, perhaps it's just another pretty mask you wear to assure yourselves you're civilized. Taunos thinks otherwise, but well, he's Haari Taunos. Sometimes it seems he lives in another world entirely."

He huffed behind her, setting one hand lightly on her waist.

She went on, the words pouring from her. "If you would be horrified to be face-to-face with a death team, with no way out, or to be caught in an explosion and left to suffer because you're deemed not important enough, but when it's a havi it's 'just the way things are,' then you might as well pick up a weapon and deliver the wounds yourself because you're only fooling yourselves that you're not as bad."

"We're sending aid," one of the women said. "If you paid attention, you'd know we're coordinating assistance to be given after the festival. These things take time, though, deciding who is responsible for what, sending out word so the people know who is coming to help them—"

"It's not about *you*," Amanah snapped. "You don't get to gain glory from the people in the square still being alive. You put those people in that situation, left them there to die. You don't get to claim you're happy they're going to be all right now."

"And what, you think you're better?" hissed another. "You come from nowhere. You have nothing. You *are* nothing. None of us had ever heard of you before. The bamimri is not for havi like you. Haari, at least we know, though what could possess him to take part in this, I don't know."

"This needs to stop," Taunos said. "You can't lift up my heroism and spit on the true hero—Amanah. How can you welcome me, a stranger, and shun her?"

"I've spent my time in Arruk trying to avoid notice. Stay invisible. I could never be small enough. I'd fight for a breath of air, and you nobles wanted it. I'd get a crumb of food, but no, that was yours. I'm done with that. I'm done with trying to avoid upsetting those in charge."

Adinna cast a glance at Rebaya. "Honestly, this girl?"

"Shut your mouth and listen," Rebaya snapped.

Adinna flattened her lips and narrowed her eyes back on Amanah.

"Maybe I won't get into the bamimri. Maybe you'll keep me out." Amanah chuckled mirthlessly. "Maybe Lamyi will have his way and I'll be tied once again to a pillar in front of Jattanu's temple, flogged and left to bake in the sun all day. Maybe my brother will once again have to cut me down and drag me into the shade, delirious from heat."

Taunos's hand tightened on her hip, as if he could tug her out of the way of her own words. As if he could save her from her nightmares.

Still, she forged on, squeezing his hand as comfort against the words she was about to say, words that would no doubt horrify him, now that she knew him so well. They needed to be said anyway, and she could say them with his strong fingers ensnared in hers.

"One of these days, maybe one of you will kill me, and why? Because you think I have no worth? It doesn't matter what you think, because I am worthy. I won't leave people to suffer and die alone. I can't imagine looking on suffering and not caring. And I will not apologize for that anymore."

Taunos's fingers closed tightly on hers, and she could feel the tension radiating off him, but he kept silent.

"You've been sent for Jattanu's justice before?" one of the women asked, eyes wide.

"I have."

"There you have it," Adinna said. "A common criminal. It's clear in the rules of the bamimri that criminals can't be bimnas, yes? Well, that's that, then. This farce is ended."

Rebaya shook her head. "Rules can be changed. And Borlim claimed that her punishment was unjust."

"And what would Borlim know?" snapped Adinna. "He's only a guardmaster. There's another person who should learn to stay in his place instead of meddling in things above him."

Amanah drew in a slow, deep breath. "I've said my piece. Your choices are on you."

"They most certainly are," Adinna said. "I wish you a peaceful rest of your festival."

She swept away, along with several others.

One woman stepped forward, the one who'd asked about Jattanu's justice, and Amanah blinked, belatedly realizing that four of the women were still gathered around her and Rebaya.

"You went for Jattanu's justice, and you're here, making enemies of nobles who no doubt could send you again? And you know this?" the woman asked.

Amanah grimaced. "I don't always choose the wise path."

"Many of you are better than this, I know," Taunos said, his voice hard and his eyes on the people who walked away. "But until you deal with your shadows, you will always be dragged down by them."

The woman's eyes flicked to Taunos, then back to Amanah. "This is so important to you, that you'd risk everything for it?"

"I didn't have the training or tools to do enough in the square," Amanah said. "And those with the training and tools didn't care to help."

The woman nodded. "Well. You and I should talk again. Perhaps we can get creative."

"Thank you, Lady Sina," Taunos murmured over Amanah's shoulder.

Numb with exhaustion and disbelief, Amanah forced a small smile and a nod. Rebaya said something, and the others began to move on to other circles, but Sina put her hand on her arm.

"Contact me if you need me. I will do what I can to help. You're not alone. But be aware, Lamyi has already publicly declared you won't get in. He's not nice when his pride is threatened."

"I have already discovered that fact, thank you," Amanah said.

Sina smiled and gave her arm a pat. "Well, perhaps I shall have to steal you away for my own guard, if things get too bad."

Amanah let out a breath, watching Sina make her way through the crowd. Taunos resumed his spot next to her, rubbing her shoulders with one hand. Had she managed to find another ally? Perhaps, though she wondered if there would be a cost from the others.

"Was that too much?" she asked.

"Who else would say it?" Taunos asked. "You were incredible. Come on, Lamyi's staring daggers. Shall we patrol?"

"Patrol sounds nice." She gave him a smile, and side-by side they left the main hall, returning the nods Biryewi's guards gave them as they stepped past.

24

THE FESTIVAL OF Dark Nights continued, blending together in a haze of sand falling, musicians changing, food, wine, patrols, jokes, desserts, stolen moments in a shadowed corner, heavier drinks, and meeting nobles.

Amanah vowed to get as many promises of support for her entry into the bamimri as she could—she'd need them to have a chance, with Adinna and Lamyi against her. And hopefully enough of those promises would pan out.

Clear divisions were forming among the nobles, like battle lines. When people were rude, Taunos and Rebaya often outright rejected their company. Every once in a while, she caught a ripple effect from those moments, where the rejected person would also be turned away by others. Worry gnawed at her, for those nobles would surely want revenge, but it overwhelmed her with gratitude, too, for how many came to check in on her. How many seemed like maybe they cared a little. Nobles like Sina, who fluttered past like birds, dropping words of support here and there as she passed by. Nobles like Biryewi, who would occasionally wander past and make it a point to ask how she was enjoying herself, as if she were any other guest. And nobles like Rebaya, who weren't afraid to chide others' rudeness as if they were poorly behaved children, shaming them publicly if need be. Even Inuwe spoke up in her support on the few occasions he was nearby.

Emin and Gurseh stuck close to Lamyi when they weren't patrolling, forming an imposing wall to face off against other guards when Lamyi and other nobles blustered at each other. Amanah and Taunos remained ready to step in if Inuwe needed them, but though tensions between the nobles remained high, and a few did scrap—or at least, their guards stood off against each other for them—Inuwe managed to stay out of it.

On the fourth day—or was it the fifth? Time was running together—of the Festival, Lamyi and Inuwe stepped into the center of the hall together. Lamyi raised a hand, and the musicians by the dance floor stopped playing. A servant rang a crystal bell, and when all eyes were on him, Lamyi's smile was smug and self-satisfied.

Amanah stole a glance at Taunos, ever at her side. She marveled at the difference between the two men in their arrogance. She'd seen similar looks on Taunos's face after completing challenges, but it only made her roll her eyes—it never sent this ripple of dread up her spine.

He glanced at her, squeezing her hand, and she leaned into him, returning her gaze to Lamyi.

"My friends and not-quite friends, thank you for your attention. I know you've all heard of the mysterious announcement Inuwe and I have to make, and I'm certain your curiosity is piqued by all the discussions we've been having. We've uncovered some terrible evidence we need to share with you."

"Get on with it, Lamyi!" someone from the crowd shouted.

Lamyi gave the woman a flat look. "Fine. Lady Adinna's a traitor."

The hall stilled for a moment, and then whispers of conversation and smattering laughter broke out around the room.

Lamyi gave the woman who'd prodded him another look full of condescension. "See, this is why we lead up to such announcements."

"What proof do you have?" someone asked.

"What do you mean, she's a traitor?" asked another.

Amanah scanned the hall for Adinna. She disliked the woman, but for her to be a traitor? She shuddered at what the nobles might do to her. The woman was standing near the tables of food, a glass in her hand, looking bored even when Biryewi's guards stepped forward from the wall to flank her. Guards all along the walls and by the doors stood alert, hands on their weapons. Along the wall by the food, a wide-eyed servant scurried between two of them and into the hall. Amanah half wished she could hide in the kitchens as well, because if this escalated, it was going to be ugly.

Lord Biryewi stepped forward, ever composed. "Enough theatrics, Lamyi. Please present the evidence against Lady Adinna to support such a claim."

Removing a stack of papers from a pocket inside his long jacket, Inuwe handed them to Biryewi. "There's more in a safe in your office, but these are a start."

"Inuwe risked much to gain such information," Lamyi said.

"And it's only thanks to our guards that we were able to come and deliver it," Inuwe said.

Lord Saawe frowned, narrowing his eyes at Amanah. "Wait a moment. If Lady Adinna is a traitor... What about that havi guard? I've seen her speaking with Adinna many times over the last days."

Amanah stifled a snort. She'd only spoken to her a few times after that first horrible conversation, and only in passing. She wanted to stay far away from the disdainful woman, and there was Lamyi's advice to stay away from her to think of, too. But Rebaya had been adamant that Adina's support would likely be needed.

"Isn't her family friends with Hinanuri families?" asked someone else. "I thought the brother mentioned that once."

At the other end of the hall, Emin folded his arms. "The brother is right here."

"Are they working together?" Saawe asked.

The smirk on his face made her want to commit violence in a way she'd rarely ever felt.

"I highly doubt Amanah is working with the Hinanuri," Inuwe said.

"My family has traded with Hinanuri families, yes, but that does not mean we're traitors," she gritted out.

"Many of you have also traded with Hinanuri, have you not?" Rebaya asked. "Does that mean any of you are working with them?"

But the crowd murmured with more suspicion.

"I would never work with a death team. I saved lives when people were attacked just days ago. Why would I hurt people who could easily be my friends, my family?" she cried.

"Greed is a powerful thing," Saawe said.

"No, I highly doubt this about Amanah. The case against Lady Adinna, however, is regrettably strong," Inuwe said, a wrinkle furrowing his brow.

How had the focus shifted from Lady Adinna to accusations against Amanah? So easily, suspicion was cast her way.

Across the room, Lamyi raised his glass to her, smiling.

He'd set her up. He'd set her up to fall with Lady Adinna, and she'd walked right into it.

"What evidence is there against Amanah?" asked Biryewi. "Surely if you're accusing her, you're not doing so without evidence."

"I haven't said a word against her, Lord Biryewi." Lamyi's voice was as smooth as the liquid chocolate that had been offered earlier that day. "Of course, we've all seen that Lady Rebaya can stick silk dresses on a havi but she's still just a havi. Have you seen those boots? And the sword belts don't in any way match their clothes."

Face burning, she gripped Taunos's arm.

"Let's turn the conversation back to what you came all this way for," Biryewi said. "Inuwe, please present your evidence."

The roaring in her ears drowned out the sound of Inuwe's voice. She had to move, had to do something. But there was nothing for her to do. Why had she come here in the first place? If she was home, there'd be plenty of tasks waiting for her, to fill her hands and calm the thoughts drowning her.

An arm wrapped around her, and Taunos's scent filled her nose. She leaned into him, letting him lead her somewhere—she didn't care where at the moment.

"This was all a mistake, wasn't it?" she murmured to him.

"It was a mistake," Lamyi snapped, and Taunos tensed beside her.

Lamyi had apparently followed them and now stood there, finger raised, as if they were errant children. Behind him, Emin was making his way toward them along the wall, while Lady Sina moved toward Biryewi, regardless of the fact that he was engaged with Inuwe's presentation of evidence.

"I warned you, but you refused to listen," Lamyi said. "When we get back to Arruk, I'll make sure everything you touch turns to dust before your eyes, until you wish you'd remembered to be grateful, to show a little humility instead of wrapping yourself up in pride. It'd be unfortunate if your brother suffered an accident, but you could care for him as you watch him wither, his strength drained."

"I warned you to stop threatening her," Taunos began.

"You leave Emin out of this!" The smart thing was to bow her head, say her apologies, and hide in the shadows. This was asking for trouble.

But she was so tired of avoiding trouble. It seemed to find her anyway.

Lamyi laughed. "Me? I won't touch him. But there are so many ways someone can have an accident in a city as large and busy as Arruk."

"Are you threatening a city guard?" Emin asked, having finally made it to them. "How interesting."

"Your reach doesn't extend so far, Lord Lamyi," Taunos said. His voice was calm but for the steel undertone, and Amanah was glad he was there, because her voice had gone, stolen by images of Gitu laying in his bed, every breath painful, except now his face was Emin's.

"It reaches far enough," Lamyi said. "You decided to move against me. I'll make sure you're all unemployable for the rest of your days. Are you proud to give all this up, Haari? You're a fool."

"Lamyi, what are you doing over here?" Biryewi's voice carried. He stood still by Inuwe, but his gaze was fixed on Lamyi, a disapproving frown on his face. Lady Sina slipped away from the center of the hall, making her way through the crowd toward them.

With a last glare at Amanah which promised retribution, Lamyi stalked away, back toward the center of the room where Inuwe stood with Lord Biryewi.

"There will be no more threats against one of my guests without proper proof," Biryewi snapped. "Guards, if anyone so much as touches someone aggressively, toss them out the front door. Let them spend the rest of the rain of the gods outside like the bandits they are."

Emin placed a hand on Amanah's shoulder.

The cold running up Amanah's spine hadn't stopped. Her eyes darted from face to face. She wished she was alone, without all the attention on her. It was too much. She hadn't wanted to make a scene in the first place, and certainly not like this.

"Are you all right?" Sina tilted her head. "Oh dear, you look like you're going to throw up."

Amanah shook her head, trying to keep her focus on Sina and Biryewi instead of everyone else. "No, I just… What is going on?"

"You're not without friends. Not anymore," Sina said, lowering her voice.

Amanah bit her lip. How far could she trust this woman?

Upstairs? Taunos's fingers tapped on her arm.

She nodded. There'd be less eyes there, and she needed a moment to collect herself.

"Thank you for stepping in, Lady Sina," Taunos said. "We'll just be up on the balcony."

With one last worried look at her, Emin stepped in, taking Sina's arm and chatting easily with her, his gaze never stopping as he scanned the crowd.

Amanah let out a breath of relief once she and Taunos cleared the top of the steps. There were more shadows up here. The oil must have run out in the lamps, but everyone was down on the main floor anyway. She was glad of it as she leaned against him, arms around his waist.

"Thank you," she breathed.

His finger trailed up and down the back of Amanah's neck. "Are you all right?"

Amanah grimaced. She didn't want to think about it yet. "I don't know."

Taunos stroked Amanah's cheek gently with his thumb, staring into her eyes as if to reassure himself she was fine. Then he folded her to his chest. "I'm so sorry."

From below, Biryewi's voice rose and fell as he chastised Lamyi. She closed her eyes, resting in the safety Taunos provided. Even though Lamyi had come after her, he'd had to organize to do it, and others had stepped in for them, including their host. That had never happened for her before.

Taunos stiffened, and she pulled away. His head raised, turning, searching, his nostrils flaring.

Something was wrong. Amanah stepped slightly in front of him, scanning the balcony. She reached back and tapped on his leg. *What is it?*

Fresh air. Breeze. He tapped back.

Movement in the shadows caught her eye, only a couple paces away around the corner of the pillar. Something blurred toward her, and she moved to duck. Taunos exploded out from behind her, knocking something away. It fell at her feet—a blackened knife. An intruder stood a few paces from them, dressed all in black, and he spun, striking Taunos in his injured ribs.

Taunos grunted, folding up. He barely managed to divert the next strike, swinging the man around. The man hit the railing overbalanced, and they both toppled over the edge.

"Death team!" Amanah shouted over the balcony. "Get to cover! Guards!"

"Amanah, down!" Taunos grunted from below, where he lay on the floor atop the intruder.

She dropped to the ground and rolled blindly, swinging a chair into the path where she had been. Crossbow bolts narrowly missed her.

"Crossbows!" she shouted.

"Amanah!" Emin's voice was also sharp with fear. "Are you all right?"

Shadows moved in front of her. She had to get some distance. Had to figure out how many they were dealing with. She'd survived one death team, but that had been a miracle.

"A little busy!" She dove to the side after saying the words. More crossbow bolts slammed into the ground just beside her boot.

She had a few moments while they reloaded, but she needed cover. She needed to make the death team leave the safety of the shadowed balcony. Had the lamps run out of oil as she initially assumed, or had someone doused them? And how had they gotten past the patrols? She shook the questions away—she didn't have time to wonder about that right now.

Amanah grabbed a tablecloth, wrapped her hand in it, and then smashed the nearest lamp. The cloth caught fire quickly, and she threw it over another lamp and table. Tossing chairs and tables behind her, she ran for the stairs, but a shadow moved in her path, ready for her.

Gritting her teeth, she took a page from Taunos's book and threw herself over the balcony.

"Tabei!" Taunos's voice was raw with horror. For her, no doubt, because he never feared a fight.

She hit the table below hard, bouncing off it and dragging dishes of food with her to the ground. Lurching to her feet, she cast a look around. Taunos was on his feet again, Emin and Gurseh next to him in the rapidly clearing center of the hall, as people scrambled for some small bit of cover and guards clustered around their employers. The black-clad figure he'd toppled over the edge with lay unmoving a few paces away from them.

The doors shut with a bang. Black-clad figures stood at every entrance and window. The room erupted into shouts and screams. The balcony was enveloped in flames. Hopefully, that would drive the crossbow-wielding enemies from their cover. The others she could see wore swords, instead. They were still far outnumbered. And outclassed—their training couldn't hope to match that of a death team. Even a death team of ten fighters could probably take on a party like this. She counted at least twenty, and they were making a show of it—how many more were shrouded by their famous stealth?

Lord Biryewi's guards seemed the least stunned, some of them running grim-faced toward the threat while others upended tables and couches. Two swept Biryewi and Esem behind a massive pillar. Inuwe stood, stunned and pale, for a moment before Sina dragged him away.

"Find cover," Amanah yelled as she headed for Taunos, Emin, and Gurseh.

Yadi took up the call, ducking from cover to cover with an armful of weapons for those who had been caught unarmed because they hadn't listened to Emin.

"I hate it when I'm right," Emin grumbled.

"Yes, yes, you're very smart," Gurseh said.

"Are you all right?" Taunos murmured to her.

She grimaced at him. "Are you trying to get hurt?"

"He was aiming at you. Seemed the thing to do."

"Can you fight?"

He nodded. "I'm not at my best, but yes."

"I'm not sure this is what Rebaya meant when she wanted chaos," Emin bared his teeth at her in a semblance of a grin.

Around them, guards were forming up into groups as well, standing between their employers and the death team.

"We have our swords, but grab weapons when you can. Disarm them," Emin said. "Taunos, I need you here." He pointed. "Amanah, right next to him on the other side. Try to get back to this formation whenever possible, this box, all of us back to back, yes? If they can take us one-on-one, we're all dead. We need to keep them away from the nobles as long as possible."

"Specifically Inuwe," Amanah said.

"No, all of them," Emin said. "Best chance we have is all of us guards working together. The more we keep alive, the more random elements they have to account for. And they probably want us all dead, guards, servants, and nobles. All of us."

She nodded. A few of the guards nearby nodded to Emin. "How best can we help?"

"Stay alive," Emin said. "Groups of four, guard each others' backs. Whenever you can gang up on them, do. Fight dirty."

Pride filled her as other guards listened, some forming up like they had while others remained guarding their nobles. They were still dead, but it was easier to face when someone had your back. And she had the best people with her. She just wished she had more time with them. More laughter. More light.

"Tenah smile on us," she breathed, drawing her sword.

Emin gave her a fierce grin and a nod. "See you on the other side. Make them hurt."

And then they were rushing forward against the nearest member of the death team.

In some ways, the fight was like dancing with Taunos. They moved past each other, moved past Emin and Gurseh, deflecting blows. Taunos was the first to snatch a weapon, plucking a sword right out of the hands of one of the death team and immediately passing it to Amanah. She slid it across the floor toward a cluster of nobles crouching behind a couch. As she straightened, an attacker plunged a dagger toward Emin's back, and she thrust her sword out, sending it flying out of the man's hand.

Taunos spun her around, leaping past her to engage another. He staggered, a hand to his ribs. She reached past him, turned aside a strike heading for him and then punched her opponent in the throat. He went down, and she grabbed his knife, one quick stab to keep him down. This one she kept, sword in one hand, knife in the other. Emin lunged past her, and Gurseh shouted from the other side.

In the chaos, she couldn't keep track of the wider room. Just each individual threat in front of her, and the glimpses of the others as they fought. Emin had two swords the next time she saw him. She didn't know where the second came from. Gurseh was most often behind her so she couldn't see him, but she could hear him fight with his calm efficiency. Beside her, Taunos's skills and impossible speed were on full display. When he was disarmed, Taunos used a wine bottle as a weapon, then a chair, then a lantern that he flung in an intruder's face, sending him screaming, on fire, into another intruder.

The exhaustion was getting to her. She swore some of Taunos's strikes didn't actually connect, but his opponents reacted as if they did. She shook her head. She didn't need her eyes playing tricks on her now. What was this day? How long had it been since she'd had a solid sleep? Five days? Six? Emin had been right—this had been a good plan, for the death team to attack near the end of the rain of the gods.

A boot slammed into her thigh hard enough to numb her leg. She went down, rolling onto her back as she fell. Her attacker was already dead though, Emin pulling his knife from the man's chest. She tossed the body to the side, scrambling up. Another one was coming toward Taunos's back while he struggled with another. She slashed out, the tip of her sword slicing across the attacker's face. As the black clad figure pulled back, hand to her face, Amanah stepped toward her. Slipped in blood. Her knife clattered away. Taunos's hand caught her arm, and she steadied herself on him, using her momentum and his balance to launch a kick at the member of the death team. The woman's knife blade skidded across the sole of her boot, the front half of her boot falling apart under the blade. The first thing she'd do with her share of Biryewi's payment was buy thick boots. She sliced the sword at the woman's blade, disarming her. The woman lunged forward, shoulder ramming into hers, sending Amanah's sword flying.

They scuffled on the floor, Amanah's strikes blocked more often than not, while her opponent's fists and knees battered at her relentlessly. She should have kept her at bay with the sword—or she should have practiced more wrestling. Even when she did hit the woman, she was too close to build up the speed to do much damage, though she focused on causing all the pain she could, as quickly as possible.

Taunos twisted, his feet staying to either side of her as he fought. In one move, he stepped forward to block someone who was coming to strike Amanah while she was vulnerable, while at the same time, kicking Amanah's sword back toward her. Emin and Gurseh quickly formed up on either side of her, each fighting desperate battles of their own, blood staining the floor.

The woman had found her knife, and she swung it up toward the inside of Taunos's leg to hamstring him. Amanah gritted her teeth against a shout—no use distracting her allies—and flicked her blade out to block the strike. Taunos startled as the flat of her blade connected with his thigh, but kept his position over her, guarding her from other strikes. Amanah did the same. Her sword was too long to be much use against her opponent but she could at least block strikes against her allies. She grunted, diverting a strike from Taunos's back with her sword and kicking her opponent in the stomach at the same time.

A grunt of pain sounded above her. Taunos fell, his knee coming down hard on her opponent's temple. Amanah seized the moment of distraction, grabbing her knife from the woman and slamming it home through the woman's throat. Leaving it there, she stood, sword at the ready in blood-slicked hands.

And then, there was no one left to fight.

Amanah blinked, unable to believe it. They'd survived?

Wailing and screaming came from various groups, but the clusters of guards still on their feet stared around in astonishment. A couple of those closest to them began to laugh, while a few shook themselves and began to check the perimeter or their employers.

Taunos was grimacing on the floor, holding his ribs and his stomach. Emin's knees gave out, too, but Gurseh grabbed him, hauling his arm over his shoulders, and bringing him to the nearest ruined couch. Gurseh flipped it over, and then guided Emin onto it. That was a good idea. Amanah stooped, groaning as she hauled Taunos upright as well. He was lighter than he looked, but all that muscle was still heavy.

"You shouldn't—" He cut off with a grunt of pain. He was clearly trying to get his legs under him to help her, but he kept sagging against her.

"I'm fine," she said. "You're not."

"You're bleeding," he grunted.

"You're worse," she returned. Step by step, she used his half-falling momentum to get him to the couch. No doubt his wounds were causing him even more trouble, not to mention any extra ones he'd collected.

"The hall is clear!" shouted one of Biryewi's guards, standing to attention by the main doors. All of his household guards had taken up stations near doors and windows, their weapons still bare, stances still ready.

Biryewi stepped out from the pillar, half-holding Esem up, and began giving orders, while others peeked out from behind cover or began shouting for help. The whimpers or screams of the wounded resounded in the hall.

She dropped Taunos on the couch beside Emin with less gentleness than she'd intended, wincing at his hiss of pain. Gurseh knelt by Emin's thigh, pressing hard on a deep gouge, and other cuts, mostly shallow, wept blood on his brown skin. Gurseh himself wasn't in much better shape, pale and shaking as blood dripped to the floor beneath him.

"We survived two death teams," Emin said. He squeezed Gurseh's hand. "Don't make me a liar."

"I think you've got it worse than me," Gurseh said.

He indicated his leg carelessly. "Oh this little thing? Couple stitches."

"Stop moving," Gurseh ordered him. "I'm trying to keep your blood inside."

"How are you two?" Emin asked, eyes darting over both of them.

"I'll be back in the practice yard before you," Taunos said through gritted teeth. He nudged Emin with his elbow and then stiffened in pain, his head dropping back against the couch.

"You must have a head wound. I'll wait until you're ready to beat you around the ring." Emin's boast was weak, but the two of them grimaced at each other.

Emin reached out to rest his hand on Gurseh's cheek. "You all right?"

"Better than you two idiots," Gurseh said.

At least the three of them were well enough to banter. That eased much of the fear in her heart. She scanned the room for their allies. Lord Biryewi sat on a couch next to Esem, who was being fussed over, while Lady Sina lay on the ground, back to her. How badly was she hurt? Inuwe was curled in a ball around Lamyi, but she couldn't see either clearly from here. She couldn't see Yadi, either.

"I should get Rebaya." Amanah shook herself, pushing down her fear for them along with the pain. She turned, scanning the desolation for a familiar wheeled chair. Was it even possible the noblewoman had survived the fight?

Her gaze snagged on a wheel, and she gasped, hurrying forward.

"Help me up," Rebaya said. She lay in a crumpled heap, a thin trickle of blood running from her temple. Her chair was half on top of her, crossbow bolts embedded in it.

It took the help of two noblemen to snap off the bolt heads that had made it through the wood and tie on fresh cushions to protect Rebaya from the splintered wood before they righted the chair and helped the Rebaya back into it.

"Thank you. This'll do nicely," she said.

"Are you all right? Please, we need your help," Amanah said, her voice tight and breathless. "Emin and Taunos need medical attention."

"Many need medical attention here," Rebaya said. "Including you. You can't help anyone without patching yourself up first."

Amanah blinked, looking down at herself. She had several cuts, including a long one up her forearm that definitely needed bandaging before she went any farther. The sole of her foot hurt—that cut must have gotten through her boot—and pain blazed up her leg. The blows she'd taken had angered the injuries she'd already been healing from, and minor wounds covered her body. She hadn't really realized how many hits she'd taken, though the scuffle on the floor had fortunately granted her mostly bruises.

As Rebaya snapped orders, sending nobles running like servants for bandages and water, Amanah cleaned and bandaged the worst of her wounds. What would it be like, not to have to scrounge for the most basic of things, like hot water? To simply know it would be at hand. If she worked in the bamimri, it would be like that.

Bodies were brought down from the balcony, some from the death team, others from the gathering. Yadi was the only one still alive from up there—his unconscious body had been halfway down the stairs. Grimly, Biryewi's guards began the process of sorting through the dead and collecting weapons. It was odd, not fearing a noble's personal guards, but they gave her nods of respect as they passed by. She returned the nods, feeling out of place.

"Finished there, Amanah? There's work to be done." Rebaya's voice snapped her back to the present. "You know what to do!"

She blinked at her. There were others with more knowledge than she to heal these people, so what could she possibly want her for? Hadn't she made enough of a scene?

Rebaya smiled. "You did well, but the work's not done. Come, help me tend the wounded."

"Triage?" she asked.

Rebaya nodded. "Good. We'll put the worst injured by your friends. I'll start there—you organize the wounded. You've shown you know how to do that. Then come find me and we'll get you working on healing."

Relief and hope blossomed in her, a painful, fragile thing. She knew too well how easily it could be crushed—but then, she also knew the resilience of it now. That strength was in Emin and Taunos's boasting, in Gurseh's quiet stubbornness. It was in Rebaya, setting her in charge of triage.

She shook her head, focusing on the task at hand. Rebaya's calm detachment never wavered, but for a quick kiss on Yadi's forehead when she came to him. She would take care of Emin, Taunos, and Gurseh, while Amanah would learn as much as she could from the woman in the meantime. She moved through the crowd as furniture was righted and people began to take stock, tasking the less injured to help her move the more injured to Rebaya and the dead to the other side of the hall. It was nothing less than astonishing how many accepted her direction, regardless of their station. Perhaps it was shock, and she'd just enjoy it while it lasted.

Above, guards were snuffing out the flames on the balcony, and curtains were raised to let out the smoke. When she finally made it back to the worst wounded, Rebaya was giving orders, sending servants and nobles alike running for supplies as she stitched up Emin's leg. Gurseh was bandaging a cut on Taunos's arm clumsily, and all three of them looked to be mostly patched up. Somehow, they'd made it out alive.

She let out a breath of relief, meeting Taunos's gaze and smiling. Guards that passed nearby tended to pause and offer Emin respect, not just Biryewi's guards, but others as well, and it made her heart swell.

Emin winced as Rebaya made another stitch, then scowled at Amanah. "I hate that you managed to stitch yourself up. It's completely unfair."

"It was only a couple stitches, and I threw up."

Gurseh snickered. "So did Emin."

Emin scowled at him. Rebaya tied the knot and cut the thread, and Emin sagged back with a sigh. "Someone needs to go through the building, make sure no surprises are left."

Taunos nudged him with an elbow, making him groan. "Say it louder."

Emin glanced at him, and then snagged the attention of a passing guard. "Teams of guards need to patrol this house."

The room fell silent, his loud voice filling the space. Emin didn't shy away from the attention though. He straightened, pushing back his shoulders. "There might be more of the death team left, leaving surprises or lying in wait for us. The house needs to be cleared of danger first. I'd say teams of four to be safe, one as a runner to carry word in case of danger."

The guard glanced at Biryewi, who stood in his ruined hall, surrounded closely by part of his personal guard.

Biryewi waved him on. "You heard him. Do it!"

The scatter, the rush of people, left her breathless, and she met her brother's gaze with a grin.

Emin laughed. "Gods above, I love being bossy!"

"Oh no," she groaned, glancing at Taunos. "You made a monster."

"He was already a monster," Taunos said, ruffling Emin's hair. "Now he's just hatched. A cute little baby monster."

Emin socked him in the shoulder, and they both fell back with matching groans.

"Both of you, be still," Rebaya snapped. "If you undo my work, I'll make it hurt worse."

"How can I help?" Amanah asked, kneeling beside the woman. "I was tired the other night and I'm tired now, but I... Anything I can keep in my head, I want to learn."

Rebaya smiled. "That's exactly the right attitude. You'll be plenty tired at times in the bamimri, too. Now, take a look at Gurseh's arm, see here?"

One by one, Rebaya took her through each injury, while a few others helped direct servants through supporting tasks including gathering even more supplies and taking away soiled linens. Biryewi's guards had captured Adinna and a few others seen working with the death team, including the servant who'd slipped out of the hall after Inuwe made his accusations.

They should have died, but somehow, she and those she loved were still breathing. She washed injuries, stitched gashes, bandaged wounds, rubbed salve on burns and bruises, and splinted one broken arm. Rebaya worked beside her, occasionally correcting a technique. Fatigue draped Amanah like a blanket of stone, but she tried to pay attention as best she could, and Rebaya answered every question patiently.

Most of the servants had only minor injuries, but several nobles were dead, arrows lodged precisely in their chests, and most of the guards were wounded. Esem was badly injured, and Lord Biryewi gave orders to the remaining guards from the couch at his master servant's side. The guards brought down four bodies of crossbowmen from the balcony. Taunos had taken down one, but the fire and the other guards must have taken down the others. By the bodies, they'd paid dearly for it, but without them, they'd all have been picked off.

And then, finally, it was done. No one was left who hadn't been tended, servant, guard, or noble. The lines of dead were laid out: ten from the death team, twenty-two guards, four servants, and over thirty nobles. Lord Lamyi was among them, his face in an expression of permanent surprise, and a crossbow bolt in his heart.

Amanah returned to the couch Taunos, Emin, and Gurseh had claimed.

Gurseh perched at one end, his arm around Emin's shoulders, and when she sagged down beside Taunos, he needlessly brushed her braids back from her face, then rubbed her uninjured shoulder. Her headscarf was askew, and she unknotted it, slipping it off.

Without something to keep her focus, the trembles began again, exhaustion and adrenaline doing their work. She tilted her head against Taunos's, grateful for the pressure of his arm around her, as if he was helping to keep her together.

Rebaya wheeled over, pressing a glass of juice into her hand. "Don't forget to drink."

"Thank you, Rebaya," she said, following the woman's order. "Will we be able to travel?"

Rebaya glanced over at Inuwe's sleeping form. "By the time he's ready to head back to the city, you should all be able to ride, so long as you aren't straining yourself. And don't lift anything heavy."

"She won't," Taunos promised.

Rebaya frowned at him, shaking a finger. "You're not to lift anything heavy either, with those ribs. And no more fights if you can help it."

"So long as no more death teams come," Emin said. "I'd like to not push our luck."

Biryewi approached, and they all fell silent. It was the first time he'd moved since settling Esem on the couch. Tugging on her scarf, Amanah swallowed hard. Lamyi was dead. Yes, Biryewi had been angry with him, but they had been employed to protect him and Lamyi was Biryewi's family. And they'd failed.

Taunos's hand stroked her head between her braids. She leaned into him and remembered how to breathe, his strength shoring up her own. Still, her tension must have been apparent.

"Relax," Biryewi said with a bland smile, stopping before their couch. "It's just some appreciation."

He turned, facing the room of injured and stunned people. All eyes were on him, on the four of them on the couch behind him. Amanah closed her eyes to shut them out.

"I believe it is nothing short of imperative that we thank these four guards from Arruk," Biryewi said. "Without them, no doubt I would not be here to give this speech. I am personally extending them my protection for any time they are in Gahimbli from this day forward. After their selfless acts, especially after baseless accusations, it occurs to me that we who style ourselves nobles could learn a lot from them."

Amanah's eyes flew open. Taunos's arm tightened around her, and he grinned at her. She clung to his arm like it was her last rope of sanity.

"My protection goes to them, as well." Lady Sina lifted a hand weakly, though it quickly fell back to her chest, to her ruined gown. Bandages covered the two holes from the crossbow bolts that had nearly killed her, but she smiled in Amanah's direction. "Any time you are in Gahimbli, if you need anything, please let me know. And when you are here, please stay in my home. We'll throw a celebration and you can dance without working for once. Agreed?"

How did one turn down a noble? Hesitantly, she nodded.

Lady Rebaya wheeled forward with a smile. "You of course have my protection and aid and that of my son," she said. "For anything you may need. But further, I am writing a letter of recommendation to the bamimri for you, Amanah. If, that is, you would still like to learn."

That was already the plan, but hearing it aloud, in front of all these rich, powerful people... The world moved beneath her. Only Taunos's warmth and steadying arm kept her from faltering. Blinking fast as tears filled her eyes, she nodded.

"Yes," she said. "I would love to be a bimna. Thank you."

"I think you've more than proven yourself, so now this is a chance for me to prove myself," Rebaya said. "And if they're half as intelligent as they should be, they'll welcome you with open arms. With hope, you'll start a new trend of havi in the bamimri."

"I will write one as well," Lord Inuwe said. He was bruised and pale, his head and chest bandaged, but he smiled at her. "You've saved my life twice now. It's past time I repay you."

The tears were falling now, rolling down her cheeks and dripping off her nose and chin. "Thank you. Thank you so much."

Taunos squeezed her, bending with a suppressed groan to kiss her temple. She brushed away the tears, even though they were tears of joy. There was still a lot of work to do—so much of it. But there was also hope that eventually things could change with that effort, and that made the work more bearable.

25

AMANAH LEANED OUT over the side of their boat, watching the ships leaving Arruk's river harbor as they entered. Her eyes drifted from one to the next until someone joined her at the railing.

Taunos was grinning at her, leaning against the hull. She tucked a braid behind her ear. "What?"

"I'm just enjoying this excitement."

She raised her eyebrows at him. "Well, maybe I was harsh before, when I said dreams didn't matter."

"I suppose I might have to forgive you," he said loftily, and she jostled his shoulder, chuckling. He joined in, wrapping his arm around her shoulders.

"Someday I will talk with Ifreesian dwarves, and I will see Kelm gnomes," she said.

"And be a bimna," he said.

She shrugged to cover her nerves. "Well everyone does get hurt. Some of us more often than others."

"There was a fight!" Taunos laughed. "I was stabbed!"

"And exploded, and all kinds of things, I know. I've seen." She smiled at him. "Maybe I'll even join you on your travels."

He leaned his head against hers. "I would love that."

"There's details to work out. And I need to complete my training."

"You're going to make a wonderful bimna."

She glanced down at the rough wood beneath her fingers. "They said I have to take an entrance exam. That was the message in Ukish."

"So you'll take it, and once again prove your worth. Maybe they'll open their eyes and see you."

"Or they could fail me. Or maybe I'm really not good enough." The words stuck in her throat with worry.

"Hey." He took her by the shoulders and turned her to face him. With great care, he kissed her eyebrows one by one. "Isn't that place supposed to teach you how to heal? So you don't need to know everything."

"Shouldn't need to." She sighed. "I shouldn't have to rely on the kindness of people like Rebaya and Sina and Inuwe, either."

Taunos glanced over, where the noble was playing cards with Gurseh and Emin. "I think we all rely on the kindness of each other at some point. But you're right, the system shouldn't be rigged against you."

She wrapped her arms around his waist. "Well, at least I'm not alone."

He rested his forehead against hers. "Me too."

She snorted at him. "You're never alone, Haari Taunos."

"Just because there are people around doesn't mean I'm not alone. I meant what I said. You see me for me. It's unbelievably refreshing."

She bit her lip, drawing designs on his back through his shirt with her finger. "Training at the bamimri will take time. If I get in."

He tightened his arms around her more snugly. "You'll get in. And I'll be around. After all, we have plans to make, if we're to travel together some day."

It was a dream, but it was a nice one. And more than that, it was nice *to* dream again.

Once they docked, Lord Inuwe took a horse to the center of the city, leaving them behind to walk and the boat's staff to unload his belongings. A servant would fetch them later, no doubt. Amanah walked with Emin, Gurseh, and Taunos through the docks to the market and up the wide road toward the palace, guardhouse, bamimri, and library. Emin wanted to report to Borlim right away, though Gurseh reminded him that Inuwe had probably already sent a report. It wasn't like they were going to beat the message to the guardmaster, but Emin's sense of duty insisted. Amanah smiled. He'd more than proved his capability as a leader, especially when he sent the guards to look for any more intruders at Biryewi's house.

Lamyi was dead. She was supposed to have protected him—they all were—and he'd died. Shudders began once the temple was in sight, its columns empty for now, but how long would that last? Would they decide that she, Emin, Taunos, and Gurseh had neglected their duty, or worse, killed him? Would the story of her fight with Lamyi have beaten her here? Probably. She had protection in Gahimbli, but not in Arruk.

"Amanah?" Taunos brushed the backs of his fingers against hers.

She forced herself to keep walking, staring at the cobblestones in front of her instead. "I'm just worried about the ramifications of Lamyi's death."

Ferocity flashed through his eyes. "If they heard about Lamyi, they should have heard about what he did. And about what you did afterward. And if they don't take any of those things into account, it's not justice."

She swallowed hard. "Lamyi's family is powerful, and they won't be happy."

He stopped her, a brush of his fingertips against her cheek. "Inuwe sent messages, and so did Rebaya and Biryewi. Inuwe promised he'd protect us from any repercussions."

It was still hard, even the thought of trusting a noble. And here in Arruk, there was no reason for Inuwe to follow through on his word. No reason, unless he really meant what he'd said.

Taunos's voice flowed over her, soothing and at the same time fervent. "Even if all that fails, I'm not going to let them hurt you. I'll do anything I have to."

"I don't want you getting hurt either," she said.

"We already had that conversation," he said, offering her a quick quirk of his lips.

His levity worked. Really, there was nothing he could do, but just the knowledge that he was with her helped. She took a deep breath, squared her shoulders, and continued forward, letting her fingers brush his as they walked.

They followed Emin and Gurseh to Borlim's office and waited as Emin rapped on the door.

"Come in," Borlim said.

Emin opened the door, and they all squeezed in. Borlim had clearly just finished running a training session. His vest was sweat-stained and unbuttoned, but he re-did the buttons as he waved them in.

"Shut the door, Emin," he said.

The door clicked shut, and Borlim sat down behind his desk, sighing. "This will be interesting."

Amanah winced.

Borlim tapped a stack of notes. "This pile is calling for your heads, or at least some punishment." He tapped another, slightly larger, stack. "While this one commends you. The problem is, most of the commendations are from Gahimbli, and we are not that city."

He fixed his eyes on Amanah and she gulped. "What does the word "invisible" mean?"

"I tried, sir. At least, in the beginning."

"Did I say *"try* to be invisible" when I saw you last?"

Amanah winced again. "No."

"And now, even more of the nobility of this city—the city you are in—want your blood, your pain, your body tied to that pole out there and whipped until bloody."

Amanah reached for Taunos's knee, pressed against hers. He covered her hand with his.

Borlim raised three of the letters. "And then these. These are even more interesting. They are notes demanding you be allowed into the bamimri. The bamimri has their own copies of these."

"Yes, sir." Amanah straightened. They'd done it then, as they'd said they would. She'd hardly dared to hope.

"Get into the bamimri," Borlim said. "If you're a bimna, Lamyi's family can't touch you. Dulara can protect you better than I can."

She nodded firmly. In some ways, nothing had changed—she was still in danger. But on the other hand, everything had changed. She had changed. And she had options, and nobles looking out for her—along with the steadiness of Emin, Taunos, and Borlim's support—even if others still wanted her to suffer.

Borlim sat back, tapping his fingers on his desk. "All right. You four look exhausted, and no wonder. I'm ordering you all to get a good meal, get at least eight marks of sleep, get another good meal, and then I want your reports—separately—on my desk by the end of tomorrow. Except you, Emin. You get to stay behind and give me your report right now. The rest of you, get out of my office. And get some baths!"

They left, Amanah flashing Emin a smile of support as she passed him. Gods, he looked like he was going to throw up. He never looked that nervous before a fight, but now he looked like he was facing lashings.

Taunos slapped his shoulder, dodging his returning smack with a snicker. And just like that, it was clear: Emin was going to be fine. She allowed herself a smile, to hold on to hope.

They headed toward the dorms, but they were only halfway there when a tall, plump woman in a bimna's uniform strode down the hallway.

"Amanah Teek?" the bimna asked, eyeing her critically.

Taunos stopped beside her, but Gurseh waved and continued on.

Amanah gulped. "Yes?"

"I am Dulara. Come with me. Your entrance exam to the bamimri begins now."

Taunos extended a hand for her bags before she could even respond, his eyes dancing. He grinned at her in silent support. Her heart hammered against her ribs as she gave him her things.

"Hurry now!" Dulara snapped.

Amanah glanced down at her travel-stained clothes. "I haven't cleaned up or—"

"There was an accident at the chemists' shop on Greenway and we need more help. Work in the bamimri does not wait for you to be ready for it."

Of course not. She knew that, and there was no way this could be worse than two death teams, could it? She'd handled that, and she'd handle this as well.

"Yes, Dulara," she said. Amanah raised her chin. "I'm ready."

Thank you for reading!

If you have a spare moment, please leave an honest review. Reviews are the best way to help other readers find books they'll enjoy, and make an enormous difference for independent authors especially! If you want to help support your favorite authors, telling others about them and asking your local library to stock their books are among the best ways to do so. Thank you so much!

Would you like to read Chapter 2 (the race) from Taunos's point of view? You can get that and/or the story of their break-up exclusively by signing up to my newsletter at skaeth.com or go to https:// dl.bookfunnel.com/4n8t446z7c

Taunos appears as a main character in the Children of the Nexus series. Amanah (and Emin) return in Let Loose the Fallen (Children of the Nexus Book Two). Don't miss them!

Terms and People

The People

Kanhu Amanah Teek — Amanah is a guard in Arruk who came to the city for opportunities, along with her older brother Emin. She is part of Murihat's Hand, a semi-organized resistance to the strict classism of Arruk, and dreams of being a bimna.

Kanhu Emin Teek — Amanah's brother, who also is a guard and is under consideration for leading a war-band

Haari Taunos — One of Emin's friends, a relative newcomer to the city who's travelled far

Guma Gurseh — Emin's boyfriend

Asi Lamyi — One of the two noblemen Amanah escorts to Gahimbli

Asi Inuwe — One of the two noblemen Amanah escorts to Gahimbli

Borlim — Guardmaster at Arruk

Yadi — a guard at Gahimbli

Rebaya — a noblewoman living in Gahimbli, also, Yadi's mother

Biryewi — a noblewoman living in Gahimbli

Esem — master of servants for Biryewi

The Place: Far Dahutad — populated by the Dahuti people of various clans.

The capital is Arruk, with Ukish being a port city and Gahimbli being another city near the border with the Hinanur Empire. The tensions between the Dahuti and the Hinanuri have been rising.

Dahuti names are ordered thus: clan or occupation name (or derisively, rank for havi), then given name, then family name.

Nine deities are worshipped in Far Dahutad:

Jattanu is the god of justice, light, and the sun. Justice is carried out in the daytime, under the sun, as a result.

Nannil - the goddess of night is also the goddess of secrets, stealth, thieves, hospitality, and knowledge. Her radiance is distributed among all the stars and the two moons.

Tenah is the goddess of women and war and death.

Kenti is the god of travelers and water and wind and sailing.

The child of Jattanu and Nannil is Kinaa, the goddess of growth and fertility, innocence and birth.

The child of Tenah and Kenti is Hayzanu, the god of luck and exploration and pleasure.

The child of Kenti and Nannil is Gashasu, the god of passion and poetry and art.

The child of Tenah and Jattanu is Ahunah, the goddess of vengeance, youth, and oaths.

The child of Jattanu and Kenti, is Murihat, the deity of deception, mischief, and mercy.

Terms

havi — a class term for the poor. Havi are looked down upon and taken advantage of in many Dahuti cities, especially havi who come from a nomadic wilderness background, like Amanah and Emin

bamimri — staffed by bimnas, this place of healing is highly respected and attracts people from countries all around Far Dahutad to come for treatment. The requirements to become a bimna and study the healing arts, however, are exclusive.

rain of the gods (or gods' rain, less commonly) — the time when stars fall from the sky for seven days. This occurs twice yearly, every year.

Festival of Dark Nights — occurs during the rain of the gods in Far Dahutad. This is a festival where people stay indoors as much as possible, celebrating, feasting, and trying to stay awake for as much of the rain of the gods as possible.

sea-wizards — people with magic abilities

Sea Peoples — a raiding force that terrorizes the coastlines of many countries. They rule the sea, coming to shore occasionally to trade, but more often to kill, raid, and take captives.

Acknowledgements

Every book I write goes through many, many eyes before I cast it into the world, and this one is no exception. Originally conceived as a free short story that I would give away to newsletter subscribers, it took on a life of its own, and clearly Amanah had things to say. I'm not sure I'll ever live down writing this 134k "short story" and I'm not sure I want to! The giggles are well worth it.

Thank you as always, to my family, for constantly supporting me even when I despair, whether that's letting me talk your ears off, or reading bits and pieces (or usually, the whole thing), or just helping me carve out the time to write, edit, and repeat. You're amazing and I love you so much.

To my stupendous critique partners, this story never would have happened without you. Yeah, you know how I nearly scrapped the whole thing after the first draft? You and my family are why it didn't actually end up trashed, and I'm so grateful. Thank you for all your support, insight, problem-solving, and all the pointing out where I can do better—and I did! R. Lee Fryar, Ariana Townsend, Kia Leep 🚀 , and Jerusha René, thank you so much. KJ, our lives blew up so you didn't get to read this, but you were in my head anyway and head-KJ's advice was super useful so thank you!

Thuy and Paulette, you are incredible first-pass beta readers and you helped this story really grow into its own. Thank you for your thoughtful critiques and suggestions—and yes, I added more steam, Paulette! Thank you also to my beta readers Raina, Léon, and John W. Vaughan for your comments, as well!

Most of this story went through my ever-patient and fantastic critique group, Parliament of Pens! Thank you for all your support. That also goes to the rest of my supporting tribe, WriteHive, my Coven (Kia, Jerusha, Justine, and Hannah, I'm not sure you know how much your generous spirits and unwavering support means to me!), and the Writer In Motion group.

To my (evil?) genius editor Justine, you are brilliant! Your reactions cracked me up and made editing a breeze, too, and thank you for catching that one bigger issue too! Your line edits helped tremendously with making my words flow and my ideas come through clearly, and without your eagle-eye I would have all sorts of inconsistencies.

Thank you also (again, always) to my cover artist, Dave Brasgalla! You did it yet again, and Amanah pops off the page! I love that you gave her Taunos, as well, shadowing behind her, and that landscape is perfect. It's incredible working with you, going back and forth with details, and your talent and support is truly appreciated. I'm truly honored to work with you on each book!

And I haven't forgotten you, my readers! Thank you for taking a chance on this book and letting me (hopefully) entertain you a bit. I hope I made you laugh, and I hope you'll be watchful of landslides and wildlife, haha!

About the Author

Ever since a college professor told S. Kaeth she'd have to eventually focus on just one thing, she's been dead set on proving him wrong.

From charging through the wilderness, wrangling alligators and snapping turtles, trapping and counting moles, or supervising prairie burns for college credits to doing research and training frogs, lizards, and a lungfish, she treats life as an adventure. She traded hikes, natural history interpretation boating tours, and creature encounters for the slightly-less-exotic-but-no-less-fun mammal training about the same time she began to get serious about her writing craft.

You can find her teaching herself languages and lesser-known fiber crafts, hiking, or playing Capoeira when she's not practicing the fine art of weaving a tale.

Stay in touch: Sign up for the newsletter at www.skaeth.com !

Other books by S. Kaeth

Windward

When dragons fight, mountains weep.

Dragonbonded Palon and her partner, the dragon Windward, are renowned for their flying skill among the dragons and dragonbondeds who make up their family. Palon's days are filled with everything she loves, especially riding the wind. Even being tasked with teaching their way of life to Tebah, a newly bonded teenager, can't bring her down too much.

But when treasures from the dragons' hordes are found in Palon's collection, her idyllic life comes crashing down. Framed, she battles to find the truth, to prove her innocence, while her every move is cast as further evidence against her. As if that wasn't enough, her teenage charge's increasingly dangerous behavior puts them both at risk. Tebah's suspicion, homesickness, and defiance would be frustrating enough even if Palon wasn't in the spotlight, with a rival smearing her name at every turn. Dragon tempers shorten, and challenges and disputes shake the ground.

Windward and Palon must find a way to clear her name while also keeping a teenager who hates her and everything about dragon life safe, before their community turns completely against them or vigilante justice succeeds.

Children of the Nexus series

Between Starfalls (Book One of Children of the Nexus)

Never leave the path.

It's sacred law, punishable by exile.

When her son goes missing in the perilous mountains, Kaemada defies the law to search for him. She enlists the help of her hero brother, a priestess berserker, and a fire-wielding friend.

But the law exists for a reason.

When the search party is captured by the mythical Kamalti, they learn that Kaemada's son was sent to an ancient prison city. As they battle for freedom, they discover a horrible truth that will change the future of both races forever.

With their world in upheaval, Kaemada must find a way to peace if she's to save her son—but tensions between the two races are leading to war.

Let Loose The Fallen (Book Two of Children of the Nexus)

The priestess searches for her faith.

The fire-wielder wrestles with her past.

The psion dreams of peace.

And the hero is torn between his heart and his duty.

While grief scatters the four protectors to the winds, outside forces write history according to their own whims. The fate of the Rinaryns lies twined with that of the boy, Eian, caught in a tug of war the heroes are unaware of.

But the evidence lies waiting for Taunos and the others to see, if only they can move past their betrayal.